Return to the 21st Century?

Can the collapsed eastern half of America, a
society still stuck in the pioneer era, be
successfully brought back into the 21st century?

Paul H Rowney

Published by: PHR Media LLC, 197 Thompson Lane, Nashville TN 37211, USA.

Coming Summer 2023: Receive a free Kindle copy of the third book in the *French Creek* series;

S.O.S-The Storm of all Storms, visit: www.paulhrowney.com

Book 1 in the series: *French Creek* is available on Amazon.

Kindle, paperback and KU.

Cover design by Yeonwoo Baik

ISBN: 9798393310486 (Paperback)

Dedication

Thank you to everyone who, not only bought my first book, *French Creek*, but also gave it so many complimentary reviews. Your kind words gave me the confidence to write this second in the series, with a third due to be published in mid 2023.

I sincerely hope you find this sequel as enjoyable. I look forward to receiving your comments, criticisms and, hopefully, positive reviews.

Paul H Rowney

Contents

Chapter 1

"Pull your hands away from your guns or the last thing you'll see are the people you're trying to shoot. Don't even turn around and look at me. Place your hands behind your head."

Pat was standing over two prone men, rifles held tightly to their shoulders, eyes glued to their telescopic sights, ready to shoot his close friends, Roger and Landy. For a few seconds both shooters didn't move, stunned by the voice behind them that had come out of nowhere. They seemed to be weighing up the possibility: could they pull the trigger and complete their mission before they were shot in the back of the head? Or do, as instructed, and live to fight another day? Or, maybe, whoever he was, might be bluffing?

One decided to try his luck. He grabbed his rifle, and started to roll onto his back in the hope of getting a quick shot at his attacker. He was too slow. Before he'd even lifted the rifle, Pat shouted "Are you friggin' mad?" and pulled the trigger of his Glock. The sniper's head exploded, spewing blood and brain on his friend and in a wide red arc across the pristine white snow.

Instinctively, the other gunman jerked away, wiping the blood from his face.

"Last warning, face down, hands behind your head." This time, the second shooter obliged.

Pat walked up and put his boot firmly on the man's neck. Pressing his face into the bloodstained snow.

"Who are you, and why are you trying to kill my friends?"

1

A muffled voice answered defiantly, "Fuck you. Those assholes, they killed my Pa and sisters down in Memphis. That's why they gotta die."

Pat immediately connected the dots, "Oh, so you're part of that scum family that kept me hostage and makes a living transporting desperate people across the Mississippi, if you don't kill them first, that is. Well, turns out, reckon we did the world a favor by getting rid of your relatives."

Keeping his anger in check, he continued, "So give me one good reason you shouldn't get the same fate as your friend here? You're nothing more than murdering trash, and I might add, shit trackers and even worse snipers. I knew you'd followed us from Memphis, saw you a couple of times getting too close to us. I found you here yesterday. Thought I'd let you spend another night in the freezing cold before I came to say hello. Here's a tip—next time you're trying to stay hidden, don't smoke a cigarette; I could see the light and smoke. Also your breath shows up in the cold, dumbass".

A furious muttering emanated from the snow, "I'll remember that next time, asshole."

Incredulous, Pat replied, "So you're telling me if I let you go, you'll still come after us? Are you serious? Have you got a death wish?"

"You bet your ass I'm serious about killing all of you. So are the rest of our group in Memphis. Either way, you're dead meat, man."

"Really?"

"You betta believe it. Our people will track you down and kill you. And they're good at it. They'll come after you, I promise."

Pat sighed and shrugged his shoulders, "Well, let's hope they're better than you. Guess that leaves me no option."

He casually leant over, put the pistol to the back of the man's head and pulled the trigger. He stood up, surveying the carnage with a dispassionate eye, turned and left the lifeless bodies without a second glance.

Chapter 2

R oger and his son Landy were just yards from the farmhouse when they heard the first shot.

"Take cover!" screamed Roger, as he dropped to the ground behind his horse, searching for the source of the shot. Looking around for his son, he shouted, "Landy! Are you OK?"

"Yes Dad, I'm fine," Landy replied. He'd quickly scooted off his horse and was now hidden behind a gigantic oak tree. Roger crouched down and ran to join him. He peered round the tree.

"Any idea where that came from?" Roger's eyes scanned the stand of trees about 200 yards from where they were hiding. He had his handgun drawn, safety off. He couldn't see any movement.

"I'd like to get my rifle from the horse, but the stupid animal's wandered off. Damn it." Roger was annoyed with himself for this rookie oversight. He knew better.

"OK Landy, you stay here, keep your eyes peeled for any movement, but no heroics. I don't need to be pulling any more bullets out of you. If you see anything, shout, but don't get involved. Got it?"

Before Roger could move, a second shot rang out, echoing through the woods. But no bullet grazed the tree or seemed to come anywhere near them. Strange. Then he remembered Pat had left a little earlier, maybe he had something to do with this?

No sooner had the thought crossed his mind than he heard Pat shout from the woods. "Roger, Landy, it's me, Pat! Hold your fire. I'm

3

guessing I have two guns pointed in my direction. I'm good here, just tidying up some loose ends."

With that, Pat appeared, hands raised in mock surrender, holstering his pistol as he did so. His army fatigues were spattered with blood. An ex-Marine, he still marched rather than walked, moving his six-foot plus frame in a determined manner through the snow.

"Christ Pat, you scared the shit out of us. You've been hunting or what?" demanded Landy, looking at the state of Pat's clothing. He was still a little shaken. He'd been shot just a week earlier and was understandably jumpy at the sound of gunfire.

"Could say that, nothing you'd want to eat, though," replied Pat indifferently.

Pat then explained how he'd found the two gunmen. They were brothers from the family of coyotes they had killed a few days earlier in Memphis. He had a feeling someone was following them all the way to the farm they were staying at near Clarksville. He kept a lookout and saw them setting up a sniper's nest in the woods. They were amateurs; he explained, easy to see and easy to surprise in their hide. He didn't go into detail about their timely demise, simply saying that they wouldn't be a problem in the future.

Roger, a former Army Captain, testily replied, "Christ Pat, why didn't you say something before? We could have helped you take them out."

"True, but everyone was busy celebrating and relaxing. I didn't want to disturb the party. Anyway, all's well that ends well. Let's leave a note for Jeff about his burial duties and start back to French Creek."

Jeff was the owner of the farm they'd been resting at after their mission to Memphis. He'd been part of the team that had helped a group of villagers from French Creek make the dangerous trip to a new life across the Mississippi. And rescue Pat, Jane, her son and husband who'd been held hostage by the same group.

Roger couldn't be too critical. Pat, as head of security in the village of French Creek, had shown some initiative, achieved a satisfactory result, even in a somewhat risky manner. No point in having a go at him now. He was a good guy who'd done something unpalatable but necessary. It wasn't the first time Pat had come to the rescue—he was reliable and capable.

Ten minutes later, the three were on their way, after leaving a note for Jeff. Pat didn't mention the bodies to Jane and her family. After their rescue they were staying at the farm to recuperate and decide what to do with their future. After the trauma of over five year's separation, kidnapping, and murder, they needed time to get their lives back on an even keel. Two more dead bodies to deal with wouldn't help in that process.

It would take three days to return to French Creek. The pace was easy, making allowances for Landy's healing wounds. The result of an ambush a week earlier, when he'd rushed back from Memphis to request Jeff's-a former Army friend of Roger's-help to take out the group of coyotes.

They camped at the end of the first day south of Bowling Green on the Kentucky/Tennessee border. The countryside was painted brilliant white with an undisturbed coating of snow. The sky was a deep, solid blue, no pollution softened the view. They bedded down in an old barn just off I-65. Soon, a fire was boiling up some water for a coffee and their MREs (Meals Ready to Eat). They relaxed for the first time in nearly two weeks.

"How are the war wounds, Landy?" asked Pat as he made himself comfortable, leaning against a large round bale of hay.

"Bit sore, but not too bad. A couple of Tylenol would help, I guess, but I'll just have to live with the pain. It gets easier each day," replied Landy as he gently massaged his injured arm. "Funny really, I was the only one to get injured, and I wasn't even involved in the whole shoot out in Memphis. Talking of which, when are you guys gonna fill me in on the details? Everyone's been awful secretive about it. It pissed me off, missing out on all the fun."

Roger stared into the fire, reliving some unseeable images from his time in Iraq and Afghanistan. With a tinge of anger in his voice, he answered his son's lighthearted complaint.

"Son, let's get this clear. This wasn't some game like you used to play on Xbox. We killed real people, murdered them. Whether or not we thought they were evil bastards, they are now dead. Sure, the group from French Creek made it safely across the Mississippi, but we have no idea what has happened to them since then. Earlier on today, two more men died. Landy, killing or watching people get killed is not fun. It's sickening and something you never forget. Truth be told, I think you getting shot and staying well away from the action was the best thing that could have happened. So, no, I'm not going to give you the details of the mission. No one is. Because it's done and nothing will be gained by knowing more than you do already."

Landy held his hands up. "Whoa, OK. Sorry I asked Dad. I figured as I got shot going for reinforcements, I was entitled to know the full story."

"You might think you're entitled to know more. I think you're entitled to still be alive and able to make your way back home. That's all." After a moment's thought, he added, "Landy, killing someone, however much they might deserve it, never makes you feel better. You never feel good about it. Having a gun doesn't give you any rights, just responsibilities and accountability. If I had my way, no one would own a gun until they'd had the kind of training we had in the Army. No one has a right to own something that can kill someone else unless they've seen the results up close. Before the Collapse, it was more difficult to get a driver's license than to own a gun. How goddamn crazy is that? Our Founding Fathers must be turning in their graves at the way the Second Amendment is distorted and abused in modern times…," he stopped himself, "Anyway, rant over. Enough said. I'm getting some shuteye."

Still angry, Roger got up, went to his horse, retrieved his sleeping gear and took himself off to a corner of the barn, leaving just Pat and Landy by the fire.

"Wow, Dad's in quite a lather. Was it that bad?"

Pat replied curtly, "Yes it was Landy, and you'll get nothing more out of me. Now go get some sleep, we've got an early start."

With that terse comment, Pat laid out his sleeping bag on the hay, doused the fire, and turned in for the night. Landy sat there for a few minutes in the dark, still smarting from the roasting dispensed by his father, before crawling into his sleeping bag and falling asleep.

Chapter 3

By six the following morning, they were on the move, the dawn gloom edged out by another sunny winter day. Conversation was sporadic as they plodded up the tracks and roads parallel to the interstate, then cut across to the Barren River Lake State Park. They stopped for the night by one of the now abandoned lake side cabins, which before the Collapse was once someone's beloved weekend retreat. Like most lakes in Kentucky and Tennessee, this one was man made. A dam at one end regulated the flow of water. However, without people or power to control this, the lake's level in winter was much higher. Now the water's only escape was over the dam itself as opposed to through its complex drainage system.

They chose a small log cabin that looked inhabitable. Inside it had been ransacked. There was nothing of value to be found. In the years since the Collapse it had been picked clean of food or useful supplies. However, to his delight, Pat found some angling gear. He decided to try his hand at fishing. He walked down to the lakeside and inexpertly cast his lure into the water. To everyone's astonishment and delight, within minutes he'd caught a massive bass. Quickly killed and prepared, it made a tasty addition to yet another cardboard tasting MRE.

It's amazing how one minor achievement, one unexpected piece of good news, can positively transform everyone's outlook. The simple delight of tasting fresh fish for the first time in months suddenly brightened their mood. They tucked in, savoring the delicate flavoring. Fish back home was a rarity. French Creek had ponds with bass and catfish, but there was never enough for everyone. Trips to nearby Dale Hollow Lake took up too much time, for an uncertain result.

It was still light after their unexpectedly delicious meal. Once they tidied up and collected more firewood, Landy and Pat explored the other cabins and houses by the lake. Land was at such a premium along the lakefront, they were built close together, often only a few feet apart. Some were barely more than spruced up manufactured homes, probably the first to be built; the more recent houses were bigger.

They explored a few, then entered one of the larger ones through an impressive oak front door. Both Pat and Landy immediately sensed someone had visited recently, or maybe was still there. Muddy footprints could be seen on the floor. They drew their guns and carefully searched each room. It was a large home, with five bedrooms, several interconnecting reception rooms, all of which revealed nothing. But they still had the feeling they were not the only ones present.

Like most lake houses, they were built on a steep slope which led down to the water's edge. The owner had created a basement from the space below the ground floor and a door from the kitchen led down to it. There was some light coming through the small basement windows. Landy and Pat crept down the steep steps, the room smelled of damp and decay.

"Anybody here?" shouted Pat. "We mean you no harm, but we have guns and know how to use them. Say something, anything, if you're here."

There was a few seconds' pause and then a young voice, trembling with fear, spoke from the gloom.

"Don't shoot, mister, it's just me and my sisters."

"OK, sonny," said Pat in a calming voice, "come out where we can see you, promise we won't hurt you."

There was a shuffling of furniture being moved. Into the fading light emerged three children of indeterminate age, all indescribably filthy.

"Hey guys, I'm Pat and this is my friend Landy. What are your names?"

The eldest, a boy, answered in a whisper, "I'm Jamie and these are my sisters, Stephanie and Shelby."

"Great to meet you guys. Are you hungry? We've got some food at our camp. Wanna come get something to eat and we can have a talk?"

"Yes please, sir, we sure are hungry. We'd appreciate that, sir," answered Jamie, looking at his sisters for confirmation they were happy with his decision. They said nothing, just clutched onto his hands for dear life.

To say Roger was incredulous when Pat and Landy appeared with three young urchins in tow, was putting it mildly. "First some fish, now three youngsters, you're on a roll Pat! Well, what do we have here?"

"Found them in the basement of a house close by. Don't think they've eaten, or by the smell, washed in a while. They're joining us for dinner." Without a moment's hesitation, Roger went into father mode.

"Of course, come over by the fire guys. I'll open up some more MREs and we can have a feast. How does that sound?"

"Sounds great, mister. Thanks. Me and my sisters haven't eaten much in days."

The three waifs sat down uneasily on the ground, legs crossed by the fire. Soon, they were scoffing down the food Roger had produced from his store of never-go-out-of-date meals. To most, these MREs were high protein, tasteless survival food. To the three kids in front of them, the meal could have been from a five-star restaurant. Roger watched as they devoured their meal. They were a pitiful sight. Their clothes were rags, covered in mud and what looked like blood. Though he could see no injuries on them. The two girls seemed traumatized, saying nothing, their eyes vacant, unblinking. All three were skin and bones, looking like refugees from some war zone. A sight Roger had seen too often around the world. What had these kids been through, he wondered?

When they'd finished the second and third helpings, they relaxed a little, realizing, maybe these grown-ups meant them no harm after all. Roger tried to get some information from them.

"So, where's your mom and dad?"

Jamie seemed to be the only one prepared to speak. He answered, showing little emotion, "Dunno where they are. Haven't seen 'em in ages. People we're staying with aren't our mom and dad, just some grown-up friends. They went out fishing one day, a snowstorm blew up and we haven't seen them since,".

"When was that?" asked Roger.

"Dunno exactly, five, six days ago? When they didn't come back, we escaped, went from house to house to find something to eat". He looked at Roger, fear in his eyes, "We…we don't want to go back. Please mister."

Jamie teared up as he told his story. His two younger sisters sat doe-eyed, looking into the flames still saying nothing. They looked in shock. Roger wondered if they had PTSD.

"Jamie, I'm really sorry to hear that. Where did you used to live?" Roger enquired.

"We lived near Scottsville, some disease came and we got out of there before it took us. Lots of people died, including most of our friends. That was last summer and we've been by the lake ever since. It's a horrible place."

"How old are you Jamie?" asked Pat, changing the subject, though still keen to know why they didn't want to return. They'd pursue that question in the morning.

"I'm thirteen, my sisters are nine and eight."

"Well Jamie, you've done an excellent job at looking after them. Why don't you try to get some sleep, we can decide what to do tomorrow? How does that sound? Do you want to sleep out here or in the house?"

"Out here be fine, sir." Jamie looked at his sisters, who nodded their agreement. Already, the warmth of the fire and a full stomach were making them dozy.

Pat and Landy found some extra blankets and made a bed for them by the fire. They snuggled together and within a minute, were fast asleep. Warm and well-fed, probably for the first time in days.

"Well, this is a turn up. What are we supposed to do with these kids now?" asked Pat, chewing on a piece of beef jerky, "we can't leave them here, can we?"

Roger agreed, "I suppose not Pat, but what if these adults ended up on the other side of the lake, and haven't made it back yet? Don't want to cause a problem with them. Maybe we need to go to their house and see what's happening there? I'm intrigued why they are scared to go back. Poor kids. Seems like they've had a rough time" He looked down kindly at the three young faces. Who, despite their awful experiences, were now sleeping peacefully as only the young can.

Landy offered up a concern. "Don't want to be skeptical, but can we assume they're telling the truth? Could it be some kind of trap?"

"Possibly," said Roger, thinking for a moment, before deciding it was unlikely, " I doubt it, these kids are starving and genuinely scared. Can't see anyone using them as some kind of bait. For what? It's worth bearing in mind, though. I think we need to find their home, check it out and go from there. Agreed?"

Chapter 4

They woke to a gloomy day with the promise of more snow. The children were up quickly devouring a breakfast of MRE omelets. Unconcerned that the contents bore little resemblance to the real thing.

Roger explained to them what was going to happen, "OK guys, we're going to your house, see what's there and try to find the people you live with. If there aren't any adults around, then I suggest you all come back with us to our home in French Creek."

Their reaction was fearful and animated.

"Please, mister, take us with you. We don't want to go back to our place. It's horrible there. They do terrible things to people. Please, can we go to your home? We're beggin' you mister." As always, it was Jamie doing the talking. The two girls said nothing, their fear showing through their wide eyes, already shedding tears.

Pat asked gently, "So what are the terrible things they do there, Jamie? What's got you so scared?"

Jamie didn't reply, just shook his head, hugged his sisters tighter to him and kept whispering, "Don't worry, I won't let them take you back."

Not wanting to force the issue, Roger suggested a compromise, "OK, OK, we won't force you to go to your home. How about we ride there? Then Pat and I will go in by ourselves. You can stay with Landy and the horses a safe distance away. Would that be alright with you guys?"

Jamie slowly nodded his agreement. It was clear the boy was petrified of going home. Roger kept wondering just what was so awful about the kid's home. They quickly broke camp, prepared the horses, and were on their way within the hour. Each of the adults had a child riding with them. They followed a road that hugged the perimeter of the lake. This time of year, it looked cold and uninviting. The trees were bare, offering no cover for the riders or anyone who might follow them. The young boy seemed to know where he was going, confidently pointing tracks or roads they should follow. It was mid-morning when he tapped Roger's shoulder, pointing to a house about two hundred yards away. He looked visibly shaken at the sight of it.

He whispered in Roger's ear, as if afraid someone would overhear him, "That's where we live."

"OK, you kids stay here with Landy. We'll be back real soon."

Roger and Pat dismounted, continuing towards the house on foot, rifles at the ready. They saw no sign of life in the log cabin, no fire smoke, noise or animals. Though clearly it had been inhabited recently. The yard had tools laying around and piles of trash. Roger warned Pat to keep his eyes out and his wits about him. Something didn't feel right about the scene in front of them. They walked warily the last few yards, then Roger banged on the door with the butt of his rifle.

"Anybody home?" Roger shouted. He indicated Pat should walk round the back of the cabin and check it out. He'd take the front. The log cabin was once someone's idea of a cute 'home on the range' getaway. Now it was in poor repair with windows broken, a rotting deck and by the look of it, a leaking roof.

There was a peculiar smell emanating from the house that Roger couldn't place. Receiving no reply to his shouted welcome, he cautiously pushed open the front door with his rifle. Walking inside, a scene of utter squalor and filth met him. Clothes were piled everywhere, dishes and plates on the floor, trash everywhere. The cabin's ground floor was one big living room with two bedrooms leading off. It had a mezzanine floor with more rooms upstairs.

The further Roger moved into the cabin, the stronger that strange smell hit him.

Pat appeared at the back door that led into the kitchen. As he walked in, he looked into the sink and stopped dead, "What the hell has happened here? Take a look Roger."

Both men peered into the sink, which was covered in blood and animal parts. It was a revolting sight that raised even more questions about what had occurred in this sordid place. They moved on to search the rest of the house.

Roger checked the bedrooms and upstairs, while Pat went down into the basement. Within seconds, he practically catapulted back up the stairs, his face ashen white. Stopping at the top, he bent over and threw up his breakfast.

Roger ran over to him, "Jesus Pat, what the fuck is the problem?"

Pat was on his knees, still vomiting violently. After a few seconds, he looked up at Roger, his face white, stricken with horror. The look of someone who'd seen something so dreadful it was impossible to describe, "Rog, don't go down there. It's a scene from hell. Oh Christ, that's not animal remains in the sink, I think they're human. The basement is where they've been processing human bodies. I think the people that live here are cannibals."

Roger looked at Pat's distraught face, sheer terror in his eyes. This man had seen unspeakable horrors, injuries, and deaths in Afghanistan and survived them seemingly unscathed. Now, down in the basement, was something worse, some harrowing vision, reducing this strapping, experienced soldier to tears.

Of course! Roger now recognized it. That sickly smell was decaying meat and blood. Death. He helped Pat across to the settee and told him to take a drink from his canteen. Slowly he began to calm down.

"It's OK Pat, take it easy, deep breaths. I need to check it out. Maybe you're mistaken. Gimme five minutes."

Pat grabbed his arm, stopping him from moving, "Roger please, trust me, it's a slaughterhouse for humans down there. You don't want to see it. If you do, you'll never unsee it. I won't, God help me it's beyond revolting. Don't go down there, you'll regret it." Pat pleaded, his voice choking with emotion.

Could it really be that horrific, wondered Roger? He'd seen some stomach churning and hideous scenes during his Army service. Men, women, children blown to pieces or left so horribly maimed and injured, he had to put some out of their misery. Did he need to see this type of carnage again? Did he want more unforgettable images of man's enduring ability to inflict pain and death on his fellow human beings, barging into his nightmares? He'd had enough of those already. Did he need more mind warping sights to ruin his sleep?

No, he didn't, he decided. He'd take Pat's word for it. In the basement was a dungeon of unspeakable horrors. By not seeing them, they'd infect his already troubled mind no further. Roger knelt down in front of Pat, "Alright, I believe you Pat, I'm sorry you had to see what you did. Let's get the hell out of here before the evil bastards who did this come back. Are you fit to move out?"

Pat nodded, standing up with Roger's help, he walked unsteadily towards the door. As he passed the wood-burning stove he saw a box of matches. Stopping, he picked them up, and with a slow, deliberate motion, struck one. Looking into the flame, he whispered.

"Let's burn this fucking place to the ground."

Roger didn't hesitate, "You got it, Pat. Do it"

By the time they reached Landy, the children and their horses, the first licks of flames were climbing hungrily out of the cabins' windows. They watched for a few minutes to make sure the fire really took hold. The flames seemed to attack the cabin with savage ferocity, as if wanting to cleanse the horrors it contained. It was an incineration of evil taking place before their eyes.

Landy looked at his father and Pat, their faces still registering the shock of what they had witnessed. He knew better than to ask what happened. His father would no doubt tell him in due time.

Roger turned to the children, "We know what happened in there guys. It's over now. You're coming with us back to French Creek—you need to be as far from this hellhole as possible. Let's move."

The three children barely acknowledged Roger's command. Inside their terrified minds they knew wherever they were going had to be better than the den of depravity now being consumed by the roaring fire. They mounted up and headed away at a brisk trot, putting as much distance from the burning cabin and any trouble it might attract.

The journey back was subdued. Pat tried to process and expunge from his mind what he had seen. It would be a long time before he could, if ever. The children, particularly the two girls, were still catatonic, staring blankly ahead, saying nothing. Pat wondered how any child could cope with living among such ghastly activities. Would they ever recover from the sights and smells of that cabin of horror? Roger said little, also absorbed in his own thoughts, while Landy, reading the vibes correctly, asked nothing of what they had seen.

Chapter 5

The frozen, bedraggled group arrived at the village of French Creek late the following day. Despite the weather, as soon as word spread throughout the village they were back, a crowd of well-wishers congregated to congratulate them on their return from a successful mission.

In contrast, the group showed little joy or pleasure at being back. They were exhausted and still shocked by what they had seen. Briefly thanking the villagers for coming out to welcome them, Roger promised everyone would hear more about their exploits in due course.

Understandably, the villager's curiosity then moved onto the three scared, grimy children still sitting on the horses. The attention clearly overwhelmed them. Roger asked Jo Brown, the village doctor, to take them to the health center and give them a thorough checkup, saying he'd be over later to get an update. "Treat them gently, Doc, you have no idea what they've been through. I'll explain when I see you. Can you arrange some food for them as well?"

Doc Brown nodded his assent and with the aid of one of his assistants, Debbie, helped the kids off the horses and into the warmth of the health center.

Roger, Pat and Landy made their way home. Having stabled and fed the horses, Roger threw together a quick meal. He then visited the Council members asking them to attend an emergency meeting at 9:00 a.m. the following day.

The Village Council comprised of ten elders, or those with specific areas of expertise such as: farming, health, security or engineering. Most had held these posts since the Collapse and steered the village through some very tough and dangerous times.

Everyone knew the purpose of the meeting as they arrived in the village hall. Roger, the Chairman, sat at the head of the table. He painfully stood up, despite a night's sleep he was still dog-tired, aching after the trials and tribulations of the last two weeks. His powers of recuperation were not what they had been.

He asked for quiet. Then recounted the highs and lows of the mission to help eight villagers get across the Mississippi to a new life in the west; meeting unexpected help in Memphis from Damian and his father, and the extraordinary help they had provided to help the group safely across. Finally, the confrontation with the coyotes. They had been expecting to transport the eight from the village—at a huge profit. As insurance, they'd held Pat and Jane's family hostage. They were not happy about being duped. He spared the Council the details of their brutal ending. Finally, Roger confirmed they had reunited Jane with her husband and son who were now near Clarksville deciding on their future.

Everyone expressed delight at the success of the mission, though surprised that Jane had not returned to French Creek with her family. Despite her inauspicious arrival they had all grown to like her. Jane arrived at French Creek many months earlier with a covert plan to recruit disaffected villagers to come with her to the west. If successful, the coyotes in Memphis, would release her

husband and son who they had held for five years. Keeping them as leverage to ensure Jane provided a steady supply of refugees.

Ultimately, Jane had admitted to the whole village her plans, and asked for their forgiveness, and help. The result: the mission Roger had just recounted with a happy ending for all concerned.

Roger finished with some background on the three children, the appalling circumstances under which they had been living and consequently why they were back at French Creek. Roger didn't provide too many details on the activities in the cabin, saying, with resignation in his voice, that some things are better left unspoken.

He spoke for a few minutes, before asking the inevitable question, "What are we going to do with the children?"

He sat down, allowing Council members to discuss the unique problem at hand. Normally newcomers to French Creek were adults, trying to find a new safe and welcoming home. Irrespective of their needs, the Village had instigated, soon after the Collapse, a strict set of criteria that would allow people to join the community. This selection process revolved very much around matching their abilities and skills with the current or future needs of the community. Put simply, those that could be of use were allowed in, others turned away.

Never before had they faced dealing with three parentless children. There was no question in anyone's mind of turning them away. The challenge lay in finding a family willing to take on these troubled children. No one on the Council could help. They either had families of their own, were too old, or didn't have enough space.

After much debate, they narrowed it down to three families who might be candidates to adopt the children. All were in their late thirties, had grown up children and big enough houses. Crucially, everyone could vouch for their solid parenting skills.

Doc Brown said he'd talk to each of them to see if they were interested in taking on this tremendous responsibility. In the meantime, the children would stay under observation in the health center, at least two people with them twenty-four hours a day.

Chapter 6

Sacramento (The new Federal capital), California. Office of Senator for Kentucky, Charles Kingston.

Charles Kingston, three-term Senator for Kentucky and now Secretary for Redevelopment of the East had a problem. Five, almost six years after the Collapse, little under his leadership had been achieved in bringing back a semblance of Federal Government control over the eastern half of the country.

As he sat in his large office overlooking the Sacramento River sipping his third cup of coffee, the Senator cut an imposing figure in his five thousand dollar suit, tailored perfectly to hide a slightly broadening waistline (he blamed too many fundraising dinners). His flowing gray hair, expertly styled, swept back in carefully coffered waves. A delicate perma-tan made him look younger than his fifty-five years. He was the archetypal, TV friendly politician, ready with a gleaming smile, firm handshake and knife to stab you in the back.

Leaning back in his chair, feet on his desk, he realized how much he missed the cut and thrust of Kentucky politics. Before the Collapse, it had been a cesspit of rival factions that took all his experience and cunning to control and bend to his wishes. Kentucky politicians had a reputation for fighting dirty, and he loved getting his hands soiled as he bribed, bought, and fought each election like a duel to the death. No matter how unscrupulous it became, he always won, while looking suave and coming up smelling of expensive aftershave. Now he wanted to get back into the fray. It was time to do something, anything, to make his mark. But the old problems just wouldn't go away.

Years of economic depression, plummeting tax revenues and supporting millions of migrants from the east, had kept the country bankrupt. What limited resources they had were used to prop up the economy of the western USA. It left practically nothing to revive the fortunes of those back east, and his former constituents in Kentucky.

However, the first presidential elections since the Collapse were slated for next year and the Senator wanted to support his president's re-election chances by showing voters they were finally reuniting America. For a longer period than any since 1776, the President had remained in office without re-election. All because of a spectacularly underhanded meeting with Congress and the Senate members as they were about to board the last plane out prior to the fall of Washington, DC. Presented with two alternatives: agree to no presidential elections for an indeterminate time in the future; or for those in the east, as representatives of ungovernable constituents, receive no pay or perks. It was a breathtaking abuse of power which left the stateless Senate and Congress members with no choice but to concur.

That deal couldn't last forever. Even if half of the country was in no position to vote, the clamor for a presidential election had reached a level that one had to be called. Two weeks earlier, he had been summoned to the new Oval Office by President Cummings.

Uncomfortably seated in a hard chair opposite a tanned and relaxed Commander in Chief ensconced behind the Resolute Desk, the Senator guessed what was coming.

"Charles, we have to face facts—the electorate wants an election. We know the main issues will be the economy and the eastern problem. Unfortunately, the economy has not recovered sufficiently to allow us to mount a full-scale restoration of the east's economy and infrastructure."

The Senator nodded in agreement, waiting for the 'but'...the President didn't disappoint.

"...But we cannot be seen to be doing nothing. Too many people in the west have friends and relatives trapped over there expecting us to help them. Our corporate donors have assets tied up there which they want access to, and first choice at any infrastructure rebuilding. So I need you to come up with a plan that will be an election winner for us. One that will reassure people we are the government to reunite this country and make it great again."

The Senator drew a deep breath before replying, "I quite understand, Mr. President. My thoughts entirely. Can you give me any idea how much we can spend on this ambitious plan? What resources will be made available?"

The President peered over the top of his half-moon glasses and looked at the Senator as though he just told a tasteless joke.

"Charles, there is no money in FEMA, the DHS or the State Department. No one has any significant funds for this enterprise. You'll have to take your begging bowl and talk to them and all the other acronyms that populate this place. If it was easy, I'd have given the job to someone else. I know I can depend on you, Charles. My future and…," the President added ominously, "…yours, depends on this initiative appeasing the electorate. I know I can rely on you to produce the goods. Any further questions?"

With a sinking feeling, he replied, "No, no, Mr. President, you've been crystal clear. I'll get onto it immediately and have an outline proposal to you within two weeks. Thank you for this opportunity."

He wasn't even sure the President heard his groveling acceptance of the task he'd dumped on him. As he left the Oval Office, the President was now screaming down the phone to some hapless assistant about a fake news report on CNN.

The Senator, with an election battle to fight, needed a big, bold, innovative and dramatic initiative to help his party win, and secure his political future as well. He knew he'd been given a poisoned chalice when offered the job of bringing the east back into the fold. His large corporate donors were delighted to know he had this new task. They saw big money coming their way when the east opened up again. Now he was getting uncomfortably squeezed from both sides: the President and those lining his pockets.

It was time; he thought decisively, to make a name for himself. To go down in history as the man who made America whole again. He asked his aides for a choice of scenarios that would fit his grand scheme. Tasking them with thinking 'outside the box', to 'challenge every conventional idea', to be 'bold, creative and ambitious.'

Unfortunately, the Senator's inner circle of advisers had little time for his plans of self-aggrandizement. They'd heard this all before. Lots of talk and no action. In spite of their doubts, if he wanted some 'blue sky thinking', then they'd give him some 'off the wall' ideas to chew on. They all knew that the government was in no position to do anything except read the reports and mothball them until some unspecified time in the future. When the country had the resources to implement a carefully constructed plan to meld America back together. That time was not now.

They knew from satellite pictures and other intelligence, the eastern and southern coastal cities were in a better position, economically and governmentally, than those in the interior. Reports indicated that imports had helped them create partially viable economies. One's still very much stuck in the nineteenth century, but slowly improving. In terms of government, it was a mixed bag: gangs still ran many areas, others had created councils or groups of powerful or wealthy individuals running the cities as benevolent dictatorships.

None of this, of course, bore any resemblance to what had been in place before the Collapse. However, it was a start. The belief in Sacramento was that moving into these areas to re-establish an acceptable form of State and Federal control would be a hard sell to those in charge. Indeed, after the corruption, toxic partisanship and ineptitude of the pre-Collapse government, the consensus of opinion from agents and informers on the ground suggested the Senator look for other areas to implement his grand ideas.

That meant considering states bordering the Mississippi. How ripe were they, the Senator asked his staff, for ReFederalization? (A phrase he had come up with and was now recommending to be used in all reports. He felt it had an authoritative ring to it, a legitimacy such a plan needed.)

The first problem was obtaining any concrete information from those areas of the country. Primarily rural states, government sources had difficulty mixing in with the local population. They were easily and frequently ousted as intruders. So getting up close and personal in these communities was a dangerous occupation. Nevertheless, keen to report something positive back to Sacramento, many of them disclosed that numerous smaller communities were slowly progressing beyond a nineteenth century societal framework, and were desperate for help.

They admitted the major cities on the Mississippi, like Memphis, New Orleans and Minneapolis, were riddled with violence and corruption. In fact, it was so endemic with gangs making fortunes smuggling people and materials across the Mississippi, many believed they were potentially lethal flashpoints for ReFederalization. Ones definitely to avoid.

Over a few days, he and his office conceived a plan to ReFederalize some states along the Mississippi and use them as a 'beach head' (he didn't use that word out loud, it smacked of invasion) but it illustrated the point. He saw his role as more rescuer and savior, though it encapsulated the approach he had in mind. Once established, they'd move towards the Appalachians and the Great Lakes.

The task was enormous. After five long years, how do you re-impose government at state and federal level? The vacuum created by the Collapse had been filled with a mismatch of local communities all pursuing their own regimes, with varying degrees of success. What would be their reaction if ReFederalization was offered to them? If the majority wanted it, then it wouldn't pose too many problems. But what if they didn't? How could you force them, without appearing as some heavy-handed colonial invasion?

Brushing aside these concerns raised by his staff, the Senator produced and delivered his report to the President entitled:

The ReFederalization of the Eastern USA

Stage 1: Kentucky, Tennessee, Alabama & Iowa.

A proposal for the Rescue, Relief and Reconstruction of the economy and government in these states.

The proposal ran to 150 pages, covering everything from: relief efforts providing vital supplies to persuading the utility companies to rebuild their infrastructure; establishing financial services to implementing healthcare, and law enforcement. Finally, the organizing of elections leading to a viable government.

Every government department read the report and had its say. Six months later, a watered-down version, now with the military heavily involved, was agreed upon. The revised plan focused on just one state acting as a test before it rolled out across the country.

Even so, it was a mammoth undertaking, one that had never been attempted before. The innumerable steps to achieving the Government's and Charles Kingston's objectives, in reality would take years, even decades to reach fruition. With blind optimism and an election on the horizon, he believed the initial phase could be done in only two.

Everyone involved had reservations, except the Senator. Blinkered in his belief and blinded by his ego, he looked forward to being the first senior government official to step foot in the eastern USA for six years.

The scene of his historic political triumph was to be, of course: Kentucky.

Chapter 7

The three rescued children had been found a caring family to live with. It had taken their new foster parents weeks of patient understanding and care for the two girls, Stephanie and Shelby, to slowly emerge from their near catatonic state. Now they were settling in at school, starting to gradually talk and interact with the rest of the family. Foster parents, Don and Jean, were delighted with their progress. The elder boy, Jamie, was faring much better and already learning new skills, particularly in farming.

Roger and Doc Brown had dropped by for an update as they had over the previous weeks.

"I do believe we've turned the corner. The girls are brighter and mixing well with the other kids. Still a long way to go, and without access to proper therapy, I'm not sure they will ever be a hundred percent normal," explained Don.

His wife Jean, sitting by his side, nodded her agreement, adding, "Jamie is much better too, though he has some pretty violent temper tantrums from time to time. We can control him at the moment, but as he gets bigger and stronger, it could cause a problem unless he grows out of them."

"Let's hope so. You've both done an exceptional job. I can't thank you enough. If you'd seen the conditions they were living in, it's a wonder they are anywhere close to 'normal' so soon. The resilience of kids never ceases to amaze me," said Roger.

Doc Brown chipped in with his own thoughts. "Let me know how Jamie's tantrums develop. We have some extracts of CBD oil and marijuana that could help calm him down, if you think that would help?"

Jean replied, "Thanks for the offer Doc, let's see how we get on, we don't want to start dosing him up quite yet."

The four chatted about the children for another half an hour before Roger and Doc Brown took their leave. As they walked down the main street of the village, the feel of spring was definitely in the air. The leaves were about to burst into what Roger always thought was almost a phosphorescent green–so strong and striking were the colors. It was a time when the Kentucky countryside was at its most verdant and prolific.

"I'm going to the spring Barter Fair in a week. I can see if there's any black market drugs that could help Jamie, if you like? It seems every time I go there's more of them available. Give me a list, I'll keep an eye out for them," Roger offered.

"Sure, let me put something together. After all this time without them, I've become quite the believer in trying to use natural remedies. No harm though having some artificial alternatives."

"Let me know, I'll do what I can Doc," replied Roger, as they went their separate ways. Roger to his home, Doc Brown to the health center.

Roger found his son Landy in the kitchen, reading a book on how to build a 'ham radio'. "What do you think of trying to build one of these?" he asked, showing his father the book.

Roger glanced at the pages, "Great idea, son. We tried in the past to see if we could communicate with other communities using this, immediately after the Collapse. From memory, not much came of it. Those we reached were overseas, so not a lot of help. I don't know where the equipment went. Some of it may have been used for other purposes. Ask Jerry, he was involved I think."

Saying he would do that straight away, he got up and left, leaving Roger a little nonplussed about his son's motives, or his ability to build such a piece of equipment. Whatever, if it kept him occupied, then no harm done. He brewed up some tea (he'd actually managed to grow his own tea plants for the first time) and settled down to make his own list of what he needed at the Barter Fair.

Each year the choice of goods available at the Fair increased. Now, you could get practically anything. It had grown to become a mammoth, twice yearly market, fun fair and meeting place. Thousands of people congregated to buy, sell, swap produce, materials, tools, in fact anything someone might need that you didn't want. It was also a place to pick up the latest news and gossip, drink, eat and enjoy company outside of one's own community. There were workshops and music, speakers, poets and plays to entertain all ages over the three days. And, of course, wherever there are sizable crowds, less salubrious activities were available like drugs, sex and gambling.

French Creek normally sent a contingent of twenty to thirty people, this time was no exception. Chosen by ballot, those going took their own wares to sell, as well as those from other villagers who weren't making the trip. Plus long lists of things to buy.

The following week, twenty-five villagers on horseback and towing two carts of goods for selling or trading, left for the two-day journey. It proved to be uneventful and late the second day they arrived at Glasgow, the venue for the Barter Fair.

Glasgow was a modest size town. Post-Collapse, its population dropped to around two thousand, a figure more than doubled during the Fair. Founded in 1799, they named it after Glasgow in Scotland, the hometown of the father of William Logan, one of the two commissioners charged with selecting the original town and county seat. Up until the Collapse, they still maintained the connection with Scotland holding a quirky annual Highland Games. It was rumored the organizers hoped to restart this spectacle at a future Barter Fair.

The Fair was already in full swing when the French Creek group arrived. People made the trek from as far away as Louisville, Nashville and Bowling Green. Tents and marquees of every shape and size were already providing cover for the countless activities that ran all day and night. Clustered alongside were hundreds of stalls selling, buying or bartering every imaginable product a family or community might need.

Roger, who attended every year, was stunned at how much it had grown. As far as the eye could see was a mass of people, animals and makeshift structures. It was organized chaos. The group split up to see what was on offer, or set up their own stalls, Roger and Pat wandered around taking in the sights, smells and sounds, almost overwhelming after the tranquility of French Creek.

On Saturday afternoon, Roger found a stall selling a startling array of drugs and pharmacy products. It was even branded Rite Aid like the old pharmacy. He doubted it was the real company, though it had an impressive array of merchandise. He presented Doc Brown's list to the 'pharmacist' who said he had most of the drugs they wanted, and to come back later when he'd have them ready. How was he going to pay, he enquired? Roger had a selection of gemstones the community accumulated over the years. After some haggling they agreed that a ruby ring would be a fair trade. As he handed the gem over, the pharmacist mentioned there was now a 'Pawn & Currency Exchange' somewhere at the Fair that would give him an excellent rate for his gems, in exchange for cash.

This was the first time Roger had heard of this at the Barter Fair. "Cash? Now there's a rare commodity. Thanks for the information. I'll go and check it out" commented Roger to the pharmacist. After an hour's search, he discovered it, housed in a very official-looking trailer, complete with a Federal Reserve logo painted above the door.

Inside sat two smartly dressed young men in suits. Roger approached the window, "Good morning gentleman, haven't seen you at the Barter Fair before. How's it going?"

One of the men, slim, with close-cropped blond hair and an earring, leant forward to answer Roger's question. "You're right, sir, our first time here. Only told to come a week or two ago, so all done in a bit of a rush." He waved his hand around the trailer as if to point out its defects. None were obvious to Roger.

"So you work for…?"

"The Government. The Treasury, to be precise. Apparently, we're part of some initiative to reintroduce the dollar back into circulation over here. Not quite sure how you guys have managed without it for the last five, almost six, years? Must have been tough not having any money," commented the young cashier with disarming innocence.

Trying to curb his sarcasm, Roger replied, "Well, it's amazing how well you can manage when there are no shops and nothing to buy. We've got used to bartering and swapping stuff instead. And surprise, surprise if we can't do that, we make it, or go without."

The young man looked horrified, "Ooh that sounds terrible, a lot of hard work I should think. Rather glad we're in the west aren't you?" he turned to his co-worker, who nodded in agreement.

"Know anything more about this 'Initiative' you mentioned? What else are they planning?" Roger was intrigued.

"Not much, except what we read in the papers and online. Seems the senator for Kentucky has the go ahead for a plan to get the east up and running again. It's not the first time this has been in the news, so who knows if it will happen this time? Anyway, getting some real money in circulation was one of the first ideas. That's why we're here. A kinda advanced guard, I suppose," he explained with some pride. Then, trying to be helpful, he added, "you can go online to find out more on their website."

Roger patiently replied, "In case you hadn't noticed, we don't have any electricity, let alone access to the internet."

"Ah yes, of course. Silly me. Well, I hear that's another of the things they'll be sorting out…sending up loads of satellites to give people access that way. Um. Not sure what they have planned about electricity though, sorry," said the young man, looking a little deflated he couldn't be the bearer of even more good news. Undeterred, he carried on enthusiastically.

"Anyway sir, have you anything you wanted to trade in for some nice new dollar bills? We offer a better exchange rate than anyone else here. And I believe there are many people here now accepting them as payment. It seems to be catching on quickly."

The cashier's gushing eagerness was getting on Roger's nerves. He decided he'd found out enough. Declining the young man's offer and wishing them a good day, he moved off back into the throng of people swarming around the stalls.

Roger continued his meanderings, this time interested to see which stall holders were now accepting dollar bills. Over the course of the next hour he counted around twenty, not a huge percentage compared to the number of stalls at the Fair, but a start.

He wandered into a bar, ordered a real beer, found a table and sat down to consider what he'd discovered. Is the Government really trying to kick start the east's economy with wads of cash? He could not imagine what would be involved in making that enormous undertaking work. Not just billions of dollars, but forging a financial, banking infrastructure as well. People with hordes of cash in their home were a recipe for attracting crime and violence, something that, by default, had disappeared after the Collapse.

The more Roger thought about this, the more absurd the whole idea became. It wasn't just about money, though the government always seemed to think it was. Was that the best place to start, anyway? Indeed, where do you start trying to resurrect an entire society that was plunged back into the nineteenth century and only now was organizing itself at the most basic, local level? Nations and societies took decades, even centuries to develop and evolve into a civilized, coordinated framework. While Roger prided himself on being an optimist, he could see no way they could do this on a broad-scale basis...unless, it suddenly came to him, are they planning to do it state by state? If that was the case–the fact that the Currency Exchange was at the Barter Fair–did that suggest Kentucky was in the front line for this plan?

With an abundance of questions, and no answers coming to mind, he made his way back to the group's campsite, deciding to talk it over with the others. Maybe they had heard something.

That evening around the campfire, Roger told them what he'd discovered and asked if anyone had similar news?

Herb, the schoolteacher, was always pretty forthright in his opinions.

"I haven't spoken to anyone or heard anything about it, though now you mention it, I have seen a few stalls offering to take cash, which I thought was unusual. As for the idea they can somehow propel us back to civilization using just money, is simply preposterous. Just think of all the services and institutions that need to be established at the same time–to make it all work? Even if it's done, as you think it might be Roger, on a state by state basis, the logistics of it are still colossal. Infrastructure, security, government, communications, transportation, education, law and order…the list goes on. One can't exist without the others, so how on earth are you going to set this all up at once? So far, the west's answer is to give us all some cash we can't spend and have nowhere to keep safe. Whoopee, that's a cracking start. I tell you, I fucking despair. As they say, you can't fix stupid."

The others around the fire nodded in agreement, though Brian, the village's 'Mr Fix it', was less critical. Stroking his beard as if it helped him to collect his thoughts, he countered Herb's tirade.

"I can't disagree with a lot of what you say Herb. It's a colossal undertaking for any government to try and get the east back on the road to the 21st century. But they have to start somewhere, somehow. I don't have the answers, but I don't think you can criticize them for trying, can you? They can't just leave things as they are. We're a divided country, something's gotta be done to stitch us back together. Though I dread to think of the consequences if they mess it up. Give them some credit for at least trying…I say, let's see what they do next?"

And so the arguments flowed back and forth. Everyone had an opinion on how it should be done, if indeed it should be done at all. People don't like change, especially if they are reasonably happy with the *status quo*. How they were living now certainly had its drawbacks, but at least they were alive, healthy and, to a large extent, free. Roger sat and listened to the discussion, adding his own comments from time to time. As the evening drew to a close he suggested:

"Ignorance can be bliss, as they say, however in this case I think we need to find out more. I don't enjoy being in the dark about things like this. Why don't we all spend tomorrow talking to people, see what they've heard, what they know, and maybe we might all learn something more? Let's get together tomorrow evening and compare notes?"

Knowledge is power, someone once said. Especially true when it comes to understanding how your life is about to be turned upside down. What the group on the second day found was a mish mash of rumor and speculation. Nonetheless, the information they'd gathered painted a picture that put the fear of God into Roger.

Chapter 8

Frankfort, the capital of Kentucky, always was, and still is, a small city compared to Lexington or Louisville. Originally called 'Franks Ford' after the name of a settler who died there in the 1780s, the local inhabitants believed its location on the Kentucky River would ensure a successful future for the town. It subsequently achieved its lofty position in 1792 by bribing the committee tasked with deciding where the capital should be established. Local wealthy residents gave them $3,000 and, among other things 1,500lbs of nails to ensure the decision went their way.

Thus the city founded on such dishonest dealings, continued on its corrupt path and prospered accordingly. Like all centers of government, it became a lightning rod for the dishonesty that runs like blood through the arteries of power. Unsurprisingly, Senator Charles Kingston felt quite at home in such a pernicious environment.

However, despite its title and position, by 2020, Frankfort still only had a population of twenty six thousand souls. After the Collapse, this had plummeted to under two thousand.

Notwithstanding its sparse population, the Senator thought it symbolic and appropriate that, when the time came, he should announce his vainglorious attempt at uniting America from this tiny, decimated capital city. However, long before that, a considerable amount of groundwork had to be laid.

The State Department had appointed Major General Anthony Redditch to spearhead the initial launch of ReFederalization by organizing and sending in the advance guard called the Rescue, Relief and Reconstruction Force (RRRF). The RRRF was the spearhead of ReFederalization bringing relief supplies to as many people as possible over several weeks. Preceding these visits, the USAF would drop leaflets, bringing the good news to all the inhabitants.

It was only days after the group returned from the Barter Fair when French Creek's residents, busy working in the fields, picked up the distant growl of a C-17's engine growing closer and closer. Everyone stopped and looked skyward at a sight and sound they hadn't heard in years: an aircraft flying over the village.

As they peered up into a perfect blue sky, it was suddenly filled with thousands of pieces of paper fluttering down like giant confetti. Most fell into the trees and the next Hollow, but enough came down close by for several villagers to pick them up.

Everyone started to read them. One man took his straight to Roger who was already on his way to retrieve one for himself. He picked one up and sat down on his front porch reading the words of one Senator Charles Kingston.

In part, they proclaimed:

GREETINGS FROM YOUR GOVERNMENT! WE ARE HERE TO HELP YOU BECOME PART OF THE UNITED STATES AGAIN!

Dear Fellow Kentuckians,

We know it's been a long time since you heard from your Government, at the State or Federal level. It has been a difficult time for all of us, but the good news is we can now begin reviving the economy of the east, starting with my home state of Kentucky. Soon you will enjoy all the benefits you once had under the care and safety of a newly established Legislature—of which you will be a part!

This is exciting and welcome news for everyone who has suffered so egregiously over the last six years. However, this will not happen overnight, a lot has to be rebuilt and put in place before we can get back to normal.

I can assure you we will be working hard on your behalf to make it happen as quickly as possible. With your co-operation, help and enthusiasm, we can achieve the impossible and make Kentucky the great state it once was.

And so it went on.

Roger stopped reading. He felt almost nauseous at the prospect of Senator Kingston leading this hugely ambitious plan. A corrupt and incompetent Senator–the only thing he successfully led was the panicked rush to leave the state as the Collapse caused the Commonwealth of Kentucky's government to implode. Now he was back, offering salvation to all. Many of the villagers came up to Roger seeking his opinion on what they'd read. Did he think it could happen? How long would it take? How would it affect the village?

"Everyone, let's just calm down," said Roger, standing up so everyone could hear him.

"I have a little more information about this. Based on what I found out at the Barter Fair, I was going to wait until the next Council meeting to discuss it. Clearly this piece of information," Roger waved the leaflet in the air to illustrate his point, "makes it more urgent. I suggest we have a general meeting for all the villagers to discuss the matter. Can you tell everyone you know we'll get together tomorrow evening at 7:00 p.m. in the village hall?"

The crowd dispersed, chattering excitedly among themselves.

Roger sat down to consider this unexpected turn of events. He decided a meeting of the council before tomorrow evening's village wide gathering would be useful to sound out their opinions and inform them in advance what he had learnt at the Barter Fair. He spent the next hour visiting the Council member's homes and suggesting they meet at 5:00 p.m. tomorrow. Everyone had heard about, or read, the missive from Senator Kingston. Already, people were forming wildly diverse opinions.

On his way back home in the gathering gloom, he saw Doc Brown leaving the health center. He walked over to warn him about the meeting and felt the need to express his early concerns. The Doc was a pragmatic, down to earth man who, despite all the trials, deaths and problems he'd confronted in the last six years, was always upbeat and positive.

"You heard the news?" Roger asked, not feeling it necessary to even explain what it was.

"Difficult not to Roger, not surprisingly it's the only topic of conversation today. I haven't read the whole leaflet but I get the drift of it. How that duplicitous bastard Kingston has the nerve to come back here playing the good guy, defies decency. I'm not saying we should criticize the idea, just in this case, I think we should shoot the messenger! That guy couldn't run a candy stall. Now he's going to make Kentucky great again? Just like that?" Doc Brown waved his hand in the air imitating a magician's wand.

"My feelings exactly, Doc. My concern is he will play on everyone's hopes and fears with lots of vague promises. Then somehow try to impose on us something we may not want, or be ready for. God knows it's about time the west started doing something. From what I've heard so far-and it's not a lot- this entire plan is programmed to fail. I'll be telling the Council what I know at the meeting tomorrow at 5:00 p.m. Make sure you're there Doc."

"I will be Roger, I will. Have a good evening, try to get some rest."

He walked into his house to find Landy surrounded by pieces of electronic components strewn across the dining room table.

"Hi Dad, Jerry gave me a huge box full of all the bits for the ham radio. He says he's happy to give me a hand trying to put it all together, see if we can make it work. Even gave me a copy of *Amateur Electronics Magazine* that explains how to make it! Might take a while. He reckons most of the pieces are here to make a basic version. Exciting eh?"

Distractedly, Roger agreed, trying to emulate his son's enthusiasm, saying, "You go for it son, a great project to get working." He wandered into the kitchen to brew up some tea, it always calmed him down and helped him cogitate on a particularly tricky problem.

Little did he know in a few weeks he would find himself in the middle of a dangerous game being played by forces for and against ReFederalization.

Chapter 9

❝What the fuck is this bullshit?" bellowed Danny Trevino at his two assistants, before crumpling up Senator Kingston's flyer and hurling it across the room. One of them recovered it, before dropping it into a trash bin. Danny didn't like untidiness. At the moment, Danny didn't like anything. He continued his rant. "After all I've done for that asshole, he now wants to come here and roll us over? No fucking way, the man's dead meat if he tries."

Danny strode across the room, scattering all before him. When he was in a mood like this, everyone stayed silent until the tsunami of vitriol ebbed away. He stopped at the floor to ceiling windows of his spacious apartment, surveying his domain like a Roman emperor. Before him stretched the shattered remains of Louisville. It might be a shadow of its former self, but it was his; lock, stock and barrel. He'd fought, kicked, and killed his way to annihilate other gangs for control of this lucrative city by the river. No sleazy two-faced politician was going to take it away from him now. *No Way Jose.*

Louisville, named after King Louis XVI of France, was founded in 1778. Its position by the only major falls on the Ohio river helped it develop a lucrative trade in portage: charging travelers to get past the unnavigable falls by land. Its principal claim to fame since then had been as the birthplace of fighter Mohammed Ali, and the annual running of the Kentucky Derby, started in 1875 by the grandson of William Clark of Lewis and Clark fame.

By the time of the Collapse, it was Kentucky's largest city with a population of 660,000, now reduced to around 20,000 hardy souls who seemed resigned to having an ambitious crime lord as their mayor. At least he made no pretense of being law-abiding, unlike his elected predecessors.

Danny turned, still furious, to a tall, gamine blonde, his current favorite assistant and occasional bed time entertainment, "Olivia, get the precinct Captains here immediately. We need to discuss this and prepare for what this asshole might throw at us."

"Sure Danny, I'll get right on it," she sashayed out of the room, Danny admiring her rear view as she left. With the other assistant following, Olivia went to a bank of walkie-talkies and began contacting the Captains that ran the different areas of the city on Danny's behalf. Her message was short and urgent. Get here now. Be warned, the boss is in a worse than shitty mood. Be late and you'll probably lose a limb.

Within the hour, the ten Captains (as Danny liked to call them, a nod to his favorite TV series, *The Sopranos*) arrived and stood fidgeting nervously, each wondering what was coming their way. Urgent commands like this normally meant bad news.

Danny stood up to address his disparate group of tame hoodlums. At just five feet, six inches, Danny's lack of height had always made him feel inferior. At school, the butt of jokes and the loser in too many fist fights. Now it was all different. His physical prowess might be modest, but he had a razor sharp mind when it came to running this gang of criminal misfits. Violence, or the threat of it, kept them under control. Olivia had told him he looked a lot like Michael Corleone, Al Pacino's character in *The Godfather*. He was thrilled with the comparison. Now with his slicked back hair and sallow complexion, he didn't just look the part of a mob gangster, he was acting one as well.

Danny believed in giving his guys clear objectives, rewarding them well if they succeeded, or showing them the bottom of the Ohio River if they didn't.

"You've probably all seen the bullshit message sent out by Senator Kingston. He wants Kentucky back, he wants Louisville back. Just like that". Danny snapped his fingers in the air. "What a fucking nerve! Well, neither ain't gonna happen on my watch. He's put together some cockamamie story about bringing civilization back, making us all happy and healthy again. He shoulda thought of that a few years ago when he fucked off to Sacramento, leaving us in the shits. Well, I reckon we're doing alright now, eh guys? We don't need his help, do we?"

There was a murmuring of assent around the room.

"So we gotta show this little asshole he ain't welcome. Nor his Major General...whatever his name is, either. We are going to create a real uncomfortable welcome for them if they come here...and make sure their crazy plans for some kind of half-assed government die a quick death."

"So whaddya want us to do boss? We're with you one hundred percent," asked one of the younger Captains, his face imprinted with so many tattoos he looked like a comic character.

"While I put a plan together, you guys are gonna go back to your precincts. You're gonna get yourself well-armed. Train your guys how to use those weapons. Start figuring out ways to defend the city. How to use the bridges, tall buildings to rain shit down on these guys. I need some anti-helicopter gear, SAM missiles, I know we got some in storage somewhere. Check 'em out. Make sure they're working and you know how to use them. Johnny," he pointed to his number two in command, "you're in charge of that, got it?"

Johnny, rubbing his hands with glee, replied, "Sure thing boss, I'll get those babies primed and ready."

"Seb, I want you to figure out ways to secure the docks and all the locks." Seb nodded. He was the only ex-military in the group. A five-year stint in the Marines before being dishonorably discharged for beating his Sergeant to a pulp, had made him something of a hero among his fellow Captains. But he understood security. The docks and locks were the lifeblood of the city, but also an obvious route of attack by enemy forces.

"Finally, I need from you, a count of how many men you got and who are armed, trained and ready to fight."

Another murmur of agreement rippled around the room. The men were excited at the prospect of some action after months of doing little except smuggling gear from the west.

Danny looked around the room expectantly…"Well, what are you sitting here for…go do it you assholes. Y'all come back here with answers this time tomorrow OK?"

As they filed out of the apartment, there were lots of high fives and fist bumps. Danny had successfully got them riled up and ready to go.

After the room emptied, Danny turned to Olivia, "Reckon that went well. Now I need a drink to calm down, fix me a bourbon and coke can you doll?"

Moments later as she handed Danny his drink he grabbed her wrist, "Baby, I'm still all wound up. I think I need a nice relaxing massage…wanna come with me?" He asked, gently pulling her towards the bedroom.

"Sure sweetheart, where do you want massaging first?" she asked coyly as they entered the bedroom.

"Oh, I'll let you decide that," sighed Danny as he lay on the bed.

Olivia knew precisely what he wanted massaging first.

Chapter 10

The Council meeting was not going well. In fact, it was chaotic. Roger was trying to calm everyone down, bring a semblance of order so that a constructive discussion could start. So far, to no avail. A despairing thought crossed his mind: if this is how a group of ten supposedly sensible people behave when presented with this ReFederalization issue, what the hell was the village meeting going to be like?

Roger tried one last time to make himself heard, by thumping his fist down on the table so hard, the glasses of water almost bounced over, at the same time bellowing in his loudest barrack room voice. "Council members, can we start the meeting in an orderly fashion? Quiet PLEASE!" This time they heard his request. They stopped talking, and the meeting came to order.

"Thank you everyone. I'd be grateful if we could make sure all future comments are made one at a time? Thanks." Before waiting for comments, he immediately waded into the topic at hand.

"Alright, we've all seen this leaflet, which is long on vague promises and short on facts. Before we go any further, let me tell you what I, and the others who went to the Barter Fair a few days ago, found out about Senator Kingston's plans."

Roger prefaced his comments by saying most of it was hearsay, except possibly his conversation with the Currency Exchange cashiers. The Government's plan, he explained, was to initially oil the wheels of 'ReFederalization' as they are calling it, by making cash available in exchange for any goods people wanted to trade.

Second, there was talk of huge amounts of aid being distributed across the state, though no one could confirm this.

Third, as best as he could ascertain, sometime in the future, each county was to send two elected representatives to Frankfort to form the basis of a new State Government, but for Kentucky only at this stage. The Army is going to be involved in spreading the word and distributing aid and assistance. To help pay for it, the rumor is, they will charge taxes on people's tangible property–houses, equipment, livestock. Each county is to appoint a sheriff to administer collection of the taxes and create a small police force once the Army has withdrawn. No one could find out anything about when utilities such as power, telecoms and water would restart.

In other words, Roger couldn't resist adding a degree of skepticism to his report, "It's a lot of big ideas backed up by zero details at this stage. A lot of the important stuff is still up in the air."

"Roger, may I make a comment on what you've said?" asked Daphne Cortez, a striking middle-aged woman, with dense wavy gray hair that fell well below her shoulders. She was one of the lead gardeners in the community, well respected, but felt by some to have a slightly superior attitude when dealing with others.

"I, for one, feel we need to give this proposal a chance to come to fruition. Yes, there's a lot of unknowns which concern me. However, they have to start somewhere, somehow, and maybe we should be grateful that Kentucky is the first in line? I think we can all see the potential benefits and we should give the idea a chance to develop. Hold off on doing anything reactionary until we know more."

"Fair comment, Daphne. Anyone else?" Roger looked around the table. "Yes, Jason?"

"I'm all for being positive," Jason was one of the two teachers on the Council. "My concern is that it's all so vague. For every potential benefit, there seems to be a downside. Do we want cops as tax collectors? Where are the 'checks and balances' between the judiciary and the legislature, as the Founding Fathers decreed? And this tax on our assets, how's that going to be calculated, especially here where most of it is owned by the community as a whole? I want to see us moving back to parity with the west, but I'd need considerably more detail on how that's to be accomplished before I get on board."

Over the next hour, everyone had their say. Roger tried to stay neutral, putting aside his natural inclination to mistrust anything the unscrupulous Senator was proposing. In reality, it was just a waiting game until more information was forthcoming. Meantime, the Council meeting showed an alarming split between those ready to embrace change without fully realizing what was involved, and those wanting to tread more circumspectly. One or two, Roger noted, were openly hostile to the whole idea.

Later on the whole village arrived to discuss the issue. Practically every able-bodied adult in the community was there. Over 130 people packed into the church that doubled up as the village hall. There weren't enough seats to accommodate everyone. Pastor Simon, standing at the door welcoming people sighed inwardly, "if only every Sunday service was this popular." Such a huge turnout was rare. This topic had people fired up.

Many were eager to welcome the changes blowing in the wind, others were distrustful of anything coming from the Federal Government and Senator Kingston specifically. They had seen him in action before, his record was less than impressive.

What everyone agreed on was the lack of trust they felt towards anything a Government who had abandoned them for six years, said or did. This distrust had a justified foundation. The Government had exacerbated the perfect storm of natural disasters that had initiated the Collapse, by allowing the economy to deteriorate to such a level it was in no position to offer any aid. Then they deserted the sinking ship and left millions of Americans to their fate.

At the end of the meeting, Roger suggested they could do no more at the moment than wait and see. Too much speculation was pointless and stoked people's fears—or hopes—unnecessarily. As soon as more was known, a further meeting would be held.

Later at home, Roger was writing up notes from both meetings in the *Record of French Creek,* as he called it. He'd started it soon after the Council was formed to record the minutes from all the meetings. To ensure accuracy, after drafting them out, he asked at least one other Council member to check them. He then transcribed them into *The Record.* This book was open to anyone to read and find out what the Council had discussed and decided. This evening he was adding a few extra details from the general meeting when his front door crashed open and Don came careening in.

"Roger, you gotta come quick, Jamie is holding Jean hostage. He's got a knife and is threatening to kill her, then himself."

Roger stood up, grabbed his service pistol from the gun safe, then followed Don as he ran towards his house. He lived about a quarter of a mile away. They reached it in just a few minutes. People were already milling around, wanting to know what the commotion was.

Roger pointed to one of them and barked, "Go get Pat and Doc Brown, tell them we have a hostage situation and to get here asap."

He turned to Don, "where are they in the house, do you know?"

"Upstairs in his bedroom, at the back...please do something quickly, he's completely lost it. I really think he might do something stupid."

"Where are the two little girls?"

"I got them out and put them with a neighbor."

"Good job. Any firearms in the house?"

"No."

"OK, do you know what brought this meltdown on?"

"I really don't, I've been out all day and came back to find them locked up upstairs with him screaming blue murder."

Doc Brown arrived, with Pat in close pursuit. Roger told them what he knew so far.

"Let's try to calm him down, and at least talk to us," advised Doc.

They moved around the back of the house and stood looking up at the bedroom window. "Jamie, it's Doc Brown here. What seems to be the problem, buddy? Come to the window and you can tell me what's troubling you."

Silence.

"Jamie...you're not in any trouble son, just tell us what's going on. We're here to help you anyway we can."

Silence. Doc tried another tack.

"Jamie, please talk to us...your little sisters are worried sick about you."

A few moments later, they could hear movement upstairs and Jamie appeared at the window, knife in hand, tears streaming down his face.

"You can't help me, no one can. Just leave me alone. Don't try anything. I've got Jean here. Tied up. I don't want to hurt her. I just want to be left alone. Tell my sisters I'm alright."

"OK, OK Jamie, that's not a problem, we'll just wait down here until you want to talk again. Whenever you like. Promise me you won't harm Jean. She's done nothing to deserve being hurt." Doc's plea elicited no reply.

"What do you suggest Doc?" asked Pat. All his military training was prompting him to storm the bedroom if nothing happened soon.

As if reading his mind, Roger said pointedly, "let's not try any heroics here Pat, give it time."

Pat nodded his assent and moved back into the garden sitting down against a large cottonwood tree. Doc, Roger and Don moved far enough away from the house so anyone inside wouldn't hear them.

Don, panic-stricken with worry, looked at both of them, asking the inevitable question, "Do you think he'll hurt her? She's been nothing but kind to him, treated him like a son from day one, she doesn't deserve this."

48

"I don't know Don, sorry I wish I could give you some reassurance. Don't get too despondent. He's a troubled young man and something has set him off today, which no one saw coming. We'll just have to…," Doc paused mid-sentence. He turned to Don asking, "he's really fond of his sisters, isn't he?"

"He adores them, very protective. Always looking out for them, why?"

"I'm thinking they might be the leverage we need to snap him out of this."

A few minutes later, Jamie's two scared and bewildered younger sisters were shepherded around to the back of the house. Pat and Roger kept well out of the way while Doc Brown and Don held the little girl's hands. They all looked up at the bedroom window.

Shelby, with a slight prompt, shouted up to her brother, "Hey, Jamie, it's Shelby. Can I talk to you? I'm scared. Whatcha doing with Momma up there?"

A muffled voice from inside the bedroom shouted down, "Shelby, you shouldn't be here. Go away. This is not your problem. Leave me alone."

Shelby looked up at Don, confusion in her eyes, "Why's he tellin' me to go away? This is my home. I want to stay here, with him."

"I know you do honey, but your brother's having a bad, bad day and we need your help making him feel better," explained Don as he crouched down beside the tearful girl.

"We need to get him downstairs so we can all have a friendly talk about it. Will you help me Shelby?"

The girl nodded cautiously.

"OK, so tell me, what's your favorite book he reads to you?"

"Harry Potter," she sniffled.

"They are great books Shelby. I love them too. Why don't you tell him you're going inside to get a Harry Potter book and you want him to read it to you? Can you do that?"

"Yes, think so."

"Good girl, so let's do that now, OK?"

They all went inside. Shelby perched herself at the bottom of the stairs, with Roger hiding behind the door of the other bedroom. She put on a bravura performance, a combination of gentle persuasion and a heart-string pulling request for Jamie to come downstairs and read with her and Stephanie.

Finally, Jamie replied with a grunted, "Let me think about it."

Shelby pleaded again with her brother to come out. Eventually, Jamie's bedroom door slowly creaked open. He peered round the landing. He looked down and saw Shelby look up to meet his eyes.

"Hi Jamie, can we read Harry Potter now? Stephanie's here too."

After a few seconds of hesitation, the distraught boy ran down the stairs to his sisters, picked them up, and with tears streaming down his face hugged them tight, blubbering words of apologies, reassurance and love.

Roger stepped out from behind the bedroom door. "Well done, Jamie, you did the right thing. I'll go check on your Mom."

With the brother and sisters still in a huddle at the bottom of the stairs, Roger quickly made his way into the boy's bedroom. Jean was sitting on the bed, crying hysterically.

"Jean, did he hurt you? Are you OK?"

Jean looked up. "I'm OK Roger, I'm crying because I'm relieved this ended without anyone getting injured. I don't think he meant me any harm, he just had a meltdown."

"Do you know what caused it?" Roger asked as he undid her bindings.

"A tragic accident, in a way. He was out at the far end of the village, helping herd cows into the slaughterhouse. I never thought of the awful connection he would make to where he used to live. As soon as he saw the carcasses and remains of the butchered animals, I guess it just triggered some horrific memories. He just couldn't stand the sight of it. I thought he might have PTSD, this just confirms it. I was in the wrong place at the wrong time. He somehow thought we'd send him back. I don't know what was going through his mind. It was scary, but the poor kid is just seriously troubled."

"Jesus, I didn't realize that he was still living on such a knife-edge. We'll have to figure out how we can manage this moving forward. He's downstairs now…are you up to being in the same room as him?"

Jean stood up and walked towards the door, "Roger, he and I live here. I'm his Mom. Now let's go down there and start working on a solution."

Once matters had calmed down, Roger left and wearily trudged back home. The adrenaline was quickly wearing off and he was exhausted. For the moment, the situation at Don and Jean's was under control, for how long he didn't know. Jamie was obviously a powder keg that the slightest incident could set off, with potentially tragic consequences. How that was to be resolved, he hadn't a clue.

As he closed the door, he heard Landy's excited voice from the bedroom, "Hey, guess what Dad? Jerry and I got the ham radio working. We need to figure out a regular source of power of course. He thinks we can rig up an old solar panel. How cool is that? Means we can talk to people all over the country now!"

Wearily Roger acknowledged his son's enthusiasm, "That's great news son, well done. Can I take a look tomorrow? I'm knackered."

"Sure Dad, that'd be fantastic. Night!"

Little did they know the radio would become an indispensable lifeline for the entire village. Indeed, the entire state.

Chapter 11

❝What's this pile of crap?" Senator Kingston looked disdainfully at a photograph one of his assistants put on his desk. He picked it up as if it had a foul smell attached to it.

"I thought you'd like to see where the first $50,000 of your currency for goods exchange has gone. That's a warehouse full of the stuff we've taken from people in Kentucky and given them cash instead. Not a bad haul in the first few weeks, eh Senator?" His aide, Houston, a young rising star in his office, tried to put a positive spin on this modest start to the grand ReFederalization plan.

"If you say so," said the Senator dismissively. Clearly not at all impressed at what looked like a large Goodwill outlet. Why do these people think he'd be interested in this pile of trash? He was a big picture man, details were for others to deal with. He moved on to more exciting aspects of the mission.

"How close is the Major General to having his troops ready to move out and start spreading our *largesse* across Kentucky? Time is of the essence."

"Pretty close," answered Houston vaguely. "They had to produce a video to brief the troops on the best way to explain how we are going to implement the RRRF mission and then the ReFederalization of Kentucky. That took a bit of time. To be honest, they couldn't go into much detail, as well, no one seems to know precisely how it's going to happen, sir."

The Senator looked at his aide in astonishment, "Well of course there are no details on how it's going to work, stupid. Because, deliberately, those details have yet to be worked out. That's the beauty of this plan. It's flexible, it can respond to any situation quickly without being bound by too many rigid rules and regulations."

Houston winced at being called stupid. The insult hid the fact that he knew the whole edifice was proceeding on a wing and a prayer, with such lack of planning, a successful outcome surely must be in doubt? Anyway, that's for the Senator to deal with, thought Houston. Typical politician.

"I understand Senator, let me go and check on the Major General's progress and I'll get right back to you, sir."

The Senator leant back in his chair, surreptitiously taking a swig of rum from his hip flask while looking at a map of Kentucky pinned to his office wall. They had decided that troops would land at major towns and cities along the Mississippi and Ohio Rivers. From Hickman in the south up to Wickville, Paducah, Owensboro, Brandenburg, Louisville and Warsaw.

Louisville was the most important launch point by dint of its size, plus it had the best road network to move quickly across the state. There was one problem, his old friend, and now adversary, Danny Trevino was running Louisville like his own personal fiefdom. How to persuade, bribe, or as a last resort, fight him, to hand over control of the city?

Money was unlikely to induce him. He had more than he knew what to do with. Courtesy of hijacking the last truck of gold leaving Fort Knox during the Collapse. He'd hauled off tons of the stuff, by his estimate, worth close to half a billion dollars.

As a result, he was heavily armed. With that kind of money he could buy practically whatever weapons he wanted. From what the Senator knew, his wealth had increased still further thanks to a highly lucrative smuggling operation, bringing in from the west whatever the people of Louisville needed, which he resold to them at a handsome profit.

It was some hours later when Houston returned with news from Major General Redditch. "We seem to be all systems go, sir. The Major General requests the pleasure of your company at a final briefing, four pm today. Shall I tell him you'll be attending, sir?" asked Houston.

"Yes of course, I wouldn't miss it for the world." The sarcasm was lost on the young man. By this time of day, his mind was a little foggy, the drip feed of rum relaxing him maybe a little too much.

The briefing took place in the bowels of some drab and stuffy meeting room beneath what was once the Four Seasons Hotel in Sacramento. It had been sequestered by the Army as its ReFederalization Communications and Operations Center. To add to the discomfort, the air conditioning worked sporadically, and the lights were at a headache-inducing brightness. The Senator immediately felt uncomfortable, and therefore irritable.

In attendance, aside from the Senator, were his aides and senior assistant Barbara, a twenty-five-year-old curvaceous redhead who was as sharp as she was shapely, according to people who worked with her. She had other attributes the Senator was currently discovering when his wife was out of town.

The Major General had come with a small platoon of experts in Logistics, Communications, PR and other job titles the Senator didn't hear, or couldn't comprehend. The Major General was a tall, imposing man, well over six feet tall and weighing in at probably 275lbs. His sheer size dominated the room. A grizzled Veteran of many overseas deployments, his staff viewed him as firm but fair. He marched into the room, confident that he could deal with any crap the Senator threw at him.

The briefing document was lengthy, though lacking any real detail. As the Senator had requested, he wanted room for flexibility and to be as reactive as possible to challenges as they arose. This, of course, went against all the Major General's training and experience, preferring to plan for every contingency, however unlikely.

Knowing his aides were taking detailed notes, the Senator asked that only the edited highlights be presented, covering the main strategic objectives.

The Major General duly obliged, condensing his briefing to a truncated thirty minutes.

The main points were:

Phase 1. The operation would launch with the 'Rescue, Relief and Reconstruction Force' (RRRF).

- Up to five thousand troops were to be deployed at the previously discussed landing points along the Mississippi and Ohio rivers. Once inland areas were secured, others would be flown in.
- There were to be no armored vehicles. The inhabitants might see this as some kind of invasion force.
- Initially, the RRRF was the carrot–a large supply train containing food, healthcare products, gas and diesel. Any supplies currently difficult to obtain in the east.
- There would also be medics, doctors and nurses to deal with any health needs they met along the way.
- These relief convoys would fan out across Kentucky, winning hearts and minds as they did so. They'd also provide invaluable feedback on the conditions in Kentucky and the inhabitant's reactions to ReFederalization.
- Timeline: eight to twelve weeks.

Phase 2. Following the RRRF's convoys, to make sure they understood the ReFederalization message, meetings were to be held by senior officers in every village and town. There they could explain the benefits in more detail, or at least as much detail as there was available.

Timeline: twenty to forty weeks.

Staff requirements: Two thousand personnel.

As the briefing progressed, the *clichés* came thick and fast. The Senator was keen on a carrot and stick approach. Objectives had to be reached with all possible speed. People had to get on board quickly. Winning their hearts and minds was the phrase that kept surfacing with a lot of emphasis on what Kentuckians would be missing if they didn't accept the RRRF's largesse–and more importantly, the subsequent plans for ReFederalization.

After an hour, the Senator announced he was delighted with the plan and made a point of thanking and shaking hands with everyone involved in its creation. (There was an election next year, after all.) He then breezed out of the room, his clutch of assistants following in his wake like so many panicked ducklings.

The Major General turned to his staff with a look of confusion on his face, "Is it me, or did the Senator not understand a fucking word I just said? Does he not realize the magnitude of what we are about to undertake? Is he stupid, deaf, or on another planet?"

"Sir," one of his senior officers stood to attention, "if I may speak bluntly, sir?"

The Major General nodded, "Go ahead Captain."

"Sir, this is, I believe, a political charade he is acting out. I don't know what his endgame is, but, with due respect, sir, I think we are just pawns in some larger devious plan he has concocted. And if I may add, sir, if it all goes wrong, they will hold us to blame."

"Thank you Captain, you have just confirmed my worst fears. It wouldn't be the first time the military are made the scapegoats when the wheels fall off a politician's grand scheme. Let's plan for the worst and hope for the best."

Chapter 12

"Awww honey, just one more time. Pleeeease?" Danny Trevino was desperately trying to get out of bed. Olivia had other plans, grabbing and holding onto his arms.

He smiled, "Jesus, woman, give a man a break. You'll be the death of me. You're insatiable, you know that?" He finally extricated himself from her lustful embrace and started dressing.

"It's you that makes me like this Danny, I can't help it, I just can't get enough of you," she purred, deploying her best *come hither* pose, the bed sheets barely covering her breasts.

"Well, darlin', you do the same for me, but I've got work to do, and so have you, this time standing up, not on your back. So let's get dressed and get going, I want to see how ready the precinct Captains are for any trouble."

Pouting, she replied, "OK, I get the message. Spoil sport." Provocatively, she let the sheet slip, slid out of bed, and walked naked into the bathroom.

Danny just couldn't stop his eyes following her lithe, taut body as she stepped into the shower. How'd an Italian runt like him from the wrong side of the tracks end up with a beauty like her? He thought for a moment, simple really, he concluded, the two things women like her love most: money and power. He had both. And he wasn't about to give up either for some smart arse politician.

Within the hour he was in the back of his camo detailed Humvee with Olivia driving. He was dressed in army fatigues, deciding the military look would be appropriate for his tour around Louisville. Getting gas for his fleet of cars was not a problem. There were plenty of suppliers down the river to keep the precious liquid flowing. Since the Collapse, he'd stockpiled more than enough to power a small army's worth of military vehicles. Danny was a man that liked to be prepared for every eventuality.

Strapped to his side was his favorite side arm, a Beretta 92, and on the seat beside him, his trusty AK-47. To enhance his appearance as their commander-in-chief, his fatigues were bedecked with a few medals, and he wore a *beret*, styled after his hero, Field Marshal Bernard ('Monty') Montgomery, the famous WW2 English Army General.

He wasn't expecting any trouble. Louisville's inhabitants were in the main, grateful to have Danny running the city. Since the Collapse, he had brought a semblance of law and order, crushing other gangs who threatened his authority. His smuggling produced a small but regular supply of gas for cars, trucks and generators. Plus, of course, food, medical supplies and other essentials. It wasn't enough for the population of 20,000 that now lived in a city that once housed 660,000 people, but it was more than a lot of other places in Kentucky. He hoped that the residents of Louisville would not forget his generosity when faced with the blandishments of Senator Kingston.

A captain simply named Ping ran the first precinct he visited. Of Chinese descent, tough as nails, he brooked no slacking from his team, and had a reputation for dealing with troubleshooters by feeding them dead or alive to his 'lambs'–in reality, two massive 400 lb pigs. Their nicknames, Hannibal and Lector, a subtle reference to the voracious man-eaters in the film *Hannibal*. As Ping gleefully explained, a drove of hungry pigs could devour a man in under half an hour.

Unsurprisingly, with that threat hanging over their heads, Ping's men were ready and very willing to defend his precinct. He informed Danny he had 150 armed men at his disposal. Some better trained than others, though he was working on getting all of them combat ready. Danny was impressed, if only all his precinct Captains were this prepared. He thanked Ping, gave him a bonus of $1,000 in gold and continued on his tour.

His prime concern were the precincts along the Ohio River. It was logical this would be the route for the Senator's Army into Kentucky. As soon as Danny had read the Senator's announcement, he expanded his network of informants that ran across the country all the way to Sacramento. Information wasn't just power at times like this, it was the ammunition needed to beat the enemy at their own game. With his contacts he knew what was happening the moment the Senator made a decision.

Based on the intel so far, he'd sent word to other gang leaders along the river, warning them that something was in the air and to gear up accordingly. How well they would perform against professional soldiers was open to discussion. Indeed, some might be quite happy to roll over, take the Senator's enticements, or bribes, and willingly acquiesce. Whatever their decision he wanted them to know he was preparing for the worst.

Those further afield, he'd contacted using his ham radio equipment. Sending a generic broadcast telling anyone who was listening what was happening. He put his own spin on the news, hoping the more trouble he could stir up, the more difficult it would be for the Senator and his Army to make any headway.

As Danny continued on his tour around Louisville, he still couldn't come to terms with how deserted it looked the further away from the river he went. Once south of I-264, most of the houses and streets were deserted. Row after row of burnt out, dilapidated shells of homes, shops and offices made for a depressing sight. Once people's pride and joy, they were now ghost streets picked clean of anything useful, abandoned, with nature now inexorably reclaiming them. Danny tried to encourage people to move into areas like Parkway village, the city center and Seneca gardens, explaining he could offer them better security and access to the goods and services he was providing. Many did. However, most of the population settled in the streets close to the Ohio, from Chickasaw Park to Glenview, where the I-265 crosses the river into Indiana. There they attempted to rebuild their lives, planting gardens, maintaining homes with no access to the proper materials, in essence living an agrarian lifestyle in the middle of a destitute city.

To help with the food supply, all the city's parks were converted for the production of fruit and vegetables, under the control of the residents and elected Food Commissioners. To the northeast of the city, a vast area of countryside had been given to farmers with an emphasis on meat and poultry production. Over nearly six years, after many false starts, Louisville, with help from goods bought legally and illegally up and down the river, had made itself practically self-sufficient. Nevertheless, the economy was still rooted in the nineteenth century, with some limited twenty-first century technology like solar panels and generators improving production and the standard of living.

No one could say they were starving-or thriving, just surviving.

Danny realized the question soon facing them was: Did they feel this was a sufficiently comfortable way of life, one they were happy to continue with for many more years? Or were the prospects offered by ReFederalization a better path to a lifestyle similar to the one they enjoyed almost six years ago?

In simple terms, was it best to stick with the devil you knew, or place your future with someone you didn't?

Danny was still mulling these questions over when they arrived in Portland by the once famous Louisville Falls, though now destroyed and replaced by man-made dams. The Falls were the reason that Louisville existed in the first place. Going around them over land was the only way to progress up or down the river. The city thrived as a stop off point while goods and people were transported overland. Now it was a crucial precinct to keep heavily guarded, as any river traffic had to make use of the McAlpin locks, now controlled by Danny.

The captain in charge of this precinct was a displaced Brit by the name of Brian. He'd come out to work at the nearby Ford factory, then found himself marooned in Louisville as the Collapse made international travel impossible. A succession of gorgeous girlfriends who fell for his Hugh Grant accent and British charm offset any disappointment at being stranded in America. Finally, a former model from Jamaica, Jessica, nailed him down long enough to get married and put his rampant womanizing in check.

Of more importance to Danny was Brian's unfailing ability to make anything mechanical work, from cars to canal locks. As the Humvee growled to a halt, Brian appeared from a warehouse, wiping his greasy hands through a mop of long blonde hair. With a matching beard, he looked like a young Brad Pitt. No wonder, thought Danny, the women found him irresistible.

In a strong London accent, which Danny at times found hard to understand, Brian welcomed him with a broad smile. "Hiya mate, how's it going? Everything swimmin' along?"

"Looking good Brian, looking good. How's it all here?"

"Not too good, sorry to say Danny...one of the storage boats sank with a ton of ammo in it, just about to put my shorts on to dive in and have a look. Wanna join me?"

"What the fuck, Brian? How could that happen? Who's fault is it? I'll blow their goddamn head off. That ammo's worth a fortune."

As Danny continued to rant and rave, he noticed Brian unable to keep a straight face any longer. Finally, as Danny seemed on the verge of exploding, Brian burst out laughing.

"Gotcha! I told the guys you'd never fall for it...but you did. That's gonna cost me a round of drinks. I'm just winding you up, mate."

"You son of a bitch, you'll give me a fucking heart attack with your stupid jokes. Don't you Brits take anything seriously?"

"Truth be told, mate, I work on the basis of never taking anything seriously for more than ten minutes. Nothing's worth worrying about for longer than that, affects your decision making. Anyway, I've got some good news for you. Come in here and have a butchers at what I found. It's the dog's bollocks I tell you."

Calming down, Danny finally saw the funny side of Brian's joke and, smiling, walked into the warehouse. His jaw dropped open in utter disbelief. He was confronted with a 1990 M4 Sherman tank, the engine in a thousand pieces strewn across a tarp on the floor.

Danny looked at the tank, back to Brian, and then at the tank again. His face lit up like a ten-year-old boy who'd just been given his first bike.

"Where the fuck did you find that beauty?"

"I'd heard whispers that the Army kept some vehicles at the airport for security. So me and the boys popped over there a few days ago and found this little darling in the corner of a hanger. The engine's fucked which is probably why no one took it, so we towed it back here with a tractor and got to work. I reckon I can have her running in a week or two, though I haven't got any ammo for her. Maybe something you could sort?"

"I'm on it. This could be a game changer Brian. I owe you one. You let me know when she's ready for action and I'll be back for a trial run. I just love you Brits, except for your warped sense of humor!"

"Get used to it Danny! By the way, loved the broadcast. Picked it up on my radio. Very Churchillian!"

Danny thanked him, practically skipping back to the Humvee, where Olivia was looking bored and impatient, he enthusiastically explained the good news about the tank.

Olivia tried to look excited. "You boys and your toys…do you never grow up?" she said condescendingly. If Danny was crestfallen that Olivia didn't share his eagerness, he didn't show it. His mind was too busy working overtime on how he could find some ammo for the tank. He had his own tank. How goddamn cool was that?

Olivia started the truck and headed for their last stop of the grand tour, the precinct by the Louisville Slugger Museum. This was headed up by a distant cousin, Fabio, who Danny couldn't stand. In his opinion, he told Olivia, "the guy is a complete dipshit who couldn't organize a piss up in a brewery."

They arrived at the precinct HQ: a riverside warehouse with panoramic views of the Ohio. No one was on guard. With increasing anger, Danny stomped into the building, shouting Fabio's name. Eventually a half-naked man staggered out of an office, clearly the worse for drink.

Seeing Danny, he stood still, saluted, swaying slowly backwards and forwards, then in a slurred voice asked what Danny wanted.

"I want that waste of space Fabio, where is the little shit?" spat Danny at the befuddled guard.

"Sorry Danny, we've been having a bit of a party. It's Fabio's birthday, whole crowd of us on the roof...shall I go tell him you're here?"

"No need, I'll find him," Danny shoved the drunk aside and, fuming, ran up the stairs two at a time to the rooftop. He crashed through the steel door and was confronted by some thirty people in various stages of drunkenness and undress. Several girls were topless or naked, sprawled across men languidly pawing or stroking their bodies. Other revelers were passed out on chairs or the floor. Rap music blared from a 1990s boombox.

Danny looked around and saw Fabio laughing and fooling around with a girl who looked suspiciously too young to be at the party at all. He roared his name across the rooftop, his voice penetrating the noise of the music and drunken laughter. It shook Fabio to alertness, his face turning white when he saw Danny striding across to him, his Glock drawn.

Apoplectic, Danny screamed in Fabio's face, "What the fuck are you playing at you stupid asshole? Any time we could be invaded and you're up here screwing around and getting drunk when you should be preparing to defend the city. Are you out of your fucking mind?" Danny's face was distorted in anger and frustration. More worryingly for Fabio, the Glock was pointed at his left temple.

"Give me *one good reason* I shouldn't fucking shoot you right now?"

Fabio tried his best to bluff his way out. Keeping as calm as he could, he looked at Danny, "Aw, c'mon Danny, it's my birthday, I'll get it all sorted tomorrow. Give us a break, cousin."

"Those, *my cousin,* are three shit reasons, not even close to one good one."

Before Fabio could say another word, he put the Glock against Fabio's head and pulled the trigger. His head jerked sharply to the side, blood, bone and brain spewing out across the drinks table, then he slumped to the floor. The rest of the partygoers suddenly lost their interest in drink and sex, all now transfixed in horror at what had just happened. Danny calmly turned to them, his anger quickly deflating, the adrenaline oozing away.

"OK people, the party's over. Get rid of him," he pointed the Glock down at Fabio's lifeless body, "clear all this crap up and get back to work before I lose my temper again."

With that warning, he walked slowly and purposefully back through the speechless group, giving them all a look that invited no comment, just imparting a clear signal. Don't fuck with Danny Trevino.

Chapter 13

It was two days after the hostage incident that Roger could sit down and finish writing his notes in the *Record of French Creek*. He occasionally took a trip down memory lane and flicked back to some of his earlier entries. Those written soon after the Collapse and the early months of French Creek's struggles to survive still gripped him. The harrowing times they grappled with: food shortages, failed crops, friends and relatives dying from injuries and illnesses. The constant attacks by marauding, desperate, starving people fleeing the cities in search of survival in the countryside. They were traumatic times, thankfully, now in the past. However, it made him realize how far they had come and what they had achieved since those dark days.

The *Record of French Creek* also contained Roger's recollections about how the Collapse had come about, much of it learned from people passing through, or at the early Barter Fairs. It was months after the Collapse before he learned its repercussions had divided America in half. That west of the Mississippi had escaped the worst and recovered. East of the mighty river, society as they'd known it, no longer existed, and the river was a Berlin Wall keeping the haves and have nots apart. In the east there was no longer any government, infrastructure, law and order. They were now living in a nineteenth century economy with none of the modern conveniences everyone had grown used to.

It was a brutal first year after the Collapse, as day after day the crushing realization dawned on the villagers that they were on their own. No FEMA convoys arriving with supplies, no handouts from any part of the government. The villagers came to terms with their plight. Now they had to deal with the myriad of problems staying alive entailed.

Roger's notes were peppered with anguished entries listing the number of people that had died defending the village. The friends and relatives (including his wife, Margie), dying through lack of healthcare and medicines. Even after all this time, the incessant bad news he dutifully recorded made for upsetting reading.

The village's survival was on a knife edge for the first two years. Frequently, his notes invoked God's help in overcoming the latest problem or emergency, praying for a break from the never- ending grind of trying to stay alive. He was not a religious man. After all, what kind and caring deity would allow such a catastrophe to befall so many millions of people? However, in those dark times, he sought help from wherever it was on offer.

Slowly, the entries became more optimistic, more positive about the future. Three years after the Collapse, the village had turned the corner. It had survived the worst and was now able to feed and protect itself.

He flicked forward reading random entries over the ensuing years, smiling at how now and then a note of good news crept into his reports..."*A record harvest of vegetables*"..."*No intruders in the past six months*"...."*Three new babies born in the last four weeks*"..."*First proper Thanksgiving, with LOTS of food and homemade beer!*"

Skipping forward, Roger couldn't resist reading the pages in the *Record* from last year. It recounted the appearance of Jane Davidson and her group, whose covert objective was to encourage people to leave for the west-and get paid by the coyotes in Memphis. They arrived with deadly force and nefarious intentions. But Jane's subsequent change of heart led her to play an integral role in a mission to help a group of villagers leave for a new life west of the Mississippi. Roger, Pat, Landy and another villager Jay, who had built himself an ultralight helped the group make the perilous trip to Memphis and the crossing. In the end the group did it without the coyote's help. A shoot-out ensued resulting in several deaths and the wounding of Roger's son, Landy. The trip also reunited Jane with her family who'd been held hostage by the coyotes for nearly five years.

Thankfully, the last few months had been absent of any major dramas. Roger wondered how long the peace would last. The missive from Senator Kingston had stirred up long subsumed concerns among the villagers. Was there a better future ahead if the Senator's plans and promises were to materialize? What would they have to give up? Was it worth the risk? Roger couldn't blame people for wanting to move towards their pre-Collapse standard of living. Life now was comfortable, but not easy. So much was beyond their control, just as it had been with their forebears. The weather could ruin a crop overnight. A serious illness could be a death sentence. No electricity or other utilities made life tough. Jobs that once took hours now took days without power tools and motors. No vacations! In sum: no real prospect of anything major changing to improve their lifestyle or prospects. It wasn't a future everyone embraced.

Roger closed *The Record*, and made himself a cup of real coffee—a luxury he acquired at the recent Barter Fair. He glanced up from his desk, saw Landy and Jerry through the kitchen window rigging up a solar panel and car battery, then trailing a cable back into the house. Landy came rushing in, brimming with enthusiasm.

"Guess what? We've got the ham radio to work in D.C. We're going to fire it up and see what happens!"

Jerry followed Landy into the house, said hi to Roger then disappeared into Landy's bedroom to help finish setting up.

Later in the day, while Roger was cooking dinner, Landy emerged from his room, a piece of paper in his hand.

"Dad, have you heard of some guy Danny Trevino up in Louisville?"

Roger thought for a moment, "Name kinda rings a bell, heard him mentioned once or twice at the Barter Fair. Bit of a kingpin up there, people reckon he runs the city. Crooked as hell from what I can remember. Why?"

"Well, he has some broadcast on repeat every few hours warning everyone against this plan of the Senator's. Seems he doesn't rate it too highly, thinks it's a massive con. Quite a speech he put together, goes on a bit. Basically, he's claiming we shouldn't trust a word the Senator is saying."

"Really? Well, that is interesting. No doubt he's got a lot to lose if the Senator takes back control of Kentucky. Next time you hear it, give me a shout. I'd like to listen. Found any other interesting broadcasts or call signs?"

"Not yet, there are a lot of wackos out there, difficult to know who to believe. I did have a conversation with a woman down in Tampa, she says it's not too bad there, they elected some kind of local government. But they are getting a lot of stuff from Mexico and places like Texas. Her call sign's 'Tampa Tootsie'. Mine's, 'Kentucky Kowboy'—what do you think?"

Roger, more in hope than expectation, replied, "I think you shouldn't spend too much time on that stuff, it'll warp your mind. Just like all those video games and TikTok crap in the past."

Muttering half-heartedly that he wouldn't, Landy disappeared back into his room, and promptly started scanning the airwaves for anything fun and interesting. It was a real novelty being able to talk to people outside of French Creek again.

Before the Collapse, like most teenagers, he used his iPhone all the time. It was part of his life. Maybe all of it. Then as the electricity failed and communications died, overnight it became a useless piece of plastic. For days afterwards he carried it around in the vain hope it would suddenly ring or ping some notification. When it didn't, realization dawned that the era of social media, texting and living your life through a phone was over. He wondered how he'd survive. The first few weeks, an electronic cold turkey gripped him as his social media dopamine fix fell apart. Now with the ham radio, he could start talking to other people, minus the visuals.

Roger, meanwhile, was building his confidence up to pay a visit to a recently widowed woman in the village, Kathy. Her husband had passed away a few weeks ago from a heart attack. His visit wasn't just to see how she was coping. He had long thought she was an attractive, capable woman, now he wondered if she might be interested in developing a closer relationship with him.

He had been a widower for nearly five years, since his wife died of diabetes soon after the Collapse. Without insulin, many, like her, suffered a slow and painful death. It devastated him, and Landy. Since then, the idea of a relationship with another woman was something he had put to one side. Running the village was a hard, all-consuming task-mistress. He had neither the time nor the energy for other interests. Now, however, times were changing and maybe he should start looking for some female companionship.

He looked in the mirror, tidied himself up, then left the house, walking towards the other end of the village where Kathy lived. With a spring in his step, he thought to himself, life could take him in a new satisfying direction.

Unbeknownst to him, at exactly the same time, 250 miles to the west, near Paducah, the first battalion of RRRF soldiers, law enforcement personnel and the National Guard were embarking onto a flotilla of small boats and barges starting their journey to landing points along the Mississippi and Ohio Rivers.

Stage one of Operation RRRF was underway.

Chapter 14

Paducah in west Tennessee lies at the confluence of the Ohio and Tennessee Rivers and has been a major trading port since its founding in 1821. Following the Collapse, the city had taken full advantage of its position a few miles from the Mississippi: trading, smuggling and profiting from the traffic of goods and people.

Over the years, security at Paducah had grown lax with little attempt to patrol the river. A mutually beneficial *laissez-faire* arrangement existed between a semi-elected local council and the gangs who paid them off to run illicit operations with their tacit approval.

They had been aware of the Federal Government's plans led by Senator Kingston for some time. They listened with interest to the radio chatter and gossip, with no mention of when or where it might happen. As a result, the City Council was caught completely by surprise when the first contingents of the RRRF began disembarking at their docks, mid-morning in late March.

The weather was not welcoming. It was pouring with rain and a brisk wind off the river kept the temperature at an uncomfortably cold level. The convoy took several hours to unload, then sloshed its way through the sodden streets. No one was around as they made their way through the almost abandoned city.

Around fifty US Marshals were accompanied by one hundred members of the National Guard and a small number of Army troops. This advanced guard made their way cautiously to the city's Kolb Park. They decided, very late in the day, to include members of law enforcement to ease people's concerns that seeing armed forces might smack of an invasion. Following behind was a convoy of trucks laden with supplies.

Quickly, vehicles with loudspeakers drove around the city, informing everyone that a public meeting would be held later that day at 2:00 p.m. Attendance was mandatory.

A temporary stage was built and generators fired up the PA system. Numerous stalls were erected to dispense free drinks, food and other supplies. Winning hearts and minds was top of the agenda, and this was the quickest way to do it, believed the senior RRRF Commanders.

By 2:00 p.m., despite the appalling weather, a huge crowd had materialized. Everyone was eager to see just what the Federal Government was offering after six years of doing nothing.

Because of technical difficulties due to the rain, it was nearly three o'clock before Colonel Sandy Duncan, leader of Section Beta of the RRRF appeared on the stage before a damp and disgruntled audience. He walked up to the microphone and welcomed the unhappy crowd. A tall, thin man with a small blonde mustache, dressed in fatigues, he exuded the confidence of a man used to giving orders. His seniority reflected the importance of the gathering. He was, however, by no means, a stirring orator. Hesitantly picking up the microphone as though it might electrocute him, (earlier, one of the techs had suffered an electric shock due to the rain), he surveyed his audience of around 1,500 expectant people. In a clipped monotone, he started his prepared speech.

"Hello everyone and thank you all for coming here today. It's wonderful to be here in Kentucky! I have some…great news for you. We come with exciting news, food and supplies…."

A barrage of jeers and catcalls muted any shouts of approval he might have anticipated.

"About time too…."

"Better late than never…."

"Why did it take you so long?"

"Nice of you to turn up after six years...."

Were some of the more polite comments, others suggested in short order he should, *"fuck off back where you came from and leave us alone."*

Slightly nonplussed by the negative reaction, the Colonel plowed on. Courtesy of the immense PA system, his voice drowned out the raucous shouts from the crowd.

Going off script, he took a conciliatory approach, trying to calm them down. "I understand your frustration and anger. I agree, it has taken us too long to get back here and help you. Um, I apologize, but my job here today is to explain how we are going to get this great city and this wonderful state back to where it was six years ago. It...it won't be easy. I can't promise you any quick fixes, but I can promise you we will deploy the huge resources at our disposal to make it happen as soon as we can...."

As the Colonel paused to check his notes, a shot echoed around the square. He glanced at his chest, then at the crowd, a look of astonishment on his face. Clutching the wound, he fell forwards, knocking over the microphone and podium. He was dead before the pages of his speech fluttered down over his body.

Total pandemonium ensued. Army personnel rushed forward, giving aid to the Colonel. As the medics tried in vain to resuscitate him, the pouring rain washed away the Colonel's blood across the stage, dripping onto the soaked grass below. US Marshals who had been acting as security, scoured rooftops for any sign of the shooter. The crowd meanwhile, after a moment's stunned hesitation, panicked and fled. Within five minutes the park was a muddy mess, empty except for piles of trampled food and drink containers carpeting the ground.

Operation RRRF was not off to a good start.

On hearing the news, Senator Kingston was apoplectic with rage. Pacing around his office he erupted into a salvo of recrimination and anger, "Those ungrateful sons of bitches. We go there to help the bastards and they thank us by killing one of our soldiers."

Paul H Rowney

He rounded on one of his cowering aides bellowing at her, "We've got to find that murdering son of a bitch who did it. Get the Marshals after him. Why didn't the soldiers fire back, for God's sake? Who handled security? I'll have their heads for paperweights. This is a fucking embarrassment. Get me Major General Redditch on the phone, NOW!"

The aide bolted out, warning her co-workers to stay well clear of the Senator's office until his volcanic temper had subsided.

Minutes later, the Senator was chewing out the Major General for his ineptitude in allowing one of his own to be shot, causing the first RRRF landing in the east to become a 'cluster fuck', as he delicately put it. More importantly, though he didn't say it, was the image it portrayed to the President and the public about the likely success of the RRRF and subsequently, Operation ReFederalization.

"The first fucking place we land, and this happens, it's a fucking disaster Redditch, have we caught the culprit? Why didn't we return fire?" The Senator continued to spew out questions and demands until he paused for breath.

The Major General kept calm in the face of this barrage of expletives and ill-informed criticism. Finally, the Senator's pause allowed him to get a word in.

"I understand your frustrations and annoyance, Senator. I have lost a good man in Colonel Duncan. But we have to be realistic. Like all the cities we are entering, we have no idea how welcoming they will be, or what the reaction to us marching into their city might create. It was, I believe, your idea, Senator, not to send in large numbers of troops so as not to antagonize or concern the residents. Therefore, we were not in a position to return fire. However, I believe if we had, the situation would have turned very ugly, very quickly.

"In terms of finding the culprit, the Marshals inform me there is little chance of success. Paducah has no law and order infrastructure, no police force, no database of criminals, no up to date records of who is actually living there. You have to understand, Senator, that Paducah could be a microcosm of the problems we will face across Kentucky as

73

a whole. I have therefore, prudently, put a twenty-four hour halt to any further landings until we review what's happened and adjust our plans accordingly."

Begrudgingly, the Senator acquiesced to the Major General's proposal. He couldn't risk any more critical news headlines. One death could be dismissed as the work of a stray anarchist. Any more and it would look like Kentucky was putting up a fight against the Federal Government's plans, which would be an acute source of embarrassment. No, another day to fine tune operations was manageable. He'd instruct his staff to send out some interference stories to the media to deflect any sniff of failure.

The Major General knew that this was the last thing any politician wanted to hear—their well-publicized plans not coming to fruition as expected. In truth, he had anticipated some resistance from the citizens of Kentucky, but not so swiftly, or so brutally. The facts were becoming clearer by the hour: they knew very little about the attitude of people to the RRRF and ReFederalization, how could they? They'd not had the chance to ask them. As a career Army officer, he believed wholeheartedly that under the right circumstances, a military approach to a problem could be the only solution. Though to ensure its success, you needed as much intel as possible about the enemy, its strengths and weaknesses. They had none.

He agreed a 'softly, softly' approach under less confrontational circumstances might yield more positive results. It would allow them to obtain more information about the attitudes, fears and hopes Kentuckians had about ReFederalization. Maybe, they should send out an army of emissaries, or goodwill ambassadors to travel the state on a fact-finding mission? Then based on their findings, decide the best course of action for the RRRF.

There was one pitfall to this idea. It would take months to complete. And Senator Kingston didn't want to wait months for his moment of glory.

He was mulling over this dilemma while on his way to the temporary RRRF HQ at Cape Girardeau when he received a call from his Comms

Chief in Sacramento. He'd been scanning the airwaves to see if there was any chatter about the RRRF, and came across the bombastic announcement by some guy in Louisville called Danny Trevino. A bit of delving turned up he was the boss there. Once a small-time thug and drug dealer who had somehow found the heft and money to effectively take control of the city after the Collapse.

Now he had taken it upon himself to broadcast a warning to everyone in Kentucky about the 'truth' behind ReFederalization and the motives of the RRRF. It seems he had a lot of sources in Sacramento feeding him intelligence about their objectives. Would the Major General like to hear a recording, asked his somewhat perplexed Comms Chief?

"Yes Captain, send it over to me on an audio file, I'll listen to it at HQ."

Fifteen minutes later, seated in his office, he sat down and listened to what he thought would be some crook's inarticulate rantings. He was unpleasantly surprised by what he heard. The recording had a lot of static, crackles and background noise. There was no doubting, though, the message was eloquent and crystal clear:

"Fellow citizens of Kentucky, my name is Danny Trevino. I am broadcasting this message to you from Louisville where I have the honor of being the Mayor of this great city.

Like all of you, I have received and read the notice Senator Kingston has distributed across the State.

I am obliged to inform you that its contents, vague as they are, should not be taken at face value. I should remind you that Senator Kingston was indicted twice on charges of corruption while in office here in Kentucky. Only the catastrophe of the Collapse and his cowardly flight to the west saved him from probable jail time.

His proposed plans for ReFederalization under the guise of 'Rescue Relief and Reconstruction' is nothing less than an attempt to take control of the State by force, so my sources in Sacramento inform me.

I have further evidence that he has considerable assets in the form of gold stolen from Fort Knox hidden in the state which he is desperate to acquire.

His proposed taxes would be crippling to the average citizen. His plans for security, law and order are tantamount to those of a police state. The fact he is using the Army and National Guard to lead, let's be honest, the invasion of Kentucky to implement his plans, is likely to cause civil war. The result will be the US Army killing innocent Americans.

We cannot let this happen! One civil war in our short history is enough! Until you know all the facts, I urge you to do nothing that could endanger your future!

Most of us are enjoying more freedom than ever before. Life is improving year by year. Don't let this be ripped away by some corrupt politician and an inept Federal Government.

Keep tuned into this radio station for more news.

Keep Kentucky Free. Keep Kentucky Independent! Keep the RRRF out!

Say NO to ReFederalization!"

With a theatrical touch, the broadcast finished, playing the 1970's song Freedom by the Isley Brothers:

"Well, I wanna say, I wanna tell you

I wanna say when you can do what you wanna do

And go where you wanna go

And live where you wanna live

And love who you wanna love."

The Major General put his head in his hands, despair descending upon him. Not for the first time in his long career, he was at the wrong end of a politician's ambition. They either want us to implement their ill-conceived ideas—and blame us when they go wrong. Or ask us to pick up the pieces once it's all gone pear-shaped. Either way, he thought bitterly, we're in a no one win situation.

Looking forward, he just knew this mission had so many unknowns, it was like walking into a cave with no lights. Every step was fraught with danger. Around every corner was an unknown trap that you didn't see until you walked into it. Stumbling around in the dark was no way to conduct a military mission. The only outcome was failure.

He got up from his desk, found his suitcase and pulled out his drink's flask. A long slug of, ironically, ten-year-old Kentucky bourbon, helped calm him down. He called his assistant requesting an all personnel meeting at 0700 tomorrow. He hoped they could come up with a strategy that could solve this mess. One primarily caused by the Senator's duplicitous behavior. Was he really doing this to grab some long-lost fortune? No, even he couldn't be that underhanded, or self-serving. Could he? Confused and despondent, he went to his cot in the corner of the office, and to his surprise, courtesy of the bourbon, was asleep in minutes.

His slumber didn't last long. At midnight, his assistant was shaking him awake, "Sorry to disturb you sir, but we've just had some news in from Sacramento which I think you'll want to hear. It's not good, I'm afraid."

Chapter 15

Louisville was on high alert. News of the events in Paducah had reached Danny within hours. He immediately told all his precinct Captains to be prepared for signs of boats coming up the Ohio. He kept using the word 'invaders' to instill a sense of fear and urgency into them. After years of peace, he knew many would need motivating and convincing it was a real and current threat. Danny emphasized on more than one occasion: "This is not a drill. They could turn up at any moment."

He sat down with Olivia and crafted another sensationalist message for broadcast. He wanted to tell anyone listening about the Paducah revolt (as he called it). He hoped it would inspire others to make life as difficult as possible for the RRRF convoys.

His problem was that while he could keep the inhabitants of Louisville under control by bribery, fear and force, he had no such leverage over the rest of Kentucky. For all he knew, most people might welcome the RRRF and the introduction of ReFederalization. Those still living on the breadline after six years might find the prospect of a return to twenty-first century living attractive. How to convince them that the ReFederalization spearhead, the RRRF, was a bad idea, when to many it might be a godsend? Indeed, if done properly, he admitted to himself, that was probably the case.

Mercifully, so far, Senator Kingston had done a lousy job explaining how ReFederalization, after the RRRF had dispensed its aid, would benefit everyone. This vacuum of information left the door wide open for leaders like Danny to keep prodding at people's fear of the unknown. Persuading them that the *status quo* was in their best interest.

How long could he rely on the Senator's ineptitude and deceitfulness to help his cause? The last thing he wanted was to take on the Army or the National Guard. Start doing that and the might of the US Military would be down on him like a ton of rocks. One thirty-year-old tank would not turn the tide of that battle. No, he needed to win the war by destroying the Senator's credibility and reputation in Kentucky. Failure here, believed Danny, would make him a toxic politician back in Sacramento he would become a pariah, forcing plans for ReFederalization to be abandoned.

He had a lot more dirt on the Senator to be sure. Unfortunately, some of it implicated him in activities that would harm his own reputation. He didn't underestimate the Senator's power of persuasion and connections he had in Sacramento. That man could sell a muzzle to a dog. Danny toyed with the idea of just taking him out. There were several people he knew, for a healthy chunk of gold, would happily put a bullet in him. However, that route could backfire in a big way. Retribution from the west for assassinating one of their own would be more than he could handle. That nuclear option would be a last resort.

Maybe he needed more help. More resources, basically more armed men. How to do that? After discussing it with Olivia, he made the decision to ask other city leaders around Kentucky to a meeting where they could discuss the whole RRRF and ReFederalization plan. Most, he figured, had as much to lose as him. Maybe they could hatch some kind of statewide resistance to this Federal interference? The more he thought about it, the more the idea grabbed him. What a bloody nose for the Senator, for the Feds, if Kentucky told them to royally fuck off, or face a war.

He called Olivia, who helped him write his first broadcast, showing surprising ability to craft some highly provocative turns of phrase. She had a deft, creative touch for words and writing. A hidden talent he was delighted to discover. There was more to her than met the eye.

"Honey, we need to do a new broadcast. I want to organize a gathering of the clans. We're gonna take that Senator's plans and shove them up where the sun don't shine."

An hour and several rewrites later, Danny's latest propaganda piece was ready for transmission.

Determined to put on a show of strength and authority, Danny's broadcast made it sound as though attendance at this meeting was almost mandatory for anyone who was anyone and cared about Kentucky's future independence. They had no idea who was receiving his broadcasts, let alone who would make the trip. Danny, confidently– and generously, offered to send transport to all the major cities and towns and collect those wanting to partake in this summit. He hoped this over the top offer would help persuade people to participate. He waited anxiously over the next few days for any response.

In the end, he was pleasantly surprised. Leaders from Lexington to Frankfort, Bowling Green, to Paducah and a dozen other large towns radioed back to say they would be there. Hardly a comprehensive representation of Kentucky's population, thought Danny, however, more than enough to make it worthwhile.

Three days later, Danny's convoys were on their way to the far corners of Kentucky. Heavily armed, the six Army personnel carriers were not luxurious, just functional modes of transport for ten people. With the bonus they looked intimidating. Danny's largesse extended to copious amounts of drink and food on board. He wanted to make a good impression on his guests. All of whom, no doubt, considered themselves top dogs and used to getting their own way. This show of wealth and power was designed to make them realize Danny, from Louisville, was in charge.

When one of Danny's trucks stopped in Glasgow, among the two waiting to get a lift, was Roger, from humble French Creek.

He'd been alerted to the meeting by Landy who'd heard the second of Danny's broadcasts. Earlier, he had listened to the first with a mixture of amusement and concern while Danny harangued his audience with cries of Liberty and Freedom from ReFederalization. Was the guy deranged or was he for real? He decided to wait and see what else came forth from the 'Louisville Nutter' as Roger had christened him. When a few days later Landy told him about the 'call to arms' meeting, Roger, with the council's permission, opted to punch above his weight and accept the open invitation as a representative of an extensive area of 'south central Kentucky'. At Glasgow, a group comprising four men and two women were already in the truck. He climbed aboard with the other new traveler.

Roger found himself in the company of a motley crew of egocentric, self-styled leaders, keen to extol the virtues of their achievements, their power, their wealth. Roger nodded in admiration at their claims, otherwise saying very little. No one questioned his credentials. After a while when everyone had run through their resumes, the conversation turned to the purpose of the meeting. Did they know much about Danny Trevino? What were everyone's thoughts on the RRRF? Who was this Senator Kingston? Did they trust him? The Feds?

The couple from Somerset, a husband and wife, knew Danny from when they lived in Louisville before the Collapse. The man, called Duncan, in his mid-fifties, with long gray hair, a beard and multiple tattoos, gave them some history on Danny.

"Danny was a local drug dealer, a real smart one, never got caught, always had contacts in the right places to get him out of trouble. Mixed with all the top dogs in the city. Somehow, as the Collapse happened, he came into a pile of money. No one knows from where. There were rumors he was mixed up with politicians in Frankfort and siphoned off some of the money they were trying to steal as they left for the west. No one knows for sure. What I know is he runs the city like a private kingdom, and violence is second nature to him."

"It was a mega amount of money," chipped in his wife. She looked about twenty years his junior, with a waif-like figure and long blonde hair framing a pale face. "I'm talking millions of dollars. It just disappeared once it got to Louisville. Poof!" She clapped her hands in the air to demonstrate the point.

"Then after the Collapse," continued Duncan, "he took control of Louisville in short order. He seems to have used the money to keep the city running pretty smoothly from what I've heard."

"So he's got a lot to lose if this whole RRRF and ReFederalization plan happens?" suggested Roger.

"Haven't we all?" said the other woman in the group. She'd been waiting with Roger for a lift in Glasgow. She was attractive, with auburn hair tied back in a ponytail. Her face had a mass of freckles and penetrating green eyes. Roger guessed she was in her mid-thirties. He stared at her a little too intently. She'd introduced herself earlier as Penny, the mayor of Bowling Green.

Penny expanded on her initial comment, "Let's be honest here, none of us want to change things too much, do we? We're all living easier each year. People are healthier, better fed and the violence has died down. Sure, we have no utilities, but I reckon we'll have electricity available within five years for everyone in our city. So we're happy with these gradual improvements, yes? Having Senator Dipshit coming over here planning a wholesale disruption of how we live, is not one I'm keen to get on board with...yet."

She looked directly at Roger seeking a response. For a second, he was too mesmerized by her eyes to say anything. Gathering his wits, he chuckled quietly, replying, "Well, you would say that, wouldn't you?! Though to an extent you're right Penny, most of us here, and probably at the meeting in Louisville, would agree. However, we can't forget the thousands who are still living on the poverty line in isolated rural areas. I suspect that if the RRRF deploys all this aid as some kind of bribe to form a new state government through ReFederalization, they could generate a lot of support. Many may see no way to improve their lot unless they go down this ReFederalization route. I think we need to bear that in mind, don't we?"

Penny smiled back at Roger. "Have we a bleeding heart liberal here among us?"

"Ha! I wouldn't describe myself as anything. Many years in the Army teaches you to be pretty apolitical. It also taught me to be a realist, and

82

never be surprised at how influenced people can be if they are fed a message they really want to hear often enough. Don't tell people the facts, just keep pumping out the same promises that appeal to their basic instincts. I think it was Rupert Murdoch who said, 'no one ever lost money by underestimating public opinion'–Senator Kingston knows this, all politicians do."

Duncan from Somerset added his thoughts, agreeing with Roger, "You're right sir, that Kingston guy will stop at nothing to win over the people. And he's very good at it. You don't remain a Senator in a cesspool like Frankfort without knowing how to win votes. We can't assume just because life for us isn't too bad, everyone else feels the same. I'm gonna be really interested to see what this meeting produces."

No one could disagree with that sentiment. Soon the conversation petered out and everyone lapsed back into their own thoughts about the upcoming meeting. A few took advantage of Danny's generosity and drank some beer left conveniently in a large cooler at the rear of the truck. They sat back watching Kentucky's verdant countryside as they trundled up I-65 to Louisville, all of them wondering what they had gotten themselves involved with.

Chapter 16

Major General Redditch listened to Danny Trevino's latest rant and his invitation to a meeting of 'community leaders' from across Kentucky. This was bad news on so many fronts. Complicating an already delicate problem, he now faced a potential armed insurrection.

"Has the Senator heard this yet?" he asked Captain Davies, hoping he hadn't, so there'd be time to plan a response.

"I had a call from his assistant a few minutes ago saying he had and was, to quote her, 'going ballistic'. Do you want me to get him on the phone for you, sir?"

"Hell no, Captain, let him calm down first. In the meantime, I want all planning and ops personnel ready for a meeting in thirty minutes. Get some reps along from the US Marshals and National Guard as well."

The Captain marched off to rally the troops, leaving the Major General digesting the latest developments. Was it conceivable that some kind of independent militia made up of this rabble would stand and fight the US Army? How would his men feel about confronting and killing fellow Americans? Just what was at stake here that made this risk acceptable? Did the Senator, the Government, have ulterior motives, hidden agendas, for this whole ReFederalization move? If so, what were they? Did the Army want to be part of it? Not that it had much choice in the matter. It was the Army's job to follow orders from the Government. Even if it was to enforce some personal mission the Senator or the President was hatching under the cover of a Government sanctioned mandate?

Before he could answer these self-imposed questions, his direct line rang. Barely had he put the phone to his ear, than a cascade of expletives spewed out from the Senator.

"Have you heard this idiot's latest diatribe? He's putting together some kind of revolutionary army. The fucking nerve! It'll never work, man's a certified lunatic. We need to take him out. In fact, why don't we take out the whole damn lot of them at this meeting? Cut off the hydra's head as it were. We need to be decisive here, Major General. I need a strategy to nip this in the bud. Suggestions?"

Not for the first time, the Major General tried to dial down the rhetoric. In a placatory tone, he replied, "Good morning Senator, and yes, I have heard his broadcast. A worrying development I agree, let's not jump the gun here. We need to know more about their intentions. We can't go in there, literally, all guns blazing. It could exacerbate the situation making any progress impossible. I have a meeting with my staff in a few minutes and we'll be discussing some options. Let me get back to you with a plan before noon."

"No later, Major General, I have to report back to the Secretary of State and the President. I want to present a clear cut strategy for dealing with this. Understood?"

Wearily he replied, "Yes Senator, leave it with me." He put the phone down. Was it too early for a nerve settling scotch? He decided it was, though it was a close call.

Half an hour later he was trying to produce some practical and effective strategies from his planning group to deal with this latest complication. All agreed the lack of intel was holding them back. Ironically, this meeting of leaders might offer an unforeseen benefit; if they could infiltrate it, they might get a more detailed insight into the attitudes prevailing across Kentucky on this entire issue. It was a risky tactic. However, the more it was discussed, the more it seemed a unique opportunity to gather information that could influence their next move.

The Major General asked for an outline plan by the end of the day. He called the Senator with the news that they were working on something and that if he and the President could wait until 6:00 p.m., he would have a draft ready. Reluctantly, the Senator agreed, ending the conversation with a barely concealed threat that *'it better be good or we could be looking at changes in the command structure'*. I should be so lucky, thought the Major General as he cut the call.

True to his word, by 6:00 p.m. his team had produced a workable plan to infiltrate the meeting in Louisville:

Two US marshals, ostensibly representing the city of Wickman, would launch a boat north of Paducah. Then make their way upriver to Louisville. This approach was not without its risks. Another unexpected attendee from Wickman could quickly blow their cover. Meeting someone who had lived there might prove awkward as well. However, all agreed that if successful, having two men at this meeting would give them the inside track on the attitudes—and plans—of these potential war lords, providing invaluable intel for the RRRF.

They relied on the fact that no one really knew anyone else attending. The US Marshals were briefed on what information they should obtain. They also gathered some background about Wickman, in case someone asked about their hometown. As far as they could tell, monitoring the radio traffic to and from Danny's transmitter, no one had accepted the invitation from there.

In a nice twist, one of the comms guys replied to Danny's invitation confirming attendance from two Wickman representatives. They'd be arriving by boat along the Ohio, so could they keep an eye out for them?

Liking the plan so far, the Major General left his team to finalize the details. Some hours later, they presented him with a worryingly thin document. It left little room for contingencies or fall-back positions. Then again, plans produced in a hurry seldom did.

As he explained the mission, Senator Kingston could barely hide his disappointment at what he obviously thought was a pretty tame strategy. He was all for hell and brimstone raining down upon the Louisville gathering. The desire for revenge and good press obliterating the original idea of a 'softly, softly' intelligence gathering approach.

Reason finally prevailed: he accepted this plan wouldn't cost any lives (well, except possibly the two Marshals if they were exposed). It would also help the RRRF plans move forward: more attuned to how the people of Kentucky were thinking. He would take it to the Secretary of State and President immediately with his recommendation. Not bothering to inform the Major General that President Cummings was only interested in hearing the good news, which meant when Kentucky was back under Federal control. Details were for lesser mortals.

Later, the Senator called back close to midnight. It was all systems go.

Chapter 17

Danny Trevino was in his element. Hosting what he considered the most important meeting in Kentucky since the Collapse. He was on hand to individually welcome guests. At his side, Olivia looked ravishing. The figure-hugging black silk dress slit up to her thigh accentuated her tall slim figure. Long blonde hair cascaded down over her shoulders. Danny was delighted, not just with her looks–and the envious glances he was getting–but also her positive impact on the planning for this important event. She'd become his business partner as well as lover. Danny was feeling at ease with the world. For the moment.

Prior to the guest's arrival, he ordered a thorough cleaning of one floor of bedrooms in the Hilton Hotel to ensure his guests were comfortable. Down in the bar and restaurant on the ground floor, the drinks were flowing like the Ohio River. A display of food that would make a Las Vegas casino proud, was available all day and evening. The welcome buffet was held in the capacious reception area allowing plenty of natural light. Even so, a few generators could be heard chugging away providing electricity for ice machines and ovens.

By the end of the evening, over forty people had arrived. Danny, an avid reader of WW2 history books, likened this event to the meeting in Tehran when Churchill, Roosevelt and Stalin had planned the final defeat of the Axis powers. The people at this meeting ruled their own private fiefdoms as they wished. This was real power. These were the men and women who would put a halt to the Fed's plans for Kentucky. Tomorrow, Danny believed, a little piece of American history would be made.

At 10:00 a.m. the following morning, the delegates congregated for the meeting. Each was given a name badge and which town or city they were representing. The two US Marshals had arrived deliberately late the previous evening, and registered last to make sure no one else had come from Wickman. Mercifully, no one had. They gave their names as Mike and Frank then wandered into the meeting room to mingle with the other attendees. They split up to cover as many conversations as possible. People stood around in groups discussing everything from crop production to fuel supplies, security to health problems. Looking at some of them, it was difficult to believe these people held so much power in cities and towns across the state. None were in attire that verged on professional. Camo and denim were the preferred color schemes. By far, the majority were men in their forties or fifties, many looking uncomfortable in the hotel's luxury surroundings. Everyone sported a handgun clamped to their waist.

For many, it was interesting to see how Louisville had survived the Collapse. Yesterday, as they were driven through the outer districts of the city, despite a creeping blanket of kudzu, vine and weeds covering destroyed buildings, it was apparent the poorer areas had suffered significant fire damage. Left unchecked, these infernos had reduced whole blocks to their concrete foundations. As they entered the downtown and financial district with more modern, concrete buildings, the damage was less severe. Most were decaying through lack of maintenance, peppered with broken windows. Even here, nature was gaining a foothold. Trees, finding root holds in the tiniest of cracks now clung to the sides and tops of office blocks and parking garages. Louisville, long bottom of the list when it came to sustainability and eco-friendliness, now found itself becoming a green city without any effort or expense. No matter which way you looked at it, post-Collapse cities were depressing places, a public tableau reflecting the fragile construct of man's achievements and a permanent reminder nature will always have the final word.

Danny and his team of precinct captains arrived from behind the stage, a small platoon of men all dressed in paramilitary uniforms. They sat down, flanking the podium where Danny now stood, unlike his audience, dressed in a smart suit, every bit the crisply turned out professional. He asked people to take their seats.

He wasn't a natural public speaker, but he knew how to deliver a speech that made complicated topics simple, and provoke a reaction. He'd save the latter until towards the end of his speech.

"Ladies and gentlemen, I am delighted to see so many of you here today. I believe it is a historic day in Kentucky's long and rich history. The fact you are attending indicates the importance this meeting is to everyone in this great state.

"Now let us get down to the crucial matter we are all here to discuss.

"You are familiar with the Governments' and Senator Kingstons' plans for ReFederalization led by the bribery of the Rescue, Relief and Reconstruction Force. From what I see and hear, ReFederalization is long on vague promises and very short on detail. Yet, we are expected to go along with this radical, unproven plan based on the words of, let's be honest—a duplicitous, unscrupulous and greedy politician. And let us not forget, he represents a government that abandoned us six years ago and has done little, actually, let me be honest again…has since then, done NOTHING for us at all!"

The last comment prompted some delegates to clap in agreement with Danny's rhetoric. Buoyed up by the positive response, he continued with a more confident voice:

"We and all the people we represent, have worked, suffered, and many died, to now finally see the fruits of our labors. All while the Senator and our Government have been sitting idly by, unwilling to help.

"Well, ladies and gentleman, what I am saying to the Senator and all those cowards back in Sacramento is this: Your RRRF is too little, too late. We don't need you now. We don't need you in the future. ReFederalization is a cover, a scam to come in and take power under the appearance of creating some form of government. Well, I want none of it until they spell out in detail exactly what they are proposing. I say to the Government, to Senator Kingston…" Danny paused then thumped the podium for dramatic effect.

"...If you come to Kentucky with your false promises, your threats, your invasion, you won't be welcome. Do so at your peril. We'll fight you every step of the way...on the riverbanks, in the cities, in the fields, in our homes. And in years to come, people will look back and say this was the defining moment in our history, this was our finest hour!"

(Danny wasn't too concerned if the audience recognized, or not, his paraphrasing of Winston Churchill's famous speech made early in WW2 when Britain faced invasion by the Nazis. Hearing it still sent chills down his spine and he believed it was particularly appropriate for the occasion).

He looked up, pausing in expectation of applause. For a few seconds, there was silence. Then one person stood cheering and yelling approval. Immediately the rest of the audience was up, shouting, clapping, stamping their feet and banging on the tables in noisy appreciation of his fiery words. Initially, the two US Marshals sitting at the back of the hall were too stunned at the crowd's reaction to do anything. They quickly stood up and clapped as well, wanting to appear equally enthusiastic.

Once the ovation had died down and the audience was back in their seats, Danny, flushed with pride that he had roused the group to such a frenzy, now took on a more somber tone.

"Thank you so much. It seems we are all in agreement? The next question is, what are we going to do? If possible, I want all of us to agree on a plan of action. Can I suggest we break into groups, with each one of my Captains as chairman, and we spend the rest of the morning discussing what we have to do to keep these westerners out of here? Let's discuss the feedback from the groups this afternoon."

Even people used to leading and making decisions, like to be organized from time to time, and this was one of them. Within a few minutes, groups of delegates were huddled around tables discussing how to keep ReFederalization out of Kentucky. Roger couldn't help himself being drawn to the table where Penny from Bowling Green was seated. The other attendees were from Lexington, London and Wickman, according to their badges.

The precinct Captain in charge of the table was the Brit called Brian. His London accent making it difficult for Roger to understand him at times, started the discussion. "OK guys and gals, now the hysteria has settled down, how are we going to nuke this wanker from Sacramento? Or do we think we should 'ear him out a bit more? Tryin' to play the honest broker 'ere. Don't want to sway you one way or t'other. We Brits lost America once. Be a shame to lose Kentucky for a second time!"

Looking across the table, he pigeonholed Roger, "What's your thinkin', Roger from the metropolis of French Creek? Where the fuck is French Creek, anyway?"

Put on the spot, Roger garnered his thoughts, chose to ignore the question about French Creek, and diplomatically replied, "As an ex-Army officer, my leanings are always to find out as much about the enemy before you decide how, and when you deal with him. We have no idea, really, what the Fed's or Senator's plans are. We have no clue what resources he has in terms of manpower and materials. Most difficult of all, we just don't know how much we can trust him. Though based on his past performance I wouldn't trust him further than I could throw him. Ultimately, I have to be fair to my community and find out as much as I can before I can make a decision on their behalf."

Brian chuckled, "Fuck Roger, you missed out on a career in politics…that nicely avoided the question! Though I do see your point. I like punters who are fair and square."

He turned and looked at the undercover US Marshal, "What's your thoughts, Frank from Wickman? Lovely tarn by the way. Great boozers there, visited it many times."

The US Marshal froze. Concealing his panic at being put under the spotlight, he fidgeted in his seat, then after a few awkward moments mumbled, "Er, well, we think this whole RRRF thing might have some merit. Need to wait and see, let's not write it off too quickly, maybe? Er, haven't got much of an opinion to be honest. Suppose it doesn't seem like a bad idea, really."

Roger's bullshit antennae began to buzz. Years in the Army, dealing with people under pressure, or in situations where there was a language barrier, had fine-tuned his sixth sense for when someone wasn't telling the whole truth. Through their body language, as much as how they spoke, or what they said. The guy from Wickman didn't quite gel with him. Something was a little off, he felt. He ran over in his mind what Frank had just said.

Why would you come here unless you were to a degree anti-ReFederalization? Best stay at home, if you believe that it is the best course of action. If he made the same comment in the bar tonight, he might find himself at the wrong end of a punch, or worse. It was a strange opinion to voice under the circumstances.

Now that he was looking at him more closely, something else was not quite right, Roger detected. What was it? Then it struck him. Frank just looked too *clean*. Too well-shaven, too neat a haircut, unsoiled clothes. This was not a man who had been living the lifestyle everyone else had for the last six years. Yes, something about this guy was not ringing true.

Roger kept his thoughts to himself as Brian turned and deployed his considerable Brit charm on Penny.

"Well, Penny darlin', such a pleasure to have you 'ere. Always appreciate a lady's point of view, normally makes more sense than the men's. Brains and beauty are a wonderful combination. What are your thoughts?"

Penny rolled her eyes and snapped back, "Brian, quit the chauvinistic crap, please. Now you ask, here's my take so far. This get together can't really be called representative of everyone's opinion in Kentucky. What it does represent are the viewpoints of those in power. Now, you could argue, what's new in that? Just how much have Senators and Congressmen and women in the past reflected the views of voters, as opposed to their own interests and those who have funded them? I think what we should all be asking ourselves is: can *we* get our communities, this whole state, back to the twenty-first century quicker than the RRRF and Refederalization can? If all the people here started working together, could we do it without any outside help? Is what we have here today actually the basis of some kind of state legislature? I don't know, but I'd be interested in other people's comments."

Both Roger and Brian were impressed with Penny's ideas, and said so. In fact, the rest of the discussion pivoted towards her plan, debating how practical it might be if developed into a workable proposition. Roger noticed Frank from Wickman barely contributed to the conversation. Later during a coffee break Roger brought up his doubts about Frank's authenticity to Penny and Brian. Penny, too, agreed he didn't seem genuine, while Brian also voiced his doubts about how 'kosher' he was. He said he'd go and discuss it with Danny. If they had some kind of infiltrator here, they had to be dealt with quickly.

As he left, Roger turned to Penny, keen to start up a new conversation. Lamely, he asked her how she'd ended up running Bowling Green, a sizable city just off I-65. Sitting down with their cups of watered down coffee, she stared thoughtfully into her cup before replying.

"More by default, really Roger. My husband was the real mover and shaker who managed to get all the warring gangs after the Collapse to see sense and work together. Bit like this guy Danny, he divided the city up into wards and gave each one control on the understanding that certain matters like food and security decisions would be made as a group. He was ex-Army like yourself, big fella, didn't take any crap from anyone. Anyway, he persuaded them all to agree with his plan, and it worked pretty well for a while. That was until last year when he got pneumonia and died."

She paused for a moment, composed herself, then continued in a quiet voice that meant Roger had to lean closer to hear her, "Then one of the ward leaders thought he'd take my husband's place. That didn't end well for him. My friends saw it coming and, shall we say, the problem went away. The rest of the group were happy for me to take the reins, they didn't want the hassle. So here I am."

"Wow, good for you. Can't have been an easy time. What did you do before the Collapse?"

Penny gave a rueful laugh. "You'll never guess, so I'll tell you. I was an accountant at the Corvette factory. Dull as ditchwater. I was looking for a change of career, when the Collapse made the choice for me. Boom, boom, I ended up running a city. Not my choice, but there you go, shit happens and sometimes you come up smelling of roses. It wasn't what I had in mind, but needs must sometimes." Deciding she'd revealed more than she wanted, she looked at Roger and asked, "Enough about me…what's your story?"

Normally, Roger was reticent talking about himself, but to Penny he found it easy. He kept his resume brief. Ten years in the Army; his arrival in French Creek, from, of all places, Bowling Green to look after his wife's sister; after the Collapse, being stuck there with his wife and son as the country fell apart; Taking over the Council that ran the village and the death of his wife from diabetes. He didn't mention about the recent excursion to Memphis and his brush with the coyotes. That was a story for another time.

"Jesus, that's quite a saga Roger. Been tough for you as well. You lived in Bowling Green, there's a coincidence!" exclaimed Penny. "Whereabouts?"

"Out near Woodburn, we had a small farm, never been back, too many memories. Maybe one day I'll see what's survived there. You?"

"Other side of the city, near Plum Springs, all very suburban…what on earth…?" Penny was looking over Roger's shoulder, a look of alarm on her face.

Roger turned to see a disturbance at the other side of the room, voices being raised. He stood up to get a better view. In the middle of a group of Danny's henchmen was Frank being roughly manhandled out into the street. He already looked in a bad way. His shirt was torn, he'd several cuts on his cheek. They both moved closer to the action and found Brian following the noisy group outside.

Roger asked him what was going on, "I think you were right, Rog me old mate, Frank here is a fraud. The boys are going to take him somewhere safe and have a nice little chat, find out who he really is and what he knows. Don't think it'll include tea and biscuits somehow!"

With that, Danny's minders dragged Frank, struggling and pleading his innocence, outside into the back of an ancient Walmart van. It sped away from the ogling crowd who'd been watching the unexpected entertainment.

With the crowd diverted, the other US Marshal quietly exited via an emergency door at the back of the meeting room. He ran down to River Road, where his small boat was docked. He knew it would only take a few minutes before someone realized the captured US Marshal had a friend they'd like to talk to as well. The streets were not busy and he worried his running would attract attention. At any moment, he expected to hear someone shouting at him, or even shots being fired. He felt guilty not helping Frank, however; it was more important to get back and tell the Major General what had happened.

He slowed down as he approached the dock. A security guard, sitting smoking at a small guardhouse looked up. He casually ambled towards him as if he had all the time in the world.

"Hi, beautiful day, how's it going?"

The guard answered, no suspicion showing on his face.

"Good thanks, sir. Hey, ain't you one of those guys who came up from Wickman? My buddy told me to keep an eye on your boat 'cos you're attending Danny's big meeting."

"Yep, that's me. Appreciate you taking care of my boat. Meeting's just about over so I gotta get going now. Thanks again. You have a blessed day."

"Where's your friend, how's he gonna get back?" asked the guard suspiciously, now standing, a hand on his gun.

The US Marshal shrugged, appearing indifferent as best he could, "Don't know, don't care, think he's met some girl and wants to stay on for a bit. Me, I gotta get back."

Not waiting for a reply, he walked to the boat, jumped in, and prepared to cast off, trying to appear as nonchalant as possible. It seemed to work. By the time the engine started, the guard was sitting back down, reading his book. He revved up the outboard, hurrying out into the river, heading south towards safety. He was sure the Major General and Senator would not be happy with the news a US Marshal had been caught. They'd also be less than thrilled at the way the meeting had made it clear they would not welcome the RRRF and ReFederalization with open arms in the good ole' state of Kentucky.

Chapter 18

Ping, the Chinese precinct Captain, was leaning over the fence that kept his 700lb behemoth pig, Hopkins, from running riot around his small suburban farm. Hopkins needed a lot of food, and several times a day. If not, he became aggressive and fractious. Not the attitude you want in a beast that size. The beauty about pigs, thought Ping, is that they'll eat anything. And with jaws as powerful as theirs, almost anything is edible. Including bones.

He'd been told to expect a visitor who might need some incentive to talk. He looked down at Hopkins, who had waddled over to see him, his nose twitching expectantly for a treat.

"No, not yet, big boy, but I may have something real tasty for you very soon. I know you're hungry. Be patient."

As if showing his disapproval at the delay, Hopkins grunted loudly and shuffled off to the other side of his pen, flopped down and looked at Ping greedily with his cold, beady eyes.

Ping went to get his special 'guest' chair, one with carefully designed restraints. These additional features of heavyweight brackets on the legs and back enabled it to be locked in place once inside of the pigpen. People tended to wriggle a lot when they saw Hopkins coming over to say hello.

Soon Ping heard the van arrive and the passengers make their way around to the back of the barn where he, and Hopkins, were waiting. A bedraggled, frightened looking man, now even more roughed up than when he left the meeting, was still making life difficult for his captors. One punched him viciously in the stomach. He collapsed, winded, making it easier to drag him over to where Ping stood behind his special chair.

Before the Marshal could regain his breath, he was bound and shackled, unable to move anything but his head.

One guard said to Ping, "This here's a guy who calls himself Frank, reckons he's from Wickman, but knows fuck all about the place. We think he might be working for the Feds. Come here to sniff about, find out what we're up to. But Frank here ain't been too talkative, so we thought you and your big fat friend over there might help him find his tongue. Danny's very keen for him to tell us all he knows."

Ping walked around and faced the Marshal. Bending forward, he put on his most welcoming voice.

"Well, hello there, Mr. Frank. I'll be honest with you, so I want you to be honest with me. We're gonna ask you some questions. If you don't answer them quickly and truthfully, I'll introduce you to my big, hungry friend here called Hopkins. Know why I call him Hopkins, Mr. Frank?"

The US Marshal looked up at Ping through bloodied, half-closed eyes, "Go fuck yourself and your filthy fucking pig."

Ping feigned at being insulted, "That's no way to talk about your fellow dinner guest. Pigs are very clean animals in case you don't know. They're also like living vacuums, they eat and swallow anything that's put in front of them—as you'll know if you've seen the film *Hannibal*, with Anthony Hopkins. See the connection now, Mr. Frank?"

The Marshal ignored Ping. He looked with his one open eye at the massive pig, who had wandered across his pen and was now only a few feet from him. He felt his insides twist in fear. This just couldn't be happening to him. It was like a horror movie. One he certainly didn't want to be part of. Could that, *would that*, pig really eat him?

His pride was telling him to say nothing. Still, the urge to avoid pain and live was a much stronger emotion than misplaced loyalty to some distant politician. Even so, deep inside he felt the need to hold out a little longer.

Through his split lip he mumbled, "Can't help you, asshole. Do you think the Senator tells me his secret plans? I know nothing that's of use to you."

"Now that's a shame you say that," replied the ever polite Ping, "because I have to believe you know something about what the Senator and the Army are planning. How many soldiers are there? Where will they be landing? When? Come on now, Mr. Frank, let's be cooperative here."

The Marshal said nothing.

Ping signaled to the men to lift the prisoner and the chair over into the pen. Its legs sank into the mud and filth. They locked the brackets onto the fence posts. The Marshal and Hopkins were now only a few feet apart, with nothing between them.

The Marshal tried to hide his fear as Hopkins ambled over and started sniffing at his feet, legs, crotch and face. He was so big that seated next to him his drooling snout could reach his head.

Ping leant over the fence, his mouth inches from the Marshal's ear.

"Giving you fair warning here, Hopkins here hasn't eaten in a few days. So he's a hungry boy. They say a pig of his size can devour a human body in about twelve hours. I guess that could be less if he's peckish? They normally start wherever there's some blood. So, all I have to do is cut you and that will be his...appetizer, shall we say? Unlike a dog, he won't be too aggressive or wild. Just a steady, how can I describe it...nibbling, no...munching, is a better word, of flesh and then bones. He can be very choosy about where he starts. I know as an appetizer he likes the softer areas of the human body. If you know what I mean, Mr. Frank?"

The Marshal was losing his self-control. The thought of this brute slowly devouring him piece by piece was beyond his comprehension. With a gut-churning sense of dread, he watched the brute move his gargantuan pink head up from his legs, snuffle around his crotch, then gradually graze his nose up until it reached his head. Hopkins' dribbling snout and mouth, with its stinking breath, was now nuzzling around the cut above his eye. He was surprisingly gentle: the caress of a killer. Up close, the pig's breath was repulsive, the animal's whole imposing presence next to him sickening and horrifying.

The men who'd brought the Marshal were transfixed, watching this giant animal almost tease the prisoner with his sniffing, licking and nudging. Though two soon walked away sickened by what they were witnessing. The others found themselves rooted to the ground like rubberneckers, watching the scene of a car crash.

Finally, the Marshal's composure and dignity collapsed, evaporating completely as the foul smelling animal nibbled his ear.

"OK, for fuck's sake, get this animal off me! Get me outta here! Please God get me out! I'll tell you anything you need to know. For fuck's sake, quickly!"

Ping nodded to the men. They unlocked the shackles and dragged the Marshal back to safety. He threw some food into the center of the pen, and Hopkins, oblivious to the terror he had caused, turned away from the Marshal, sauntering over to munch on his snack.

"OK," said Ping, looking down at the shaking and terrorized Marshal, "shall we start again?"

The Marshal told them everything he knew about the RRRF's plans. Which wasn't a lot, though probably more than Danny had learnt from his contacts. They called Danny on the walkie-talkie and told him what the Marshal had revealed, all courtesy of Hopkin's close attention.

"Put him in one of the secure stalls in the barn and keep a close watch. Might have a use for him later on," ordered Danny.

"Sure thing Danny. Glad me and Hopkins could be of help," replied Ping, pleased he was on the right side of the boss. The men dragged the still shocked Marshal into the barn and locked him in a horse stall.

He slumped down in the straw, shaking and whimpering before throwing up and passing out.

Meanwhile, Danny, though a little disappointed at the paucity of the information extracted from him, was happy to be a little wiser about his enemy's plans. More importantly, he also had a hostage for leverage in any future negotiations.

Danny sent word to the delegates at the interrupted meeting that they would reconvene for dinner. He was keen to see if a consensus viewpoint was emerging from the groups. The Marshal episode was a little embarrassing, the fact another may have gotten away, particularly galling.

Roger and Penny had spent most of the day chatting about their pasts and how they were running their respective communities. Both admitted to themselves it was one of the most enjoyable afternoons they'd spent in a long time. Away from the stresses and pressure both their roles imposed upon them. They returned to their rooms to freshen up and met again at dinner. They sat together after helping themselves to an impressive buffet, washed down with real wine.

Reading the label, she asked incredulously, "Where the hell does he get Merlot?" as she poured herself, and Roger, a generous glassful.

Taking an appreciative sip, "I'd rather not know, might spoil the taste," replied Roger. He hadn't had a wine like this in years. It was exquisite.

They continued to enjoy Danny's sumptuous hospitality before the man himself stood up, glass in hand. He tapped it gently with a spoon. The diners politely stopped their conversations and waited to hear what he had to say.

"Firstly, thank you all, again, for coming to this meeting. I hope you found it both enjoyable and informative. I apologize for this morning's disturbance; it appears we had two Government informants in our midst. One escaped, the other has proved most...*cooperative,* and provided me with some useful intelligence on the RRRF's plans." He paused, took a drink, then continued.

"It appears the RRRF is headed by a Major General Redditch with some five thousand Army personnel at his disposal, along with US Marshals, and the National Guard. They intend to land at various ports along the Mississippi and Ohio Rivers, then move out across the State spreading the Government's propaganda. Unfortunately, the Marshal knew no details about the ReFederalization of Kentucky.

"Huge amounts of food, medicine and goods are to be dispensed to our citizens to bribe them to come on board with their plans. The RRRF is the soft, carrot, approach. However, the killing of their Colonel in Paducah a few days ago has put plans on hold. The two US Marshals were sent here to try and discover our intentions. Unfortunately for them, they will learn nothing, thanks to the detective work done by...," Danny looked down at a piece of paper, "my precinct Captain, Brian, Roger from French Creek and Penny from Bowling Green. Thank you!" There was a round of appreciative applause. Roger and Penny reluctantly acknowledged their thanks with a quick wave. Brian across the table winked and raised his glass in salute.

Danny then resumed his address, clearly enjoying being the center of attention with such a rapt audience.

"Secondly, the discussions this morning produced a variety of opinions. All agreed we don't want the Senator and the Feds here until we know more about their plans for ReFederalization. I believe until we know more, we should do everything possible to stall their progress. Some of you were advocating to take the fight to them before they land. Others wanted to take a less proactive approach, and see if we can get more concrete information from them. As one of the leaders that would be in the front line of any Government invasion, I would like to propose, before we start shooting, we send a delegation to meet the Senator and the Major General to see if this whole situation can be resolved without force."

People were a little surprised at Danny's conciliatory tone. They were expecting a call to arms. He had decided on this approach after talking to Olivia. It was his way of testing the revolutionary waters, as it were. If this less aggressive direction was voted down by the attendees, then he would willingly agree to up the ante. If not, then he'd be seen as a man of reason for proposing a cautious approach.

There were some murmurings from the audience complaining that this was a sellout. They wanted action, to kick some ass, as the leader from Lexington was heard to say. Others nodded their agreement at Danny's more diplomatic route.

As if to appease those who thought he was being too easy, Danny then explained that sending a delegation to start negotiations gave them all the more time to prepare for any eventual conflict. This brought a more positive response from pro-fight delegates.

Penny nudged Roger and whispered in his ear, "What happened to my idea of us all working towards our own government?"

Roger whispered back, "Guess that sounds far too sensible. Sorry, I thought it had some merit."

She flashed her eyes across the table at Brian who must have guessed why she looked so angry. He looked at her and shrugged his shoulders as if to say, 'I tried'. Still smarting at being overlooked, when Danny asked for volunteers to head up a negotiating group, she was the first to put her hand up, nudging Roger strongly in the ribs to do likewise. He did as instructed. Few others were so keen.

Danny looked round the room at the paltry show of hands and picked Roger, Penny, and three others to form the delegation. The meeting rambled on for another thirty minutes with various people offering up viewpoints, none of which progressed the discussion in any helpful direction. Realizing he should quit before noisier elements in the crowd started to whip up the idea of immediate violence, Danny wound down the proceedings. He thanked everyone for their participation and informed them transport would leave at 9:00 a.m. tomorrow.

Danny signaled for the delegation members to meet him for a coffee. They gathered round in the bar and introduced themselves. Aside from Penny and Roger, there was the representative from Lexington, who had earlier been keen on taking the fight to the Feds. Of the two other members of the group, one was from Frankfort, and the other from Richmond. Representing Danny's interests was the irrepressible Brian.

After the introductions and small talk, before Danny could say anything, Roger cut to the chase.

"OK, I need to be clear about a few things if I'm going to be part of this exercise. Are we serious about finding a compromise? Or is it just a delaying and fact-finding exercise? What are our objectives? If we don't get what we want, what are we threatening them with? If this is just a charade, then I want no part of it. If we're serious about finding a peaceful solution, then I'm happy to be involved."

"Whoa!" exclaimed Danny, "here's a man that doesn't mince his words. My kinda guy. Fair question Roger. Here's where I stand. I don't want those Fed assholes putting a single foot on Kentucky soil. And I've got a thousand armed men ready to defend Louisville if they even think about it. That said, no one wants any innocents getting killed. If we can persuade them to just go away and leave us alone, then I'm all for it. But they need to understand, if they start moving the Army over here, we'll put up one helluva fuckin' fight."

Frankfort man, who went by the name of Jack, spoke for the first time. He was built like a linebacker, in his forties, with close cropped gray hair, his bulging arms and neck covered in tattoos. Despite the street brawler looks, he spoke in a considered tone, "I agree with Roger. I have a lot at stake here as I'm guessing Frankfort is where they'll want to establish their half-assed government. That isn't happening on my watch. Things are rolling along pretty well. I don't need any outside help, thanks. I'd really prefer to tell them to go take a hike without starting a war. So how much negotiating room have we got here? What are we offering them to go away? What leverage do we have?"

Penny joined in before anyone else could have their say. "From day one I've wondered why they chose Kentucky as the first place to 'ReFederalize' as they call it, and with the crooked Senator Kingston leading the charge. The guy was as dirty as a shit shovel before the Collapse. Why does he want to risk his political reputation on a high-risk plan like this? I wonder if he has a hidden agenda? Revenge maybe?

Can't be for the power trip…who wants to take on dragging Kentucky back into the twenty-first century? Hell, half of it was barely in the twentieth century before it all went to shit six years ago. The pieces don't fit together for me."

Everyone turned to Danny for an answer. For an instant, he looked uncomfortable, almost embarrassed. Awkwardly, it was his precinct Captain, Brian who made matters worse by commenting, "Yea Danny, you told me once you knew him before the Collapse, any idea what his real motive might be?"

Danny brushed aside any speculation he knew the Senator well, "I had a few business dealings with him years ago, nothing special. No, I've no idea if he has other reasons for wanting to take over Kentucky, except he's a typical power-hungry politician looking for glory. We have to stop him. I'm also guessing the move isn't entirely his, that the President has some skin in the game too. I gather there may be an election coming, perhaps that has something to do with all of this."

Penny picked up on Danny's reply. "So you think we're just pawns in some power play back in Sacramento? Win Kentucky, win the next election. That's a high risk strategy I would suggest."

"I wouldn't put it past both the Senator and the President to try something like this. In a way it's a win-win for them: if ReFederalization works, they're the good guys, if it fails because Kentucky sends them packing, they can say they tried, and those ungrateful folk in the East didn't want their help." Reasoned Roger. "You gotta admire their devious thinking."

Grateful for the way the conversation had been sidetracked, Danny had, for the moment, avoided explaining his past involvements with the Senator. He had a good idea why the Senator wanted to see Kentucky under his control, and also Danny out of the frame. He wasn't about to reveal that now. He'd deal with those problems later.

"So," asked Frank, "how is this first meeting to be arranged–assuming the top brass at the RRRF want to negotiate at all?"

In the end, the simplest way was chosen. An invitation broadcast on their ham radio to talks, hoping the other side would pick up the message. The captured Marshal said they had heard Danny's previous broadcasts, so it was likely they would hear the latest one. Now it was a case of waiting for a response.

Chapter 19

The US Marshal took two days to reach Cape Girardeau, the RRRF's new HQ. Now he was standing, disheveled and exhausted, in front of Major General Redditch for his debriefing. In reality, he didn't have much information. All he could relay was that the group at the meeting had seemed not just united, but enthusiastic about repulsing any kind of Federal sponsored RRRF mission that might arrive on Kentucky's shores. Well, at least that's the impression Danny Trevino had given, admitted the Marshal, aware that he had, for the most part, failed in his fact-finding mission. On top of that, the other Marshal was no doubt being interrogated about his knowledge of the RRRF's plans.

The Major General quickly grasped the fact that Danny now knew more about his strategy, than he did about theirs. The Senator would create merry hell over this *snafu*. He questioned the Marshal for a few more minutes, realizing there was little more to be learned, he dismissed him. A few hours later, his Comms Sergeant came in and he snapped to attention.

"Sir, just received this broadcast from the rebels. Sorry sir, the people in Kentucky. Thought you'd want to see it immediately." The Major General took the proffered note. The message was only a few lines:

"Attention Major General Redditch and Senator Kingston. We would like to meet to discuss the current situation concerning your intended invasion by the RRRF. We wish to avoid any unnecessary violence or bloodshed. Our delegation is ready to meet you. We propose Stewart Island near Birdsville, noon on April 26th. Please confirm your attendance."

The Free Kentucky Army.

"Shall I send a reply, sir?"

"Let me talk to my senior officers and the Senator first. Sergeant, was this an open broadcast?"

"Yes sir, anyone could hear it."

"Thank you sergeant, that will be all."

He sat back in his chair, feet up on his desk. Practically before it had started, this entire mission was becoming a nightmare, with the real possibility that some kind of civil war could break out between the US Army and the newly formed Free Kentucky Army, whoever they were. He began to feel his next promotion slipping away, his reputation forever sullied as the man who started a conflict that killed thousands of fellow Americans. Moreover, all of this being done at the behest of a Government and politicians who had entered this arena with no clear plan of action. But then again, when did they? Smoke and mirrors was their normal M.O., it ran in their blood, making it impossible to get a straight answer out of them. He braced himself for the call with Senator Kingston who no doubt would expect some instant solutions to this increasingly intractable problem.

He was still mulling over this quagmire of complications when his Comms Sergeant reappeared, looking flustered, clutching another piece of paper.

Sharply the Major General looked up, "Now what Sergeant? It better be important." Wordlessly, he took the message from the nervous messenger, and read its brief contents. "You may go Sergeant. Tell Captain Davis to come in here at once."

He collapsed into his seat, the piece of paper scrunched up in his hand. He desperately controlled the urge to smash something against the wall in sheer annoyance and frustration. Within a few minutes, the Captain appeared at the door standing to attention.

"You wanted to see me, sir?"

Yes, Captain. Tell me what you make of this message."

The Captain took the ball of paper, unpicked it and read the carefully hand-written message the Sergeant had transcribed:

"Attention fellow Kentuckians,

You have heard the ramblings of the man known as Danny Trevino, so called Mayor of Louisville, the self-appointed leader of the Free Kentucky Army. He claims to represent the will of the people of Kentucky. He claims that the RRRF is going to invade and enslave our state and they are not wanted here. He even organized a meeting in Louisville of people who want to fight the RRRF and ReFederalization.

This broadcast is to tell anyone who hears it that these people do NOT represent the views of everyone in Kentucky. Let it be clear there are a lot of us who would welcome the RRRF's assistance, and these are the people we speak for today.

We demand a seat at the negotiating table at the meeting on April 26th and demand our voices be heard. Flood the airwaves with your support. Let them know we will not be ignored!"

The Kentucky People's Movement.

The Captain looked up at the Major General, "What do you think, sir?"

"I think, if this is for real," said the Major General wearily, "we have a Grade A clusterfuck on our hands. Keep listening for anything else they broadcast, or any reaction from other people or groups. We need to get a handle on how serious these people are."

He dismissed the Captain with a perfunctory wave, asking him to reconvene a meeting of all senior staff within the hour.

He picked up the phone and called Senator Kingston. For once, he was ahead of the politician with the latest news. No one had heard, or informed, the Senator about the appearance of the Kentucky's People's Movement. In a perverse way, he took some pleasure in hearing the Senator explode at the other end of the phone. If the prospect of negotiating with those 'fucking murderers' had him incandescent, the emergence of the Kentucky's People Movement into the equation had him almost foaming at the mouth with indignation. How many more complications could arise to derail his plans?

"Do we know anything about these Kentucky People's Movement assholes?' demanded the Senator when he had come down from orbit.

"Not much Senator, though since that broadcast the airwaves have certainly lit up with both sides claiming to represent the majority of the populace. They probably haven't got the resources Danny Trevino and his group have, but they may have the numbers. Who knows?"

"Well, I fucking want to know, and soon. And what about this meeting? I think we should go tell them to take a hike. Fucking nerve demanding negotiations. Don't they know who they're dealing with here? The goddamned US Government, that's who. And it doesn't negotiate with terrorist thugs. Can't we go in and take a few of the leaders out?"

"I understand all of that, Senator. The fact is to fight an enemy, you have to know where they are. We have no idea where all these leaders have gone after the meeting in Louisville. We don't want our own domestic Vietnam or Afghanistan, do we? As for this pro-RRRF group, they are spread nationwide. We have no way of harnessing their energies for our purposes. Also, it's not just people in Kentucky who have heard these radio broadcasts, they can be heard anywhere. My comms guy said social media in the west is already blowing up with posts and comments supporting all sides of this issue. If we start killing other Americans without some real justification, we'll all be out of a job. On the plus side, it does appear that the RRRF plan has its followers. I think we should try and find ways to cultivate them? In the meantime, reluctantly Senator, I think we should go to this meeting and see what happens."

Hearing the words 'Vietnam' and 'Afghanistan', the Senator recoiled at being compared to Lyndon Johnson or George Bush who had led the country into two unwinnable wars.

With a resigned growl, the Senator agreed, "Jesus, OK let's talk with these people and see where it gets us."

He put the phone down, picked up his third glass of scotch for the day, and wondered if this was all worthwhile. Then he quickly reminded himself it wasn't just his and the President's political future at stake, more importantly, a lot of money. That made it eminently worth the effort.

Chapter 20

Sitting in his double wide a few miles outside Paintsville, in the far east of Kentucky, Jodie McFadden had long been a keen user of CB and ham radio. There wasn't much else to do in this tiny Appalachian town. Paintsville had a long and undistinguished history going back to 1780, when the first white settlers arrived. They noticed carved paintings on trees created by the local Indian tribes and dutifully called the original settlement Paint Lick Station. Its population peaked at just over 4,300 in the 1960s, however after the Collapse it had fallen to just 850.

Jodie, once a long-haul truck driver, was familiar with CB radio. He'd used it extensively during his travels around the US. Laid off just before the Collapse, he'd acquired a ham radio to keep in touch with the outside world. For the past six years there had been little traffic on the airwaves, so he contented himself with harmless chats among contacts across the US and occasionally in countries far away he'd never heard of. Suddenly, in the last few weeks, his radio was buzzing incessantly with chatter about some Government plan to rescue Kentucky, and now, a bunch of people who wanted to stop it. Were they mad?

Paintsville had one of the lowest median incomes of any town in Kentucky. For years, even before the Collapse, people had been living on the breadline. Now there was a promise that some Government assistance might be coming their way! Jodie had mentioned this at the monthly farmer's market—most had heard nothing about it. None of the Senator's leaflets had made their way to this rural backwater. Jodie informed his rapt audience about the Senator's plans and the resistance to it being led by someone called Danny Trevino in Louisville. They were horrified that someone would be opposed to receiving any help. What was the matter with these people? Anyway, who was this Trevino guy to speak for them? The rumblings of discontent quickly became angry and vociferous among the tiny Paintsville population. Something had to be done. It was decided that Jodie should broadcast a message telling everyone that this Government organized RRRF idea was one *they* welcomed. They co-opted a reporter from the now defunct local paper, *The Paintsville Herald*, to write a reply.

It was this message the Major General–and the rest of Kentucky heard. Little did they know it was from a small town in the middle of one of the poorest areas of America. How could they know its effect would ripple and grow in strength as it flew across the state at the speed of light? Within twenty-four-hours, more and more ham radio enthusiasts were dusting off and firing up their stored equipment, helping Jodie's message bounce back and forth across Kentucky and America like some ethereal pinball.

The problem was, no one in Paintsville stood any chance of getting to the meeting on April 26th. It would take about a week on horseback to get to Stewart Island. In any case, no one was too thrilled about traveling so far from home. Did anyone have any relatives or friends in west Kentucky who might want to go? The answer was no from all his contacts in the town.

Undeterred, Jodie broadcast a message asking anyone close to Stewart Island to attend and represent the views of people like Jodie, prepared to hear out what the RRRF was all about. If, on the face of it, the ideas sounded reasonable, make it clear to all concerned that those involved in the Louisville meeting weren't the only players in town. Within a couple of hours, Nathan Burke, former mayor of Salem radioed back to say he would go. The town was only about ten miles from Birdsville, adjacent to Stewart Island on the Ohio River.

Major General Redditch ordered all radio traffic be monitored to discover just what the chatter revealed about this new development. Did the Kentucky People's Movement really have a groundswell of support, or was it just a few isolated individuals? Either way, he wanted to know.

Meanwhile, there was one person distinctly underwhelmed at the emergence of the Kentucky People's Movement: Danny Trevino. He paced around his penthouse, like a tomcat who could scent a cat on heat.

"Just who the fuck are these people?" he roared at Olivia, who hastily poured a vodka to calm him down. "All this time and effort, all my planning, and then these fucking rednecks are over us like a bad rash. If they fuck this up, I'll personally go find them and blow them away."

Olivia handed Danny the glass, he downed the contents in one gulp. Calming down a little, he told Olivia he wanted to see the group that were going to the Stewart Island meeting. Now.

Thirty minutes later, they dutifully arrived to hear Danny's rant about the appearance of the so-called Kentucky People's Movement and how inconvenient it could be. How dare they disrupt his plans? Who the hell did they think they were getting involved in his negotiations? No one answered his rhetorical questions, safer not to.

When his temper tantrum finally dissipated, he demanded to hear the group's ideas on dealing with these fucking upstarts. To his surprise, the reaction from them was to let these Freedom people send someone to the meeting, see what they have to say? What harm could come of it?

Roger added, as diplomatically as possible, "While we all, to some degree, don't want the RRRF here, at least until we are one hundred percent clear about their objectives. We have to accept there are thousands of people across Kentucky who might welcome their help. Under any circumstances. Also it will be an opportunity to found out more about them."

The man from Richmond, Jake, added his thoughts, "Can't see we've got a choice Danny. We don't know who they are or where they are, so going after them isn't an option. I've got a comfortable set up down in Richmond. Go fifty miles into the boondocks though and some people are still having a rough time, real subsistence level stuff. Hardly blame them if someone offers a carrot, they wanna eat it."

Danny wasn't used to having people disagree with him. However, he had to admit they were probably right. Within the confines of Louisville, it had been easy to keep people under control through bribery or coercion. Across a thousand small villages, it was impossible. They would need a different approach, one he couldn't think of at the moment. Worry about that later.

Penny added her thoughts, "I agree with you guys…to a degree. It's all very well for us sitting here, content with our lot, to forget there's a whole bunch of people out there who are not. As I said during our discussion yesterday, maybe we should look to work together, try to do what the RRRF is offering? We have to face facts. If it's not this RRRF, then it will be another variation in the future. I believe if we can be involved in the process–and control the narrative, as they say–then we might all get what we want in the long term."

Penny thought her comments were well reasoned. She was furious when Danny brushed them aside.

"Nice idea Penny, but it ain't gonna happen. We've all got too much to lose if any type of RRRF is successful…."

"You mean you've got too much to lose Danny," interrupted Penny angrily, "maybe we need to stop being so goddamn selfish and look out for everyone in the long term, not just ourselves? All these little fiefdoms scattered across the state controlled by fear and violence aren't sustainable, in my opinion. I'd rather be part of the solution than the problem on how we tackle this in the future. Sorry if that doesn't fit in with how you see it." Penny wasn't sorry at all. Someone had to tell this bombastic little shit that his way wasn't necessarily the best way for everyone.

To Danny's annoyance, the rest of them nodded in agreement with her sentiments. Except Brian, who knew what Danny would do to him if he sided with them; he wisely stayed silent.

"If I'd known you all thought this way, I'd have chosen some others to go to this meeting," replied Danny with barely concealed contempt. "All I can say is if I hear you're trying to shaft all the people who attended my meeting yesterday, things won't turn out well."

Roger bristled at the threat Danny was making, but still tried to be reasonable, "I think we all understand where you're coming from Danny. We are all going to this meeting with open minds, knowing full well what everyone wants out of it. We won't let you down."

Danny decided to end the fractious meeting on that note. The group went back to the hotel and prepared themselves for the trip. They left Danny quietly seething in his penthouse.

Within the hour they were ready for the Stewart Island meeting, as it became known. One from which not everyone would return.

Chapter 21

The Louisville Group arrived in Birdsville early for the meeting. Stewart Island sat in the middle of the Ohio River, a few minutes by boat from the town. Turning up in an old military truck created a lot of interest among the locals. One or two entrepreneurial types had heard that the island was to be the venue for this meeting. They hastily acquired a few boats to ferry attendees across (for a small fee). Stewart Island covered over forty acres and was a wildlife preserve once open to campers and hunters. Now denuded of any huntable wildlife, it hadn't been visited in years. Nature had quickly reclaimed the primitive camping facilities.

The site was cleverly chosen by Danny. A neutral meeting place, it offered no opportunity to try anything underhand or launch any surprise attacks. By the time Roger and his group arrived, the representatives from the RRRF were already there. They'd erected a large tent, with tables, chairs and refreshments. Roger led them towards some Military personnel. When he saw one had the rank of Major General he instinctively stopped and saluted, "Captain Roger Makefield, pleased to meet you, sir."

The Major General returned the salute, "At ease Captain, I'm guessing you're retired so we can skip the formalities, though I appreciate the courtesy."

Off to a good start, thought Roger. Every officer likes a little brown nosing. He introduced the rest of the group, then the Major General did the same. There were representatives from the Army, the National

Guard, US Marshals, and Senator Kingston's office. Some fifteen people in total.

They were invited to help themselves to the refreshments then take a seat at the large, makeshift, conference table. Roger looked at the other participants. Sat opposite him had to be the Senator's man. He was slickly dressed in an expensive suit, had dark swept back hair and what looked like a fake tan. Called Houston, he opened the conversation with a barely concealed smirk, "We're waiting on the Kentucky People's Movement guys to turn up. We want everyone to have their say. Only fair after all. Must've been a surprise that lot turned up all of a sudden? Kinda rained on your parade, I guess?"

No one in the Louisville group rose to the bait. They ignored his taunt and continued eating and chatting amiably about everything except the matter at hand. Eventually, two people made their way from the dock to the tent, a man and a tall African American woman sporting a dazzling set of dreadlocks. The man introduced himself as Nathan Burke from Salem and the woman as Destiny Nolen from Birdsville itself. Introductions were made around the table, it was all very civilized. For the time being.

The Major General started by thanking everyone for attending. He then laid out the RRRF's plans in the broadest terms. Everyone listened without interruption. When he finished, he turned to Houston and asked if there was anything else to add from the Senator's office? Houston confirmed there wasn't. He then asked each person around the table to air their concerns or ask questions.

Roger kept quiet, wanting to hear the views of the two Kentucky People's Movement people, to try and gauge just what they wanted. Nathan Burke obliged, in an overly formal manner.

"Thank you Major General, for explaining the RRRF's intentions, albeit somewhat vague, towards the people of Kentucky. As I understand it," he began ticking off the points on his fingers, "you'll use some five thousand troops and other personnel to travel the length and breadth of Kentucky as the RRRF dispenses food and supplies. How long might this take?"

The Major General, sensing these questions could turn awkward, replied, "I think the Senator's representative here is best able to answer that–Houston?"

Smart move thought Roger, pass the poisoned chalice to someone else.

At last, thought Houston, I can begin to really earn my keep. After six years in the CIA as a Russian spy, he had transferred to the Senator's office after a chance meeting with him at a Washington security summit. The Senator was impressed with Houston's experience at the Agency. When a vacancy arose in his office, he persuaded the CIA to release him, claiming his security clearance would be ideal for the impending launch of ReFederalization. For Houston and his handler in the FSB (the Russian equivalent of the CIA), it was a perfect opportunity to sow discord and confusion, the ultimate aim: to disrupt the reuniting of America.

"Ah, yes...thank you Major General...happy to, er...answer that question...." Houston stammered.

"We haven't projected yet how long this might take. There are too many unknown factors involved, ease of travel, security, road conditions and so forth."

"Thank you. Mr. Houston," up went the second finger, "you say that you will distribute food, health supplies and other materials. How will you decide who gets what?"

"That's an excellent question, Mr. Burke. As of now, we haven't drilled down to sorting those details out. We thought we'd ask the locals about that."

"OK, Mr. Houston, how about this one?" up went the third finger, "What are your plans to reconstruct utilities such as electricity, water and gas supplies? And how long do you think that might take?"

"Another excellent question, Mr. Burke. We don't have a timescale on that either until we bring in engineers and specialists to discover what needs to be done. Not quite sure when that will be...."

Undaunted, and passing no comment, Nathan continued with a fourth finger, "You intend to create some kind of state legislature by asking residents to provide two representatives per county to come to Frankfort, I am led to believe? How can you ensure this is done fairly?"

"Well, er, we haven't ironed out those details either. It's just a proposal at this stage."

For another ten minutes, the former mayor deployed his considerable political skills trying to elicit useful information from the squirming, embarrassed young Houston. When he'd finally reached finger number ten, he concluded by saying:

"Well, thank you, young man, that was a masterclass in how not to be prepared for an important meeting. Let me be clear to you, and everyone else here. There are many, many people who want and need this RRRF initiative to succeed. For six years, they have struggled to survive. Countless numbers have seen friends and relatives suffer and perish. The prospect of, finally, some action by the Federal Government is to be welcomed. But from what I have heard, this RRRF plan is full of ill thought out ideas that could make matters worse, not better, for those in need."

Sitting by his side, Destiny nodded vigorously in agreement with his withering criticism of Houston. She now spoke up, not mincing her words, "I'm believin' ya'll got us here under false pretenses. Know what I mean? This is a load of bullcrap. If this is the best the Federal Government can offer, you just go back and talk some more with that Senator man and get us some real practical help. You hear me now?"

The rest of the table sat unresponsive. No one was sure how to follow up such a thorough massacre of the Government's plans. Then Brian looked up and delivered his two cents worth. He'd scribbled a few notes on a piece of paper, which he now read:.

"I, we, are here representing a group that met recently in Louisville. I want to say on behalf of this group and in particular my boss, Danny Trevino, mayor of Louisville, that we do not want the RRRF in Kentucky in any way, shape or form. Mr. Trevino asks me to make it clear to you that if you persist in your current course of action, he reserves the right to defend his city by any and all means. He cannot speak for all the other groups who attended the meeting, but he believes they feel the same way too. Thank you."

The Major General acknowledged Brian's comments, "Thank you for your contribution. So as the representative of Mr. Trevino, could you please inform us of the whereabouts of the US Marshal you captured?"

Expecting this question, Brian simply answered, "He's in good health, alive and well. He'll be released when the RRRF confirms it no longer intends to invade Kentucky."

The most senior US Marshal at the table looked daggers at Brian, growling, "If anything happens to that Marshal, everyone involved will be hunted down and arrested. Mark my words, sonny."

Brian bristled at the Marshal's patronizing tone, "Thanks for the threat, Mr. US Marshal, I'll pass it onto Danny. I am sure he'll be quaking in his boots. Now here's a message from my boss to your boss, that wanker Senator Kingston. Kiss my ass!"

Before the meeting degenerated into a slanging match–or worse–the Major General stood up and in a no-nonsense voice suggested the meeting adjourn for further refreshments. As everyone moved away from the table, he leaned across to Houston and said with a smile, "I'll leave you to call the Senator and report on how the meeting's gone, shall I?"

Roger gathered the Louisville Group to one side, "That was interesting, if not productive. Love the subtle negotiating approach Brian! Unless someone feels otherwise, I am not sure we can achieve much more here? I may have a quick chat with the Major General, soldier-to-soldier stuff, he might give me something useful?"

No one disagreed with Roger's suggestion. They went to get some food and gather up their belongings. He found the Major General conversing with one of his aides.

"Excuse me, sir. A word if I may?"

"Certainly Captain, what can I do for you?"

"Wanted to try and give you a quick heads up, sir. Broadly speaking, what Brian said is true, there are a large number of people, mainly from the cities and towns who really don't want the status quo changed. They are doing OK. From what I can gather, they are all pretty well-armed and ready to fight. This guy Danny, in particular, has a small Army at his disposal. I have no idea about this whole Kentucky People's Movement lot. They came out of nowhere."

"That's useful to know, Captain, thank you."

"Can I ask you a question, sir?" the Major General nodded.

"I have a sneaking suspicion there is more to this Senator's, and the Government's plans, than hauling Kentucky back into the twenty-first century. What's your feeling, sir?"

"Obviously, I cannot divulge any confidences, Captain, but I can tell you two things that concern me. First, while this has the backing of the Government, they want it to be operated at arm's length. I assume to protect the President if the wheels all fall off. I think they call it plausible deniability. Second, the Senator is a true politician and seems to delight in keeping everyone, including me, on a 'need to know basis.' Which means I am, at times, operating with limited resources and information. Confidentially, I believe he has a hidden agenda, though I do not know what it is. I can't say any more, Captain."

"Thank you, sir for your time, and for coming to this meeting. In truth, I'm not sure what we have achieved here today. Unless you think we should stay and talk further, we'll be on our way. I should add from a personal point of view sir, that I am in no way advocating what this group in Louisville is planning. I went along as an interested observer. It worries me this could all get out of hand. Obviously, I'm not opposed to the people of Kentucky seeing their quality of life improve. Just not sure the current M.O. of the RRRF is the right way to go about it. With all due respect, sir."

The Major General listened, seeming to nod his head in agreement, "I understand where you're coming from, Captain, and I appreciate your candor. Some aspects of this entire plan I have reservations about, too. However, as you know, the Military are here to carry out the orders of our political masters. Even if we believe them to be, how can I say this…unhinged?"

With that telling comment, he wished Roger well. The group collected their belongings, walked to the boat and took the five-minute ride across to Birdsville.

They all piled into the old Army truck. Brian fired up the ancient diesel and chugged through the town. Suddenly, out of a small side street, shot an old APC at high speed in a cloud of dust and squealing tires. It careered in front of them, stopped, blocking any movement forward. A second later, an ancient Ford F-150 roared up behind, preventing Brian from reversing out of trouble.

Four men from each of the vehicles piled out running full pelt towards the truck, pointing shotguns and pistols. They had masks on, though they didn't disguise their US Marshal badges. One reached the driver's door demanding at the top of his voice, "Get out, all of you, hands behind your heads. Go for a weapon and you're dead. On the ground now!"

Caught completely unawares, Roger and his fellow travelers had no chance to grab their weapons from the storage container under the seats of the truck. Slowly, reluctantly, they climbed out and lay on the ground.

"Which of you fuckers is Danny's man?"

Brian raised his head and unwisely said, "That would be me mate, you miserable little toe rag."

For his flippant reply, Brian received a thumping kick in the ribs and another to the head. His sense of humor temporarily left him.

"OK asshole, you're coming with us. You're our insurance we get our Marshal back in one piece. You other fuckers can go tell his boss we have him, for the moment, unharmed. Might even make him a cup of tea if he's a good boy. If anything happens to our man, your mouthy boy here is toast. Now you lot get up and get the fuck outta here."

With six guns trained on them, they watched impotently as two men cuffed Brian and dragged him into one of their trucks. The rest of the ambushers jumped into their vehicles and hurtled off towards the center of Birdsville.

Penny stood up and dusted herself down. In a shaky voice she asked, "Everyone OK?"

The three men nodded, still in shock over what had happened. It wasn't the violence that concerned them, it wasn't even the unexpected kidnapping of Brian that temporarily rendered them speechless. Most worrying of all, they knew this had just ratcheted up the animosity level between Danny and the RRRF, with potentially terrible consequences for everyone.

Chapter 22

The situation quickly deteriorated on all sides over the next seven days:

- Danny put his Army on full alert along the banks of the Ohio as far south as Shepherdsville. He put a call to action across the airwaves that incited anyone with an ounce of anti-RRRF sentiment to do likewise.

- He offered a reward of $100,000 in gold for any information that would lead to Brian's whereabouts. A futile gesture, as the captive was now back in a St. Louis prison.

- Hearing about the breakdown of talks, Jodie and his disparate group of pro-RRRF supporters were left deciding which of three options they should follow: side with the RRRF, throw their lot in with the Louisville Group, or do nothing?

- Senator Kingston conferred with Government officials in Sacramento, his objective to demand a large-scale deployment of troops and security personnel into Kentucky. In addition, he wanted sanctions imposed on all boat traffic on the Mississippi and Ohio Rivers to prevent supplies reaching Louisville and other river ports.

- Anti-RRRF groups in Paducah, Owensboro, and five other towns along the Ohio and Mississippi announced they were ready for any assault by Government troops.

- Publically, the Sacramento Federal Government backs down, refusing to authorize any force against fellow American citizens. However, privately, they agree to Senator Kingston's alternative request for small scale, covert actions to remove Danny Trevino and any other active anti-RRRF leaders. Major General Redditch resigns from the Army citing illness and the need to spend more time with his family.

- In response to the proposed sanctions, Tennessee and Indiana said they would oppose any interruption of river-based traffic, pledging to help keep Kentucky supplied with essential goods.
- Hardline Delta Force Commander, General Samuel Banks is put in charge of the RRRF's Army contingent.
- Under 'enhanced interrogation', Brian finally gives up all the names and locations he knows of the Louisville Group. Including Roger's and Penny's.
- Senator Kingston announces the Government has no intention of inciting an insurrection that may lead to Kentucky's seceding from the Union. He will pursue 'less confrontational and more discrete' methods to allow the RRRF to achieve its objectives.

Chapter 23

The Reverend Josiah Wedgwood of the First Church, Resurrection of Christ, took his beliefs and sermons from the most zealous interpretations of the Bible. Based in Montgomery, Alabama, he was a large, rotund African American with even larger ambitions to spread his extremist gospel amongst the godless of his state, and beyond.

Before the Collapse, he'd built a steady following on social media for his cacophonous fire and brimstone sermons. His 'Likes' and 'Followers' numbered in the tens of thousands. A TikTok video showing him sermonizing against a backdrop of lambs being led into the inferno of hell (all CGI generated, no animals were harmed during the making of the video, he assured his human flock), had garnered a jaw-dropping one million views. He was on the verge of becoming an internet sensation; a viral evangelizer. After the Collapse, that all came to a crashing halt.

With the internet no longer accessible, he lost a lucrative and easy way to reach the great unwashed across the country (and, crucially, their money). He now contented himself with bombarding the sinful residents of Montgomery with his fiery rhetoric.

When one of his followers played him the broadcasts, both in opposition and support of the Fed's RRRF plans, he spotted an opportunity. It was time for God's word, liberally interpreted by him, to be part of this discussion.

He prepared his first broadcast sermon to the unknown masses across Kentucky and beyond, with great care. People out there were confused! Being misled by men with evil intentions! Loyalties challenged! Facing life-changing decisions with no divine guidance! They needed help and succor in these confusing and dangerous times! Fear not, the Reverend Josiah Wedgwood was here to help them overcome these challenges, make the right decisions. With his, and the Lord's help, of course.

His first sermon hit the airwaves with an appeal, as all good propagandists do, to the basest of his listeners' fears. He started with plagiarizing a quotation from George Orwell, not from the Bible:

"The choice before us is not between good and evil, but between two evils. You can let one side win–that is evil to some, or you can let the other side win–which will be evil to others. There is no good choice before you. Whichever you choose, you will come out with blood on your hands."

He then painted both sides as, "Lying from their very core. Misleading and duplicitous in their messages and their practices." He prophesied, "death, destruction and God's punishment will befall you and your family if these harbingers of evil have their way."

Adding, reassuringly, "The only way forward, the only truth to be heard and to be believed, will come from the words of the Lord and his Holy Book."

His mesmerizing, terrifying rant lasted a hackle rising thirty minutes, dredging up every conceivable fear his listeners had lived with since the Collapse. It was a spellbinding performance. The radio chatter following it was almost universally positive. (At least from the Southern states.)

The Rev. Josiah Wedgwood had found a new audience. In turn, they had found a new leader. Now he could start to really stir things up. His end game, money. Lots of it.

Chapter 24

With the help of a large whiskey, Senator Charles Kingston felt like he was in the eye of a hurricane. Cool, calm and untroubled. For the moment anyhow. He had welcomed Major General Redditch's resignation, and the President taking his advice to go easy on sending in the Army to deal with the Louisville Group. He felt he was now in control. He liked being at the epicenter of this mammoth enterprise, so he could manipulate it towards his own goals.

Finally, the best news of all, the thought of Danny Trevino spitting blood, now that his right-hand man was in jail. He chuckled to himself, that'll teach the goddamn Brit to stay here. He should have gone home while he had the chance. Bloody colonialist, serves him right.

The Kentucky People's Movement had gone quiet, which was a shame, as he'd hoped they would induce a groundswell of help for the RRRF. Unfortunately, that had apparently evaporated. Never mind, at least they hadn't sided with the Louisville Group as seemed likely after the Stewart Island Meeting. He hadn't been optimistic that the meeting would produce anything useful. Though it was worth going through the motions–it made him look good back in Sacramento. Now, however, he knew where everyone stood. Negotiations were no longer an option.

As for the young Houston, he'd proved, as expected, depressingly incapable and was now on his way back to Sacramento for a career in political limbo land. That meeting was always going to be beyond his capabilities and he'd loused it up as the Senator hoped he would.

The only small cloud on his currently clear blue horizon was the Bible-thumping nutter down in Montgomery. It seemed Rev. What's-is-name, sensed an opportunity to make his voice heard above the fractured politics of this whole circus. We'll worry about the wrath of God later on, thought the Senator, never a religious man. These opportunists came and went. The Senator had no time for religion in politics, their sanctimonious contributions only stirred things up among the Bible-bashing electorate. He dismissed the self-aggrandizing religious lunatic. Let's hope he was just a pirate ship floating across the political horizon that would soon sink without a trace.

He was more excited with meeting his new, covertly formed, Action Group. They would undertake what the Delta Force had been originally tasked with. This time they'd be answerable to no one but him. Their mission: to wreak havoc among those Louisville renegades.

Creating the Action Group had not been cheap. His shadowy contacts had found ten former Military personnel still unable to wean themselves off the fix of violence and death. For a considerable fee, they would work for him now. It was an enormous investment for the Senator, who was rich but not cash rich. They were costing close to a quarter of a million dollars a month, plus expenses. It was the promised bonus at the end that had really motivated them: get Danny Trevino and a jackpot could be theirs.

The calm before the storm was passing quickly. All hell was about to break loose and the Senator knew it. He felt ready and prepared. That devious shit Danny in his sights, and he had the wherewithal to get him at last. He could almost smell the money.

Chapter 25

After Brian's abduction in Birdsville, the rest of the group headed dispiritedly back to Louisville. Danny, predictably, was spitting blood at the news his right-hand man had been kidnapped. He threatened death and damnation on the whole US Marshal Service. He was beside himself with anger. In reality there was little he could do, which made him even more frustrated. He went into a day-long funk, not wanting to see or talk to anyone.

With Danny *incommunicado* and believing nothing could be achieved staying in Louisville, Penny and Roger decided it was time to return to their home bases. They calmed Danny down enough to persuade him to lend them a vehicle. He agreed. They filled a banged up Dodge Ram with enough fuel to get them to Bowling Green, via Glasgow and left. Glad to be out of the orbit of someone who was hellbent on revenge against the Senator, the Feds, in fact anyone who disagreed with him. Danny was a loose cannon, and they didn't want to be in the firing line when he finally exploded.

The journey back revealed how much Roger and Penny had grown close to each other. They chatted about anything and everything, opening up and revealing things about themselves they hadn't done with anyone for a long time. They both expressed how much they'd like to see each other again, accepting the physical distance between them made it difficult. By car, the journey was under two hours, by horse more like two days. Each gave the other detailed directions where they lived…just in case. By the time they reached Glasgow they despondently agreed it could be a long time before they saw each other again. Though at least they could talk by radio.

"Just think," said Penny with a smile, "I'll have to say 'Roger, Roger, over and out' at the end of the conversation. What a hoot!"

Roger smiled, "Very droll. Maybe I'll ask you, 'Penny, a penny for your thoughts'?" They both started giggling like a couple of teenagers.

They stopped by the stables in Glasgow where Roger had left his horse. He got out of the truck, gathered his backpack, then lent across and kissed Penny full on the lips. She responded with an urgency that surprised and delighted him. They pulled apart after a minute, held hands for a few seconds, then Roger said, a thickness in his voice. "You take care Penny, call me if you need anything. I will see you again soon. Count on it. Be safe. I think it's going to get shitty out there for a while."

Penny, her eyes moist with tears as yet unshed, whispered, "You too Roger. I'm so glad we met. It's been fun, to say the least! You look after yourself, too. I want to see you again soon."

He closed the truck door, tapped the roof and watched as Penny roared off back onto the Cumberland Parkway heading west to Bowling Green.

By the time Roger reached the stables, it was late afternoon. The owners offered him a room for the night, which he gratefully accepted.

He left at daybreak and was back in French Creek by mid-afternoon, looking forward to seeing his son and sleeping in his own bed. He'd debrief the Council the following day.

Drinking his coffee the following morning, he wondered if his son Landy was ever going to tear himself away from the ham radio and say good morning. He could hear bursts of static, then a few words, more static, then a longer conversation, and so it went on. Eventually he came out, gave Roger a hug and sat down at the kitchen table.

"How was the trip Dad?"

"I met some interesting people who seem hell bent on having a war with the Government's ReFederalization plan. Then went to a meeting

133

with some of the other parties involved in this whole bizarre situation. At the end of the day, not sure how much was achieved."

"How do you think this whole Government, what's it called…RRRF will pan out? Do you think it's good or bad news for us?"

"That's a damn good question, Landy, and I have no definite answer. It's all up in the air. Everyone's into a pissing contest at the moment. Only time will tell. What news have you been hearing on your radio?"

"Lots of people are spouting opinions. Day or two ago, some Reverend from Alabama broadcast a sermon. Real Bible-thumping stuff like those Revivalists that used to come here from time to time. The chatter afterwards seems he might gather a few followers. You know the south, Dad, they like that kinda stuff."

"Really, now some Reverend getting involved? That's all we need. Religion and politics is a recipe for disaster, in my opinion. Let me know if you hear anymore from him."

Their conversation then drifted away from the current swirl of rumors about the RRRF to what had been happening at French Creek. Thankfully, nothing of any major importance. They finished their coffees, Landy went back to his radio. Roger decided to walk around the village visiting the Council members about the impromptu meeting this evening.

Kentucky in the spring is so vivid and verdant, the fresh foliage is almost fluorescent green at times. The trees seemed to vibrate with colors so rich it was as though someone had sprayed them with luminous paint. As Roger walked through the village, he stopped and chatted with people, complimenting their efforts at planting some early vegetables, or preparing the fields for spring sowing.

They all knew he'd been to some important meeting in 'Lurville', as they pronounced it. For the first time in years, he sensed a frisson of excitement among the people he met. The Federal Government's plans, were practically the only topic of conversation. He curbed his skepticism. He had precious little detail to tell people on how this mammoth operation would actually affect them. Roger didn't want to dampen people's enthusiasm. After all, they had waited six years for the Federal Government to come to their aid. Now it appeared something was happening. On the other hand, raising people's hopes, only to have them crushed if it all came to nothing, would be cruel.

After the Collapse, with the disintegration and subsequent flight of the Federal Government to Sacramento, the population's opinion of their political leaders had plummeted. Consequently these runaway politicians had a long way to go to convince people they had serious intentions to help. Let them down again and they wouldn't get a third chance: *fool me once, shame on you; fool me twice, shame on me.* However, people's eternal optimism created short memories.

Roger continued his perambulations through the village. There was a positive bustle of activity wherever he went. He felt himself choking up as he observed the industriousness of the villagers. The last couple of years they had begun to reap the rewards of all their past efforts. Life wasn't easy, but it was more predictable, more under control. People were, in the main, happy with their lot. It was gratifying to see less stress and worry on their faces, replaced with a sense of purpose and pleasure.

Suddenly, in the far distance, a slight buzzing in the air caught Roger's ear. He looked up and around but could see nothing. The sound was getting louder. After about thirty seconds, over the hills to the west of French Creek, flew a small aircraft. As it grew closer, Roger realized it was an ultralight machine. It circled once, then lined itself up to land on the meadow behind the village.

Roger stood there, dumbfounded. Could it be? No way, he was out west somewhere. Wasn't he? Roger ran to the field, along with several other villagers, then hung back as the ultralight taxied to a halt close by. The pilot clambered out, took off his helmet and, laughing, said, "Hi everyone, surprise, surprise, I'm back!"

It was Jay. Back from the west, where he'd been left seriously injured after playing a vital role in helping the group of villagers cross the Mississippi.

Chapter 26

Danny was worried. The last two weeks had been too quiet. News that the RRRF and all its Military and law enforcement personnel were standing down, didn't mean they were going away. He believed it meant that, in all probability, the devious bastard, Senator Kingston was planning something else. Something below the radar of political and public opinion, he guessed. But what? His sources in Sacramento had dried up. The radio chatter was equally unhelpful...lots of hot air and threats, including a raving lunatic preacher down in Alabama. Even the Kentucky People's Movement had gone MIA.

Later that day, as shared a beer with his second in command, Johnny, the walkie-talkie squawked into life. He picked it up.

A flustered voice stammered into Danny's ear, "Danny, it's me, Ping. A guy has just ridden into town from Frankfort in a real panic. Seems some kinda hit squad has snatched their top guy. Think he said his name was Jack Cheney? Do you know him? Over."

"I remember Jack, he came to our meeting. Send the messenger over to my place, I'll be there in ten. Over."

"What's that all about, I wonder?" said Johnny, finishing off his beer with a noisy gulp, "maybe someone's trying to take him out, be the new top man?"

"Could be Johnny, could be. Let's go see what this guy has to say."

By the time they arrived back at Danny's apartment, Ping had delivered the still shaken and disheveled bearer of bad news from Frankfort. His name was Davey, and he'd been one of Jack's guards. As he told the

136

story of Jack's abduction, Danny knew this was not some other gangster trying to take over his turf. Davey described the group of six men as professionally equipped, organized, and commanded. They had burst into Jack's office, scattered stun grenades around and, before anyone could react, tranquilized Jack, dragged him away then disappeared in one of his cars. Most tellingly, when it was found outside Frankfort soon afterwards, a local farmer claimed that all the occupants were flown off in a helicopter going westwards.

Danny digested this worrying news. He just knew Senator Kingston was behind it—or at least some part of the RRRF military. So was this abduction a one-off? Or the first of many? With the end objective of removing all those who objected to the RRRF's plans? That, he couldn't answer for the moment, but what he could do was warn those who came to the Louisville meeting. Knowing the Senator as he did, Danny believed he was a prime target.

First action was to beef up his own personal security. He couldn't appear to be 'running scared' by his people, however it made sense to have some extra bodyguards discreetly in place. Maybe more security at his apartment, too. He'd sit down with some of his trusted lieutenants to see what they suggest.

What he couldn't sit down and discuss with anyone were his stashes of gold spread around the city in various redundant bank vaults. The amount was huge in value and weight—close to fifteen tons. No one but he knew where it was all hidden. The men who helped him snatch it from the Fort Knox convoy six years ago had either died in the process or come to sudden ends. In the post-Collapse chaos, no one noticed their disappearance.

Just then, one of the women in the office monitoring the ham radio broadcasts came rushing in. "Danny!" she stopped in front of him, "I heard someone saying that two top guys have been shot. One was from Paducah, the other from Elizabethville. Both dead, so he said. Can't be one hundred percent sure it's genuine, though some other radio guy in Paducah confirmed his top man was murdered."

Danny tried not to look surprised. Don't show any weakness, he inwardly told himself. Just think this through. While being cautious wasn't his style, he knew a rash move now was not a good one.

"Thanks Jean. Keep monitoring the airwaves. Let me know if you hear anything else."

First things first: he told Johnny to find a couple of good guys to keep guard downstairs. Once by himself, he walked over to the apartment's large windows, hastily pulling the blinds and drapes. This isn't being paranoid, he reminded himself, just taking sensible precautions. Clearly, these hit teams were highly trained killers, to it appeared, one-by-one, snuff out the leadership of all the cities and towns who had shown they weren't prepared to be bulldozed by the Fed's RRRF juggernaut.

If the Senator was behind this—and he had every reason to think he was—then Danny knew he was near the top of the hit list. Maybe the first three were meant to scare him into surrendering, or doing something rash that might give Senator Kingston's killer squads the chance to snatch or kill him.

Danny Trevino hadn't survived the last six years by just holding his hands up when some problem presented itself. In the past, it had been easy to take out any local wannabe who threatened his authority. These covert operators were a different breed. They appeared well-trained and had the resources to travel across the state and hit their targets with impunity. No grand ambitions to take over a city. Operating from the west meant they could scoot back quickly and safely after every op, making it difficult to capture them or anticipate their next move.

Danny grabbed a bottle of bourbon, gave himself a generous measure, poured in a little water, and sat down to consider his options.

On a personal level he could protect himself from these assassination squads. While a worry, he was confident he was safe. On a broader scale he had some one thousand armed men at his disposal. They could certainly make life difficult in the short term for any invading force. In the long run, they would just be a delay tactic. Overwhelming force and munitions would soon grind them down. Granted, if every town and city along the way put up a fight, the Senator faced the prospect of a backlash in Sacramento if the body count started to mount. Americans killing Americans didn't make for good headlines, no matter how worthy the cause.

Cherry picking the resistance ring leaders was a low-risk way of undermining any armed opposition and avoiding widespread killing. Made sense to Danny the more he thought about it. Probably something he would do if he was in their shoes.

He swirled the sweet smelling liquor around in his glass, took a sip, then another. He was getting to the stage where drinking relaxed you enough to make rational decisions. A few more, and bravado overcame common sense. He was at that perfect cusp of logical thinking. He mulled over the options, then, after his second glass of bourbon, decided he'd worry about all this crap tomorrow. In the meantime he needed a little diversion. He called Olivia in from the bedroom where she'd discreetly kept out of the way.

"Olivia, honey, can you come here? I'm feeling kinda wound up. I think I need one of your very special massages, know what I mean?" he said, smiling up at her as she walked in the room. She must have anticipated his request, provocatively wearing one of his shirts, with nothing underneath.

"Sure do honey, you just sit back and let me ease your worries away," Olivia replied in a soothing voice, kneeling down between his knees and slowly unclipping the belt of his jeans.

Tomorrow the fight back begins, Danny thought, before Olivia's ministrations took his mind in other, more pleasurable, directions.

Chapter 27

The Senator was crowing at the initial success of his Action Force. Frustratingly, as a covert operation, he had to keep the good news to himself. Normally, any triumph like this would see him bragging on TV, and the rent-a-talking-head online sites, or any other news outlet that his PR team could get him on. Not so this time. His involvement had to stay below the public's radar. So he kept repeating to himself the progress so far: two dead, one captured and already spilling the beans about the Louisville meeting.

His hit list, courtesy of Brian the Brit, and now Jack of Frankfort, had grown to over twenty-five individuals who had made their anti-RRRF feelings clear at the Louisville meeting. He realized he was dealing with a Hydra of considerable size and geographic spread. The first three victims had been easily accessible via helicopter from the west. As the hunt moved further east, the logistics and distance heightened the risk. Not that he was concerned if a few of his Action Force didn't make it, it kept the costs down and the eventual payout less. Just as long as enough survived to see the operation to a successful conclusion.

Of course, the ultimate prize was Danny Trevino. He hoped these early hits might spook his nemesis into a knee jerk reaction that could leave him exposed to capture. So far, nothing. Never mind, there was still time to sow more havoc to achieve the desired result. He'd waited six years, a few more weeks was nothing. The Senator certainly didn't want Danny dead. It would be catastrophic, he had to get Danny to talk…before killing him.

Here in Sacramento, deliberately a long way from the action, the Senator was relying on regular updates directly from the Commander of his Action Force. It was a motley crew led by a disgraced former Marine officer with the improbable (and false) rank of 'Colonel'. The Senator knew he was neither a Colonel, nor called Wayne Flowers. He was a loose cannon, a ruthless killing machine whose thirst for murder was only matched by his greed for money. The Senator was happy to oblige him with the opportunity to fulfill both addictions.

After every sortie, Colonel Flowers called the Senator and in his almost incomprehensible Louisiana accent gleefully provided the gory details of their successes. He'd cut the Colonel off midway through the graphic description of how they'd obtained information from 'Frankfort Jack'–the less he knew the better, for his conscience and his stomach. As the latest conversation with his effective, but repugnant Colonel was finishing, the Senator interrupted asking, who was next on the list?

"Sir, we plan to concentrate on the west of the state for the moment, so we'll be moving in on targets on the hit list in Owensboro, Henderson and…some place called Bowling Green."

Chapter 28

"What brought you back here? Never thought I'd see you again. In fact I thought you were dead!" exclaimed Roger as he drank a beer on his front porch with a decidedly healthy looking Jay. His unexpected arrival on the ultralight was the first time in almost a year Roger had seen him. After playing a crucial role in helping the group of people from French Creek to reach Memphis and across the Mississippi, he'd then flown to Missouri with Jane, ending up wounded in a local hospital.

Looking relaxed and happy to be back home, Jay recounted his story, "Well, I almost died from a broken arm that turned bad. Some quick thinking by Jane and those folks in the Missouri safe house saved my hide. To be honest, a lot of it is still a blur. Anyways, I made it through, that's what matters! Heck! Enough about me, what happened to everyone...did they all make it over the river?" asked Jay.

"Yes they did," explained Roger, "some really kind and well-connected people at a Memphis church helped get the group across unharmed. Then we went and confronted the traffickers who had Pat and Jane's family hostage. That got a little messy, with a few casualties on their side. In the end, she and her family were reunited. I left them with a friend near Clarksville, haven't heard what happened to them afterwards. Landy was shot. He's OK now. He, Pat, and I eventually made it back home safe and sound. So what happened to you once Jane left?"

Jay at this point began to tear up, "The last thing I remember is Jane saying goodbye to me before she drove down to cross the river to meet up with you guys and rescue her kin. Then I ended up in hospital, recovered, and escaped. The cops were after me so I didn't hang around. Managed to rescue my ultralight from those lovely farmers and skedaddled out of there darn quick. Decided to find my cousin, thankfully he'd moved from California to Arkansas. Not sure my ultralight was up for a two thousand mile flight."

"So why on earth come back here? Thought you hated the place! That's why you built the ultralight in the first place, wasn't it?"

Jay explained, "Roger, I didn't hate French Creek as such. I wanted to leave to go find my crooked brother-in-law in Atlanta. If you remember, Jane's husband was a cop there. The idea was he might be able to put me in touch with people to help find him. The whole trip over the Mississippi was part of the deal. Unfortunately, the wheels came off and I had to hightail down to Arkansas, so I never got to meet him. After a few months down there, I discovered my cousin had gone off the rails, into drugs and illegal stuff. So once I was fit again, I decided to get out before he mixed me up in it. Thought I'd pay y'all a flying visit!" Jay laughed at his pun.

Roger couldn't believe how this dour, taciturn little man, who kept himself to himself during his years living in the village, had transformed into an outgoing, cheerful individual.

"Well, I'm really pleased you survived such a hair-raising escapade. No one had a clue what happened to you. Now I can finally thank you for your help in that mission!"

"Aw, thanks Roger, it was kinda fun. Jane was a real star. What a lady, a real firecracker and a damn good shot, too. Saved our lives more than once. And she even learned to fly my ultralight. Yep, that was quite an adventure. Pleased it worked out for her, too."

"So what are your plans now? Off to Atlanta, find that crooked brother-in-law of yours?"

"Yes and no Roger. I'd still like to go there and beat the shit out of him. Before my wife died I promised her I'd get some payback for him stealing all our money. In the meantime, I was wondering what all of you were doing about this whole Federal takeover of Kentucky, or whatever they're calling it? It's all over the news out west. That Senators face is on TV all the time, well, up until a couple of weeks ago. Anyway, before I move onto Atlanta, I wondered if you needed any help?"

He grabbed Jay another beer, sat back and thought for a moment. Having an ultralight on hand could be a real asset. He wasn't sure how as yet. His first thought was getting to see Penny in Bowling Green. They'd spoken once on the radio after the news that three of the people at the meeting in Louisville had been abducted or murdered. They both agreed they must be targets, too. Roger had made Penny promise to increase her personal security and have her people be extra vigilant. They set a weekly time to call each other with any news or updates. Or any time, in an emergency.

"That's a mighty kind offer, Jay. How long are you prepared to hang around? It looks as though behind the scenes it's turning a bit nasty. Can't quite figure out what's going on. If you can stay for a few weeks, I'd be eternally grateful. I guess your house is pretty much as you left it. If you need some food supplies from the central store, I'm happy to get some."

Jay shrugged his shoulders, indicating he was pretty relaxed about the whole idea, "Sure Roger sounds great. It will be good to see some of the French Creek folks again."

Before Jay left, Roger took the opportunity to update him with what he knew about the Fed's plans, the RRRF and the latest worrying attacks on those who'd gone to the meeting in Louisville. Jay, in return, provided what information he could, based on news and TV reports out west. They didn't add much to what Roger knew already.

It was getting late in the day, Jay needed to get back and make his house habitable again. He downed the rest of his beer, stood up, shook Roger's hand, saying with real warmth, "It's good to be back and see you again Roger," then walked off the porch towards his house.

Roger watched, pleasantly surprised, as Jay wandered back through the village nodding 'hellos' and 'long time no sees' to people he met. What a transformation from a curmudgeonly antisocial individual, to Mr.

Sociable. Amazing what nearly dying will do to make you appreciate what you have, however little it might be.

Jay's walk through the village laid bare to him the stark contrast between life in the west and here in the east. No cars, noise, loud music. It was all much calmer, even civilized in a basic, rural nineteenth century kinda way. Of course, there were no utilities to keep houses warm and lit. No easy ways to have water (hot or cold) on tap, or gas to cook with. Everyone created their own ways to make life as comfortable as possible. Still, compared to where he had just come from, the difference was startling. It was all so much…simpler, he thought. Here people adapted to their surroundings, not the other way round. Jay had to stop himself. It was easy to get a little wistful, even jealous about what life was like in French Creek. To be honest, no matter how you looked at it, life was still tough here. Was it better or worse, he wondered, than the never-ending technology-driven treadmill he'd left just a few hours ago?

The romantic illusion of living off grid painfully hit Jay when he opened the front door of his house, that he'd not been in for months. No turning on the lights to brighten up the gloomy interior. No air conditioning to help clear the stuffiness. Absolutely no chance of a hot bath. Only a cold shower awaited his aching body. No fridge containing food, or a cold Budweiser. It was back to the pioneer days. Christ, he'd forgotten how even the easiest of jobs was a chore. Inevitably, you ended up simplifying everything to save time and effort. The more complicated the solution to a problem, the more likely it was to go wrong. K.I.S.S. was the order of the day.

The supply of water to the house was one example. Yes, there were ways to run pumps from wells using some of the solar panels they'd acquired. They required maintenance and in winter were not so reliable. A simpler method most of the residents had employed was to use large two hundred gallon containers that collected rain water from the roof and could be gravity fed straight into the house. Some had one tank on a south facing roof that in summer produced hot water, while another on the north side, which when suitably insulated, gave a supply of cool water. The bonus was you could drink it without boiling it first.

Jay had both kinds of tanks at his house. The Kentucky spring sun had not yet raised the water temperature to comfortably hot, but neither did it take his breath away as he stood under it washing away the grime and oil from his four hour flight.

He finished, put on some clean clothes and went outside to his cold store and cellar. Hopefully some food and homemade beer might still be usable. They were. The cold store kept temperatures at a steady forty degrees Fahrenheit. With an extra thank you to the twenty-first century, protection from rodents and dampness was provided by large, firmly sealed plastic storage boxes. Rows of airtight glass and plastic storage jars kept a small arsenal of food ready to eat.

He selected smoked beef, potatoes and carrots, took them to his outdoor cooking area and lit a fire to heat up a saucepan of water and a griddle to fry up the meat. He risked the salty taste as he was so hungry. It wasn't Waffle House, but it was more than a passable dinner.

An hour and two beers later, Jay was sitting on his front porch at the northern end of the village doing nothing but watching the wildlife and the sun slowly sink behind the trees atop the hills to the west. In a reflective mood, he calculated he was only about three hours by ultralight to the Mississippi, and back into the twenty-first century. How can such an insignificant amount of time and distance separate two societies, living lives two centuries apart? Could this whole government initiative bring them back together, he wondered? Could the Feds finally bridge that gap? He had his doubts. From his brief stay in the west, he saw that life had carried on as though the Collapse had never happened. Same dreadful toxic social media, same thirst for more and more material possessions all being led by the latest technological marvel. Same old frenetic pace of life. Certainly what hadn't changed was the divisive, poisonous politics that contributed to the Collapse being a lot worse than it needed to have been.

All of which in a perverse way, made him happy to be back home. No doubt the time would come when it would change, not for a while here in French Creek he thought. He made his way to bed, tiredness quickly closing his eyes before he could ponder the future any more.

Far less than three hours away, six men jumped from a helicopter four miles west of Bowling Green. Their mission to capture and kill the city's leader, named on their list as one Penny Davenport.

Chapter 29

The Reverend Josiah Wedgwood had embraced the internet as a way of spreading his gospel with as much fervor as he put into his sermons. His fiery words of biblical wisdom had reached millions via smart phones, computers and importantly, their wallets. Oh praise the Lord for the person who invented Paypal, Venmo and other ways to relieve the gullible of their cash so quickly and so easily. Now, tragically, they were a distant memory.

Then a miracle: praise the Lord he had discovered ham radio. And what a blessing it was! Without the need for expensive backdrops, costumes and singers, radio broadcasting allowed him to again start spreading his fear-mongering beliefs to (so he believed) a spiritually starved audience. The only downside at the moment, there was no easy way to collect the donations.

The Collapse had dried up the flow of money like a sluice gate closing in a dam. He'd lived sumptuously on the money diverted away from the good causes he was supposedly supporting with his donor's cash. That was now running out. He needed to find a new infusion of funds. The confusion, partisanship and feuding between Kentuckians and the RRRF was a sign from the Almighty he should be out there, involved in finding a solution through God's words. His belief and ego telling him: insert yourself into the problem so you can become part of the solution.

His audience may not have money, but the Feds and the anti-RRRF leaders had lots of it.

The Reverend Josiah Wedgwood saw a heavenly sent opportunity in the making. There was no doubt he was a charismatic preacher. Part Billy Graham with his simple, homespun beliefs, add in Joel Olsteen's low-key, wholesome approach, then stir in the soaring oratory and unforgettable wordsmithery of Martin Luther King, Jr. and you had a potent mixture. He had spent years perfecting this persuasive brand of rhetoric. Before the Collapse, his followers had numbered in the hundreds of thousands, especially in the Southern Bible Belt. They had faded away as quickly as the batteries died on their cellphones.

Now he was going to take his faith out on the road to meet his believers in towns and cities across the south and Kentucky. As he declared to his listeners, "I believe the forces of evil are at work on both sides of the pro- and anti-RRRF debate. I believe it is my God-given duty to help pave the way to a successful meeting of their minds. As I speak to you, I am awaiting a sign of divine intervention that will reveal God's intention for Kentucky: should we welcome the RRRF, or send the evil invaders back across the Mississippi?"

With his ego expanding in direct proportion to the size of his congregation, the Reverend had faith he would hold the reins of power and decide, with God's blessing, which side they should support.

That would come at a price. A very big price for the chosen side.

Chapter 30

Penny took Roger's words to heart. She increased her personal guard, and moved residence to a more secure house, at Hobson's Grove, in the city's north. It sat on a golf course that offered limited cover to attackers. Built solidly of brick, it would withstand gunfire better than her previous wooden frame home.

She also took the precaution of implementing a ring of watch posts around the outskirts of Bowling Green who could communicate with each other, and her, if any unwelcome intruders approached. Well-armed with night vision glasses, they'd been in place for over a week with nothing to show for their efforts and sleepless nights. They didn't mind. They were all devoted to Penny and would follow her orders no matter what. Life in Bowling Green since she and her husband had tamed the wilder gangs was better than it had ever been. By no means was it easy, but they were safe and able to work hard to provide for their families. Some Fed sponsored assholes would not disrupt this by taking out their top lady. No way. So they buckled down and sucked up the anti-social hours, knowing it was a vital cause they were protecting.

Bowling Green was founded in 1795. Some controversy exists over the source of the town's name. In 1798, it was known as "Bolin Green" after, some say, Bowling Green in New York City, where patriots had pulled down a statue of King George III and used the lead to make bullets during the American Revolution. Others claim it derived from Bowling Green, Virginia, where early migrants had come from, or the personal "ball alley game" of founder Robert Moore.

Whatever the source of its name, the city was well defended, ready to fight for its top lady.

It was 2:00 a.m. when Penny's walkie-talkie squawked to life. A disembodied voice blurted out, "Penny, the post at Downing Museum has spotted six armed men moving towards the town center. Over."

Despite being abruptly awoken from a deep sleep, she was wide awake within seconds. Climbing out of bed, she held the walkie-talkie to her ear as she scrambled to get dressed.

"I'll wake Hunter. He'll direct operations. Whatever happens, we need one alive. Do the guards have the capability to take them out? Over."

"Negative Penny, there's only two guys in each watch post. I can get some more together to intercept them as they get closer to the town. Guessing they're heading to your old place?"

"Do that. We'll meet at the Corvette museum in thirty minutes. Keep eyes on that group, no matter what. Over and out."

Penny called her brother, Hunter. A former Army Sergeant, he had the Military experience she lacked at a time like this. She explained to him what was happening, and he agreed with her decision to get the men to meet at the Corvette Factory. Then move to cut the intruders off long before they reached their target, he assumed, of her old home at Plum Springs.

It took the Senator's Action Force nearly an hour to move through the deserted, dark streets of Bowling Green towards Penny's previous residence. They had slightly underestimated the distance from the drop off point. No matter, the six men moved swiftly through Bowling Green. At that time of the night, no one was around. Or so they thought.

Reports came in from lookouts closer to Penny's old base that the intruders were hugging the banks of the Barren river heading northeast towards their objective. Hunter now had around thirty armed men on either side of the river in Weldon Peete park.

Soon he saw for himself their progress through the park. He chose it because in many places, decades old stone walls crisscrossed the park. They provided great cover. It was behind these his men waited. Through his NVG's he saw the six intruders slowly, unknowingly, moving towards the waiting ambush.

Colonel Flowers was cautiously optimistic this mission would go the way the other three had: a surprise attack on a poorly defended target, in and out, with a quick and deadly resolution. Followed by a well-planned extraction courtesy of a nearby helicopter. Boom. Another bonus.

His five men were strung out along the Barren River's banks, knowing it would lead them close to the target's house. For a minute, the cloud cover dispersed and moonlight radiated across the park, creating dark shadows behind the trees and walls. He and his men took this opportunity to climb up the low bank to confirm their course and direction. It provided Hunter and his defenders with a perfect sighting of their targets.

All hell broke loose. A cacophony of shots erupted on Colonel Flower's left side. Flashes of light exploded from every angle. He heard the whizz of bullets all around him. In the dark, the sound of gunfire 150 feet away was ear-splitting and disorientating. He dropped down against the river bank seeking cover, hugging it like a frightened cat. He looked behind to see two of his men hit, flung like rag dolls backwards, splashing into the river. Another was clutching his head, falling to the ground with a cry of pain. The remaining two were wildly returning fire with little idea where to shoot.

Colonel Flowers peeked over the river bank, trying to triangulate where the shots were coming from. Before he could, from across the river came another volley of bullets, smacking into the ground and water. Only the covering of the moon by clouds, reducing his attacker's visibility, kept him alive. He and his men had no protection against fire from that direction. He loosed off a magazine of shots from his trusty AK-47, giving him a few seconds to decide what to do next. With no safe option, he shouted to retreat back along the bank, in the direction from which they had come.

The injured soldier, half in the river, half on the bank, was feebly trying to crawl out of the water. "Leave him!" he yelled at the two soldiers as they bent over to pick him up.

"Let's get the fuck out of here. Follow me." He waded into the river until his head was just above the surface. Weighed down with his rifle, ammo, and other equipment, all he could do was half walk, half swim. In the dark it was a terrifying experience. Shots followed him, spurting water all around his head, then gradually petered out as the gentle current took him painfully slowly away from the field of fire. After a few minutes, with no more shots fired, he climbed out of the river and waited for the two others to join him.

"Are you hurt?" he asked curtly. Both confirmed they were fine. Then one asked about their injured comrade. Should they go back for him?

The Colonel peered at them through the dark, dismissing the suggestion with a growl, "He's history, forget him. You both keep watch. See if they're following us." He sat on the bank, radioing for an urgent extraction, giving the pilot coordinates to the nearby Kereilakes Golf course.

Within fifteen minutes, he heard with relief the familiar 'whumpf, whumpf' of the helicopter's rotors. Before it had even touched down on the third green he and his two bedraggled combatants were scrambling aboard and whisked westwards to safety.

An hour later, the injured intruder was coming round to discover he was tied to a chair. In front of him were three men in masks and a woman with auburn hair. One had a baseball bat, which he nonchalantly swung, practicing some non-existent home run strike. His head throbbed like no tomorrow, but he could feel it was bandaged and the wound no longer bled all down his face.

"Why didn't we go after those bastards and finish them off?" asked one of the masked men to Hunter.

"We could have, but I thought it more important to bring this piece of shit back for questioning before he died of blood loss. Chasing the others exposed our guys to an unnecessary risk, in my opinion."

Penny interrupted the conversation, "You all did a good job. Let's see what this guy has to say. I want everything you can squeeze out of him, quickly. Don't be gentle on him. But don't kill him, at least not yet," Penny instructed as she left the room. She wasn't squeamish. However, seeing Hunter and his team in action with prisoners in the past was a horror show she'd rather miss.

It didn't take long for the prisoner to talk. A couple of well-aimed hits with the baseball bat smashing each kneecap, had the man howling in agony and talking to anyone who would listen. He had no loyalty to the psycho Colonel, just the next paycheck. At twenty-one, he thought this was an easy buck. The recruiter at a dive bar in St. Louis promised he'd earn $100,000 for a few month's work guarding some Senator. Unemployed, fighting a drug addiction, it was manna from heaven. He signed on the dotted line asking no questions. A couple of weeks training somewhere in the boondocks of Mississippi and the Colonel said they were ready to go. He never saw the Senator, or even discovered his name. A last minute change of plans meant they were going east to deal with some bad guys.

The first three missions had been scary but fun. They'd got their men and came back to a healthy bonus of $10,000. It was money for old rope. Admittedly, killing some of the captives didn't sit easy with him. Though ten grand miraculously eased his conscience.

Money was the last thing on his mind as the baseball bat crunched into his right kneecap. Quickly deciding this was no time for heroics, he told them what he knew, and what he thought they wanted to hear.

"The guy's just a no good hired hand," explained Hunter to Penny the following morning, "he knew sweet fuck all, and I'm convinced threw in a few scraps of fake info to keep us happy. All I believe is, he's part of a group of mercenaries charged with finding, capturing, or killing all those who went to that meeting in Louisville. You went, so you're on the list."

He continued, "Who's behind it, he didn't say. These types work on a 'need to know basis', in case they're caught. He said they recruited him to be a bodyguard for a Senator, but that all changed. He just answers to some wacko Colonel. I can keep going at him but I think that's all we're gonna get."

"Thanks H, as ever you've been a star," Penny slumped down exhausted onto her couch, clutching a cup of cold coffee. She looked up at Hunter through her sleep deprived eyes, unable to keep the concern out of her voice, "Do you think they'll be back for me?"

Hunter shrugged noncommittally, "Can't answer that sis. They've got a long hit list, so maybe they'll move on to easier targets. As we don't know who's behind this, or what their end game is, it's difficult to predict what they're gonna do next. I'd keep yourself well protected and move bases every few days. And don't tell anyone except close friends where you're going. Seems their M.O. when they land is to arm twist a local resident into telling them where the target stays. Most people around here know you and where you live. Not a difficult thing to find out. They still have the benefit of GPS, too."

"OK, H, I'll take your advice and keep on the move, at least for a while. Can I leave you to increase protection for the city? Brief anyone who should know about what's going on. I hate to cause all this extra hassle. Hopefully, only for a few weeks?"

"Will do sis, that's why we're here. I'll report back if bozo talks any more. What do you want us to do with him when we're done?"

"I'll leave that to your discretion H. You're better at making those kinds of decisions than me."

He nodded and winked at her as he left the room, "No problem, leave it with me. Now you go and get some rest, you look like shit."

"Thanks brother, don't look too hot yourself...go get a bath."

Not for the first time, she knew if anything happened to Hunter, she would be lost, and probably dead soon after. He dealt with all the crap, the unpalatable situations, without ever showing any fear, or regret. She'd never wanted to be in this position: running a derelict city of 15,000 people all scrabbling to survive. Sure, things were a vast improvement compared to six years ago. Very little crime; no one had much worth stealing. Everyone was just trying to put their lives back together, keep food on the table and not get despondent about the future. Which made her wonder: if the RRRF provided more details about how, what and when they were going to get Kentucky back on its feet, would she have no option but to go along with it? For the thousands who were on the edge of starvation, as Destiny and Nathan had expressed so eloquently at the Stewart Island Meeting, the RRRF offered a potentially life-saving opportunity.

Bone-weary from lack of sleep and worry, Penny crawled back into bed. She dreamed of many things. Among the disjointed, silent images, the face of Roger kept appearing, looking worried and shouting something at her which she could not hear or understand. She woke up with a start, "God how I wish you were here to help me," she whispered to herself.

She couldn't know, she'd be seeing him again sooner than expected.

Chapter 31

In the days following the botched attempt on Penny's life:

- In a tearful radio conversation with Roger, she recounted the events surrounding her attempted murder. He suggested she come to French Creek for her safety. Penny said she would seriously consider his offer.

- Pat, head of security at French Creek, increased the number of guards around the village. Everyone feared Roger could be next on the assassin's hit list.

- Senator Kingston, smarting from the failed Bowling Green attack, was mulling over the Colonel's demands for more men and better equipment.

- Danny remained practically a prisoner in his own home, rarely venturing out. He stayed inside planning his next move against the RRRF, and Senator Kingston in particular. Louisville was now secured like a fort.

- The Reverend Josiah Wedgwood, in Southern Kentucky, was drawing sizable crowds to his 'Revival and Resurrection' rallies. Preaching loudly and consistently, he was expecting anytime a revelation from God to resolve the RRRF conflict.

Chapter 32

Danny Trevino looked up and down the Ohio River from his vantage point on the roof of the Louisville Slugger Museum, though well hidden from any snipers that might be across the river in Jeffersonville. Mentally, he was keeping to the right side of paranoid, just. After all, people were out to get him. Since news of the failure to kill Penny in Bowling Green had reached him, there had been no further attempts to take out anyone else. Not much of a consolation. No news wasn't necessarily good news in these crazy times.

He could see up and down the south bank of the Ohio, his men on patrol between the heavily armed watch posts he'd built. He'd acquired some M60 heavy machine guns, though not a lot of ammo. They'd cause some real havoc until they ran out. Otherwise, his men had a wide selection of less destructive firepower at their disposal. He was hoping Brian's team could get the tank ready for action. Getting shells for it had been a challenge. As always, everything and everyone had their price. To his delight, a shipment had arrived yesterday by boat.

Now that his defenses were in place, Danny was concentrating on how he could take the fight to the Senator. He needed to find out when he'd move closer to the border with Kentucky, within easy reach of Louisville. Danny's well-paid spies had found out nothing, as yet. Communication with them was always a little hit and miss, relying on coded radio broadcasts or messages brought up the Ohio by friends and allies.

He wondered if he could flush him out with the proposal for another meeting. This time just one-on-one? It was a dangerous gambit: if the

Senator double crossed him, Danny could find himself the prey, not the hunter. No, he couldn't trust that shit to keep any such meeting private. His middle name was duplicitous

Alternatively, he could wait the Senator out, see what he did next. Or pay an exorbitant amount to some hired killer and get him assassinated in Sacramento?

None of these options thrilled him. What Danny knew is, he hated being a target, and he detested waiting around for someone to try and take him out. For the last few years, he'd been master of all he surveyed, he could walk around the ruins of Louisville in safety. It was his domain. He thrived on being in control. This game of cat and mouse was not to his liking at all. As a result, he'd become ill-tempered, shouting at any perceived slight or criticism. Occasionally even threatening to shoot those who particularly pissed him off. Even Olivia's delightful distractions were losing their appeal. Maybe he should find a replacement for her? Then again, she did have some amazing tricks that he'd miss. They would be wasted on someone else.

He was temporarily daydreaming about Olivia's ability in the bedroom (or anywhere, really), when he saw one of the watch posts at the far west of the city send a red flare into the air.

Simultaneously, his walkie-talkie burst into life. Danny clicked the receive button and demanded to know what was going on.

"We're on the Sherman Bridge watch post Danny. We've got visitors, looks like our friends, the Navy Seals. Do you copy?" asked Johnny, one of the precinct captains.

"Yes, I copy, I'll be there in five. Don't do or say anything. Understood?" directed Danny, as he flew down the outside fire escape into the back of his waiting Humvee. He barked the destination to the driver and hung on as the Humvee rocketed through the deserted streets, horn blaring up onto I-64, over the Shawnee golf course, straight onto the bridge.

Danny jumped from the truck, crouching behind the defensive barricade making his way to the watch post. Two guards were peering down the river at a boat some six hundred feet away.

"What's happened? Have they said anything?" Danny asked as he ran up to Johnny.

"Not much boss, just said they were the Navy and wanted to speak to the person in charge. So I buzzed you."

Danny grabbed the binoculars and focused on the boat. He spotted a man who appeared to have a megaphone in his hand. The patrol boat flew the American Navy flag. On the bow was mounted a heavy machine gun. Danny counted six other sailors on board, all armed. Danny didn't have a megaphone so cupped his hands around his mouth and bellowed.

"I'm in charge…what do you want?"

The officer with the megaphone then read out a prepared set of instructions.

"On behalf of the United States Government, we are here to inform you that all unauthorized boat traffic on the Ohio and Mississippi as far south as Memphis is hereby subject to stop and search by the United States Navy. They will confiscate any goods or materials found on board considered illegal. The ship and crew will be detained until further notice. There will be no exceptions to this rule. This comes into immediate effect. Thank you."

"What a fucking nerve!" screamed Danny. "That river is for everyone to use. It's a lifeline for this city. They stop stuff coming here and we'll starve to death." He turned to Johnny, in a fit of anger demanding he take a shot at the Officer on board the boat.

"Danny, steady down man, that's the fucking Navy. We start firing at them, all hell's gonna break loose. Please think this through, don't do anything hasty," Johnny pleaded.

Danny was so mad that he was deaf to any reason, "Gimme your gun. Now, Johnny. That's an order."

Before Johnny could move, Danny had wrenched it from his hands and was resting it on the barricade, taking aim. As the officer on the boat came into focus through the sights, for a second, Danny hesitated. Maybe Johnny was right, killing someone from the US Navy might not be a good idea. Still, no harm in putting a shot across their bows as it were? He lowered his aim and let loose half a dozen rounds that splashed harmlessly into the water fifty feet in front of the boat. The boat crew scurried for cover after the first shot. When he stopped, the officer reappeared, rifle in hand.

Danny shouted at the top of his voice, "That's just a warning. Next time it's for real. Now go fuck yourselves and tell that Senator he can go fuck himself as well!" As an afterthought Danny shrieked, "You can tell that slimy Senator we're comin' for him!"

The boat crew did not return fire. Danny guessed that would be a last resort. He hadn't pissed them off enough for that to happen. The boat fired up its engine and circled back heading south away from the bridge and Louisville.

Danny was cock-a-hoop. Jumping up and down, letting loose a series of expletives as the Navy boat disappeared from view. He turned to Johnny grinning like a maniac, "That showed the mothers who's boss didn't it? They don't come up to my city and start telling me how to run it!" Danny positively skipped off the bridge back to his Humvee.

The streets of Louisville were busier than normal. Today was the monthly market for this part of the city. Feeling a little reckless and impulsive after his successful skirmish with the Navy, Danny asked the driver to stop at the end of Jefferson Memorial Forest. The parking lot was packed with stall holders selling not only food, but all kind of supplies. Unlike at the Barter Fair, dollar bills were in circulation, though not everyone had them. A lot of business was still transacted by bartering. Some regular stall holders would also keep a tally, or give credit to local customers who they knew well.

As Danny strolled through the market nodding hello to people, shaking a few hands, it struck him how much being sold clearly had not been grown or made locally. In other words, smuggled from the west. He stopped and asked a few sellers if they thought the Navy blockade would affect their business?

Most laughed. One elderly lady selling cigarettes and alcohol scoffed at the thought, "Those guys have three or four boats to patrol five hundred miles of river. I'm pretty sure my contacts can find a safe time to cross with the goods. I don't see those sons of bitches causing us too many problems."

Danny smiled and thanked the woman. After another half an hour of wandering around the market, he walked back to the Humvee, relieved that at least one part of Louisville's economy seemed to be safe from disruption. On a whim, he asked the driver to take him to Brian's precinct to see if they'd made any progress getting the tank serviceable. To hell with security, at this moment he felt almost invincible.

A few minutes later, the vast warehouse that was once Brian's domain came into view. Stopping by the enormous roll up doors, Danny strode inside to find several men in greasy overalls in, or under, the tank. To his delight, the engine was running, albeit belching out flumes of noxious diesel exhaust.

"Hey, Danny, good to see you!" shouted one man over the din of the engine, "we got her going yesterday, just doing a bit of fine tuning now. She runs ok, the tracks seem to be in good condition. Just a bit rough still, but should be running like a Caddy soon."

"Have we got anyone who knows how to drive this thing? Even operate the gun?" shouted Danny back at the mechanic.

"Think so. One guy from Middletown was in a tank battalion years ago. He came and had a look yesterday and reckoned he can get this old girl going and popping out a few shells."

Danny smiled, delighted at the news. He had his own tank! He'd place it on the Sherman Minton bridge. It would provide a clear line of fire down the Ohio, over the North Bank and some of downtown Louisville. He was under no illusions that this was more for show than an effective weapon. It could be quickly immobilized by the Army's anti-tank weapons, nevertheless in the short term, it would act as a sign of intent to the enemy and a morale booster for his men.

Leaning into the mechanic so he could be heard, his mouth close to his ear, he shouted, "I'll be back in a few days to see it in action. Well done to all you guys. Awesome job."

The mechanic nodded his appreciation at the compliment, then slid back under the mammoth engine, wrench in hand.

It had been a good day for Danny—seeing off a naval boat in grand style and now his tank was ready for battle! Only a continuing lack of news on the whereabouts of the Senator dampened his elation. For a publicity hungry shark, he sure had gone quiet, thought Danny. He'll have to break cover eventually, then I'll go for him.

He arrived home, reassured to see his guards alert and in place at the building's entrance. He went inside, skipping up the stairs two at a time. Danny decided he deserved a drink and maybe something extra if Olivia was around.

The guard at the door told him she had gone out to the local market. Momentarily aggravated at her absence, he opened the heavy, bulletproof doors. Immediately checking all the blinds were down and the drapes closed before he sat in his favorite chair with a bourbon and water. Thankfully, as the apartment was on the top floor, it had skylights helping to keep the room from being too gloomy. As the drink took effect he began to relax. There was a knock at the door. Now what? He drew his pistol and walked warily down the hall, looked through the spy hole, only to see one of his radio operators, Tim, clearly agitated. Danny unlocked the door and the man practically fell into the hallway, excitedly waving a piece of paper in the air.

"Danny, we know where he is. The Senator. One of our guys in Sacramento got a whisper he's coming to the Navy HQ at Evansville in a few days time."

"Tim, how sure are you of this intel?" demanded Danny.

"Can't be one hundred percent, but we also picked up some other chatter about navy movements around Evansville, so it looks like something's cooking boss."

Danny thanked the operator, got on the walkie-talkie to Johnny, and ordered him to get all the precinct Captains together at his place. Time to start preparing for action.

Chapter 33

The Reverend Josiah Wedgwood stood on his makeshift stage–an old hay wagon–looking at the noisy, adoring crowd of nearly two thousand adherents who had come to hear his words of succor and salvation.

He was in Somerset, Kentucky, a no nothing town, where he estimated practically the total population had turned out to see him. Somerset's historical claim to fame was being the furthest upstream navigable port on the Cumberland River, which connected to the Mississippi via the Ohio River. For over a century, it had been a major artery for the transport of timber, and people from Kentucky all the way to New Orleans. With the advent of motor cars and the dam near Jamestown, boat traffic had ceased and Somerset had died with it.

There was no doubt the Reverend's inflammatory words were lighting the torches of hope in the thousands of people as he preached his way across the state on his 'Resurrection' pilgrimage. He had pummeled into his audience that he saw, "not one, but two Resurrections coming our way. One, for their souls through prayer and believing the word of God. And second, the saving of Kentucky, either through the RRRF, or acceptance of the *status quo*. God would choose the best path and it would be revealed very soon."

The crowd drank his words of hope up like people who had been in a spiritual desert all their lives. The Reverend had them in the palm of his hand. He could work a crowd like a seasoned stand-up comedian. Knowing what to say, when to say it, then repeat it again and again, until it became their truth, their belief, their emotional lifeline. When it came time to decide the future of Kentucky, these people would follow him without question.

Dressed in his normal preaching attire of an all white, heavily sequined suit, he cut a flamboyant figure as he stalked back and forth across the small stage exhorting the crowd to follow the word of God. His oration lasted a crisp thirty minutes. There's only so much soul searching, haranguing and demagoguery, you can hammer into people before they switch off. Leave them wanting more, the age-old trick of every good entertainer. The Reverend was a professional at finishing on a high, leaving the adrenaline still pumping, the crowd on the verge of hysteria. He inhaled the adoration like a drug, feeling the high every speaker does when they have an audience under their spell. As the applause and 'thank the Lord's' died down, he descended the steps from the wagon, mixing with those who wanted him to lay hands on them, pray with them, or, most satisfying of all, give him a donation.

He was saying farewell to the last of his worshippers when a young man approached him. "Reverend Wedgwood, I'm Jodie McFadden, the one who's been broadcasting on behalf of the Kentucky People's Movement. Do you have a few minutes to talk?"

Concealing his surprise, the Reverend shook the proffered hand, "Mr. Jodie, so good to meet you. I have been an avid listener of your broadcasts. Please come into my modest home."

The Reverend led the way to a small four wheeled, Conestoga styled wagon. Inside was furnished in a simple, spartan style. There was a bed, desk, nightstand and a chair. Jodie sat in the chair, accepting the offer of a glass of water. He was nervous, turning over in his head the short rehearsed speech to be delivered to the preacher. Once the Reverend was settled, he explained the reason for his visit.

"Reverend, we've been following your tour with interest. Seems like you're generatin' quite an enthusiastic audience in some of these parts. When it comes to deciding if you're pro- or anti-RRRF and ReFederalization, us in the Kentucky People's Movement can't figure out which way you're leanin'. I'm not a godly man myself Reverend, but it seems to us God's also sitting on the fence here, which seems mighty odd, if you'll forgive my rudeness."

The Reverend looked at this sorry specimen in front of him. So this was the voice of the KPM? The kid couldn't be older than twenty-five and looked like he hadn't had a decent meal—or wash, in months. His hair was a haystack of dirty blonde spikes, his patchy beard a poor excuse for a grown man. A torn khaki jacket and pants completed a vision of poverty and neglect. In his most unctuous tone, he answered the young man's question.

"Not at all, my son. Your question is a fair one. One which I wish I could answer today. Unfortunately, God, as yet, has not spoken to me about his intentions. It may well be he will want Kentucky to accept the help the RRRF is offering, with all its shortcomings. Then again, he may not. I am merely the messenger. We have to be patient."

His sanctimonious tone did not sit well with Jodie. He and many of his fellow KPM'ers saw more than a touch of Jim Bakker in Josiah Wedgwood's words and antics. Bakker was an American televangelist and convicted fraudster. He milked his enormous number of followers for immense sums of money in the 1970s and 80s, then misappropriated the funds. Jail time followed with no divine intervention for him.

Jodie, seeing through the Reverend's evasiveness, countered, "Well if I can speak bluntly, Reverend, we would be concerned if this delicate and potentially dangerous issue became one in which the church got itself mixed up in." Jodie was speaking from a list of carefully memorized points he and his group had discussed back in Paintsville. He continued without waiting for a reply, "Reverend, we see this matter as one between the haves and have-nots. Those in power who've created a comfortable life for themselves since the Collapse, and keep that position by force and threats; and the rest, who the Kentucky People's Movement speaks for. Those that are struggling to survive. They see the RRRF as a way of making their lives more bearable. To be honest, we can't see why you or your church should have anything to do with this. Isn't there something in the Constitution about the separation of Church and State?" Jodie knew nothing about this, it was a suggestion his journalist friend thought might add credibility to his argument.

The Reverend showed no reaction to this upstart's criticism. His poker face belied some quick thinking to deflect these criticisms. Before he could answer, Jodie blurted out one last point.

"Finally, Reverend, you seem to have collected many donations from people who can ill afford to part with their money and valuables. That also concerns us. We wonder what you are going to do with all this money?"

Deploying every politician's best defense, he ignored the questions by adroitly diverting the conversation and asking some of his own, "They are excellent points you raise, Mr. Jodie. Perhaps I can first ask you exactly what the Kentucky People's Movement has in mind to fight the anti-RRRF factions? I think you will need all the help you can get. Just how widespread is your support? I'm guessing it is patchy, and disorganized? You need someone who can unite and focus your people if they are to be effective. Somehow I don't think a series of radio broadcasts is going to do the job, do you Mr. Jodie?"

Jodie was no politician, and his carefully scripted argument didn't stretch to answering these awkward questions. He had to admit, though; the Reverend had a point. They weren't at all organized. So far they had made a lot of noise, attended a short, useless meeting with the other parties in the dispute, and that was it. They had no leader, no effective spokesperson. No plan of action.

He looked up at the Reverend, who had a slightly pained expression on his face as if offended anyone could challenge his motives, "Well yes, guess you could be right Reverend. Sorry, didn't intend to be rude."

Quickly reverting to a benign, calming tone, the Reverend replied, "I quite understand your position. I am only here to help the people of Kentucky in their hour of need. I would surely be happier back in Alabama with my faithful congregation, than spending weeks on the road offering aid to the disaffected and needy. I suggest we keep in regular touch and I am sure God will show us a way to help each other when the need arises."

With this polite dismissal, the Reverend stood up and wished Jodie god speed back to Paintsville. Jodie walked off, slightly nonplussed at the way the meeting had ended—with no genuine answers to his questions. Once out of sight, the Reverend called over one of his bodyguards and whispered some instructions. The man nodded and lumbered off, beckoning two of the guards to join him.

It was early evening, the crowd was thinning. Jodie chatted with a few of the remaining people, trying to gauge their reactions. They all seemed fervent in their support for the Reverend and his beliefs. These people needed a spiritual crutch, and the Reverend was providing it. Jodie and the KPM would reluctantly have to accept this man had inserted himself into the argument and couldn't be ignored.

As the evening ended, darkness creeping in, he decided to find a place to stay and start out early the next morning on his two-day journey back home. Collecting his horse, Jodie rode a short distance east of the town before finding an old barn to spend the night. He ate some of his meager provisions—beef jerky and some fruit—before settling down to sleep.

It was still dark when he heard the barn door squeak open. Before he could get up, someone hit him over the head, then kicked him in the stomach. The beating continued for a few minutes. Jodie tried, unsuccessfully, to fight back. There were too many of them: he guessed at least three, attacking him from all sides. One stunning hit to the back of his head sent him tumbling to the ground, where all he could do was roll up in a ball to protect himself from the worst of the kickings.

The men said nothing until leaving, when one shouted, "That's what you get for sticking your shitty nose in our business. Next time we meet, we'll kill ya. So shut the fuck up on that radio of yours."

Chapter 34

The chopper touched down in a mini tornado of dust on the old baseball field outside of Cape Girardeau. Senator Charles Kingston ran from the cockpit, crouching under the slowing rotor blades.

He was met by Colonel Flowers, with a sloppy salute and a, "Hiya Senator, good to see ya again."

They moved to one of the old dugouts. It had not been used in years, it was damp and the floor was covered in rusting beer cans, trash and even, the Senator saw, recoiling in horror, used condoms. He'd met people in some disgusting places before, but this must rank as one of the most repugnant ever. Needs must, he thought to himself; no way did he want to be seen in public with this hired killer.

"Got the money?" asked the Colonel a little too aggressively for the Senator's comfort. Leaning over to look at the large holdall the Senator had put on the bench.

"I have. However, we need to be clear what I expect in return for this extra cash," the Senator spelled out his requirements, "replace the men you have lost and get another six in case you lose some more. Try to be more careful next time. Losing two men is careless, three is downright reckless. Second, I want Danny Trevino in Louisville to be your next target. I want him captured alive. This is non-negotiable. Fail to do this and your contract ends, no bonus. Understood?"

"Yes siree, loud and clear. Already got some extra bodies in training. You know getting this Danny guy ain't gonna be easy? He knows we're coming for him. He's probably got guards all over the place. Hey, just wonderin', can we get any help from those Navy guys on the river?"

"Not directly. However if they were, say, to come under attack by what appears to be hostile forces, they are permitted to return fire…," the Senator deliberately didn't finish the sentence.

For a second, the Colonel looked blank, then the penny dropped, a toothless smile crossed his face. "oh, gotcha drift there man, stir it up a little, light a fuse, then stand back. Woohoo, what a gas!" he slapped his knee excitedly as the scenario played out in his mind.

"I leave the details for you to sort out–I don't want to know anything about your plans. In fact, I'd rather not hear from you or meet you again until this is all over. Here's $250,000 dollars. That's all you're going to get from me until you earn your success bonus. If you fail, or are caught, I will deny any knowledge of this. Am I clear?"

"Yes siree, crystal clear. You can rely on me, Senator. I won't let you down," he grabbed the proffered bag, climbed out of the dugout and disappeared from view.

The Senator heard a motorcycle engine start up, then fade into the distance. He shuddered, thanked god that abhorrent little shit had gone; he hated even talking to him, let alone meeting him. He walked back to the waiting helicopter, giving the pilot instructions to fly him to the Navy Patrol's temporary HQ on the west side of the Ohio River at Evansville.

The helicopter touched down on the grounds of the Evansville Wartime Museum. To meet the him was Commander Jerry Williamson, officer in charge of the Navy Patrols up and down the Mississippi and Ohio Rivers. They went into the Museum's Cafe, sitting down with coffee and stale doughnuts.

The Commander was all business, starting his debrief without waiting to be asked, "we currently have five boats on patrol. To effectively patrol nearly five hundred miles of waterway, we need many more than this."

Why do the Military always want *more*, no matter how much they already have, wondered the Senator. The Commander sipped his coffee, and continued.

"No serious incidents to report so far, sir, except a minor confrontation in Louisville with the person there who seems to be in charge–a Danny Trevino? He fired off a few rounds across the bow of one of our boats, made some threats against us, and you, Senator. We declined to engage as per our orders to only do so if our lives are at risk. We diffused the altercation by withdrawing. In addition, we have stopped and confiscated the contents of eight smuggler's boats, mainly goods and provisions destined for the east."

"That's excellent news Commander. I'm sorry we cannot provide more resources at this time, however I'm sure you'll do an excellent job with those you have," a pat on the back went a long way with these Military types, the Senator knew. They chatted for a few more minutes, then he stood up, abruptly ending the meeting. He needed a drink, "it's getting late Commander, if you could show me to my sleeping quarters? What time are we reconvening for the patrol?"

"0800 hours sir, I'll have my aide collect you at 0745?"

"Perfect, I'll see you in the morning."

A waiting car took the Senator to his room at the local Holiday Inn. He ordered a pizza, clicked on the TV news to catch up with the happenings back in Sacramento. He didn't expect to see any news of his trip, this one was definitely below the radar. It was both enervating and worrying to be on a clandestine visit such as this. No aides, PR people, TV cameras, also no security. He had told only a handful of people where he was going and when. The Senator felt safe in the hands of his Navy hosts and was looking forward to a few hours out on the Ohio seeing the patrols in action.

He found the flask of vodka at the bottom of his case, took a long slug, feeling the liquor course through his body, relaxing him as he lay on the bed. He made one last phone call before calling it a night.

Colonel Flowers listened to the Senator's instructions, replying briefly, "You got it Senator."

No matter how hard you tried to cover your tracks, nothing was secret in the claustrophobic world of politics. Enemies and friends alike can't help but pass information on if it might be useful to someone, or to curry a future favor. The Senator, like all longtime politicians, had made his fair share of adversaries as he trampled his way to the top. Like the rejected Houston, who, after his humiliation at the Stewart Island Meeting, had been sidelined into a menial job in the Senator's office.

Outwardly, he seethed and complained to anyone who would listen at this unreasonable treatment. How could he be expected to answer questions on the RRRF's plans when no one knew what the hell was going on? He now realized, failing to have a reply to any question is a recipe for disaster in politics. If you don't know, bluff, lie, or better yet, ask a question back. Houston had not been skilled or adept enough to handle that awkward situation on Stewart Island, so was now deemed a liability and sent to political purgatory.

All of this public display of disaffection did not divert him from providing intelligence about the Senator and the Fed's plans for reunification to his handler at the FSB, and a newer source of income, Danny Trevino.

Conveniently, he was still sleeping with one of the Senator's secretaries, who after a particularly satisfying session between the sheets, had carelessly mentioned that he was taking a trip east to see the Navy's activities on the Mississippi. The following morning, he called his contact who knew how to reach Danny. His father had always told him to have contacts with both friend and foe, because you never knew when they may prove useful. Now was such a time.

He had little compunction about putting the Senator's life in danger. The man was a terrible human being that had stayed in power despite, or probably because of, his total disdain for the way he treated other people. Houston knew there was an ulterior motive in the Senator's whole RRRF and ReFederalization plan, though he'd been unable to find out what it was. No, the man deserved whatever was coming his way; he reasoned. He wouldn't lose any sleep over it.

As the Senator awoke after a dreamless night's sleep, he donned some carefully tailored Navy blue camo fatigues and waited for the driver to collect him.

While he'd been asleep, Danny Trevino had been very busy after receiving the intel from Houston revealing the Senator's travel plans. He was organizing quite the welcoming committee.

Chapter 35

Evansville sits on the north side of the Ohio River in Indiana. It was once the state's third largest city. Famous for its Indian burial mounds going back ten thousand years and infamous for its ambitious plans to build the world's longest canal connecting it to the Great Lakes. A plan that bankrupted the city and, when finally finished, unfortunately coincided with the railway's arrival, that proceeded to take all the intended canal traffic away.

It is only a two-hour drive from Louisville, or at least to Henderson, a small town just south of the city on the Kentucky side of the Ohio. Conveniently sitting in the middle of the Ohio is Henderson Island, where Danny intended to put two of his best snipers. To the north was a small unnamed island close to the improbably named Scuffletown. Now a ghost town, it acquired its name from the regular wrestling matches between the Cherokee and 'flat bottomed' boatmen coming down the Ohio in the eighteenth century. Here, Danny put two more sharpshooters. Finally, another two would be in a boat on the Green River where it flowed into the Ohio, just north of Henderson.

These three points covered all potential routes the Senator might take on his river trip. They also offered quick escape routes for the shooters once the job was done.

His men were in position twenty-four hours before the Senator's intended visit to the Naval docks at Evansville. They didn't know his exact itinerary, so patience was the order of the day. It hadn't been difficult to find six men who were expert shots, indeed one was a former Army sniper. Brought up with guns and hunting, hitting a human being at up to nine hundred feet was well within their capabilities. Positioned where they were, at some stage the Senator would pass them much closer than that. The Ohio was only about 2,500 feet wide around Evansville. The Navy Patrol Boats would be within range of the shooters no matter which side of the islands they passed.

Danny' men arrived in three trucks, enabling one to be close on shore to each of the shooters' locations. In addition, two small dinghies were used to ferry them to their island lookouts. A local fisherman lent a third larger one to the men on the Green River.

With his men in position, all with walkie-talkies, Danny pulled back a mile into the countryside near Spottsville. The two other drivers stayed close to the island shooters.

Danny hoped whoever shot the Senator could quickly escape any retaliatory attacks, getting back to the Kentucky bank of the river and making a quick escape.

The day dawned cool, with a light mist sitting gently on the Ohio, waiting to be dispersed by the midmorning sun. At the dockside, Commander Williamson escorted the Senator aboard the patrol boat. On his order, the engine's note grew from a barely audible burble to a deep growl as the boat edged away from the dock. The mist still obscured the far shore as they cruised along at a steady ten knots, in a northeasterly direction headed for Louisville.

"I thought we'd patrol a few miles in this direction for about an hour, sir," said the Commander.

"Sounds perfect Commander, beautiful day to be on the river. Have you seen much traffic since you started patrolling?"

"It's decreased in the last couple of weeks as the smugglers know we're here. Most of the action is overnight. We're still apprehending a few, mainly further south. But as I said yesterday, it's a lot of river to cover with a handful of patrol boats."

Paul H Rowney

"You're doing an excellent job with the resources you have, Commander. I commend your effort, it will help the RRRF get off to a safer start, knowing our backs are covered."

"Thank you sir, it is good to know our efforts are appreciated."

The patrol boat was now passing where the Green River emptied into the Ohio. They couldn't see the boat hiding in a small creek a few yards down from where the rivers met. Danny's two men waiting there heard the patrol boat, though the mist prevented a clear sighting. One picked up his walkie-talkie and quietly informed Danny that he thought the target had passed them and was heading towards the tiny island across from Scuffletown.

Danny changed channels on the walkie-talkie and told the two shooters, Joey and Christian, that the Senator was headed their way– ETA five to ten minutes.

The two men double checked their rifles and settled themselves down, peering through their scopes into the mist. Visibility was three to four hundred feet, so they wouldn't get much time to pick out the Senator, aim and shoot. They prayed the boat would go to the north of the island, allowing them to escape south to Kentucky. If it didn't, life could get interesting.

For a few minutes there was almost no sound, just the mist muffled cries made by a few distant birds. Then…the unmistakable sound of a diesel engine chugging towards them. Joey and Christian sighted up the boat as it broke through the mist. Initially, they could see no sign of the Senator, then he came into view standing on the port side! This gave the gunmen only a few seconds to shoot. If the boat went on the north side of the island they would lose sight of him behind the wheelhouse.

As the boat glided towards them, Joey and Christian waited for the optimal moment: close enough to ensure a clear shot, but not too close to find their field of vision blocked.

"Ready, Joey?" whispered Christian, his right eye glued to the telescopic sight on his rifle.

177

"Yep."

"In three, two, one...."

The sound of two rifle shots echoing across the still water was audible to Danny in the truck and the two gunmen hidden in the boat on Green River.

Danny pulled the walkie-talkie to his mouth. Before he could ask if they got the Senator, a fusillade of shots shattered the silence.

On board the patrol boat, the Senator slumped to the deck clutching his chest. Two seamen ran to the bow mounted machine gun and let loose a ferocious volley of shots towards the island. The patrol boat moved closer taking the south side route. Effectively cutting off Joey and Christian's escape to Kentucky. The island was only about a thousand feet long and a hundred feet wide, with a few trees for cover.

The gunmen crouched low to the ground, crawling to avoid the raking gunfire from the patrol boat. Sometimes it came perilously close, then moved further away. Joey and Christian had left their small inflatable craft in the middle of the island and were now dragging it to the north side, meaning an escape into Indiana. Not ideal, but they could easily make their way back over to Kentucky further downriver.

The two men jumped into their getaway boat and started paddling the few hundred feet to the Indiana bank. Suddenly the sun broke through, providing clear visibility across the river. They were now totally exposed. The patrol boat was on the far side of the island, but could turn around and head back towards them in a matter of minutes. They paddled furiously away from the island. They were within two hundred feet of the river bank, when gunfire erupted towards them. The water churned up all around the boat as dozens of bullets missed them by inches. But not for long. Within seconds, the craft was punctured and sinking, leaving Joey and Christian floundering in the water, unable to defend themselves. Mercilessly, the shooters on the shore zeroed in on their splashing targets. Within seconds they riddled the two men with bullets. In an instant, they perished and began drifting face down in the Ohio, slowly floating back towards Evansville.

Danny heard the gunfire and radioed for the shooters in the boat on Green River and on Henderson Island to get the hell back to shore, dump the boats, find their trucks and get away. Something had gone drastically wrong. As Danny roared along Route 60, he was frantically calling Joey and Christian. Before long, he was out of range. He told one truck to wait a few hours near Scuffletown to see if they returned. Scared, humiliated and furious, Danny gunned it back to Louisville.

On board the patrol boat, Senator Kingston gingerly peeled off his kevlar vest. The Commander had done a smart port turn and traversed the north side of the island to see if they could find the shooters. They did, two pieces of human flotsam still oozing blood. They were dragged aboard and put in body bags.

The Commander looked perplexed, "Senator, were you expecting this attack? Do you know these people?"

The Senator, looking pale and shaken, replied in an unsteady voice, "I thought it was a vague possibility something might happen. I don't know these men, though I can guess who they work for."

"And who were the men that killed them?"

"Some, shall we say, freelance bodyguards I use from time to time."

The Commander barely contained his anger, "Why put yourself in danger of being killed? I would venture to say it was extremely risky for you and my crew members. I am responsible for your safety and theirs. If anything fatal had happened, all hell would be let loose on me."

The Senator sighed, then patiently explained his actions, "if I had told you I was planning this, you would have refused to go. I do apologize, but my purpose in doing this was twofold–to show the man behind this, Danny Trevino, I am not running scared of him; and secondly, to confirm I have a mole in my organization with connections to these terrorists. I now intend to use this information to my advantage. Now, could you kindly get me to a doctor just to check that nothing is broken?"

The Commander gave him a withering look, then tartly commanded the helmsman to make haste back to port, and radio for a doctor to be waiting.

Later that evening, when the last team of shooters had returned without Joey or Christian, Danny assumed the worst. They were dead or captured. He was sure that bastard Senator had set them up. He couldn't be sure if his guys had shot him before they were attacked themselves.

By the next day, his sources confirmed the worst. The Senator had been hit but not seriously injured. The whole assassination plan was a flop, and he'd lost two good men as well. On top of that, he could no longer trust his sources close to the Senator. It was a triple whammy of bad news.

Chapter 36

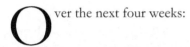ver the next four weeks:

- Colonel Wayne Flowers and his team captured or liquidated six more attendees from the Louisville Meeting.

- Penny became seriously ill. Jay flew to Bowling Green in his ultralight, bringing her back to French Creek for safety and medical attention.

- The Reverend Josiah Wedgwood continued his triumphant sweep across Kentucky garnering support for his pilgrimage and promises of salvation.

- Senator Charles Kingston, believing the anti-RRRF faction was losing ground, asked the RRRF Army to be readied for action.

- Nothing more was broadcast by the Kentucky People's Movement.

Chapter 37

Roger wasn't a great nurse, he'd be the first to admit. Dealing with sick people was not his strong point. Nevertheless, he was happy to look after Penny as she recovered from what turned out to be a bout of pleurisy. Time, rest and a good diet were Doc Brown's suggestions, and it seemed to work. Penny was now out of bed and moving gingerly around the house. She'd even ventured outside once or twice, taking advantage of the early summer warmth.

Landy, taken aback a little by the sudden arrival of a female into the house, had grown to like Penny and found a shared interest in, of all things, post-apocalyptic fiction books. For hours while Penny was laid up in bed, Landy would read to her, or later, bring her books as she recovered. It delighted Roger the two were getting on so well. He even took over some of the non-embarrassing nursing duties when Roger was busy.

They had kept up to date with happenings in the outside world, via the ever-increasing number of people using ham radio to spread news, gossip and (dis)information. Roger wondered where all these radio sets had been until now? He was grateful that communications were improving across Kentucky, but worried about the accuracy of the information. News that a further six city leaders had been murdered or kidnapped, was a source of continual concern. These vigilantes were not going away. They were on a witch hunt for everyone who attended the meeting in Louisville. He and Penny felt safe in French Creek. Its relative isolation and increased security reassured both of them.

Jay helped with security too, venturing out on regular reconnaissance flights to spot any unwelcome visitors. So far, seeing nothing of concern was spotted.

At council and village meetings, the discussion always returned to the RRRF and the ultimate ReFederalization of Kentucky. Many, like Roger and Penny, were ambivalent. They knew something had to change. People were moving beyond survival mode to wanting more of what they had before the Collapse. With many of the leaders from the Louisville meeting now dead or captured, they wondered whether those towns and cities were more likely to embrace change? Or had they just found a new leader who carried on the role of benevolent (or maybe not so benevolent) dictator, as before?

'If you're not moving forward, you're going backwards', is a phrase used by many business gurus to describe the way a company should be run. The same could apply to a country, in particular, one that had once been a beacon of twenty-first century progress. Now the east of America was in a state of limbo. No one liked uncertainty, and that's what many in Kentucky faced.

As Roger said to Penny over dinner one evening, "I believe most people would go for this whole RRRF thing, if they had a reasonable idea what to expect and how they'd benefit. The Government's vague promises have the opposite effect–particularly when their front man is a historically corrupt politician."

Penny agreed with a smile, "He's the latest in a long line Kentucky has produced regularly over the decades. They have had little choice when it comes to voting for squeaky clean candidates, have they?"

"Too true Penny. Why do the very people who should run for office never bother, leaving us with such a lousy choice?"

"Who was it that said, 'we have the best money congress can buy'?"

"I think it was Mark Twain," Roger answered. "I wonder if we ever get back to full elections here in the east, will it change? Talking of famous quotes, I always liked Churchill's, 'Democracy is a lousy form of government, but it's better than any of the alternatives.' Never were truer words spoken."

The two continued to discuss ideas and outcomes as they awaited further news. Penny was nearly back to normal. Her strength had returned. She now helped around the house and in the garden. She was enjoying the relaxed atmosphere of French Creek, happy to leave the running of Bowling Green to her brother. Slowly, it dawned on her that she had no desire to go back there. She didn't feel safe and was practically a prisoner in her own house. Running the town had never been her choice, it was foisted upon her when her husband died. Hunter, her brother, was better suited to it, and seemed to relish the responsibility, and power. Finally, she wanted to start a family and Bowling Green was not a conducive environment, especially at the moment.

Then there was Roger. It wasn't surprising how close they'd become. He had been at her side for weeks, seen her at her worst, and helped her get back on her feet. She'd caught him staring at her when he thought she was asleep, and it wasn't just concern she saw in his eyes, but a look of care and affection. He hadn't said anything, Roger was hardly the demonstrative type, but she recognized the looks he gave her, the tone of his voice. He'd fallen for her as much as she had for him.

All these unspoken emotions finally came to a head one evening after a simple barbecued supper and maybe just a little too much homemade wine. Landy was out hunting with friends. Roger and Penny sat alone on the front porch in the dimming light, watching storm clouds bubble up above the distant hilltops. The conversation between them had been about nothing and everything, just the idle chatter of people comfortable in each other's company. Even the long silences, as they listened to the frog's rasping calls, the incessant chirping of insects, while sipping wine, never felt awkward. You don't have to fill in the quiet moments when you're with a soulmate. There are no expectations, no demands to make conversation. The silence is enough–or was.

Penny finally felt the need to have a 'it's decision time' conversation with Roger. They'd been hedging around just how they felt about each other for some time, now she wanted to target it out in the open.. As casually as possible, she asked, "I guess we need to discuss when and how I'm getting back to Bowling Green? I can't stay here forever. I don't want to overstay my welcome."

Silence. Roger stared into his wine glass. Not sure how he should reply to this not very subtle ultimatum.

"Do we have enough gas in the truck Roger?"

No response.

Penny doggedly carried on the one-sided conversation, "I suppose Jay could always…."

Roger finally interrupted her, "You don't have to go. You can stay, however long you like."

Pause.

"Penny, I've really, really enjoyed having you stay. It's been wonderful to have some female company. And, well, you don't have to go yet…."

She laughed at his uncomfortable squirming, "For fuck's sake Roger, are you saying you'd like me to stay here, like permanently? Or not? Spit it out man! This is like pulling teeth!"

Roger looked up from his glass, his eyes moist with emotion, "Yes Penny, that's exactly what I'm trying to find the words to say. I am sorry, I'm not very good at this kinda thing."

"Ya think?" said Penny gently, mocking him. She stood up and took his hand.

"OK, that's settled. I'd love to stay. Now let's go to bed."

Stunned at this unexpected suggestion, Roger didn't move, rooted to the spot, "Jesus Penny, where's all that shy southern lady stuff I hear so much about?"

"As far as I'm concerned, that's a load of horseshit. Now come on Roger we could play this courting game, but we know where it will end up sooner or later. We're not teenagers. So why don't we save ourselves a lot of time and start at the finish line? I'm horny and I'm guessing you are, too. So let's quit talking and move straight to the action. Are you coming with me?" she tugged his arm, dragging him into the house.

Roger followed her inside. For the first time in a long while, he was happy to be at the receiving end of orders, not giving them.

Within minutes they were undressed and in bed. Suddenly feeling a little nervous Roger said, "It's been a while since I've done this…."

"Me too, so guess we both have to treat this as a bit of a refresher course?"

"Well, they say it's like riding a bike, you never really forget," laughed Roger.

Penny looked at him with a straight face, "Hey, are you saying I'm like an old bike?"

Roger groaned in embarrassment, "No, no, Penny, I'm not saying that at all. Oh Jesus, I'm sorry that came out all wrong."

"At ease captain, I'm teasing you. Now quit talking and let's start working our way up through the gears!"

Later that night, Landy returned with nothing to show for his hunting trip. He noticed Penny's bedroom door was open, with her nowhere to be seen. Putting two and two together, he smiled. Dad finally had someone else to take care of. Maybe the distraction would make his life a little easier!

By 8:00 a.m. the next day, Landy was making the rounds of his ham radio buddies to see if anyone had any news. When he finally heard from 'Paducah Paul' it was not good. Transmissions then started coming in from several radio hammers along the Mississippi and Ohio rivers:

A large flotilla of boats were heading northwards, some estimates put the number of personnel at well over three thousand. There also seemed to be air support with helicopters flying up and down the river informing residents by megaphone that the RRRF was landing at several points along the river and not to be alarmed.

The RRRF, the soft spearhead of ReFederalization was on its way, for the second time.

Chapter 38

Under General Samuel Banks, the RRRF had been reconfigured and would enter Kentucky from several directions. Not only would nearly three thousand men and women from the Army, US Marshals and National Guard be landing at a dozen places along the Mississippi and Ohio Rivers, but mechanized convoys would use temporarily opened bridges at Paducah, Memphis and St. Louis, with more crossing the Ohio having traversed Illinois and Indiana.

The convoys contained hundreds of trucks packed with food and supplies run by the Military. Airports, once secured, would enable plane loads of additional supplies to be airlifted in. There would be doctors, nurses and engineers. The latter to assess and prioritize basic infrastructure reconstruction needs.

The ham radio fraternity exploded across the airwaves as operators throughout western and southern Kentucky reported the convoy's progress. To the delight of General Banks, and the Senator, the early reactions to their arrival were, in the main, welcoming. Though caution dictated celebrating too prematurely as they had yet to reach any of the major cities. It would be several days before that happened. Based on these positive reports, General Banks and his senior officers bypassed the major centers of population and concentrated on covering as much ground as possible elsewhere in the state. In this way, they hoped to isolate the areas that posed the most risk.

It was day four of the RRRF's incursion when they reached French Creek. Jay had spotted them from his ultralight hours before they arrived. Pat had several guards hidden along French Creek Road. Roger and Penny went to meet them at the intersection with SR90. They wanted to find out exactly what was going to happen before allowing them into the village.

To their surprise, it was all very low-key. While the convoy had several vehicles in it, only two intended to turn into French Creek. The others would continue eastwards to replenish their stores at Somerset Municipal Airport, two hours away.

A man and woman in Army uniforms jumped down from the leading truck and walked towards Penny and Roger. Shaking hands, they introduced themselves as Sergeant Jennifer Nowalski and Lieutenant Michael Drondale.

"We're the advanced guard of the RRRF. Here to offer you food and medical supplies. We have a nurse on board, too," the Sergeant explained with a bright, engaging smile. She was probably only twenty-five, tall, slim, with short cropped hair and an open, honest demeanor. She was an ideal ambassador, thought Roger.

"Welcome to French Creek," replied Roger, introducing himself and Penny by first names only. He wasn't sure if they had a hit list of names from the Louisville meeting though they wouldn't expect to find Penny here. He continued, "We are delighted to meet you guys. I like the low-key approach. Some of the stuff we've been hearing made you sound like an invasion force."

"Yes, I know," agreed the Lieutenant. "We're taking it softly, softly. Seems to be working so far. How can we help you people of...," he looked down at his clipboard, "...French Creek? To start with, can you tell me how many people live here?"

"Just under two hundred. Why don't you guys drive down to the village? There's a lot of folks keen to meet you. Can we ride with you?"

As the trucks lumbered down French Creek Road, Roger radioed Pat telling him what was happening and to remain on standby.

"You got people watching us?" asked the Sergeant with a quizzical look.

"You bet. Wouldn't you do the same?"

The Sergeant nodded in agreement. Within a few minutes, they were stopping by the church where most of the population had come out to greet them. They thronged around the two large trucks.

Roger stood on the tailgate and raised his hands to quell the excited hubbub, "Everyone, listen up. Here, at last, is the advanced guard of the RRRF. They have supplies on board for us, and we are most grateful for them. I will let the Lieutenant here explain what they have in the trucks and what else they can do to help us in the short term. Before I do, remember, we are lucky here. We have sufficient food and supplies. I ask you to be fair and not take things which other communities might have greater need of than us. Thank you."

Roger jumped down and Lieutenant Drondale took his place on the tailgate. He introduced himself, and the other people in his team. Then itemized what he could dispense now, and take a list of other things people needed with the promise a second convoy would attempt to bring those along in a few weeks. As he flung open the roll up doors on each large truck, people clambered around to peer inside at this treasure trove of provisions.

Doc Brown was first in line, enquiring about medical supplies. He'd become a great believer in using nature's remedies, however, some antibiotics and painkillers would be a godsend. He was given a generous supply of both, plus bandages and antiseptic products.

"Thank you so much Lieutenant, this will make my life so much easier, and help so many people," he went away with a broad smile on his face, Christmas had come early!

Then in an orderly fashion, the RRRF crew yelled out a long list of supplies they had to distribute. Most took Roger's plea to heart and didn't ask for food or items they didn't need. Though when it came to the likes of chocolate and candies, few could resist. Likewise, coffee and...Coca-Cola!

People gratefully took everyday pharmacy items like Tylenol, bandages, antiseptic cream, sanitary towels, and a host of other long forgotten products.

Within an hour, the residents of French Creek had gone back to their homes clutching armfuls of supplies and goodies they had only dreamt about over the last six years.

"They're certainly winning the hearts and minds, Penny. Getting everyone on their side before politics makes its unwelcome appearance," observed Roger, as Penny nodded in agreement.

Penny walked back to the Lieutenant and Sergeant who were busy tidying up empty boxes, throwing them in the back of the truck, "Can I offer you some refreshments? Least we can do after all your generosity."

"That's mighty kind of you, ma'am. Can you give us a few minutes to finish up here, then we'll join you?" Jennifer replied gratefully.

"No problem. We'll get the coffee going. In fact, we'll have the coffee you brought today! We haven't had freshly ground coffee in a long time. It'll be a real treat. We're just over there," Penny pointed to Roger's house across the road.

Once inside the house, Roger turned to Penny, "We have to be careful to not say anything about our trip to Louisville, or that meeting on Stewart Island. I nearly gave them a false name when I introduced myself. I really don't want them jumping to any conclusions here. Don't know about you, but I'm pleasantly surprised at what they've said and done so far?"

"Yes, all seems pretty honest and above board. No doubt they've made a good impression on the villagers. Then again, anyone arriving here bearing gifts like they have will be welcomed as heroes!"

Roger agreed, "True, this is the easy bit for the RRRF. Imposing some kind of government and all that goes with it is a whole different ball game. Be interesting to see what these two know about that side of things."

Ten minutes later, there was a knock on the door. Roger invited the Sergeant and Lieutenant to sit on the porch, then brought out the coffee and homemade cake. Both Roger and Penny sighed appreciatively as they sipped the freshly brewed coffee.

"Oh my god, that is nectar to my taste buds," said Penny dreamily as she savored the tangy, rich taste for the first time in years, "you forget how damn good this is after years of reusing the same coffee dregs six times over. This is bliss, thank you so much."

"I can't imagine going without a good coffee, it must be hell! How do you get up in the mornings?!" asked Jennifer.

"You get used to it, but then again, I could get really used to this," Penny replied.

Jennifer and Michael seemed at ease, willing to answer questions as best they could. They obviously relished being part of what they saw as some kind of huge rescue mission. Doling out supplies to grateful people, delighted to be seen as the good guys.

Roger tried to extract more information. Surely it couldn't all be good news? "So, how have you found things as you moved across from the west?"

Michael looked at Jennifer, "Do you want to answer that? You're the one that's got to write the report."

"Sure, happy to," she paused, running her hand absently through her short hair, "as you can imagine, it's a mixed bag. Seems the further east we go, the less we see stuff that's obviously come from the west, legally or otherwise. Things which make a real difference to people's comfort. There's no doubt some folks up in the hills and remote valleys, sorry, hollows–as you guys call them–are at subsistence level. Barely growing enough to feed themselves, so nothing to barter or sell. We've seen a dozen such communities so far. Not surprisingly, they were happy to see us. We can't, at the moment, do much for them in the long term. All we can do is give them what they need to survive another few months. It's so sad. Some of those kids look like refugees."

She paused, fanning her arm across the view in front of them, "Then we come to a place like this which clearly has got its act together and is doing well. Hell, you've even got an ultralight! That is different! From what we can see, you've made fantastic progress. You deserve congratulations."

Roger thanked her, feeling the need to add, "It wasn't easy and there were times we came very close to starvation. We survived by having a very strict regime of sharing, cooperating, and working together as a community. If we hadn't, it would have ended up very differently. Go look at our graveyard to see how many didn't make it."

An awkward silence followed Roger's words. Night was drawing close, the frogs and crickets were beginning their nocturnal chorus. The occasional firefly randomly stabbing the darkness. The only light came from the few candle lamps on the porch now being attacked by moths and insects.

Jennifer broke the silence, almost whispering, "It's so quiet here. I'd forgotten how much noise we live with back home. And so dark! It's like I'm in a room painted completely black. Makes me slightly envious of the peaceful life you live here."

"As I said, it came at a price Jennifer," repeated Roger, an edge to his voice.

Jennifer looking pained, said, "I'm sure it did Roger, I cannot begin to appreciate what you all have been through since the Collapse. You have every reason to feel aggrieved about the way the west treated you."

Michael added an attempt at an apology, "Over in the west we had no idea what was going on here. It was almost like a news blackout once the Mississippi border was secured. Overnight there were no more videos of desperate people clamoring into boats to get across. It all went silent. We just carried on like nothing had happened. Being part of the RRRF has been a real eye-opener. We just didn't realize how…how…*basic*, life is in the east. I did not know that it was so…so…," he struggled to find the right words.

Roger, unable to keep quiet, finished off his sentence, "...Backward, forgotten, abandoned, how about: primitive? Kinda words you were looking for, Michael?"

Before Michael could reply, Penny hastily steered the conversation back to the RRRF's future plans, "So tell me, you've given out the aid, the goody bags, everyone's got a temporary fix: what happens after that? There's all this talk about forming a new government, getting the infrastructure up and running. But that could take years and billions of dollars. Do you know anything about how this will come about?"

Jennifer and Michael for the first time, looked a little uncomfortable.

Michael shook his head, "That's a good question, Penny. I have to be honest and say we don't know much at all about the next stages in the RRRF's strategy and ultimately this whole ReFederalization thing. Only what we hear second hand."

"Which is?" asked Penny.

"Well, as you know, Senator Kingston is the prime mover here. He's not given any indication as to how much the government has to spend on this whole idea. Everyone knows it's a fortune. All we know is, once we've distributed the supplies across Kentucky, and that could take months, we go back to the west. And wait."

Roger felt he had to ask, "Have you heard anything concerning the places that are hostile to the RRRF? Louisville, Lexington, we reckon there's around twenty of them. Is the Army getting involved there?"

"Roger, I wish I knew the answer. We've been told to steer clear of any confrontation. If it gets bad, we call in for support, so far that's not happened. We are trying to avoid it by not going to places where we'll not be welcomed," Michael shrugged his shoulders in a 'what do I know?' manner and took another sip of coffee.

After a moment's thought, he continued, "Everyone realizes these convoys are a quick fix, a sticking plaster, but better than nothing. At least it's a start. My guess is they'll see how this goes, then plan their next move. Typical government: great thinking up the ideas, not too

Paul H Rowney

good at seeing them through to the end." Feeling he'd said enough, looking at his watch, "Jennifer, time for us to call it a day? Early start tomorrow. Been great talking to you both, and glad to see your thriving community. Thanks for your time and hospitality."

Penny stood up and shook their hands, "No, thank you all for your supplies and information. It's been wonderful meeting you."

As Michael turned to leave, his demeanor changed. The glow of candles lighting his face against the dense black of the night sky, suddenly made him look a little intimidating. Turning to face Penny and Roger, his hand resting casually on his gun, his voice took on a more serious tone. "Before we go, can I mention one other thing, Roger, Penny? We know you were both at the Louisville Meeting. You're on the list we have; everyone in the RRRF has one. I know from talking to you now that you're not the radical anti-RRRF types like the others. So we're not going to detain you, or tell anyone you're here. There's no point. Just thought I'd warn you, though, others may not be so relaxed about it."

Roger glanced at Penny, his eyebrows raised in surprise at being called out, "That's mighty kind of you both. I think it's fair to say we went to that meeting to see what it was all about. Not to support their objectives. There were a lot of firebrands there spouting off how they'd fight anyone who tried to take over their city. Personally, I don't think they stand a chance against a well-coordinated attack, though it could be costly to both sides. Down here, we are just waiting and seeing how the dice will roll. Whichever route is best for our communities, we'll support. I have to be honest and say, it'll take more than truckloads of Coke and coffee to persuade us!"

Michael nodded in agreement, "We know Roger, we know. I suggest you guys keep your heads down, wait and see how it all develops. What the next few weeks and months hold for you and your community, I can't say. All I can do is wish you the best of luck. Thanks for your time, we'll be leaving before dawn."

195

He shook hands with Roger, as did Jennifer. They stepped down from the porch and within a few steps were swallowed up by the darkness. The heavy Kentucky night absorbed them like a black sponge.

"I need a drink," said Roger, walking into the house. He emerged clutching a bottle of wine and two glasses. Both sipped at their drinks, mulling over the conversation with Jennifer and Michael.

Penny spoke first, "What did you make of that? Should we hope–believe–they won't shop us to their officers?" Penny was trying to be optimistic, though the uncertainty in her voice betrayed a sense of unease.

Roger answered with a resigned sigh, "Not sure we have a choice but to believe them. It makes you wonder what else they know, but didn't tell us. It was a real disappointment they knew nothing about ReFederalization. Handing out cookies to hungry kids is one thing; starting a new government from nothing is quite another. It's a huge undertaking. Why do I have this nagging feeling this is all going to end in tears?"

They continued swapping thoughts and hopes for the future before going to bed. There were no easy answers to the questions that worried them most. Neither heard the RRRF's trucks leave early the following morning. They woke up, still wondering whether the next contingent of RRRF's soldiers might be there to arrest them.

Chapter 39

Of course, it wasn't God that was going to decide the Reverend Josiah Wedgwood's next move. Something more prosaic, money or people: the Reverend had a decision to make: drag his increasingly unwieldy band of pilgrims across Kentucky, where the impoverished might be more accepting and believing of his message. Or, head north towards Lexington and Louisville, where the money and donations were to be found. But with a danger the audience might be more skeptical and partisan.

He'd met two of the RRRF relief convoys on his travels. Worryingly, they left in their wake a population enthused with the prospect of a new beginning under ReFederalization. Even if they knew little about it. The RRRF's statewide bribery campaign was yielding positive results. Having too many people in favor of this didn't suit his purpose. He needed a fragmented, undecided population he could meld to his way of thinking. Crucially, he needed to position himself as the kingmaker between the two warring parties. Who, for the right inducement, would recommend the RRRF stay, or not? Put another way: ReFederalization was Kentucky's salvation from its present, dismal existence or a threat to its independence.

Increasingly, he believed he could take over the role the Kentucky People's Movement had started. He wouldn't need that upstart from Paintsville to be on his side, sending out pathetic propaganda from some godforsaken place he'd never heard of. No, what he needed now was to get in touch with the Senator behind this whole ReFederalization idea and convince him that a modest preacher from Alabama was the solution to his problem. He also needed to feel out the attitudes of the anti RRRF faction and how malleable they might be to his involvement.

He decided after much deliberation that a trip to Louisville would give him the opportunity to meet one of the most ardent anti-ReFederalizationists, some hot head called Danny Trevino. Assuming a successful meeting of minds could be reached, with some careful finessing, he would make them realize he was an indispensable part of their success. This was playing all ends against the middle—a poker game where the stakes weren't just vast amounts of money, but life or death as well.

It took him nearly a week to lead his train of aides, supplicants and camp followers, now numbering over two hundred, up through central Kentucky to the outskirts of Louisville. They were a motley gathering, to be sure. When he'd started, there had been just over a dozen of them. A victim of his own success, the Reverend's fiery words of hope and salvation had galvanized many to leave their homes and join him in his pilgrimage around the state. Feeding and caring for the increasing numbers was causing logistical problems. Most towns could handle an influx of twenty or thirty visitors, now it was more like a small invasion. It stretched their hospitality to the limit.

They pitched camp at Broad Run Park on the southern edge of Louisville. Crowds soon gathered to see what was happening. After all, two hundred plus people carrying banners proclaiming salvation and answers to all their prayers, was a rare sight. Add to that a flamboyant African American preacher dressed in a white suit, inviting them to join him in prayer, was proving an irresistible attraction.

Before he knew it, the Reverend had an audience of over a thousand. They settled down in front of his hastily erected stage. He wasted no time in deploying his well-rehearsed words of hellfire, and damnation, followed by reassurance and salvation. As he moved towards the climax of his fiery sermon, encouraging the increasingly excitable crowd to respond to his exhortations, he again revealed himself as the conduit from God in these momentous and confusing times. He would, in due course, impart to them the divine wish for the State of Kentucky. No longer would they have to worry about which was the best way forward. God would do the thinking for them and guide them into making the right choice. After six years in the spiritual wilderness, his message was devoured *en masse*, the audience clutching at his promises like a drowning man grabs a life jacket.

As the Reverend stepped down from the stage, the crowd scattered as two Humvees careered through them, coming to a sudden dust swirling halt only feet from where he stood.

The doors flew open and a gang of heavily armed men formed a cordon around the preacher as Danny Trevino exited the vehicle and walked towards him. With no introduction, Danny launched into a furious verbal attack.

"Just who the fuck do you think you are and what the fuck are you doing here getting my people all riled up? This is my city and you get my say before you preach all this bullshit. I've heard about you, and as far as I'm concerned, you're a load of unwanted fucking trouble. So get your shit together and leave now, and take all these groupies with you," Danny waved his arm at the crowd, who had gathered to see what the ruckus was all about. No one seemed to object to being called a groupie.

The Reverend showed commendable calm in the face of this onslaught. He wasn't fazed by the vitriol; it came with the territory, though the display of heavily armed men was a little unnerving. Taking a few moments to compose himself, he replied in his most accommodating manner, "Sir, I do apologize if I have offended you, or caused any trouble. As God is my witness, I had no intention of making any speeches before contacting you. However, the people here seemed anxious to hear what I had to say. Who was I to disappoint them? If I can offer help and reassurance in these...."

"OK, I hear you Reverend," Danny interrupted. He was not a good listener, especially when it came to preachers, "You've come to save all our souls, and that's just fucking fantastic. However, in case you hadn't noticed, this state is in danger of being overrun by the Feds. So I have better things to do than deal with people like you, stirring things up, putting ideas into people's minds. So fuck off outta here before I put you where even God can't find you."

A lot earlier than he had planned, and certainly not under these combative circumstances, the Reverend thought now might be the time to put into action his initial game plan. This man, he knew, was a major player in the anti-RRRF movement. He also had a pile of money, by all accounts. Perhaps this was the moment to test the water and see if Danny Trevino would take the bait and recognize that having the Reverend on his side—and his state-wide army of devoted followers—was worthy of consideration? A large consideration? It was an enormous risk, but as his daddy, an inveterate gambler once told him, 'You don't win big by betting small'.

"Mr. Trevino, perhaps we can discuss this more in private? I have a proposition that I think you'll find very attractive. It could be worth a lot of money to you and ensure the safety of your fine city."

Danny stopped himself from launching another tirade…money…saving his city? Could this bullshitter really be in a position to offer these? Well, no harm in listening, "OK, Reverend you've got five minutes. Let's go sit in the truck for some privacy. If you're wasting my time, you might not live to regret it."

They moved across to the Humvee, Danny asked his guards to form a circle around the vehicle. Once inside, Danny turned to the Reverend, "Your five minutes start now."

An hour later, they were still talking. Suddenly, Danny was an excellent listener.

While they were discussing the Reverend's proposal in Danny's vehicle, lost in the crowd, Jodie McFadden of the Kentucky People's Movement. Underneath his coat he gripped the handle of an ancient Colt 45 revolver. Hell bent on revenge, not just for the beating he'd received at the hands of the Reverend's thugs, but for hijacking his Movement's purpose and agenda. How dare he try to sideline them, even ridicule the Movement he'd helped start? That so-called Reverend had even called them 'Redneck Roosters, making a lot of noise, but not a lot of use to man nor beast'. What sort of preacher said things like that?

Most of his friends in Paintsville were prepared to ignore the Reverend's jibes, believing he was all talk and no action. Jodie was not. Having met the Reverend, and his violent sidekicks, he knew the man was a dangerous fraud. One that had built a substantial following. It was time to reveal he was no more than a snake oil salesman. Jodie was determined to bring this charlatan preacher's litany of lies to an end.

Chapter 40

Senator Kingston was in a self-congratulatory mood: he'd given that odious little jerk Danny Trevino a bloody nose, dispatched two of his sidekicks, unearthed a mole in his ranks, and best of all, early reports coming back from the RRRF convoys were almost unanimously favorable.

"Don't you just love it when a plan comes together so well?" he mused out loud to one of his aides.

She nodded obsequiously. Keen to leave, she asked if there was anything else the Senator needed? He looked across the room at the young girl, probably in her mid-twenties, black hair, cute, slim and well dressed in a body hugging white blouse and dark skirt.

"Yes Monica, how about you join me for dinner this evening? Let's celebrate!"

She was well aware of the Senator's wandering eyes, and hands, if you got too close. Yuck! Christ, the man was older than her father! He just couldn't keep it in his pants.

"Thanks for the invitation sir, but I have dinner tonight with my parents, maybe another time?" In your dreams, she thought as she hurriedly left the office before he could suggest an alternative time to try his luck.

Unperturbed by the girl's refusal to join him, he picked up the phone and called his ever ready standby and senior assistant, Barbara. She quickly agreed to his last-minute invitation. She valued her job far too much to say no when the Senator asked for her company. Even if it entailed some less than spectacular sex.

To pass the time before dinner, he poured a generous finger of bourbon into his cut crystal glass, letting his mind wander to the pleasures in store later that night.

The following morning, he convened a meeting with his team and political advisors to discuss how to follow up the success of the initial RRRF 'feed the minds and bodies' mission. Now he wanted to know how the non-compliant areas were to be subdued, or persuaded to welcome the RRRF. Many of the larger towns and cities, now minus their anti-RRRF leaders, (courtesy of Colonel Flowers) were by all accounts 'open for business'. Not so in Louisville. Despite the best efforts of his covert military force, they'd been unable to get close to Danny Trevino.

"It'd be easier to kidnap the Pope," claimed the Colonel in a recent call with the Senator.

The trouble was, he needed Danny alive. Dead, he'd never find out where the goods were, one of the main (though by no means, only) reasons for this whole goddamn exercise. True, he would like to see Kentucky re-emerging into the twenty-first century. Even better if he was at the helm to steer it back to prosperity. A guarantee his name would be remembered as an integral part of Kentucky's history. Though in his darker moments, he had to admit this could take years, probably far longer than his tenure as a Senator. That failure could be softened by having several (hundred) million dollars in the bank. Danny Trevino was the only one who could provide that cushion.

Two hours into the meeting, feigning the need to make an important call, he departed. He told his staff to produce a list of the most important action points, prioritized, with suggestions as to whom they should be delegated to. Having dispensed with such mundane matters, he left them to it.

He had to put a call into General Banks, and try to convince him that military force was the only way to take Louisville. He knew the General would be very wary of using US troops to fight US citizens. The trick would be to make it sound like a Military, rather than political, imperative. Something was needed to provoke the Army into a retaliatory move. Stopping mid-dial, he smiled to himself. He didn't need to convince the General of anything. He knew the perfect man to make sure the General made the decision himself.

Colonel Wayne Flowers was relaxing in a bar in downtown St. Louis when he took the call. He listened patiently. The longer he did, the more incredulous he became. He had to repeat the Senator's idea back to him to make sure he'd heard it correctly.

"Have you any idea how difficult, how dangerous this will be? Let alone what will happen to us if we're caught? Are you out of your mind? No fucking way Jose."

The Senator, expecting pushback to his idea, had lined up a few incentives to persuade the recalcitrant Colonel to see his way of thinking. He explained them in simple terms, "Colonel, I am not sure you're in a position to argue. With one call to the authorities I can have you arrested for murder, robbery and a litany of other crimes. Who are they going to believe, a Senator or a disgraced Army Veteran? I can even say you were the one who opened fire on me when I was on the boat. Your list of crimes is long, so let's not be too hasty in turning my proposition down. On the plus side, I'll pay you a $100,000 bonus if you pull it off. Think again for a moment...do we have a deal?"

Silently wishing the Senator would die and go rot in hell, the Colonel reluctantly agreed. He had little choice, though the prospect of another $100,000 made it more palatable. All he knew was, once this was over, he would be out of the country leaving the Senator to deal with any fallout.

Two days later, the Colonel and a duet of his more capable soldiers were a mile from Cape Girardeau, Missouri, still the operations center for the RRRF US Army forces. Most of them were in Kentucky, however, around a thousand were still billeted there on the fringes of the city's airport. Security was modest. No one had any reason to think the camp would be under threat. Colonel Flowers surveyed the sea of tents from the safety of the woods to the west, trying to plan an attack that would cause maximum destruction with minimal risk to himself and his two men.

As he scanned the area with his binoculars, he saw an opportunity. A large fuel tank, probably holding, he estimated, fifty thousand gallons of gasoline. He wished he had some kind of RPG to shoot straight at it from a safe distance. Unfortunately, the Senator's budget didn't run to such exotic weapons, so he'd have to improvise.

At 2:00 a.m. that night, he crept up to the base of the fuel tank. The other soldiers were following his instructions to complete their tasks. To ignite the tank he was going to use a small amount of explosives and a flare gun. The first to breach the fuel tank walls, the second to set alight the gasoline as it flooded out.

The sleeping soldiers were awoken minutes later, with a tent flattening explosion followed by a plume of fire and smoke spiraling two hundred feet into the Missouri night sky. Tragically, two soldiers were killed and another twenty injured. By daybreak, the fire was under control and the true extent of the damage could be assessed. It wasn't too extensive–three nearby buildings had windows blown out and roofs torn off. What astounded and infuriated the soldiers and officers was the graffiti sprayed on the hangers in bright red paint:

Fuck the RRRF!

No! To ReFederalization!

Fight for a free Kentucky!

The Colonel's soldiers had plastered plenty more insulting slogans around the Army base with similar expressions of anti-RRRF sentiments. They made for incendiary reading.

The camp Commander was immediately on the phone to General Banks.

"Sir, we have been attacked, two dead, twenty injured, so far. Based on the evidence, it seems elements of the anti-RRRF faction are responsible. I'll send you pictures. We've increased security and the police are on the lookout for the attackers. Though I have to assume they have escaped across the Mississippi and are miles from here by now. Do you want us to send out search parties across to the east side, sir?"

Controlling his rage, the General replied, "Negative Major to the pursuit, it could be a trap. Send me what evidence you have and I'll let you have my orders in due course. I expect a full report on my desk within twenty-four hours, understood, Major?"

Without waiting for a response the General cut the call and ordered his assistant to organize a conference call with all his senior officers, wherever they were, in an hour's time. If those agitators over in Kentucky wanted a fight, they were going to get one, right on their front doorstep.

That evening, a hundred miles away, Colonel Flowers stopped his beat up truck at the end of a long dusty track and walked warily into a dilapidated barn on an abandoned farm. He thought it was a strange way to collect the $100,000, the Senator normally liked to deliver it in person. This time, the he'd explained, it would be too dangerous to meet and one of his aides would drop off the money as soon as he saw on the news the mission had been successful.

The Colonel cautiously opened the barn door and saw a large bag hanging from one of the stalls. He waited for a few seconds, scanning the barn for signs of a trap. Feeling confident he was alone, he walked over to the bag and opened it to check the money was inside. His last puzzled thought was, "What the f...?"

The old barn did a good job muffling the explosion and it would be weeks before Colonel Wayne Flower's decapitated body was discovered.

Chapter 41

General Banks ordered three battalions, almost three thousand soldiers, to move towards Louisville with the objective of encircling the city within the next twenty-four hours. He also directed six fully armed Apache helicopters to be on standby. And finally, for ten M1 Abram tanks to head for Louisville via the bridge over the Mississippi at Wickliffe.

This wasn't so much an act of revenge, the General reasoned with himself, more a way of showing the likes of Danny Trevino that murdering his soldiers was unacceptable and would invoke a swift, painful response, "No good deed goes unpunished," he explained to his aide, "we go in there with the best of intentions, distribute millions of dollar's worth of aid, then they turn round and start killing us. Some thank you."

Within a few hours, Danny's contacts and the ham radio lookouts alerted him to the Army's maneuvers. He toured his defenses once he heard the incursion was likely to happen. His tank was now stationed on the Sherman Minton Bridge. Depending on your viewpoint, this was a clever, brave move to defend his Louisville at all costs, or an exercise in hubris and vanity. Danny didn't care; he was proud of his efforts to defend the city, *his* city.

Danny's conversation with the Reverend had been illuminating to say the least. He had to admire the man's *chutzpah*. The price he was demanding to deliver what could be a knockout blow to ReFederalization was huge. With luck, it would also end the career and demands of the Senator and his Fed friends. It was a tempting offer.

He could afford it, though five million dollars was still an eye watering amount. The question was: for this money could the Reverend deliver his end of the deal? A promise to mobilize thousands of his followers to fight the government, based on the belief it was 'God's choice' they should do so?

Never a religious man, Danny had a real problem believing anyone would follow God's word to their probable death. He found the entire premise barely credible. The reverend was an egotistical maniac...but, but, what if he could? In a day or two, his city could be under attack by the Army. His men would put up a good fight, no doubt. In reality, they could only hold out for a few days. Would the Reverend's followers heed his bidding or run for the hills when they saw tanks and Apache helicopters raining death and destruction down on them? Were they a force to be reckoned with or a figment of the Reverend's imagination and ego?

Alternatively, should he follow his gut, ignore the Reverend's questionable promises and accept the inevitable: he would lose any long-term siege of Louisville and in the process people (and probably himself) would die. Instead, why not use the time available to make plans to escape, taking as much of his fortune with him as possible? He had men, equipment, fuel and arms to fight his way to the Appalachians if necessary. Or even buy a plane and fly to South America. With enough money, the options were always there.

Later in his penthouse suite, brooding over his future, Olivia sat across from him with an expectant look on her face, "Danny, are you OK? What did that Reverend guy have to say? Was he any help? You seem distracted honey, can I do anything?"

Irritated by her endless questions, Danny snapped back at her, "Olivia, just shut the fuck up for a minute. I've a lot to think about. Gimme some peace and quiet will ya? Go make me a drink, that would be really helpful."

Stung by his response, Olivia stood up and stared down at him, eyes blazing, on the verge of tears, "Don't you talk to me like that Danny. I'm not your friggin' slave. Go get your own damn drink. I'll come back when you're in a better mood," with that, she grabbed her coat and flounced out of the apartment, the heavy front door crashing closed behind her with a force that shook the pictures on the wall.

Fuck it, that's all I need, thought Danny; her throwing a hissy fit at a time like this. Women could be so goddamned selfish. Putting her tantrum to the back of his mind, he continued to wrestle with the problems facing him. Then he realized, in an ironic way, Olivia's behavior probably reflected what most people in Louisville were thinking: great to have you around Danny, but when the going gets tough we ain't gonna put ourselves in harm's way to help you out. Sure, his precinct bosses and some of their men would fight; until they realized they'd be on the losing side, then they'd drop him like a hot coal. So why wait around for the ax to fall?

Of course, he could really throw the whole invasion into complete chaos by getting the Reverend's hordes to swamp the Army with their sheer numbers. It was a perfect smokescreen. Allowing him time to coordinate his escape along with a serious amount of the gold he had stashed away at various locations around the city.

He called up the precinct Captain closest to where the Reverend was camped in south Louisville, with a message to bring him to the apartment. Twenty minutes later the walkie-talkie squelched into life. A voice cut through the static, "Boss, bad news, the preacher has been shot. It looks pretty bad. Some guy in the crowd waited for him to go into his trailer, then tried to kill him."

"Is he alive? Can he talk?"

A worried voice replied, "He's conscious, just. A nurse was in the crowd and she's looking after him. Looks like he was shot in the chest. What do you want me to do with him Danny?"

"Take him to the nearest medical center and find the best doctor you can. Don't you dare let him die, do you hear me? Otherwise you'll be next. Call me when you're there. By the way, who shot him"

"Some guy who says he's part of the Kentucky People's Movement. He was still sitting in the trailer when we got there. He's down at Ping's at the moment."

"Good, keep him there."

Danny broke the connection and threw the handset across the room, his anger boiling over. He screamed at no one in particular, "Well, that is just fucking fantastic. Today just keeps getting better and better. Jesus fucking Christ gimme a break!" He took his temper out on some glasses, bottles and a table lamp, all of which went crashing against the apartment walls.

Still fuming at his misfortune, he stomped out of his apartment shouting at the guard to get his truck and drive him to wherever the damn preacher was being taken. Within twenty minutes, Danny was standing over a very pale and shocked Reverend, his pristine white suit now drenched in blood. A female doctor was cutting away the clothing around the wound, exposing a mass of pulverized flesh, blood still flowing copiously from it.

Skipping any sympathetic formalities, Danny demanded, "What's his chances Doc?"

The harried, overworked doctor, called Joanne, knew better than to make any promises to Danny, let alone a firm prognosis at this stage. Get it wrong and she could be the one on the hospital bed. So she vacillated on the safe side. "Difficult to say Mr. Trevino, I'll have to do a more thorough examination. He's lost a lot of blood and we are low on supplies for a transfusion. He'll need an operation to remove the bullets. I'll know more in an hour or so. Most immediate problem is to stop the bleeding. I'll, of course, do what I can with what we have available here. Now, if you'll excuse me, we need to get him into surgery. I'll get a message to you later with more news," with that, she barked instructions at the nurses and ignored Danny, who took the hint, and left the room.

Compared to most places in Kentucky, the hospital was well-equipped. For certain hours of the day, generators provided limited electricity for the air conditioning, lights and refrigeration allowing operations to take place. Danny's money and the city's location on the Ohio enabled them to smuggle in the basic drugs like painkillers and antibiotics, though not in the quantities needed. It was hardly a fully functioning hospital by western standards. Still, Danny was proud to see under the difficult circumstances of the past six years, it had provided an adequate service.

As he was leaving, the hospital's administrator accosted him, "Mr. Trevino! Do you have a minute, sir?" A tall African American man in his sixties came limping across the reception area, his walking stick clicking on the tile floor. He moved as quickly as he could to intercept Danny.

"Not really Casper, what do you want?" Danny could guess what he wanted: more of everything. It was always the same refrain from these hospital admins.

"Just a quick word Mr. Trevino, thank you." he reached Danny out of breath, struggling to talk. He regained his composure and asked between rasping coughs if the rumors about a battle for the city were true, and if they were, when might it happen? He continued, "I ask Mr. Trevino, because we would be ill-equipped to handle a large number of casualties. As you know we only have one functioning hospital in the city. We would be overwhelmed very quickly if such a scenario happened. Is there any way to get more medical supplies in case this occurs?" Casper looked at Danny, worry written across his face as he imagined scenes from a civil war field hospital happening right here in his facility.

"Casper, I know you're worried. I'll see what I can do. At this short notice, not a lot if I'm honest. I think your best plan is to prepare for the worst and hope for the best. Sorry, I have to go."

Danny didn't like the prognosis for the Reverend. All the gold in the world couldn't persuade a dead man to support you from the grave. He also had little time for the preacher to regain consciousness and (hopefully) tell his followers that Danny and the anti-RRRF movement were the God given choice to follow. Unless that happened soon, Danny's future didn't look too healthy, either.

He was slowly coming to terms with the fact that maybe his tenure as the leader of Louisville was ending. The reports from around northern Kentucky and across the Ohio in Indiana gave him every reason to believe a substantial force was ready to attack him. His source in the Senator's office had smuggled out news that the forces numbered over three thousand men, complete with armored brigades in support. Three, five, ten thousand men, whatever, the numbers were, they were overwhelming. That was some serious firepower Danny couldn't hope to defeat.

His gut told him this was all heading towards an uncomfortable end to his regime. Better quit while you're ahead and keep control of the situation, than leave it to the last minute and face some hasty, uncomfortable choices. Danny headed back to his apartment to plan his exit. He'd wait a few hours until he had news of the preacher's condition, then make a final decision.

Entering the apartment he noticed the mess of broken lamps and glasses had been cleaned up, meaning Olivia must be back. Time to mend some fences.

"Hi honey," Danny crooned, setting the scene for a groveling apology, "I'm back, sweetheart. I'm real sorry about what happened earlier. Been a shitty day. One problem after the next. Forgive me?"

Receiving no reply, he padded across to the bedroom, wondering if Olivia was asleep. He poked his head around the door. Olivia was far from asleep. She was lying naked on the bed. A smile spread across Danny's face as he walked into the bedroom, loosening his belt.

"Does this mean you forgive me, honey?"

Olivia, with a coquettish grin, simpered, "Depends on if you're going to be a good boy; a really good boy who can make me a happy girl."

Playing along, Danny climbed onto the bed, hastily discarding his pants, "OK sweetheart, I'll be delighted to make you happy, baby. Tell Danny what he needs to do? Where would you like me to start?"

Silently, she grabbed his head and pushed it down between her thighs. Olivia sighed, "That would be a great place to start making me happy, very happy, Danny darling."

For a glorious half an hour, Danny forgot his troubles. Olivia bringing on a severe case of what he liked to call 'sexual amnesia'.

Chapter 42

To everyone in Kentucky with a ham radio, news of the Army's move towards Louisville was a source of fascination. Landy was no exception. Every few hours he would tune in, scan the airwaves to pick up the latest developments. He relayed them to his father and Penny whenever they were around. Most of the village became absorbed with the news as Landy repeated what he heard to anyone who would listen. The trouble was: how much of it was accurate, or truthful? Even the Army's own broadcasts Roger knew from first hand could be economical with the truth if it suited their purposes.

Was Louisville the start or the end of the campaign? Did the RRRF believe that if they removed Danny Trevino and took over the city, the rest of Kentucky would fall into line? The convoys of aid no doubt had softened the resolve of a lot of anti-RRRF communities. What would they do about those who weren't welcoming them with open arms? Was there a chance of a guerrilla war between those communities and the Army?

Even within French Creek, opinion was mixed. Some were all for giving ReFederalization a chance, others wanted nothing to do with 'big government'. Could Kentucky again be in the position it was during the Civil War where families were divided between Union and Confederate beliefs—and ended up fighting each other? It was a dreadful prospect.

While talking this over with Penny, an outlandish idea came to Roger's mind. Could he act as a peace broker between the RRRF Army and Danny Trevino? He knew both sides, though his Army contact had been replaced, he still believed both sides would trust him to represent their views honestly. He outlined his idea to Penny, "If I can persuade Danny to let Louisville be taken peacefully, it might set a precedent for other cities and towns. Even allow for him to leave without being arrested or even shot? He might go for that. I mean, the Army has already shown the RRRF mission can be accomplished without bloodshed. Maybe I can get them to hold off doing anything heavy handed while we try and get the other anti RRRF parties to talk some more. It might mean at least all the supplies get distributed quickly to the people that need them?"

Penny was perplexed at Roger's apparent change of heart, "I thought you were against this whole 'Fed's invading us' process? Now you want to persuade Danny to give in gracefully? What about all the other people at that Louisville meeting? Going to convince them as well they should hand over the keys to their cities?"

Roger tried to explain his thinking further, "I've never been against the whole ReFederalization idea, just the way it might be implemented. There's a hundred holes in my idea, I agree. All I want to do is avoid a bloodbath in every major city in the state. ReFederalization with all its shortcomings, will never succeed by force. I think if I can persuade Danny to leave Louisville under some kind of pardon arrangement, it could set a peaceful precedent."

Penny looked skeptical, "Phew, you're shooting for the stars here, Rog. If you think you can do it, then you've got to give it a try. I think it's a real long shot. Though I admire you for even willing to risk your neck."

They discussed Roger's idea further, trying to refine his approach, anticipating the push back from the different parties. Ultimately he admitted a lot would be played by ear. Neither side might be prepared to see, or listen to him. He just felt compelled to try.

"Nothing ventured, nothing gained," was Roger's parting shot before he went to discuss it with the Village Council.

Their reactions were mixed: ranging from declaring it foolhardy and pointless, to worthy of serious consideration. Eventually, the council agreed that the final decision should be Roger's. He did it at his own risk.

Herb, ever forthright in his opinions, argued that Roger's desire to act as some kind of peacemaker was, "at its best, misguided, at worst just plain arrogant." Adding, "What makes you think these two sides even want some kind of settlement?"

Roger argued back, "Someone has to do something Herb, I happen to know people on both sides. Not many do. I can't just sit here and watch two giant egos lock horns while people die. If they don't listen to me, or I end up wasting my time, at least my conscience is clear, I tried."

Herb still believed it was a fruitless exercise. In the end, he accepted he wouldn't weaken Roger's resolve, "I think your sentiments are genuine, but I really doubt you have much chance of success. That said, I wish you well, come back safely. We need you here more than they need you in Louisville."

Now Roger had to get down to practicalities. Firstly, he had to get to RRRF HQ. A light bulb moment hit him: enter Jay and his ultralight.

Jay took a little persuading to participate in this risky venture.

Roger convinced him that, "It could be the difference between a peaceful transition to a resurgent Kentucky or one imploding into civil war." Possibly a little hyperbolic, but Roger's persistence that he had to try something to avoid bloodshed, finally convinced Jay to agree.

The RRRF HQ at Cape Girardeau was around three hundred miles from French Creek, or a four-hour flight. The extra supplies of gas they'd acquired at the last Barter Fair would be more than enough to get them there.

Penny still thought Roger was out of his mind. Scared he might be shot down, taken prisoner, or worse. She admired his desire to find a peaceful solution. However, in reality, what could one person do? Was Roger in a position to broker some kind of compromise? Would the Senator, Danny or the Army take him seriously? How open would they be to him playing peacemaker? Roger just kept repeating: he had to try.

Roger's game plan was thin on detail. He would get to Cape Girardeau, then use his Army rank and experience to, hopefully, deal with the service bureaucracy and bluff his way into a meeting with the General. He packed a minimum of supplies and discussed with Jay the best route and landing area, based on an old AAA map.

Two days later, the day dawned clear and warm, not a cloud in the sky. Without further delay, they were in the air soon after dawn. Roger said his goodbyes to Penny and Landy, assuring them he'd be OK. He'd try to keep in touch by radio if the opportunity arose.

The flight was uneventful. Jay took them up to five thousand feet, keeping them safe from anyone wanting to take a shot at them. In pre-Collapse times, regulations restricted such craft to twelve hundred feet, but nowadays no one was checking. After nearly four hours, they spotted Cape Girardeau's small regional airport. It seemed almost deserted. As they landed, the scorched buildings and burnt out gas holder were plain to see.

They taxied over to a hangar and parked alongside a few other small aircraft. Roger walked into the control tower office and brazenly asked for the RRRF's HQ.

The girl behind the counter showed little concern about Roger's request and told him it was in a local hotel, helpfully giving him directions. Then she added in a bored voice, "It would have been a bit different if you arrived last week. Place was crawling with soldiers until some guys from the east blew up the gas tank and killed some of them. They all cleared out pretty quick after that, going to Louisville, so I heard. Serves those easterners right if they get blown away."

Jay had to ask, "How do you know it was people from the east?"

The girl pointed to one building on the far side of the airfield, "They left their calling card, painted graffiti all over the place telling us what they thought of this plan to invade Kentucky. Go take a look, no one's cleaned it off yet."

"We will ma'am," replied Roger, "thank you for your help."

Jay said he'd wander over and see the damage. Roger went into the restroom and changed into his old Army uniform, then left for the hotel. It was about a mile away. He set off at a brisk walk, leaving Jay to get a coffee and something to eat at a nearby McDonald's. He'd sensibly brought some cash from his recent time in the west.

Twenty minutes later, Roger saw the hotel. There were armed guards at the parking lot entrance, and the hotel itself. He walked straight up to one guard announcing in a commanding voice, "Captain Roger Makefield, I've some vital information for your commanding officer. Could you tell me where I can find him? Thank you," Roger looked down at the guard's name tag, "Corporal Appleton."

The soldier frisked Roger, then with no further checks, pointed him to the hotel's main entrance. "Certainly sir, please make your way over there."

Roger's bluffing got him as far as the Sergeant at reception in the hotel, then it became a lot more difficult.

It took twenty minutes of phone calls to Army records, Major General Redditch's office to confirm Roger had been at the Stewart Island Meeting and some other checks, before the Sergeant and the Commander's aide agreed Roger could see General Samuel Banks. However, he would have to wait a few hours until he returned to HQ.

Roger grabbed a free coffee from the dispenser at reception and kicked his heels until late afternoon when a Humvee drove up and General Banks strode into the hotel. They had obviously warned him of Roger's attendance. He walked over, Roger sprang to attention and executed a perfect salute.

"General, thank you for seeing me at such short notice, sir."

"You're welcome, Captain. I've got twenty minutes to spare. What have you got that I should find of interest?"

"Is there somewhere a little more private, sir?"

The General, his aide, and Roger moved across to the far side of the deserted hotel reception area and sat down.

Roger explained where he came from in the east, his knowledge of Danny Trevino and his attendance at the infamous Louisville meeting. Adding his participation at the inconclusive get together on Stewart Island. He believed because of these connections, he was in a unique position to head off a full-blown war. The General listened, making no comment. Once Roger had finished talking, the General quickly zeroed in on his connection to Danny Trevino.

"Now tell me more about this Trevino guy, and what he's got waiting for us in Louisville. Will he put up a fight, or run for it? How many men does he have at his disposal? Finally, why do you think he'll listen to you?"

Roger knew better than to bullshit a General, he decided honesty was the best policy, "Sir, I can't offer any guarantees, of course. But he's not stupid. He knows the forces lining up against him are way more than he can handle. He's looking for a way out I'd bet. One that doesn't look like he's had his ass whupped. An option that will allow him to stay safely, or leave with his entourage and money–of which I gather he has a lot–I think would appeal to him. I believe the other priority has to be the safety of Louisville's population. To be honest, what have you got to lose, General? If I go over there and achieve nothing, well, you and the Senator can tell the world you tried the peaceful route; then send your boys in with a clear conscience. If Danny takes the get out of Dodge option, you get what you want and no one gets hurt. He knows me, and I think he trusts me."

For a further fifteen minutes, Roger argued his case with the General who raised several objections and asked some pointed questions. In the end, the General knew a 'nothing to lose' strategy when he heard one. He leant back in the chair, relaxing for a moment while he considered his decision.

"OK Captain, you have a deal. Bear in mind that that son of a bitch killed some of my men here the other day. I won't lose any sleep if we have to take him out. So I'll give you forty-eight hours to convince this

Trevino guy to see sense. I don't care what option he takes as long as it doesn't involve shooting at us. If I don't hear from you one way or the other by then, you can tell him my version of 'shock and awe' will quickly make his life unbearable. I'll get you to the outskirts of Louisville by chopper and give you a satellite phone to keep in contact. I'll tell the Senator what's happening."

"No need for the chopper sir, I have my own transport."

The General looked surprised, "Your own transport?"

"Believe it or not, one of our people in the village has an ultralight. We used that to get here. Landed at the local airport. Though if you could supply some gas, and that phone, that would be useful, sir."

"An ultralight? Very enterprising. As you wish, Captain, use your own transport, rather you than me!"

The General stood up, bringing the meeting to an end. He instructed his aide to take Roger to the stores, then give him a lift back to the airport. Wishing him success, he walked off, hoping to God this wannabee Henry Kissinger from Podunk county could pull off his crazy idea. He doubted he would. In two days he'd know whether to give the guy a medal or order the invasion of Louisville.

The General went to his office, sat down at his makeshift desk and put a call into Senator Kingston. To cover his back, he'd give him some details on the plan he'd just hatched with the Captain. The Senator's reaction took him aback.

"General, as I've said before, it is imperative we capture Danny Trevino alive. I, we, the Government, believe he has extremely useful information we need to extract from him. Do not let him escape or allow him to leave. Most of all, don't kill him. If this Captain can help achieve that, so much the better."

The General controlled his temper at the Senator's imperious demands. "Shall I take him a case of scotch while we make him comfortable in his penthouse? Heaven forbid we make life difficult for him. This guy is a murderer, Senator. Would you care to give me an idea why this information he has is so important?"

"Sorry General, that's classified. Suffice to say I, the Government, need him alive and well. Is that understood?" The Senator had to sidestep any appearance it was a personal reason he wanted to meet Danny face to face. Throwing in the word 'Government' inflated the importance of the request, the Senator believed. Though he wasn't sure it worked too well with a grizzled veteran Army General.

"OK Senator, I'll do my best to bring this Kentucky terrorist back to you alive and well. After you've finished with him, hand him back to me, I'd love to see him fry for what he's done."

The Senator was quick to agree, "Quite General, my sentiments entirely. Sending men over here to kill our brave soldiers has to be punished. I'll leave it with you to bring him to justice in the end." Satisfied he had moved the discussion onto common ground, he then enquired about the progress of the mission so far.

"The troops will all be in position around Louisville within twenty-four hours, together with armored and air support. So far, we've had no push back from the rest of the population. In the main, they seem pleased to see us. While I don't hold out much hope for this Captain's peace brokering effort, if he does succeed, it will save a lot of lives and keep the local inhabitants on our side. If we shoot our way into Louisville, we'll lose a lot of local support. And the more the body count increases, the the greater the likelihood they'll turn against us."

The Senator concurred with the General's assessment, "Let's hope this Captain can produce the goods. Once you've taken Louisville, I believe the rest of the state will welcome us with open arms and ReFederalization can start in earnest. You establish the peace and we'll maintain it, General."

Sensing a speech in the making, the General brought the conversation to a close. He had better ways to spend his time than listening to this bombastic politician, "OK Senator, I'll keep you updated on our progress. Good talking to you."

He pressed the disconnect button on his phone and ordered a meeting with his senior staff to run through the final arrangements for the taking of Louisville, unless one Captain Makefield could pull a rabbit out of his hat. And the General was not a big believer in magic.

Chapter 43

Jay and Roger, restocked and refueled, took off late afternoon with an estimated flying time to Louisville of around three hours. They had asked the General's aide to inform any forces northeast of the city to be aware they intended to land near River Bluff.

With the help of some prevailing winds, they arrived into River Bluff as it was getting dark. Jay expertly landed on a minor road near the Louisville Yacht Club. They hunkered down for the night in an abandoned school, ate their tasteless MREs and tried to sleep. By sunrise, Roger was up and ready to walk into the city. He would first have to convince some of Danny's overeager, nervous guards that he had a genuine reason for meeting him.

He didn't have to walk very far before a patrol pulled up beside him, demanding to know what he was doing. Roger explained who he was, that Danny knew him and that he had important information for him. He suggested that a quick call to Danny would confirm his personal connection with the man's boss. After a few minutes of walkie-talkie conversations working their way up the short chain of command, someone decided to wake Danny up.

A grumpy, sleepy voice came crackling through the static, "What? This had better be important."

"Hi Danny, it's Roger, Roger Makefield, we met at the Louisville meeting. I went to Stewart Island?"

Suddenly alert, Danny's voice took on a sense of urgency, "Hey Roger, good to hear from you. Why are you calling? Where are you? What's happened?"

"I'm right here in Louisville Danny, I'd like to meet and have a talk. I've got some information about the RRRF I know you'll want to hear."

Danny sounded doubtful, "You working for them now, Roger?"

"No Danny, I'm not working for anyone. I'm just trying to see if there's a way we can avoid a god-awful shit show descending on Louisville, and you. I'm trying to save lives here Danny. I only need a few minutes of your time. If you think I'm blowing smoke up your ass, then I'll just leave. No harm, no foul."

Fifteen minutes later, Roger was in Danny's apartment. While Olivia made coffee and breakfast, the two men sat down and got straight to business. Danny was still wary of Roger's motives.

"You're a long way from home buddy, what's the big deal that brought you to the middle of a likely war zone? Before you answer that, how'd you get here anyway?"

Roger briefly explained about Jay and the ultralight, then moved on to the main purpose of the meeting. Danny's interest was clearly piqued by the ultralight, but said nothing.

"Danny, I understand if you're skeptical, but hear me out. I'm trying to avoid Louisville turning into your own personal war zone. I've been to see the General leading the Army that's camped outside your city, or soon will be. He's given me forty-eight hours to try and persuade you to hand over the city peacefully and negotiate a way for you to exit without being killed. You must realize you are backed into a corner here Danny, unless you're on some kind of kamikaze mission?"

Danny listened to Roger, his attitude suspicious. He was still unsure just what clout Roger had in all of this, or was he just some time-wasting do-gooder? At the back of his mind, he was wondering whether the preacher still had a role to play in all of this. He clung to the hope that the support of the preacher's thousands of followers could still stall the Army. In truth, he wasn't convinced—he'd not heard back from the hospital, so that trump card he couldn't bring into play yet. In the meantime, no harm in hearing what the peacemaker sitting in front of him had to offer.

He waited while Olivia served them both coffee, then sat back in his oversized armchair and invited Roger to continue, "OK what's on offer? I'm all ears. It better be good," he said, a note of doubt in his voice.

For the next hour, the men discussed the options. Needless to say, Danny was as much concerned with his own welfare as everyone else's. Sure, he didn't want to see a wholesale slaughter of the city's inhabitants—or his own personal Army. Nonetheless, always churning in the back of his mind was how he could safely exit Louisville, even the country, with as much of his fortune intact.

Unfortunately, most of his fortune was in gold and silver bullion—not easily transportable. He kept these thoughts from Roger as their negotiations went round in circles.

Finally, sensing he was getting nowhere, Roger held up his hands in frustration, "Danny, you need to come clean with me, just what do you really want from all of this? I keep making suggestions and you keep shooting them down. So, tell me, what's your agenda here? Give me your wish list. Otherwise I'll stop wasting everyone's time and go home. Leave you to whatever fate is coming your way. Which, by the way, doesn't look too healthy after your people went over at Cape Girardeau and killed some soldiers."

Danny reacted angrily to Roger's comment, "I didn't kill any soldiers, anywhere. Who told you that?"

"General Sanders to start with, he firmly believes it was you. The graffiti your guys left behind all over the airport makes it pretty clear who was behind it."

With a hint of desperation, Danny replied, "I swear to you Roger, none of my guys did that. I didn't order any such attack. I'd be stupid wouldn't I? It would bring the whole Army down on me like a shitload of bricks," he paused, "I think I've been set up somehow, by people who want to get the Army beating the shit out of me. Someone's trying to hang a murder rap on me." He stood up and started pacing around the room, trying to make sense of this upsetting news. Sure he'd pissed off a lot of people, but who'd go to this extreme…suddenly the answer came to him.

"It's that motherfucker of a Senator, I know it. I know he's behind this, bet my mother's life on it," Danny railed to Roger, "he and I have a bit of a history. I won't bore you with the details. I know he's the one behind the attacks on the other city leaders who came to the Louisville meeting. This has his play-dirty M.O. all over it. Get the Army all riled up over something they think I did, then they come in here all guns blazing. Take the city, then arrest me. That asshole! More I think about it, the more I'm convinced he was behind the attack on those soldiers—just so he could put the blame on me. No way I can prove it though."

Roger looked disbelievingly at Danny, "Sorry, let me get this straight. You are suggesting that Senator Kingston deliberately arranged for some soldiers to be killed so the Army would attack you in revenge? Danny, that's a stretch for me. I know these politicians are corrupt, but that's an accusation too far to be honest."

"Is it though?" countered Danny, "he wants to take over Kentucky in a blaze of glory. Get back on his own little gravy train, skimming money off all the RRRF funds coming into Kentucky and this ReFederalization crap. When he was Senator here before the Collapse, he had his sticky fingers in so many pies he was creaming off money by the millions. I know, he demanded a slice of my action in return for keeping the cops off my back. Everyone was in his pocket. I'm guessing this Collapse has been bad for business, now he sees a way back in. This whole RRRF thing is just the start. It's all beginning to make sense to me now."

"It might be making sense to you Danny, but I'm finding all this a little hard to swallow, sorry. I agree the guy is a grade A asshole, but you're making him out to be a real evil murderous piece of work."

"Trust me Roger, he is," Danny answered simply, "that's a great way to describe him…an evil piece of work. Who for reasons I can't tell you, wants me where he can beat the shit out of me until I hand over something he believes is his."

"What's this information he wants from you that's worth all the time, cost and who knows how many lives?" Roger demanded.

Danny turned and smiled, "As they say, Roger, if I told you that, I'd have to kill you."

It was clear to Roger he was not going to persuade Danny to do a deal that would end up with him facing a trial. Danny would have an impossible job convincing anyone in law enforcement he had nothing to do with killing the soldiers; let alone putting the blame on Senator Kingston: who would people believe, a drug dealer turned godfather, or a Senator?

Ironically, if the Senator was behind the scheme to kill the soldiers and turn Danny into a wanted criminal, it backfired badly. He would now accept no deal from the Feds and likely make a run for it. Whatever the Senator wanted from Danny was now a non-starter. Anyway, thought Roger, that's their problem, not his. He'd tried to avoid a confrontation, but developments outside his control had scuppered that.

Deciding he could accomplish little by staying any longer, he told Danny he was leaving, "Danny, I'm sorry, I don't think there's any more I can do here. I understand your position not wanting to end up in jail. I can't change what's not in my control. I'll leave you to decide what to do next. I wish you well. All I ask is you do everything you can to avoid any bloodshed. You and your people must realize the Army can crush you with the forces they have sitting outside the city. Please try to figure out a way to end this whole thing without violence. That's all I ask."

"I hear you Roger. But I didn't get to run this city without making tough choices and spilling some blood. It's not in my nature to cut and run."

"I know Danny, but a good general knows when to fight and when to accept the inevitable. Choose your battles. I'm guessing you have enough resources to live comfortably anywhere in the world. Live long enough to enjoy what you have. Every empire in history has to come to an end sometime. Maybe this is your Waterloo. Quit while you're ahead."

Danny looked at Roger, thoughtfully digesting his advice, "Maybe, maybe not. I'll sleep on it."

"Just make sure you hear the alarm clock!" said Roger jokingly. They shook hands, said their goodbyes. Danny organized Roger's ride back to Jay and the ultralight.

After Roger's departure, Danny sat down with a large scotch to mull on his words deciding what to do next. Based on Roger's timeline he had less than two days before the Army started to move on Louisville.

He weighed up his options–Roger was right, he didn't stand a snowball's chance in hell of defeating the Army. He could hold out for a few days no doubt, in the end though, it would be an ignominious defeat. Then he'd be forced to run for the hills with a posse of Feds after him.

Danny didn't know the precise value of the gold bars he had stolen from the Fort Knox convoy. Six years ago, gold was worth around $1,000 an ounce. Each bar weighs four hundred ounces, so, equal to probably half a million dollars now. He had roughly four bars left from his haul. So, $200 million and change: weighing in at four tons–a lot to transport surreptitiously. Plus other gems and valuables he had retrieved from safe deposit boxes in the city's banks.

Next question: where to escape? Now he had (an undeserved) murder warrant on his head, staying in the country could be risky. Areas of the east would be a safe haven for a few years, but if the ReFederalization plan eventually rolled out there would be no place to hide. Plus, he knew some of the other kingpins around the country would turn him in for a handsome reward, or just steal his gold and kill him.

Finally, what to do about the Senator? He was after him big time, wanting to crush him, while at the same time, no doubt desperate to extract information from him. To add insult to injury, he had fabricated the murder charge, provoking the interest of law enforcement. The guy was making life very difficult for him. What if he could meet the Senator face to face? Negotiate some deal, bribe him? Hey, even take him out as a last resort? How could that be arranged?

Of course…there was a way! Danny leapt up, grabbed the walkie-talkie and spoke to the guard who'd taken Roger back to the ultralight. Had they taken off yet, he asked? The answer came back, "No, he and his pilot decided to stay the night at the school and leave first thing in the morning, why?"

Danny was relieved, "That's good news! Go back there immediately, with reinforcements, and a trailer, and bring the ultralight and the two men back into the city to see me. ASAP."

To say Roger and Jay were pissed at being put under guard and prevented from leaving Louisville, was putting it mildly. When they heard what Danny had in mind for them, they were scared witless.

Chapter 44

The Reverend Josiah Wedgwood was in pain, a lot of pain. Coming round from a lengthy operation to remove two bullets from his shoulder and chest, he groaned out loud in agony as he reached for a glass of water. A nearby nurse came and helped, offered some comforting words, but nothing to ease his agony. They were out of any powerful painkillers; she offered her apologies.

As instructed by Danny, once Joanne, the surgeon, heard the Reverend was conscious, she contacted him with the news.

Amazing how quickly things can change, thought Danny. A few hours ago, he was seduced by the Reverend's promises that he could persuade his flock to rally behind him in exchange for a large amount of gold. Now, the prospect of an all-out conflict with the RRRF seemed pointless. He had a new game plan, and it no longer included the Reverend. Crucially, he didn't want him rushing off to the RRRF offering his services to them either. Suddenly the Reverend was a loose cannon, therefore expendable.

He contacted the ever faithful Ping and told him what to do– immediately.

Semi-conscious, they manhandled the Reverend out of the hospital, despite the protests of the nurses and doctors. His final resting place was to be with Ping's favorite carnivorous pig, Hopkins. Ping showed some final mercy, putting a bullet in the back of his head before Hopkins came for his evening meal. Within a few hours, there was nothing left of the Reverend Josiah Wedgwood.

Paul H Rowney

Chapter 45

The Senator had forgotten the name of the intern currently getting dressed in his hotel room, after a hasty, but amazing, sexual interlude between a never-ending series of RRRF meetings. He certainly wouldn't forget her gymnastic abilities. Where did they learn such tricks at such an early age, he mused? She sashayed out of the room, saying nothing, only throwing him an air kiss as she left.

Recovering from his horizontal workout, he dragged his mind back to the imminent capture of Louisville. All was going well, except he hadn't heard from the General about the peace-making efforts of some Captain Whats-his-name. He didn't really care which way the negotiations went, as long as they took the city and caught that irksome man, Trevino, alive. He had a lot to answer for—and a lot to give back after six years of waiting. Trevino owed him big time.

A plane took the Senator to Cape Girardeau that evening. He wanted to be close to Louisville when the final *denouement* happened. He decided that as Louisville proved to be the final bastion of anti-RRRF sentiment, it should now be there that he would make his grand entrance. That he'd announce the 'beginning of the end' of Kentucky's isolation from the west and a welcome back to the twenty-first century. He felt sure there were some other Churchillian *bon mots* he could regurgitate to make him sound suitably statesman-like—he'd get his speechwriter onto it at once.

The Senator was going to savor the moment. It had been a long time coming. He could see the congratulatory headlines in the press, the anticipated phone call from the President and the cheers of relief and gratitude from the citizens of Kentucky. This would not be his fifteen minutes of fame. It was his claim to a place in American history. *It would be his finest hour!*

The Senator wasn't a churchgoing man, so he may not have known the phrase: *"Pride comes before a fall,"* or how true it would become.

Chapter 46

Developments over the next few hours came thick and fast.

- News of the Reverend Josiah Wedgwood's 'failure to survive extensive surgery following his shooting in Louisville' left his followers and adherents shocked, then confused. Suddenly leaderless, they disbanded and made their way back home, dejected and unsure what the future held for them without their charismatic leader.

- Danny, with the help of a few trusted (and extremely well-rewarded) guards, loaded his gold and valuables into a Humvee. They also prepared four other identical vehicles, all for a long journey.

- The Kentucky People's Movement never saw Jodie McFadden again. Caught by Danny's guards at the scene immediately after his attempted murder of the Reverend, he was detained. Danny told them to deal with him quickly. They handed Jodie over to Ping and the ever-hungry Hopkins.

- The final element of the RRRF's plans for taking Louisville fell into place with the arrival of the armored division fifteen miles from the city center.

- Showing a total disregard for his security, the Senator arrived in a blaze of publicity at Cape Girardeau, ready for his moment of glory in Louisville.

Chapter 47

"Sorry guys, but before I disappear, there's one job I need to tidy up—and only you can help me," Danny was addressing Roger and Jay, now back in his apartment after unceremoniously being forced at gunpoint to the meeting.

"And just why should we do that?" demanded Jay. He objected to being bossed around by some little wannabe Mafia mob leader and was making his displeasure very clear.

"Because Jay, I have no choice in what I'm about to do, and...," Danny waved his arm around the room at the six guards pointing guns at them, "...you have no choice but to help me." He continued in his most reasonable voice, "I just need you and your flying machine to take me on a little trip, then back again. Roger will remain here as my guest. It shouldn't take more than a day, tops. Plus, to show my gratitude, I'll give you $500,000."

"I'm not a fucking flying Uber service. Who do you think you are, holding us prisoners like this?"

"Jay, just calm down. I'm asking you a small favor in exchange for half a million dollars. Think about it. How else will you ever get your hands on that kinda money?"

Jay was thinking about it, very hard, "Can Roger and I have a private word?"

"Sure, but make it quick, I don't have a lot of time."

Roger and Jay moved over to the windows, as far away as possible from Danny and the guards.

"What's he playing at, do you think Roger?"

"I don't know Jay. If I had to guess, he wants to make a hit on someone or something, and then get back here as quickly as possible. Obviously too far, or dangerous, to do it by road. In truth, Jay, it's your decision. I'm the spectator here–it's your ultralight and pilot skills he needs. Unless you want to feel some pain, or worse, not sure we have much choice here."

"And the half a million dollars?"

Roger was philosophical, "It's worth diddly squat at the moment, but in the future, who knows? He sounds desperate. Ultimately, it's your call."

From the other side of the room Danny shouted, "OK, mother's meeting is over. Let's get on with it before things turn nasty. Are we going to do this the easy way or the hard way?"

Jay looked at Roger one more time, who shrugged noncommittally.

"Alright, alright I'll do it," agreed Jay, "for a million dollars."

Danny looked stunned for a moment, then burst out laughing, "You ballsy son of a bitch! You're surrounded by armed guards, my prisoner, and now negotiating for more money? I love it. I should have you dumped in the Ohio River with a couple of concrete blocks for company…."

"And then you'd never get off the ground," Jay interrupted. Pressing his advantage, "so pay up and I'll fly you to wherever you want to go. Give Roger a truck loaded with the money so we can be on our way when we get back…that or it's no deal."

Danny had few options, and they all knew it, "Alright, you got it. You won't need a truck, I'm not giving you cash, just a couple of gold bars worth, I'm guessing around a million. Put them in your backpack! Good enough? Do we have a deal?"

Thinking they would get holdalls full of cash, both Roger and Jay were so dumbfounded at the idea that two gold bars could be worth this amount of money, they could only nod their heads in agreement.

Roger then asked the inevitable question, "Right, now we have a deal, where is Jay taking you?"

"Can't see there's any harm in telling you as you can't do much sitting here. We're taking a little trip to Cape Girardeau. To see an old friend of mine."

Roger took a moment to digest what Danny was proposing, "That's RRRF HQ. You want to talk to the General in charge? General Sanders? You're mad, they'll slap you in jail. Are you serious?"

"As an AK-47," replied Danny coolly, "but it's not the General I want to see, I want to talk to the main man himself, Senator Kingston. I need to, shall we say, straighten a few things out."

Chapter 48

Danny hadn't been so scared since he'd first ridden an unbroken horse at the age of six. A thousand feet up in a flimsy contraption held together with duct tape and hope was his idea of hell on earth–if he made it down in one piece. He was strapped in the seat behind Jay, trying to keep his breakfast under control, as the ultralight bumped its way through the thermals, headed west. How did this thing stay in the air, he wondered not daring to look down. He closed his eyes and, for the first time in years, prayed. The three-hour flight would get them to Cape Girardeau airport late in the morning, in the meantime Danny hung on for dear life.

For a disguise, Danny found an Army Major's uniform stolen from a local base when they were scavenging after the Collapse. It didn't fit too well due to his diminutive size, but would probably get him past the inattentive guards. After that, Danny reckoned he had to wing it to get a one-on-one with the Senator.

The same bored girl at the Cape Girardeau airport was there to ignore their arrival. As Jay attempted to start a conversation with her for the second time, Danny marched off to the RRRF's hotel. He arrived at the guard post feigning a broken down truck, making him walk to HQ. He demanded to deliver his urgent message in person to General Sanders. He also casually enquired if the Senator had arrived? The guards confirmed he was at the hotel, letting him pass with a lazy salute. He headed for reception, then, instead of going inside, veered around the side of the hotel to check out the rear of the building. Not surprisingly, all the doors were locked. By one of the dumpsters a man was washing a silver Mercedes 500SL. Danny confidently strode over and introduced himself as Major Devito.

"Just getting a breath of fresh air, gets stuffy in there. Beautiful day I must say," Danny chatted amiably to the man who'd stopped wiping down the car and stood back to admire its gleaming finish.

He laughed in reply, "Probably rain now I've washed the car! Not that the Senator will mind. He's always too busy to take notice of anything except what's on his phone."

Danny agreed, "Isn't that typical? Probably shouldn't say this, but these politicians just don't seem to be connected to the real world, do they? So you are...?"

"I'm Manny, the Senator's temporary chauffeur. The other guy's ill. Shouldn't complain, it's not a bad gig. Do nothing most of the time. Drive him to and from the airport, clean the car, then sit around waiting for something to happen."

Danny felt the germ of an idea forming. He probed further, "Not too bad a way to pass the day I guess. Tell me, do you know when the Senator's going out next? I may need to arrange security for him. I'm normally the last to know!"

Manny nodded in sympathy, "You and me both, Major. I've been told he may need me around lunchtime, in a couple of hours. He doesn't usually bother with much security, occasionally just takes one of the guards at the front gate with him."

"Thanks for that info. You've been most helpful Manny. I may see you around later. Good job on cleaning the car, looks great."

Manny beamed with satisfaction at the compliment and wished Danny well, "Been a pleasure talking to you, Major."

Danny now had two hours to kill until the Senator ordered his car. And surprise! The chauffeur wouldn't be Manny. He hid behind a stand of trees that separated the hotel's manicured lawn from another next door. Nearly three hours later, Danny saw someone come out of the rear of the hotel, walk across to Manny and start a conversation.

Quickly, he ran to the side of the hotel, then walked around to where the two men were still talking. The man was finishing the conversation confirming that Manny should be at the front of the hotel in ten minutes to collect the Senator. He walked back to the hotel without acknowledging Danny.

Danny said in his most welcoming voice, "Hello again, Manny. Still here?"

"Not for long, Major, just got my marching orders, as it were. The Senator needs a lift in ten... what the fuck?" the color drained from his face as Danny shoved a gun in his stomach.

"Now Manny, here's what we're going to do. I'm going to tie you up and leave you in one of those dumpsters. You'll stay there for one hour before you do anything or even shout for help. If you try to escape or attract anyone's attention, I have people watching the hotel who'll kill you. Understand me?"

In a quivering voice, Manny whimpered agreement to Danny's demands, "Sure, sure, anything you say, don't kill me, please. I won't do anything, I promise."

"I'm sure you won't, Manny. Just do as I say and you'll live, I guarantee it. Now move."

Within five minutes, Manny was hog-tied and wallowing in a dumpster full of rotting trash. Danny drove the Mercedes around to the front of the hotel. Barely had he stopped when none other than Senator Charles Kingston emerged, along with some young blonde girl Danny assumed was his assistant. This was an added complication, but one he could handle.

The Senator slid into the back seat, the girl followed. Without looking up, the Senator barked, "Take me to the airport via ABC, I need to get some drinks."

"Yes, Senator," Danny replied in an even voice. He found it difficult to control the adrenaline firing up his nervous system. Finally, after six years he was face-to-face with the person who had been hounding and threatening him. Who had made his life a misery, sending armed people to capture or kill him. Payback would be so sweet. Finally, he'd get this asshole out of his life. Danny slipped the car into gear and drove towards the guards, who, without question raised the barrier, letting them through. He looked in the rear-view mirror–the Senator had one hand on the girl's knee, the other on his phone. Danny was invisible to him.

Taking advantage of the Senator's preoccupation with matters other than where they were heading, Danny drove up onto I-55 towards the airport. He quickly diverted at the next exit heading east on a narrow country road towards the Mississippi. On either side were fields and woods. No word from the back seat about their change of direction. Danny was looking for a way into the woods where he would have his long delayed conversation with the Senator.

As the car slowed down, the girl looked up, exclaiming, "What's going on? Where are we? This isn't on the way to the airport, is it?"

Just a few more seconds was all Danny needed to drive up the dirt track and stop before his passengers realized not all was going to plan. He came up with a weak excuse but one that would buy him a little time, "Call of nature ma'am, sorry, only be a few seconds."

With that, Danny drove up a track into the woods, stopped the car and ran around to the Senator's door, pulling his gun as he did so. He yanked it open.

The Senator's jaw dropped when he saw the gun pointed at his head, "What is the meaning of this? Who the hell are you? What do you want? I insist you take me to the airport at once. The police will be looking for me if I'm not on the plane in a few minutes."

The girl was clinging to the Senator's arm like a limpet, already crying, whining she hadn't done anything and to please let her go.

"Lady, just shut the fuck up and I'll try not to kill you. The Senator and I have some unfinished business. Keep quiet, stay in the car and you'll be safe," Danny turned his attention back to the Senator, pressing the gun to his forehead.

"Both of you give me your cellphones." They reluctantly handed them over and Danny smashed them against the car roof, "Now you asshole, out of the car, get walking. Please don't try anything heroic, it'll only mean I have to kill you now before we have our little chat, not afterwards."

The Senator eased himself warily out of the car. He stood up towering over Danny, trying to assert his authority, again demanding to know what this ridiculous situation was about.

"Glad you asked that, Senator. You don't remember me, do you?" When the Senator shook his head, Danny helped him out, "I'm Danny Trevino, we did some business together before the Collapse. I'm the one you've been sending hit men to kill. Ringing any bells now, asshole?"

The Senator stared down at Danny, realization gradually dawning on him, "Oh yes, I remember you, Mr. Trevino. I haven't forgotten your duplicitous, thieving behavior. What I had forgotten is what a little weasel you are. The sunglasses, beard and uniform fooled me for a second. They do nothing for you, by the way."

Without saying a word, Danny raised the gun and pistol whipped the Senator's face. Blood poured from a deep gash on his cheek. He slumped to the ground, clutching the wound, crying out in pain and anger.

"You little piece of shit, I'll make you pay for…."

Danny finished his sentence with a kick to the Senator's gut, sending him rolling onto the ground.

The girl jumped out of the car and ran towards the Senator, screaming, "Stop it, stop it, you'll kill him!"

Danny replied calmly, "That I fully intend to do. In the meantime, get back into the fucking car NOW, otherwise I'll shoot you too."

The girl stopped, hesitated, then walked backwards to the car, never taking her eyes off the groaning Senator lying on the ground. She crawled into the back seat, glaring at Danny.

"Good girl, now stay there." He looked down at the Senator, who was trying to get to his feet. Danny walked over and casually brought the gun down again with a vicious swipe to the back of his head. The Senator crumpled to his knees, "Now I have your attention, Senator, you just listen to me. This is what happens when you start threatening me, trying to kill me, then framing me for the murder of two soldiers. I kill people all the time Senator, as you'll find out. However, I get really pissed when I'm accused of something I didn't do–and it brings a whole fucking Army to my front door."

The Senator looked up at Danny, blood running down his face, turning his white shirt a sickly red. He gathered his breath, determined to have his say too, "Danny, you're a scheming low- life drug dealer who struck it big when we made a deal to share the truck loads of gold from Fort Knox. But you stiffed me. I was due half, and all I got were two lousy bars. A measly million bucks. You owe me, that's why I've been after you."

"You have a selective memory Senator, it was you who broke our deal. It was quite simple, let me remind you. You provided the information on the Fort Knox convoy's timing, route and number of guards. In return, me and my men would hijack two trucks, one for you, one for me. The plan fell apart because you gave me crap intel about the number of armed men that would be in the convoy. It was crawling with them. I lost a lot of good men getting that gold. In the end, we only got one truck. So I left you some of the haul where we agreed. Not as much as you expected, but I reckon a fair reward for what you did or didn't do."

The Senator, ever the politician, fired back, "How the fuck was I supposed to know they upped the number of guards at the last minute? Still, you owe me half of that load–but I'll take fifty bars now, say $25 million, and we can call it quits. I'll go away and you'll never hear from me again."

"Wait a minute here Senator, are you telling me this whole RRRF and ReFederalization crap is just a front for you to get this gold? You cannot be serious? Are you that desperate that you'd risk millions of government dollars, maybe thousands of lives, *for some shitty gold bars*? I always thought you had a warped sense of right and wrong, but this is just fucking unbelievable."

The Senator looked up, and despite only having one open eye, gave him a withering stare, "No, I'm not that stupid or arrogant. The whole RRRF plan is pure politics. There's an election next year. The President needs to be seen doing something about the east. It would pull in a lot of voters who have relatives over there to see them getting help. I'm getting grief from my donors who still have assets over there they want back, and a slice of the billions that will pour across the Mississippi if we can make it work in Kentucky. Me, I'd get my state back. If I don't, then at the next election I'll be out. I can't remain a Senator for a state that, in effect, doesn't exist as far as Sacramento is concerned."

Danny shook his head in despair as the Senator finished his explanation, "So it's all about you, not the people of Kentucky at all, really? You'll sacrifice people, money and countless resources so you don't get kicked off your gravy train? You are one selfish prick, you know that?"

The Senator wasn't in a position, or the mood, to argue, "Call me what you like. Piss all over my motives. Just remember one thing–whatever you do to me, there's still an Army camped on your doorstep and one severely pissed off General who thinks you killed two of his soldiers…."

"Glad you brought that up," Danny interjected, "guess you were behind that scam to try to frame me?"

With a half-smile, the Senator answered, "Needs must Danny, needs must. And it worked like a charm. Hell, you were never going to live long after we took Kentucky anyway. What's another murder rap to add to your long list? To hell with you, I'm finished explaining myself. I need to get my share of that gold, otherwise…."

Danny cut in, tired of the Senator's warped reasoning, "Otherwise what, Senator? From where I stand, you haven't got much to bargain with. I can shoot you now and be back in Louisville before the cops get their shit together. Once I'm back there, they'll have no chance of finding me."

The Senator hadn't given up yet, "You seem to forget Louisville is surrounded by the Army. Which can annihilate you and your thugs in a matter of hours. Your gold is not worth a lot then is it Danny?"

Much as he wanted to ignore the Senator's threats, Danny knew he had a point, nevertheless he wasn't about to roll over quite yet, "Guess it's all a bit of a stalemate then, isn't it, Senator?" Danny was interested to see if the Senator would offer up some kind of compromise, start negotiating.

Ever the politician, he was quick to grasp at the 'get out of jail free' card. Danny was offering. He played his now: suddenly Mr. Reasonable, the Senator came back with his idea of a solution, "Give me my half and I can get the Army and RRRF off your back with a single phone call. Really, Danny, I can make this all go away."

Danny kept his best poker face, thinking that wasn't a bad first offer. Though he thought it was improbable he could really do that. "Keep talking Senator, I'm listening. I have my doubts you can make all this disappear. You have a General and his Army itching to invade my city. Plus, I have a murder charge hanging around my neck. Can you make that disappear too?"

Sensing he was making progress, the Senator continued, "Yes, yes. You let me go now, I'll make those calls, I promise. I'll get the Army to stand down, and tell the President the whole ReFederalization plan is a non-starter for another year. I'll talk to the Feds and get them off your back too. I can do all this. You have to believe me. Just get me my gold and we go our separate ways. Deal?"

"Not so quick, Senator, let me think for a second. There is one obvious flaw in your offer of course."

"Like what?"

"That you're a lying, duplicitous bastard who'll say anything to get out of this hole you've dug yourself—then change your mind the next day. Why should I believe a word you're saying? Your track record of honest dealings makes Donald Trump look like a saint."

Still dazed, clutching his throbbing head, the Senator tried again to convince Danny, "You have my word. This can end well for both of us. Why would I double cross you and lose millions of bucks? At the same time, I can get you off the hook for murder, leaving you to carry on as boss of Louisville, or leave with your gold. It's a win-win!" the Senator tried not to sound desperate as he scrambled to put some icing on his hasty proposition.

Danny was thinking quickly, too. Was he underestimating the clout the Senator had with the RRRF and the Federal Government? Could he make all his problems go away so easily? He was skeptical. This guy was a politician, who even when he wasn't fighting for his life, lied for a living. If, and it was huge if, he could deliver, then it was worth considering. He'd be a little poorer, but alive and still running the city.

However, If he reneged on the deal, then the Army would take over Louisville. Within days he'd be on the run from the Feds and who knew what other law enforcement agencies.

Then again, if he killed the Senator, sure as hell the wrath of the Government, Army and probably the Pope, would descend on him with a ferocity reserved only for people who assassinate politicians. It was a Hobson's Choice, one partially of his own making. Maybe coming here was a bad idea. Revenge may be a dish best served cold, but perhaps after six years, he should have left it stewing a little longer.

He pointed the gun at the Senator's head, "Senator, I don't trust you further than I can throw you. But I'll give you one last chance to prove to me you're not a lying piece of shit. Here's how we're going to play this: I'm gonna leave you and the girl here, alive. I'm going back to Louisville. If you don't call off the invasion of my city within twenty four hours, the deal is off. If you double-cross me, I will come back for you one day, some day, and kill you. Understand?"

Hope, relief, surged through the Senator. Struggling to stand up, he leant against the tree for support, "Yes, yes I do. You have my word. I'll keep my promise…and the gold?"

Typical, thought Danny, just spared his life and now he wants paying for it. These people never know when to call it quits. Danny thought for a moment, "I'll arrange for fifty bars to be delivered to Paducah. How you get it across the Mississippi is up to you. Oh, one other thing, I want you to free my guy, Brian. The Feds snatched him in Paducah a few weeks ago. I want him back in one piece ASAP."

The Senator, grateful to be alive, nodded. He'd agree to anything at the moment, "Sure, I'll get it done. Now, I need a doctor before I bleed to death."

"Trust me, Senator, you're a long way from bleeding out. I'll leave you in the capable hands of that bimbo in the car, I'm sure she'll take care of you. Remember, you double-cross me and today is just a taster of what I'll come back and do to you. Clear?"

Danny walked over to the car and pulled out the petrified girl. "Your boss needs some help. Do whatever you can to make sure he lives–and keep reminding him that if he doesn't keep his word I'll come back for him–and you." For dramatic effect, he held the gun briefly to the girl's head. Danny jumped into the car, slammed it into gear and scorched away in a cloud of dust.

The girl ran over to the Senator. "Are you alright, sir?"

The Senator looked at her, amazed at the stupidity of the question, and snapped back, "Do I look fucking alright? That asshole just beat the shit out of me. I need a doctor, quickly. Go find one."

"But he's taken the car, and smashed the cellphones!" she wailed.

"Then start walking you stupid bitch, and don't come back until you've called EMS."

Obediently, Diana trudged down the dirt track to the main road, hoping to attract a passing motorist's attention. Part of her was tempted to leave the ungrateful Senator where he was. She wisely concluded this course of action wouldn't do much for her work prospects. It took nearly half an hour to reach the main road and finally flag down a driver, who thankfully, believed her strange story of a US Senator lying beaten up in the woods and let her use his cellphone. A further twenty minutes passed after the 9-1-1 call, before an ambulance arrived. Diana guided them into the woods where a very sorry looking Senator sat propped up against a tree, looking like he'd been attacked with a chainsaw.

Grateful as ever, he demanded, "What took them so fucking long to get here, Diana? Did you call the police as well? Get them after that shithead that attacked me!"

Realizing her blunder, Diana guiltily avoided his stare, "Er no, I didn't do that yet, sir. I'll borrow one of the EMS's phones and call them right now."

Before the Senator could scream his disapproval, he emitted a howl of pain as the EMS team dumped him on a gurney and piloted him smartly into the ambulance.

Diana joined him in the back and dialed 9-1-1, again. This time relaying the details of what happened, and the car Danny was driving. The dispatcher told her she'd contact the police immediately and send someone to the hospital to get a statement.

It was all too late. Danny had taken just ten minutes to get to the airport. Jay was fueled and ready to take off as planned. Before Diana had even called the EMS, the ultralight was in the air headed east.

Chapter 49

General Sanders was close to ordering his troops to full alert, ready to move on Louisville within the next twenty-four hours. He'd heard nothing from Captain Makefield and his negotiations with Danny Trevino. No news in this case, was probably bad news. The whole exercise was one more of hope than expectation. However, he was willing to go the extra mile to reach a peaceful conclusion that avoided bloodshed. He really did not relish slaughtering fellow Americans on their home soil. He didn't want that stigma attached to his name in the history books. He decided to wait and see what developed over the next few hours. After six years, it would make little difference to the outcome. He put a call in to his aide, telling him to pass an order to the field officers and commanders to remain on standby and await further instructions. He went down to the officers' mess for some lunch, hoping against hope that the Captain would contact him with some good news.

Later that afternoon, he received a disturbing call from the Senator, who sounded groggy and a little distracted.

"Hi…General, I have spoken with the President and we have decided to give negotiations between ourselves and the, er…Louisville leader more time. Can you please pull your men and…and your equipment back, especially on the west side of the city? We want to…to allow for any evacuees to leave in peace. Um…I think we all agree that we want to be seen by the rest of America as doing all we can to avoid this conflict."

The General was bemused, though happy to give the order, "You must have been reading my mind, Senator, my thoughts entirely. I'll order my men to pull back immediately. Do we have a timeline for these negotiations?"

Trying to ignore his throbbing head, he attempted to string a sensible reply together, "Good question General. I…er…anticipate a week, no more…can that be done?"

"Certainly Senator. Can I ask, is everything alright?"

"Yes, yes, hunky-dory…good to hear from you General. Thanks for calling."

The line went dead. The General looked at his phone. Did he hear the Senator correctly…'hunky-dory'? Where had that come from? And he called me, not the other way around. What was the guy on? Well, not his job to wonder why…the Military just followed the politicians' orders. So (not for the first time), it wasn't up to him to question the sanity of the Senator.

Within hours, the RRRF's military contingent west of Louisville was heading back towards the Mississippi, leaving the main interstates clear for anyone who wanted to leave. The General couldn't imagine there would be a mass exodus. These people had nowhere to go that offered them better living conditions.

He pondered if the Government was beginning to get cold feet over this whole exercise. The cost was huge and the outcome was far from certain. The main driving force was, without a doubt the Senator, and that man, he wouldn't trust not to steal his grandmother's last meal.

The General had cause to be skeptical, As he would discover, the next few days would see the whole RRRF/ReFederalization plan fall apart, but not in the way he, or anyone, could have foreseen.

Chapter 50

Back in his apartment, Danny related to Roger in the briefest of details his 'conversation' with the Senator. He finished by explaining that, "The next few hours will show whether the little shit will keep his word and start withdrawing the troops or not. What are you going to say to the General, unless he's already got some word from the Senator to do what he promised?"

Roger was not enjoying his role as middleman any longer. It was starting to feel like he was trying to separate two fighting dogs, with him, in all likelihood, the one to end up bitten. Danny's impromptu meeting with the Senator had pulled the rug from under his feet, he really had nothing more to contribute.

"I don't think I'll say anything, Danny. Actions speak louder than words now. Either the troops withdraw or they move onto Louisville. Either way, I've no control over what happens. If it's all the same to you, first thing tomorrow, I'd like to go back home with Jay."

Danny contemplated whether keeping the two of them here would be of any benefit. The ultralight was a useful toy, but if hostilities broke out, it could be easily shot out of the sky, he preferred to take his chances on firmer ground. Plus, it couldn't carry any useful weight of gold. Danny liked Roger. He had enough problems. Making an enemy out of Roger was pointless. On balance, letting him go was no great loss.

"Sure, Roger. I'm a man of my word. I'll get one of the guys to give you a couple of gold bars. Might be worth swapping for real cash one day. Otherwise you're good to go. Like to thank you and Jay for the use of that frightening flying contraption! Suggest you get some sleep and I'll see you before you go tomorrow."

Roger and Jay quietly breathed a sigh of relief. Amazingly, this murdering mobster had kept his word. Though they'd believe it once they were in the air on their way home. They said their good nights and went off to one of the spare bedrooms to get a few hours of sleep.

Danny wasn't around at daybreak as they prepared to leave. True to his word, Olivia appeared and pointed at a leather holdall containing two shiny gold bars weighing about twenty-seven pounds each.

"He's not all bad, you know," Olivia explained as she made them a coffee, "he can turn real nasty at times, but he's mostly a good guy. Don't be surprised he kept his end of the bargain, he appreciates loyalty. He likes you guys, he told me last night."

Roger acknowledged the compliment, "That's good to know, Olivia. I wish him, and you, all the best. Uncertain times ahead for everyone, I hope it all ends how you want. We'll be on our way now. Thanks for your hospitality."

"Safe flight back guys, that ultralight of yours looks lethal. Like something out of Mad Max!"

Jay feigned a hurt look, "It's a fine machine, Olivia, first class all the way!"

Olivia shook her head in disbelief, "Rather you than me. Anyway, you better get going. The weather is supposed to take a turn for the worse later."

With that warning, they bade her farewell and went to the ultralight, parked in a huge deserted car lot. The minimal pre-flight checks made, they were airborne and flying south over Louisville within minutes.

"Can't say I'm sad to be leaving, I think we dodged a bullet!" shouted Roger into Jay's ear, over the din of the engine. Jay simply gave a thumbs up and concentrated on flying. Roger sat back and enjoyed the view. As they flew over I-65, he tapped Jay on the shoulder, pointing at what looked like columns of Army vehicles heading southwards away from the city.

Wonders would never cease, thought Roger. It looked like the Senator was keeping his word–the Army was withdrawing. Was that the end of the whole RRRF exercise? Was ReFederalization dead in the water? Or was this just a feint, a move by the Federal Government before trying a different tack?

Jay broke into his thoughts, Olivia's warning about the weather proved prescient. Looking west, they saw a huge dark band of cloud stretching north and south as far as they could see. He shouted over his shoulder, "Roger, that weather front looks like bad news. This baby won't like getting caught up in that mess. I hope we can outrun it." Roger nodded, well aware ultralights were fragile machines not designed to ride out severe thunderstorms.

Normally, on the ground, such a vicious cloud formation would be a signal to make your way indoors and sit out the storm. No big deal, just an inconvenience. At three thousand feet, it was a different matter. The wind speed and torrential rain would make flying an ultralight impossibly dangerous.

Roger bawled at Jay, "Can we go quicker, get ahead of it? Or do you want to land somewhere and sit it out?"

"Only worth landing if we can find cover for the ultralight. Even on the ground, in one of those storms, it could get damaged. I'll open her up and hope for the best."

For the next two hours, they flew south, parallel to the approaching storm, watching it remorselessly close in on them. As they flew over Columbia, the leading edge of the front started to soak them and buffet the ultralight. The sky was as dark as if it were midnight. Within minutes, they were being pummeled by rain, hail and ferocious turbulence. It was as though they were inside some giant washing machine. Jay fought for control as they were bounced around the sky by the conflicting gusts of winds. Visibility dropped to nearly zero. Roger used his compass to guide them south towards French Creek, now only a few minutes away.

A crack; the sound of splitting wood, saw one of the wing's struts torn off, leaving just two more to keep it rigid and providing lift. Jay was now flying just above the treetops when the tower of French Creek's church came into view. Despite the ferocity of the swirling, spiraling winds, Jay managed to line up for landing. Just when Roger thought they had made it, with only a few feet to touch down, an updraft threw the ultralight fifty feet into the air before dropping it to the ground like someone smashing a rock into a frozen pond.

For a second, all Roger heard was a cacophony of wind, rain and breaking machinery, then, nothing.

Chapter 51

Penny leaned over Roger. He was still asleep, three long days after the crash. Recovering from a concussion, broken leg, arm and cracked ribs. Doc Brown had administered copious amounts of painkillers after resetting the broken bones and bandaging up his ribs.

As for any internal wounds, the Doc explained, "I've no way of knowing what trauma he may have suffered internally. Can only hope and pray it's no more than bad bruising. Keep a close eye on him, take his temperature regularly. Let me know if there's any change for the worse."

She sat down beside the bed looking at her stubborn, kind hearted, brave man. Even when he was asleep, having him near her made her feel safe, happy and wanted. She looked back at her days in charge of Bowling Green and the never-ending squabbles, fights, struggles she had to deal with on a day-to-day basis. She thanked God and Roger, for bringing her to this small slice of Kentucky that blended in so well with her personality. Peace, harmony and an unbreakable sense of community.

He had looked after her when she was seriously ill. Now it was her turn, a responsibility she took willingly, for however long it was necessary. It turned out to be four stressful days until Roger regained consciousness. He opened his eyes to see a tearful Penny crying with relief, "Oh thank God, Roger, you're back with us. I've been worried out of my mind. How do you feel? Are you in pain?"

Roger opened his one good eye, focused on Penny's face just a few inches away and whispered hoarsely, "I feel like shit. Guess that was a pretty spectacular landing?"

Penny answered, "It was, thankfully, one of the farmers was putting his tractor away and saw you guys come crashing down. It wasn't a pretty sight apparently, you're lucky to be alive."

He closed his eyes for a few moments, then opened them slowly and with a huge effort asked, "How's Jay, he OK?"

Penny took his hand, "I'm so sorry Roger, Jay didn't survive the crash, he's…dead."

Roger broke down, his voice choking with grief, "Dead? No, no, I can't believe it, oh please God, it's all my fault for forcing him to take me on that trip…."

"Roger, Roger, calm down, you're not to blame. Jay knew what he was doing, he knew the risks. Please let's talk about it later. You need to rest…."

Exhausted and upset, Roger lapsed back into unconsciousness. Penny reached down and softly stroked his cheek, wiping away a solitary tear as it ran from his eye.

It was three more days before Roger was able to sit up in bed, eat and talk without the effort knocking him out. His concussion had made focusing and remembering troublesome. It was a week after the crash that he remembered about the gold bars. Beckoning Penny over to his bed, he asked, "Have you been to the site of the crash?"

Penny answered that she'd only been there briefly to help extricate Roger from the wreckage, then carry him back. Other villagers had gone back after the storm to clear up the debris, "Why are you asking?"

Roger hesitantly explained the reason for his question, "You won't believe this…but there was a small leather holdall by my seat, containing…well how can I put it…two gold bars worth about a million bucks!"

Penny's jaw dropped, "Sorry, did you say a million dollars? Are you feeling OK, sure you're not imagining all this? Bangs on the head can do strange things to people."

"No, I'm serious Penny, that's what Danny gave us, or rather Jay, for flying him to meet the Senator…I'll tell you all about that later. In the meantime, I'm intrigued to know who's got those bars now?"

Chapter 52

By the time Roger was well enough to meet some of the Council at his bedside, news of the RRRF's withdrawal from Louisville had left everyone confused. Was that it? Had one man in Louisville sent them scurrying back to the west? All those promises of a bright new future disappearing like melting snow in the spring. Here one moment, gone the next?

As Roger recovered, he discussed his trip with Penny: the visit to see the General. Jay's unexpected return trip with Danny to talk to the Senator, and the subsequent pull back of the RRRF's troops.

Penny was confused. "What do you think he did, or say, to the Senator that caused this change of heart? He must have had some leverage to make that happen. There's a lot of people involved who'd spent a ton of time and money pulling all this together. Then it all goes in reverse."

Roger agreed, "I don't know what it was, but my guess it involved money, lots of it. Danny is rolling in it. Remember, he gave us those two gold bars? From what I can guess, there are plenty more where those came from. Now I can get up and about, I need to find them. No one has said anything to you, no whispers around the village?"

Penny shook her head, "Not a word. Very strange, it's difficult to keep any secrets in this place."

Roger agreed, "I'm wondering how best to persuade whoever has the bars to hand them over without making them feel like criminals. It could be an amazing resource for the whole community, now it's only useful to buy stuff at the Barter Fair. Its value in dollars is of no use to us at the moment, mind you, that could all change if the RRRF does, sometime in the future, get its way."

At that moment, Landy walked into the house carrying firewood, "Hi Dad, how are you feeling?"

"Much better son, thanks," Roger paused, indicating to the seat beside him, "come sit here, I have a favor to ask, but you need to be discreet." Roger then explained about the leather holdall from the crashed ultralight and asked whether Landy had heard anything around the village.

"No I haven't Dad, I know a couple of the guys who helped clear the wreckage away, I can see if they picked up something?"

"That would be helpful, Landy, thanks. Maybe suggest to them or anyone they know who might have the bag, if its left on my front porch, anytime, day or night, no questions will be asked. What's in those bags was left to the community by Jay. They should honor his memory by doing the decent thing. You'll have to be discreet about it. Let me know if you hear anything."

Landy's inquiries produced no information. Whoever had the gold was obviously intent on keeping it for themselves. By Sunday, with no news of its whereabouts, Roger asked the pastor to say something in church, emphasizing the importance of returning the bag for the good of the whole community.

As the pastor delivered his sermon, Roger placed himself near the front of the church to see if there were any uncomfortable reactions from the congregation. He'd asked Pat, the village's security chief, to stand by the door and check on people as they left to catch any whispers, or averted looks.

The pastor started by asking, "Can we all pray for our dear departed friend Jay McDonald, who we laid to rest last week. And thank the Lord for saving Roger from that terrible crash, helping him regain his health and well-being and that his continued recovery be swift."

He continued by reminding everyone of the need for honesty and sharing of their resources to ensure the future prosperity of French Creek, "For six years, we have been blessed with every one of you believing and acting in the best interest of our community. It is, I believe, the reason we have survived and thrived through such terrible ordeals. However, it pains me deeply to reveal that certain contents from the ultralight crash have not been returned to Roger who, with Jay's help, had obtained them at great risk for the benefit of the community. I would ask anyone with any knowledge of these items to return them to Roger."

No one seemed embarrassed by the pastor's words. Most wondered what on earth he was talking about? As the congregation filed out of the church, people were confused and concerned at the accusation someone could be hoarding something of value. But no one came forward with any information. By day's end, Roger had seen and heard nothing more. Pat reported a similar lack of progress, and none of Landy's friends knew anything either.

The silence was broken the next day, with news that Stu Featherstone, his wife and teenage son had left the camp on horseback in the middle of the night. Pat told Roger the news early in the morning, just hours after the family's hasty departure.

"No one has left French Creek so suddenly in years. So I have to come to the conclusion they've got the gold, Roger," Pat was clutching a cup of coffee leaning against the porch in the hazy morning light, rifle propped against the chair, "shall I go after them?"

Roger replied despairingly, "I really hoped it wouldn't come to this. I'm almost tempted to let them have the damn gold. It seems to bring nothing but bad luck. In truth, though, it's the Government's. We should just keep it safe until we can hand it back to them, assuming we can find the family and the gold."

Pat wasn't having any of it, "Roger, you're being too nice. The Government's done SFA for us. I'd argue that gold is just reasonable compensation for all the damage they've inflicted on us. I've no hesitation in claiming it's ours. Be real, it's never gonna find its way back to those Sacramento sleaze balls. So, what do you want me to do?"

Roger thought for a moment, "Unfortunately, I can't come with you, nowhere near ready to ride a horse. I can't order you to chase them down and bring it back, but I can't stop you either. If you decide you want to go, then, well, I'd take a couple of people along for security."

Pat drained his coffee mug, grabbed his rifle, and offered up a phrase Roger had never heard before, but understood only too well, "OK sir, *a nod is as good as a wink to a blind man.* Catch you later."

Within thirty minutes, Roger saw Pat and two friends canter down French Creek Road. Roger crossed his fingers, half-hoping they'd never find the fleeing family. That gold was proving an unwelcome gift.

It was the next day when Pat and his team arrived back. He trotted over to Roger's house, tied the horse to the railings and called his name.

Still walking slowly and with difficulty, Roger came to the door with Penny supporting him, "That was a quick trip, Pat, how did you get on?"

Dejected, Pat was brief and to the point, "It's bad news all the way, Roger. We found the family near Glasgow. They'd been ambushed by the look of it. All three dead, and surprise, no sign of the gold. It's gone. Whoever attacked them lucked out. They made off with a fortune."

Penny was remarkably philosophical, "That's awful, those poor people, even if they were thieves, they didn't deserve that. Maybe that gold is tainted, perhaps we're well rid of it?"

"I think you're right Penny, it was ill-gotten gains to start with and it's brought nothing but grief along with it. Easy come, easy go. The Featherstone's didn't deserve to die, but maybe that gold is cursed. Let it be a lesson to all of us. Nothing good comes from a bad decision."

For the next few days, as his health improved, Roger immersed himself in the day-to-day running of French Creek, household chores, preparing his garden for vegetable planting and all the jobs that had been put off for too long.

Penny had quickly taken charge of re-organizing the house and created a 'honey-do' list of items to repair or make. For many of these, it was easier said than done. Like everyone in the village, post-Collapse, Roger had to acquire a new range of skills: carpentry, plumbing, gardening, preserving, poultry and animal care, anything needed to keep your household running and well-stocked, all without electric tools of any kind. Now a job that before the Collapse might have taken a few minutes, took hours, and was a lot harder on the muscles!

Penny came out from the back door and wandered into Roger's workshop, "How are the new shelves coming along?"

"Slowly Penny, I'm getting there. Reusing old nails and screws makes it all a little more difficult. A piece of Chippendale furniture it will never be."

Penny moved behind Roger, putting her arms around his waist and nuzzling into the back of his neck, "I've been thinking…."

Roger interrupted, "Uh oh, I've told you not to do that. It normally means trouble."

Penny continued, ignoring his jibe, "I'm so happy here, I'm loving every minute of it. I'm loving you too, even if you do go off on these maniac missions. So…."

Roger turned to face Penny, "So…you want to get married?"

Exasperated, Penny asked, "How'd you guess I was going to say that?"

Blithely Roger replied, "Oh, over the years I've had women proposing to me all the time, can see it coming a mile off!"

"Yea right, lining up were they? In your dreams!" Penny laughed, "you should be so damn lucky. Well, thinking about it, you are, because that is exactly what I was going to propose: literally. I'd like to make an honest man of you!"

"Here we go again. That modest southern gal reticence disappears when you want something. Seem to remember that's the kind of thing you said to me while you dragged me off to bed for the first time!"

Penny, rising to the accusation, replied, "Fuck the shy southern girl crap! It's a myth! So…don't make me ask again. Let's get married, yes or no?"

Roger got down on one knee, grabbed a hose clamp from his workshop bench and slipped it on her finger, "Penny, will you marry me? I can adjust the ring with a screwdriver later!"

"God, Roger, you are just so romantic, and practical! Yes, let's do it. Soon, very soon."

Later that day Roger and Penny announced their plans. The rest of the village celebrated the news of the impending marriage and started making plans for the big day.

Chapter 53

Danny paced around his apartment like a proverbial caged tiger. However, unlike the animal, he did have a way to escape–if he wanted to. He'd seen, and heard, the RRRF's forces had withdrawn, though he couldn't tell if it was all of them, or how far westwards they'd gone. It appeared the Senator may have kept his word–a rarity indeed. Now he faced the prospect of keeping his side of the bargain: shipping the gold bars to him in Paducah, and hoping that would be the end of it. Trouble is, he couldn't trust that man to take the gold, then come back to Louisville with the Army as he'd originally planned–a win-win for the crooked Senator. And what if the Government decided they still wanted to go ahead, could the Senator really persuade them otherwise?

Or he could revert back to Plan A, take his truck already loaded with gold and valuables, leaving Louisville to its fate at the hands of the Feds. (Though he didn't believe they would do its inhabitants, his people, any harm, it still would be a humiliation Danny found difficult to stomach.)

He had confided in Olivia, who in recent weeks had become a trusted confidant, a source of practical and sensible advice. He normally wasn't so indecisive, but this time he was faced with some life-changing decisions, so different from the day-to-day ones he'd dealt with while running Louisville. He had to admit the odds seemed stacked against him. So much was beyond his control, an unusual position and one he found frustrating. She had suggested sending the gold to the Senator and wait to see what happened. If he kept his word, the city would remain untouched, and Danny could stay.

However, as Olivia had also wisely pointed out: that would mean a complete about face on the RRRF's plans, and ReFederalization. It would require some deft footwork and hefty spinning by the Senator to avoid any negative fallout and accusations of incompetence back in Sacramento. The Federal Government would face the same problems too. In an election year, that was bad news no one wanted to own.

Alternatively, he could stay and fight it out. To what end? He and countless others would die and the Army's overwhelming superiority would crush them. Danny would be accused, dead or alive, of causing an unnecessary bloodbath for his own vainglorious reasons. A legacy he did not want to be remembered for.

The final option was leaving the city and heading for a safe haven away from the Feds. So where to? Olivia wanted to go east to the Appalachians and use their gold to establish a remote sanctuary that would take the authorities years to find. They'd be surrounded by people who had a natural enmity to any Federal interference. (Infamously, years before, Bill Sparkman, a fifty-one--year-old part-time Census field worker, working in the Appalachians asked too many questions for the local's comfort and was found lynched with the words 'Feds" carved on his chest.)

Danny was keener on going to South America; some place like Ecuador, that he'd heard had limited extradition agreements with the US, and a relaxed attitude to immigrants with significant wealth. Traveling there would be a challenge, though over $100 million in gold and valuables should grease the palms of enough people to arrange transport out of the country without many questions being asked.

They'd make a decision in the morning.

Chapter 54

The Senator was discharged from the hospital with a heavily bandaged head and strapping around his chest to protect three cracked ribs. Through a drug-induced fog, he flew back to Sacramento after being summoned to brief the President and Secretary of State about the RRRF's change of plans. He hadn't been into the Oval Office for many weeks, not since this impossible job had been dumped on him. All communication had been via the Secretary of State or the President's Chief of Staff. The request to meet the President face-to-face caused him some concern. He worried he was in for a dressing down based on the lack of progress.

The Senator and the Secretary of State were ushered into the Oval Office. The President strutted around munching on McDonald's, clutching a Diet Coke in the other hand. Three televisions were on, sound muted, with the captions scrolling jerkily across the screens. Fox News, CNN and CNBC played continuously, ensuring the President could react instantly to any piece of news, good or bad, firing off a tweet or post on his personal social media site. It also meant his attention span for what was happening in the room was that of a five-year-old with ADHD.

President Cummings reluctantly dragged his attention from the televisions and turned to the Senator and Secretary of State, Michael Crapo, "You look like you've been in the wars, Senator," commented the President. Not waiting for an explanation, he continued, "I hear this RRRF invasion is turning into a pain in the ass. Kentucky's a lovely state, great people, we've gotta be nice to them. I've got a hotel in Lexington I want back. Bet it's a fucking mess at the moment, it'll cost

266

me a fucking fortune to remodel it. Sure as hell they've looted all the gold-plated faucets. Fucking animals. Why don't we just send in the Air Force and bomb them to hell?"

Both men looked at each other in despair. The President's illogical rants were sometimes impossible to follow. As long as there was an adult in the room, most led to little of note happening. Occasionally, an overeager assistant took them literally with almost dire consequences. Once, the President demanded that anyone looting or stealing should be made to draw money from their ATM and pay the victims back immediately. He was about to tweet he'd made an executive order to this effect, when it was pointed out that such people probably didn't have a bank account.

The President was astounded, "What, some people don't have bank accounts? Fucking morons. What can we do to make everyone have a bank account? I know the CEO of Bank America, he'll help. Get him on the phone."

Mercifully, before that call could be made, Fox news called wanting a quote about a lost dog on the White House grounds and an embarrassing incident was averted.

Secretary Crapo answered the President's contradictory suggestions diplomatically, "Excellent ideas Mr. President; shall we explore the least unpopular option first? Negotiating a peaceful RRRF entry to Louisville, avoiding any bloodshed? A few days grace can do no harm, and would certainly bolster your humanitarian credentials with the election coming up? After all, every dead Kentuckian is a potential lost vote."

"True, true, can't afford to lose votes like that. What about the Cummings' hotel?"

"We'll make sure that it is secured as soon as we enter the city, Mr. President. We'll get contractors in there as soon as possible to make any urgent repairs."

Senator Kingston painfully sat back in wonderment. How had a discussion involving a decision that could cost billions of dollars and thousands of lives be diverted to one concerning hotel renovations? He tried to bring it back on track.

"Mr. President, if you can give me just a few more days, I think we can bring this to a satisfactory conclusion. One less problem for you to deal with. That's if Secretary Crapo is happy for this temporary halt to proceedings?"

The Secretary, happy to bring the meeting to a close, agreed, "It's good with me, Senator. No more than a week to get it done? Are you OK with that arrangement, Mr. President?"

Suddenly distracted by CNBC showing a downward trend in his corporation's share price, President Cummings replied dismissively, "Yes, yes, sounds good to me…do it. I'll send out a tweet later." He picked up the phone and yelled at some hapless secretary, "Get me Jim Cramer, immediately!"

The two men left the Oval Office. In the corridor outside, Senator Kingston turned to Secretary Crapo, "Is he always like that?"

"Senator, that was a good day…you have no idea what a carnival it is here most of the time. Go back to Kentucky, it's saner and safer there."

As Senator Kingston took a cab to his hotel, he questioned whether he should be doing anything to get this madcap President re-elected. The man couldn't string a sentence of coherent thought together. He knew all about the revolving door of senior aides who lasted days, occasionally weeks before being fired, frequently via Twitter. Now he understood why. The man was impossible to work for, or with. As the cab passed the statue of Abraham Lincoln outside the Sacramento Law School, Senator Kingston wondered what Lincoln would make of the current President. He smiled to himself, pretty sure the hum he heard was the sixteenth President of the United States spinning in his grave.

By the time he arrived back at his hotel, his mind had moved onto more important matters. Had Danny Trevino shipped his gold to Paducah? It was twenty-four hours since the RRRF pullback and the road should be clear to transport his share of the Fort Knox bullion. He'd given General Sanders strict instructions to keep an eye out for a convoy coming from Louisville. When it arrived, it was to be stored in a secure facility, guarded twenty-four seven. He intimated that the trucks contained 'classified papers' that Danny Trevino had stolen, and as part of his ceasefire agreement, they would be returned. It was a flimsy excuse, one that would have to do for the time being.

The Senator was to wait in vain. The gold would never arrive.

Chapter 55

In the end, the decision was an easy one for Danny and Olivia. They simply didn't trust the Senator to keep his word, so why send him the gold, only for him to give the go ahead for the RRRF's Army to take over Louisville? The answer was obvious: they needed to flee the city as soon as possible. It would help if they had a few days start. To that end, Danny asked all his precinct Captains to come see him immediately.

He decided to be honest with them. He needed their help and lying would mean they'd be unlikely to do what he asked. By mid-morning, the Captains had all arrived, coffee and breakfast were provided, and they all took advantage of Danny's hospitality. It was the last time it would be offered.

Danny had rehearsed what he wanted to say. It would be an emotional farewell speech. He had known some of these men for over a decade. They were like brothers. It felt like he was breaking up a family, a kind of divorce. He stood clutching a cup of coffee, staring into the dark, steaming drink, seeking inspiration. The captains waited expectantly for him to say something. They knew it was likely to be news about the RRRF, exactly what, no one could guess.

Danny looked up from his cup and started explaining the situation he now found himself in.

"Captains, what I'm about to say is not easy, and some of you won't like it, but I have no choice. The RRRF and their Army, as you must realize, has resources and manpower way beyond what we have. I've never run away from a fight in my life, but sadly, this one is impossible for me, for us, to win. I don't want to put you, your families and the people of Louisville through a battle we cannot win."

"So I am ordering you all to stand down and let the RRRF move in and run the city. I have no reason to believe they will do any harm to the people of Louisville. They want peace and an easy transition of power. We should help them do that."

Danny paused to see what reaction he would get from the Captains. Inevitably, it was mixed. Some were for fighting to the last man, but thankfully, most seemed to accept the reality. Danny continued, his confidence increasing.

"There is one other matter I need your help with. I am a marked man, with a false murder charge against me and a Senator hell-bent on revenge for something he believes I owe him from years ago. As you know, the man is a crook and liar. He can't be trusted. He has promised me a pardon if he takes the city...."

Johnny, one of the senior Captains, interrupted, "Hey Danny, are you saying you've recently met this Senator? How come you never told us? What did he say? I think we have a right to know?" a few other Captains murmured in agreement.

Danny inwardly cursed himself for his inadvertent admission about meeting with the Senator. There was no point denying it.

"Yes, you're right Johnny, I did meet him a couple of days ago to try and do a deal to save all of us. He refused, wanted to blackmail me, the whole city, for his personal benefit. I wasn't having any of it. You'll be pleased to know I gave him a few bruises to take back to Sacramento with him!"

The group broke into smiles and shouts of approval, before quietening down to hear what else Danny had to say.

"So I have no choice but to leave Louisville. If I don't, I face life in prison or even execution. Because of this, I have one last favor to ask. I need you all to say nothing about my whereabouts. Let them assume I am hiding somewhere in the city. Give them as much misleading information about me for as long as possible. I also need some volunteers to help me in my escape. I intend to leave Louisville within a few hours. Who is with me?"

Everyone held up their hands to volunteer. He picked men who were single with no families. He couldn't guarantee their safe return.

Danny drew the meeting to a close, trying to conceal his emotions. The words stumbled out, "Brothers, friends, we have had some great times together…ones I'll never forget. We survived the Collapse and lived well afterwards. We helped the residents of Louisville as well. We all have a lot to be proud of. To show my thanks, I'd like to give you all a present as you leave, Olivia?"

As Danny called her name, the bedroom door opened and Olivia pushed in a cart carrying ten gold bars.

Danny walked across to the cart, "There's one bar for each of you. From what I understand, they could be worth up to half a million bucks. Hopefully that should soften the blow when the RRRF comes into town!"

The Captains gathered around the cart, touching the lustrous gold bars before each picked up his reward, clutching this universal symbol of wealth to his chest. It was a windfall beyond anything they could have imagined. The room was silent as they tried to digest what they held in their hands, and what it could mean for their futures. The silence was broken by the pop of champagne corks.

Danny raised his glass, "Everyone, please grab a glass and drink to this momentous occasion. It's a time for celebration," remembering his favorite Churchill quote, with a flourish he added, "now this is not the end. It is not even the beginning of the end. But it is, perhaps, the end of the beginning." He went round to each of the Captains, shook their hands, hugged them and wished them well. The volunteers that had one last job to do for him, he gave instructions as to where and when to meet.

Within minutes, after a few tearful farewells, the room was empty. Danny's reign as the Boss of Louisville was over. Now to make his escape before the Senator and the Feds realized what was happening.

Chapter 56

Senator Kingston was almost vibrating with rage. It was three days since the RRRF had withdrawn from Louisville. No gold had arrived in Paducah, no contact of any kind from that little conniving shit Trevino. The Senator knew he shouldn't trust him, and he'd been proven right. To further confirm his fears that no gold fortune was on its way, an Army drone had reported seeing four identical Humvees leaving the city, each heading in different directions. Was Danny in one of those vehicles? If so, which one? Or maybe none of them?

The Senator had to admire this apparent deception being played out to cover Danny's escape–if that's what was happening. For the moment, they were under the eagle eye of the drone, soon they'd have to decide which one to follow–the spy in the sky couldn't follow all of them.

Meanwhile, believing Danny had left, the RRRF slowly began to approach Louisville to see if any resistance was offered by the inhabitants. General Sanders ordered the relief convoy to go in first. It was a massive display of goodwill. Three hundred trucks heavily laden with food, medical and other essential supplies. His comms team had been flooding the airwaves with news of their approach, making it clear they were unarmed and bearing life-saving supplies. The trucks fanned out around I-65 and I-265 then entered the city stopping every few blocks to meet people and dispense the provisions. They were welcomed warmly by everyone they met.

No violence was reported. No armed militia were seen, even the tank had been removed from the Sherman-Minton bridge. It was worryingly quiet, reported the division commanders. General Sanders, however, breathed a sigh of relief. This was going far better than expected. Next was the delicate matter of trying to ascertain where Danny Trevino was, or had, gone. He believed the flight of four vehicles were camouflage for his escape. Currently, one was heading southwards on I-65 towards Nashville, another heading east for Lexington. The remaining two were seemingly going to Cincinnati and Indianapolis.

It was a clever ruse. Not one that would have worked in the west. There, by now, a platoon of cop cars and helicopters would be tracking each vehicle's move, waiting to pounce and arrest them. Not so in the east. With no law enforcement in place, the progress of the vehicles would be difficult to follow. The General couldn't ask for several multi-million dollar drones to criss-cross the east simply to apprehend an alleged murderer. Even the Army had a limit on the resources it could deploy; a problem the Senator failed to comprehend. He wanted the fugitive caught and brought to justice immediately.

Well, you can kiss my ass, Senator, thought the General. I have more important fish to fry: namely securing Louisville in a timely and peaceful manner, and install some gentle martial law, until the Senator and his cronies decide what to do next. Then he wanted to be out of there in double quick time.

Chapter 57

The Humvee containing Danny, Olivia and his two guards, Seb and Ping, were passing Knoxville by late afternoon. They had seen no sign of anyone following, on the ground or in the air. Despite their outward size, Humvees are not particularly spacious inside, or that economical to run. With the gold bars and other crates of valuables, most of the remaining storage was filled with tanks of gas. A dozen more were strapped to the roof. Danny estimated they had enough for 1,500 miles–to get him where he wanted to go. Where he felt safe. He wanted to drive nonstop all the way to his destination in Florida.

He'd told the three decoy drivers to keep driving for four days, before returning to Louisville. They too, were laden down with gas to ensure they had enough fuel to get back. All in all, Danny reckoned he had four days before the Feds realized which vehicle he was in. Then they'd have to make a decision whether they wanted to track him down in the inhospitable, lawless east. He doubted they would. Nevertheless, he was not going to give them the chance.

Chapter 58

It was some small consolation that the General confirmed two days later that Louisville was under his control. There had been no violence or resistance of any kind. He was suspicious and grateful. Law enforcement was making inquiries to see if anyone knew what had happened to Danny. Frustratingly, they were met with a wall of silence and little cooperation from the city's population. They were happy to accept the RRRF's largesse, but the generosity wasn't reciprocated with any useful information. Even a large reward had produced nothing except a few false leads. Danny might be gone, but his influence lingered on. His well-paid Captains made it known: anyone who knew anything was to keep quiet.

Louisville wasn't the only city to welcome the RRRF and its truckloads of good news. Across many Kentucky cities anti-RRRF sentiment had been diluted with the removal by the Colonel of their vociferous leaders. Others decided discretion was the better part of valor and quietly disappeared, leaving the cities to their fate.

It took a few days to organize and secure a venue for the grand pronouncement that Kentucky was now 'ready for ReFederalization'. The Senator and his writers spent hours preparing his speech to the people of Louisville, Kentucky, indeed the whole country. The venue for his 'truly historic event" (the Senator's words) was Louisville International Airport (ironically there were never any international passenger flights in or out of the airport). His staff had persuaded several high profile absentee politicians from eastern states to attend, intending to show them this was a successful example of, and launch pad for, the RRRF to move into Tennessee, Illinois and Indiana.

Senator Kingston had proved it could be done in Kentucky. Let the other states follow his lead.

For sure, Phase Two, the introduction of critical infrastructure, systems of government, law and order had yet to be planned, let alone implemented. A process most constitutional experts thought would take at least five years.

Ignoring the naysayers, the Senator followed one of the immutable laws of politics—claim your successes even before they become fact. Wait until they've happened and someone else will take the credit.

It was all great political theater. A win is a win, even if it is but one step forward with a thousand more to go. And Senator Kingston was going to milk it for all he was worth. This, he believed, was a stepping stone to a future cabinet seat-if President Cummings won re-election. The President was currently refuting accusations he'd diverted government funds to upgrade one of his golf courses. He and his security detail had severe reservations about attending. The last time he was this far east, there had been an assassination attempt which killed his Vice President. In the end, the President would not be seen at this momentous, self-congratulatory fest. Never mind, the show must go on, he'd only be a distraction.

The Senator's helicopter landed close to the stage where two hundred dignitaries sat waiting for his overblown entrance, complete with a band and fly past by the USAF. It was meant to impress not just the attendees, but the TV audience as well. The Senator had removed his bandages with some difficulty and was in considerable pain. Ample makeup covered the bruises and cuts on his face, though his cracked ribs made for slow progress to the stage. He waved magnanimously to the politely clapping audience, relishing every moment in the public spotlight.

Even after taking several pain killers, the adrenaline flowing and the warm feeling of basking in the glory of the moment, the Senator did not feel well. He was perspiring heavily by the time he reached the stage. Secretary of State Crapo was there to make the introductions and then hand over to the Senator who had worked hard on a speech that was both visionary, yet practical, paying homage to JFK's legendary, "Ask not what your country can do for you–ask what you can do for your country," by substituting the word 'country' for Kentucky. He was ready to deliver the speech of his political career. Except, he just couldn't stop the palpitations in his chest that made it feel like his heart was beating at twice the rate it should. Granted, it had been a stressful few weeks, normally he coped with such problems with ease. A few Prozac and a couple of brandies usually did the job.

Was he having a panic attack, he wondered? He sipped some water, wishing for the Secretary to finish quickly so he could start his meticulously prepared speech. He really did feel awful. Please God, don't let me pass out now, prayed the Senator. By the time the Secretary had finished, the Senator was feverish. He stood up and lurched towards the podium, gripping it to stop himself falling over.

"Honored guests…ladies and…."

Three hundred yards away, Grant Muirhead was lying on the roof of the UPS Training Center. A thirty-year-old former Army sniper, he was now one million dollars richer courtesy of Danny Trevino. He'd spent the previous twenty-four hours in a cramped HVAC duct avoiding the security sweeps. Staying hidden in uncomfortable places was part of the job. For a million bucks, he would have hung from the rafters for a day.

Now he was getting down to business. Tucked into his shoulder and resting on a custom tripod was his Barrett M82 sniper rifle with an effective range of two thousand yards. Grant had been waiting motionless for six hours under his carefully constructed hide; he was invisible to any drone or someone scanning the area through binoculars. He'd spent the time continuously checking his line of sight, wind speed and direction, and most crucially his exit route. He'd easily taken out enemy combatants at eight hundred yards. At last count, his kill tally was forty-five. This one should be a breeze.

Chapter 59

They reached Miami in the early evening. Olivia was delighted to tell her fellow travelers, courtesy of her ten-year-old travel guide, that Miami is the only major city in the United States founded by a woman. In the late nineteenth century, Julia Tuttle, a local citrus grower, was the original owner of the land upon which the city was built. She persuaded Henry Flagler to extend his railroad down to the city in the 1890s, encouraging northerners to vacation in the warm winters. It was described by earlier settlers as 'a promising wilderness'. A description that still sadly fitted the city after the Collapse.

Once Florida's second biggest city, its population had been decimated by a series of hurricanes, then a succession of other disasters that hit it, and the rest of Florida. While Miami avoids the bone-numbing chill of the winters in the northern states, the brutally hot summers with no electricity for air conditioning led to a devastating death rate particularly among the elderly population. Two further hurricanes during the last four years had also done nothing to improve the conditions many residents now lived under.

On the plus side, being on the coast enabled the city to receive aid from other countries. Many were willing to help in return for bartered yachts, luxury cars, private jets and valuable works of art from the city's museums and galleries. Others stole thousands of acres of land in anticipation of civilization returning in the future.

Danny had never been to Miami, in fact, none of his traveling companions had. So they just headed towards the Atlantic. Like all cities in the east, even six years after the Collapse, Miami still bore the signs of widespread neglect: streets of abandoned houses, no electricity, trash and burned-out vehicles littering the silent, dark streets; graffiti adorned every surface. It resembled the bombed out blitzed cities of WW2: Dresden, the East of London, Berlin.

However, as they drove slowly towards the beach, signs of 'modern' life appeared. Cars driving around, people walking the streets, many bars, restaurants and hotels had lights on. By the time they reached downtown, they were seemingly transported back six years. The twenty-first century was alive and well, right here in front of their astonished eyes.

After a few minutes of driving around, Danny suggested they find a hotel. Of serious concern was protecting the multi-million dollar valuables in the back of the Humvee. They could hardly lug the gold bars and other crates up to their room without attracting attention. Danny ordered Seb and Ping to sleep in the Humvee overnight, guns at the ready. He and Olivia went into a modest motel and booked a room for the night. Danny had remembered to bring cash with him as well as the other assets.

After luxuriating in the almost forgotten experience of a hot shower, one that lasted as long as you wanted, they lay next to each other on the bed. Olivia propped herself up on one elbow, looking at Danny, she couldn't contain her curiosity any longer, "Alright Danny, I haven't dared ask, but you've said nothing about where we're going. Think it's time to spill the beans now. What do you have in mind?"

Danny wasn't sure if he wanted to reveal his thoughts quite yet. Then again, Olivia had proven to be a source of practical ideas in the past. Maybe she could help fine tune the details of his far from finalized escape plan.

"Fair question Olivia, my love, sorry I haven't been more open. My thinking is we can't stay in the US. Not because of the Feds, I think they won't follow us here. I'm scared shitless some local gangster will hear about my stash and take it, more than likely killing us in the process. I have the idea of buying a good-sized boat and sailing it to Belize or Panama. Somewhere that doesn't ask too many questions."

Olivia didn't look shocked, "I figured as we got into Miami that a boat trip might be on the cards. Why don't we check out extradition agreements with South American countries, see if one is safer than the others? I'm assuming now that we're back in the modern world we can use the good old Internet to do some research. I'll go chat up the manager to see if he'll let me use his computer."

Danny smiled and kissed her on the forehead, "Now I know why I brought you with me, you're a star. That's a great idea. Off you go and discover our next destination! In the meantime, I'll take some food to the boys in the truck."

He was dozing when Olivia came back an hour later, smiling broadly, "Seems we have quite a choice of countries who don't like dealing with Uncle Sam. The bad news is, only one is on the Atlantic coast, all the others are on the other side of South America. I don't think going through the Panama Canal would be a good idea. Flag up some questions, I'm guessing. So…we are off to…Nicaragua!"

"Wow, great work, Olivia. That sounds like a plan I can work with. Why don't we grab some sleep and start getting things moving tomorrow? Jesus, Nicaragua. I've only been abroad once, and that was to Canada. This will be interesting, to say the least."

The following morning, Danny and Olivia used the motel manager's computer to try and find names of anyone selling boats. They found nothing of interest. Feeling despondent, they casually asked the manager if he knew anyone? Via a series of 'friends of friends' they were told to head for a marina on Miami's Dodge Island where they'd meet a man who could help them.

Getting around Miami was a revelation. Most of the taxis were Teslas, or other EVs. Their cab driver explained that many homes had charging points that worked when charged by solar panels. Apparently, it entailed some innovative changes to the technology, way beyond Danny and Olivia's understanding, but the net result was a few hundred cabs ferried people around the city—a small nod to the way it was a few years earlier.

The marina was part of the docks once crammed with vast cruise ships, now used by private boat owners. Their new found friend, yacht broker José, quickly realized this was a 'below the radar transaction'. Not unusual in this part of the world, he told them, as he puffed on a large Cuban cigar. Dressed in white chinos and a Ralph Lauren polo shirt, he looked as though he had just come from a round of golf. Discretion was his middle name, he went on to reassure them. Just like in the old days, Miami was still a major hub for the smuggling of drugs; he had done plenty of deals with no questions asked for people involved in that trade. When Danny cautiously inquired about methods of payment for these ocean-going boats he was told by a poker faced José that 'gold would do nicely'.

There was one problem. Neither Danny nor Olivia knew the first thing about boats, especially large ones. They couldn't sail, navigate or run such sized vessels. José, of course, knew plenty of captains and crew who would be able to help them out—for a fee. Leave it to him.

It took two days of searching before they found a boat they liked. A whopping 117 foot, Ocean Alexander. It was a stunner—scorchingly sleek lines, opulent and luxurious inside. José assured them it would get them wherever in the world they wanted to go…which was, he casually inquired? Olivia blurted out Cancun in Mexico, as she'd been there once on vacation. Whether José believed her or not, it didn't matter, he merely confirmed the boat they had chosen, *The Mary Jane,* would be more than capable of such a voyage.

The Mary Jane required a minimum of four crew, plus the captain. José said he would make a few calls and present them with a shortlist of people to interview for the various positions on the boat.

The next few days were a succession of meetings, interviews, and dubious financial transactions. The total cost for the boat, crew and all the necessary stores, fuel and countless other 'necessities' was a staggering, inflated, $4.5 million. Not an eye blinked as Danny handed over nine gold bars. Since the Collapse, no one asked questions anymore.

A week after they arrived in Miami, Danny and Olivia were ready to leave the US for good. Danny gave Seb and Ping a more than generous bonus and sent them on their way back to Kentucky.

As *The Mary Jane* was preparing to depart, news came through. Hurricane David was barreling across the Atlantic heading for Cuba, and Florida. They had to stay in port.

Chapter 60

G rant Muirhead, put his right eye against the telescopic lens, sighting the crosshairs on the Senator's chest as he stood at the podium three hundred yards away. He steadied his breathing, slowly, gently, curling his finger around the trigger....

"What the fuck?" he said to himself, "what the hell's happening?" He shook his head and refocused his view through the high-powered lens. The Senator was now lying immobile on the floor. The lens was so clear and the image so close, Grant could see the Senator's eyes were closed. Within seconds, he was surrounded by people, making a kill shot now impossible.

It didn't matter—the Senator was dead. A massive heart attack brought on by (as the post-mortem described it, "excessively clogged vascular arteries"), felled him in his moment of glory. He would have liked his legacy to be the politician who had united and rescued Kentucky from the abyss of nineteenth century living. Instead, the images of him sprawled lifeless on the stage became the enduring images associated with his name.

Social media wasn't so kind either, they were soon awash with videos of his dead body. The comments were not flattering—from *"Dead on arrival: The Senator and the RRRF,"* to, *"He died doing what he loved, talking bullshit,"* and, *"ReFederalization: his heart just wasn't in it!"*

Chapter 61

The wedding was a simple ceremony. Roger and Penny wanted it that way. The whole village was there, it was the first wedding in two years, and they were in the mood to celebrate. Everyone crammed excitedly and noisily into the Village Hall.

Penny was dressed in an elegant pale yellow dress that clung to her slim figure. Her flowing auburn hair coiffured (courtesy of a hairstylist living in the village) for the first time in years, looked stunning.

Roger dug out his old Army uniform, and looked resplendent in dark blue with his medals pinned on his chest. He, too, had a haircut for the occasion.

The two rescued girls, Stephanie and Shelby, were bridesmaids. Acutely embarrassed at being the center of attention, they nevertheless did a grand job at scattering flower petals on the aisle as Penny and Roger walked behind them.

In a stunning surprise Penny's brother, Hunter, turned up to help celebrate. Penny dissolved into tears at seeing him after so many months. Hugging him tightly she weepingly exclaimed, "it made a perfect day even better."

Pastor David officiated and Pat was the best man, also dressed in his Army uniform. Penny was given away by Landy. Ensuring a long and happy marriage, Roger found a proper wedding ring, once worn by his grandmother to substitute for the hose clamp.

After the brief ceremony, the celebrations began with food and drink provided by everyone in the village. It was a carefree, relaxed day, helped by perfect weather. The festivities went on well into the evening, before the newly married couple staggered home drunk with happiness, and too much wine.

Over the next few days, news came across the ham radio network of the takeover of Louisville and the sudden death of Senator Charles Kingston. No one in the village knew how this news would affect them. For the moment, Roger and Penny didn't care. They had each other–soulmates, lovers and best friends–neither could believe how lucky they were. In amongst all this chaos, they had found an oasis of calm, and happiness. Every day they surprised each other with the depth of feelings that grew between them.

To top it all? Penny was pregnant.

Chapter 62

Hurricane David was a Category 5 when it smashed into Miami, mercilessly hanging over it for thirty-six hours. The devastation was worse than Peter or Sophie, the dual storms that had started the whole Collapse in Florida six years earlier. Parts of the city looked like Hiroshima after the nuclear bomb–nothing was left standing. Yet again, the east coast had been subjected to a natural disaster of biblical proportions. It would take weeks or months to discover who had survived, especially on the badly hit islands off Miami's beaches where the marinas and ocean going yachts were located.

Chapter 63

Allowing for a decent interval following the death of Senator Kingston, Secretary Crapo appointed a new interim Senator to represent Kentucky. Senator Davina B. Shankill was formerly a Congresswoman representing the fifteenth district in Louisville. Known for her no nonsense, bi-partisan approach, she was shocked to inherit a plan lacking any real detail or structure.

No fan of the deceased Senator Kingston, she quickly announced there would be a 'thorough root and branch review' of the proposal to ReFederalize Kentucky and the east. She would return to Sacramento immediately and put together a senior level team that would report back to the Government within the year on how they should move forward.

General Sanders was ordered to withdraw all troops and equipment to their bases. Any remaining members of the RRRF were to stop distributing relief supplies and return to the west too. The money was running out and with ReFederalization on hold, there was little point in continuing the winning of Kentuckian's hearts and minds.

Interim Senator Shankill issued a statement that, in part read:

"Kentucky. Our thoughts and prayers are with you all. We are deeply sorry the promises made by Senator Kingston and the Government cannot be honored at this time. We will continue to offer our support, while a new plan for the ReFederalization of the east is discussed with all the appropriate parties in Sacramento."

Everyone knew this was political-speak for 'ReFederalization wasn't happening any time soon'. The mood across Kentucky was one of resignation. Yet again, a government had led them up the garden path only for them to find a cliff at the end of it. There was nowhere to go but back to the starting point.

The failure to make any significant progress in revitalizing Kentucky, let alone bringing it back to the twenty-first century, cost the Government dearly. A year later, President Cummings was ousted by a landslide vote against him. He complained it wasn't a fair election because only half the country had voted.

His opponents, after ten years of his chaotic leadership, dismissed his claims. Tail between his legs, he sulked back to Palm Springs, taking up residence on one of his golf courses.

Cummings' successor, a Latino Senator from New Mexico, Peter Santoz, in his inaugural speech promised the problems in the east would be his administration's top priority once the economy was out of recession. Privately the newly minted President told his advisors he didn't expect the economy to be in any position to help the east for at least five years, if not longer.

So, Kentucky and all the states east of the Mississippi would likely remain rooted in the nineteenth century for the next decade. French Creek and its inhabitants would continue as before, resigned to living in the aftermath of America's greatest natural disaster.

One which everyone said would never happen.

The End

"We have surmounted all the perils and endured all the agonies of the past. We shall provide against and thus prevail over the dangers and problems of the future, withhold no sacrifice, grudge no toil, seek no sordid gain, fear no foe. All will be well. We have, I believe, within us the life-strength and guiding light by which the tormented world around us may find the harbor of safety, after a storm-beaten voyage."

Winston Churchill

Thank you so much for reading
Return to the 21st Century?

As you know reviews are the lifeblood for self-published authors like myself. If you enjoyed the book, please take a few moments to write a review, or at least give it a 'star' rating.

Thank you in advance for taking the time to do this, I very much appreciate it. <u>Follow this link.</u>

If you'd like a free Kindle copy of the third book in the French Creek series: *S.O.S. The Storm of all Storms*

just sign up at: www.paulhrowney.com

Regards, Paul Rowney.

PREVIEW TO

French Creek (Published in November 2022)

Book one in the *French Creek* series.

This takes place before Return to the 21st Century?

Chapter 1

Billie never saw the shooter. He never heard the shot or felt the bullet as it entered his skull, instantly ending his twenty- eight years of life.

Alone in Sentry Post One, he was supposed to be on guard, protecting the French Creek community from the people who slowly crept through the moonlit Kentucky night towards his unsuspecting village. But the work was boring (there had been no intruders in over six months), and keeping his concentration proved difficult. He fell asleep, never to wake up.

Billie wouldn't be the first to die that night.

"Got 'im" said the group's leader, Hal, with a hint of self- satisfaction in his voice. He put down his rifle and turned to the rest of the group with a smile on his face. "Good shot, though I say so myself", he whispered. Not everyone thought the same.

Jane, one of the three women in the group, was not impressed. "Was that really necessary? We could have taken him out some other way, surely?"

"Best be safe than sorry, wouldn't want him creeping up behind us. Come on, let's keep moving, we've got work to do." Brooking no further argument, Hal urged the group of four men and three women quietly along the dried-up creek bed towards the village

Except for Hal they were not trained killers, or professional soldiers. Just, it appeared, a desperate, hungry, homeless group of vagrants who by necessity had become adept at the art of killing to survive.

Compared to the years immediately after the Collapse, they were now a rare breed. But when they did appear, the fact they had survived so long meant they were dangerous and determined.

They crept up French Creek's almost dry riverbed, hugging the banks of overgrown vegetation that offered good cover as they advanced towards the village.

They had spent a couple days watching and waiting, seeing what defenses the Community had built to keep people like them away from the residents, the food, and their valuable, life-saving resources. Now, they made their move to take them.

From their lookout just off SR 90, Billie had been easy to spot, and the lack of attention he displayed made him easy prey. Once he was disposed of, they advanced up the river, determined to reach the village.

They were moving into the unknown, unable to reconnoiter any further from their lookout on SR 90 due to the nature of the hilly terrain. The group had no idea what awaited them—a well- fortified encampment? Or a village ripe for the taking?

Billie may have been sleeping on duty, but Pat in Sentry Post Two wasn't. The shot jolted him to high alert. He knew a hunting party had been sent out for deer, but this shot sounded different. For the first time in six months, there was someone out there with humans in their sights.

Pat was one of the few in the village with any military experience. A three year deployment in Afghanistan had ended abruptly. The whole US presence was pulled out at a few days notice, because the millions of dollars required to keep them armed and supplied each day had dried up. They were needed back in the US to keep law, order and discipline in the midst of economic chaos brought on by an unforeseeable 'perfect storm' of natural disasters. The fragile physical and economic infrastructure that had kept the country running on the edge of catastrophe for so many years, buckled, then finally collapsed.

By the time Pat and his fellow soldiers were back in the United States, not even the mighty American military could keep control of millions of citizens facing starvation. Within days of his arrival at Fort Bragg, he and most of the base deserted to find their way home and protect whatever family they had left.

Five days of walking, stealing cars, and defending himself against hapless looters frustrated by the empty Walmart shelves had brought him to French Creek. Like most of his fellow soldiers, he kept his Army-issued M4 rifle and stole whatever he could easily carry that could be of use in the future. One such item was the scope fitted to his rifle and the other, night vision goggles.

Now here he was, scanning down the valley from his high vantage point on what was known locally as the Indian Burial Ground, waiting for the ghostly green images produced by the goggles to come a little closer. Seeing them, he knew the shot he'd heard wasn't for a deer, but for Billie.

Flashing pinpricks of light from fireflies sporadically burst into his goggles and faded away. He brought the walkie-talkie to his mouth and clicked the send.

"Billie, do you read me? Over." Not even static returned his call.

He tried again, then a third time, then switched channels in case the idiot had forgotten the correct one for this night's watch. Nothing.

"Oh shit, no," he murmured under his breath, a nagging feeling of fear clutched at his stomach. Now fully alert his senses were heightened as he methodically scoured the dark landscape beneath, praying the lack of response from Billie was not bad news. But three years of watching out for the murderous Taliban, night-time killers of astonishing skill who could travel across open terrain and be upon you before you knew it, had fine-tuned his senses to danger. And that's what he was feeling right now. A sickening sense of trepidation. But, as the adrenaline kicked in, a sharpening of focus and calm.

There. On the third scan across the riverbed, he saw movement. The long hair of one of the female intruders poked briefly above the undergrowth. He held the goggles steady while he picked up the walkie-talkie to rouse the other sentries and the rest of the village. He saw two, then three, finally seven more bodies moving slowly parallel to him about six hundred feet away.

"Home base, do you read me? That shot was not the hunting party. We have intruders. Seven, maybe more, in the riverbed close to Marker 400. This is not a drill! Go to Code Red now!"

One of Pat's first moves upon returning was to set up a series of watch posts at intervals along the road leading into French Creek, which was about a mile from the SR 90. The three manned sentry posts looked towards the road to Albany across to the hills and the Western end of the valley. Alongside the road into French Creek, were small marker posts every two hundred yards indicating how far from the main road any visitor had traveled. They were meant as easy reference points as most of the houses and barns at the East end of the French Creek near the intersection with SR 90 had been demolished for fuel, building materials, and to offer no protection to intruders.

French Creek started as a trickle of spring water at the far East of the village and gradually gathered in size as it flowed towards the main road. At times, the banks were almost six feet deep, offering ideal cover for the group moving towards the village. Ironically, it made for an easy route into the village without being seen.

"Copy that, Pat. I'll get the reserve crew up and ready for action." The disembodied voice of Night Watch Commander Eddie South came over the airwaves into Pat's earbuds.

The other post nearer the village confirmed receiving Pat's Code Red call, and a prearranged defensive plan went into action. Though it had not been deployed for any genuine emergency in a couple of years, it was rehearsed every four weeks.

Satisfied that he had alerted the village to the danger, Pat was now concerned about the hunting party still somewhere in the woods. They were separated from the creek by a large pasture several hundred feet wide. They obviously didn't know what was happening, though hopefully they heard the solitary shot which alerted them to return to the village.

Pat's focus returned to the unwelcome party creeping along the riverbed. Pat assumed they had done some reconnaissance but probably didn't know the level of French Creek's defenses. He could have taken a shot—they were five-hundred feet away now—but the defense plan allowed a small intruder group to proceed up to Marker 600. At that point, they would have moved past Pat's hidden watch post, closer to the village, and into a welcoming committee of well-armed villagers.

The plan also sent six armed men through the woods to come up behind any intruders at Marker 200. Thus, effectively preventing them from retreating back to the main road. They had planned and trained for several different intruder scenarios. Pat hoped he'd called the right one.

He radioed into night watch command in the Baptist church, a tall building in the center of the village that allowed for better communications and defense.

"CC, let me know when Marker 200 by SR 90 is covered. Over."

"Will do." Eddie's reassuring voice, a farmer and one of the more level-headed members of the village, came through loud and clear.

"Their ETA is a few minutes, I'm guessing. Will confirm when I know. Over."

Pat kept watch as the group, all armed with a variety of rifles, shotguns, and handguns, continued to move forward, unaware they were being tracked.

The Kentucky night was cool and calm; dawn began to break through and enhanced the half-light provided by a vivid full moon. It was early fall, and the trees still provided some cover for the intruders. There was a little cloud cover, but the moon allowed reasonable visibility despite the dark. Pat figured that's why the intruders had chosen tonight to make their move.

In a few weeks, French Creek would be a torrent of flash floods and dangerous roiling currents of water. But now, after the summer season, it was dry except for occasional pools of shallow water, good only for horses and cattle to drink.

Eddie radioed to Pat that the men would be at Marker 200 in two minutes. The stillness of the early dawn was suddenly broken as he heard the hunting party come noisily out of the woods, staggering under the weight of a large deer. Thinking they were under attack, the intruders opened fire at the hunters.

Caught completely by surprise, initially, the hunters had no clue where the shots were coming from. In their panic, they started running towards the river-and the shooters- resulting in two being hit, the third diving for cover behind a fallen tree. It seemed the intruders had night scopes too.

Pat radioed Eddie.

"Tell the group going to Marker 200 to stay put when they get there. Our hunters have alerted the intruders. In five minutes, get the guys at the village barricade to move towards the intruders. I'll try and keep them pinned down. Let's gradually close the trap and send them back down to the team near the main road. Over."

"Roger that, Pat. Will do. Over."

Pat put the radio and goggles down and brought his rifle up to firing position. He looked through the scope: 390 feet. The intruders were at ninety degrees to him, still trying to put down the last hunter behind the tree, who was wisely sitting tight.

Pat aimed at the first intruder who had opened fire on the hunters. With a practiced and steady hand, he put the cross hairs on the leader's body and fired. Instantly, it slumped to the ground. The others looked confused at first, then scared as they realized an unknown firing position had opened on them. In quick succession, Pat fired twice more, hitting one of the women. Panicked, they started to run back down the riverbed, straight towards the men at Marker 200.

For a minute, there was silence. Then a stuttering of rifle and machine gunfire. After no more than two minutes it stopped as abruptly as it had started.

The echoes of the brief crackling of gunfire ricocheted around the valley before going quiet. The crickets resumed their night time chatter. The fireflies continued to dance in the dark.

Available on Amazon.com, click here for more information.

COMING SUMMER 2023:

S.O.S. The Storm of all Storms.

Here's a preview of the third book in the *French Creek* Series. This is a 'prequel' and looks at, from numerous viewpoints, how the Collapse happened across the USA. Including the early days of French Creek's desperate fight for survival. A combination of fact and fiction, it lays bare how close we could be to a real Collapse.

Chapter 1

October 15th. Cushing, Oklahoma.

If God has a sense of irony, then there's an example to be found in Cushing, Oklahoma.

The Oklahoma town of Cushing is home to nearly eight thousand people. It is also home to the largest concentration of oil storage facilities in the USA. Up to ninety million barrels of the black liquid gold rests there in hundreds of tanks, above and below ground waiting to be pumped across America via thousands of miles of pipelines.

What also sits four miles under these vast and fragile tanks is the Wilzetta-Whitetail fault zone, the name for the meeting of two geological plates lying deep below this unsuspecting town.

On October 15th at 4.52am the Wilzetta-Whitetail fault zone awoke from its million year sleep. The resulting movement was only a few feet on the surface, more than enough to create an earthquake of six magnitude. In geological terms it was a mere shudder, a tiny release of the irresistible pressure between two immeasurable forces deep in the Earth's crust.

On the surface it was cataclysmic.

Within minutes it had ruptured 65% of Cushing's oil storage tanks. The aftershocks in the following days took care of the rest. The surrounding countryside was awash with some eighty five million barrels of crude oil (by way of comparison the huge BP oil spill on the Gulf of Mexico in 2010 released…3.1million barrels of oil).

(Cushing had experienced numerous smaller earthquakes before (magnitude 1 or 2). Prior to 2009, the area saw one to three of these minor earthquakes every year. Now it was suffering between one and three mini quakes per day. The cause? Years of fracking which involves pumping millions of gallons of water at high pressure into the rocks thousands of feet below the ground to extract…oil).

This magnitude six earthquake wasn't six times more powerful than the minor daily occurrences. The way earthquake strengths are measured meant it was *500-600 times more deadly*. The result was an economic and ecological disaster that would have ramifications across the USA for years to come. One created by the oil industry itself. Big Oil hadn't so much as shot itself in the foot, but in the head. The effect would be fatal.

It was also the first in a series of biblical sized natural and manmade calamities that would, during the next few months, plunge the eastern half of America back to the 19th century.

Nature, when she's abused, takes no prisoners.

Chapter 2

October 16th. Miami, Florida.

On Miami's NBC 6 TV station, Debby, the curvaceous weather presenter, euphemistically called a meteorologist, was beside herself with excitement. Another hurricane was forming in the Atlantic, just a month after Peter a category 4 had smashed into the city. This news meant she would appear on TV numerous times a day with minute by minute updates. It was great for her exposure ratings, boosting social media numbers and advertising revenue, too.

Unfortunately, the network owners were frantically repairing damage to their studio and broadcasting facilities after Hurricane Peter, so would be in no position to capitalize financially on this newsworthy event. Early reports indicated it could be as strong as Peter. The station's CEO, Damian Fulton told his wife, Barb, that morning, "The network sees this as a ratings bonanza. Ratings be damned, realistically, we might not even be around to report on it. Three of our four studios are still inoperable, the underground cables are waterlogged. To be honest I think we're screwed honey. You and the boys should head for your Mom's place in Atlanta until it's safe to come back."

Barb agreed, and by mid-morning their Cadillac Escalade was packed full of a month's worth of clothing. Squeezed in the back seats, Damian Jr and David sat strapped in ready for the eight hour drive.

Damian leant in and kissed them both, hugged his wife and promised he would "see them soon". As they pulled out of the driveway he waved goodbye. Sadly, he would never see them again. A few days later,

Hurricane Sophie would reduce News station NBC 6's remaining studio to rubble, killing all the staff inside.

Miami is a city gradually sinking to below sea level. (One Cassandra repeated the warning that buying a beachfront property on a 30 year mortgage was an unwise move: there was every chance by the end of it, the building would be underwater). Hurricane Peter had inflicted huge damage to the beachfront, marinas and the outlying islands. With over seventy miles of canals, with an elevation of around five feet above sea level, they helpfully allowed the storm surge to funnel its way across the city destroying thousands of waterfront homes.

In places the storm surge reached a terrifying ten feet, reversing all the sewage and water processing plants, causing millions of gallons of untreated wastewater to flow into the nearby Everglades. Environmentalists had long warned this could happen and now watched as the delicate Everglades ecosystem was poisoned. It seems with help from a Hurricane, shit can flow upwards.

The destruction caused by Hurricane Peter, its associated storm surge and torrential rainfall, extended all the way up the Florida peninsula to St Augustine and inland as far as Orlando and Lake Kissimmee. Normally Lake Kissimmee averages a slim five feet in depth, This was temporarily doubled by the dumping of six inches of rain in 48 hours. The ensuing run off all the way down to the Everglades caused rivers to burst banks and homes to be flooded creating a two hundred mile swathe of carnage, and yet more lethal runoff into the fragile nature reserve.

Florida's infrastructure for years had been starved of funding and investment. Florida Power and Light in particular, could never seem to understand that a power grid built above ground in a hurricane prone state was always going to be a liability. In the past when their power grid was decimated by bad weather neighboring states would send thousands of repair crews to help rebuild the damaged grid. Not so this time, Georgia, the Carolinas and Tennessee had their own problems. They were too busy repairing their own infrastructure. Florida Power and Light were not going to receive any outside assistance. And that was before Hurricane Sophie hit.

When Sophie did, once it had pummeled Miami and the Keys, again, its path veered across Florida grinding slowly towards Sarasota and then careered into Tampa. The city founded in 1823 and famously never at the receiving end of a hurricane (at least since 1921) was hit with a vengeance. The carnage in Florida's largest city was on a scale that dwarfed Miami. The storm surge funneled by the confines of Tampa Bay, swept aside the downtown area like a house of sticks, reducing it to a scene from WW2 akin to Dresden's destruction. It pulverized its way as far as Busch Gardens. Flooding went as far east as Lakeland.

With a stunning lack of foresight Tampa International and nearby St Pete/Clearwater airports had both been built adjacent to the seafront. Any hope of using them as portals for relief supplies were washed away along with the terminals and hangers. Few commercial jets suffered any damage, they had long since fled once the airlines had been warned of the impending hurricane.

Thousands perished immediately, a preliminary death count that would be multiplied a hundred fold as the storm's aftermath made close to two million people homeless. Without any immediate rescue operation mounted by the overstretched and under-resourced FEMA, they were left to fend for themselves. Pleas for Federal Assistance by Governor Dessault were heard and ignored by Washington. They had too many states asking for help. The resources would go to states that had been, shall we say, more friendly towards the President, than the Governor of Florida?

By mid-November over half of Florida had been on the receiving end of two hurricanes, torrential rain and flooding. Relief efforts were stretched to and beyond the limit, exacerbated by the influx of over a million 'snowbirds' who flock down to the warm climes of Florida to escape the brutal winters of the North. Many would later wish they had stayed put and learned to live with the cold.

Every emergency resource was splintering under the pressure of never ending demand for their help-exacerbated by depleted supplies or personnel. Worryingly, the hurricane season had yet to end. The government in Tallahassee was on high alert watching weather formations off the coast of Africa and praying none would start forming a third hurricane. On November 20th, just in time for Thanksgiving the National Hurricane Center emailed Governor Dessault. Hurricane Thomas was forming off the Azores. It was too early to be precise about when and where it would make landfall, but it would do no harm to take the necessary precautions and evacuations, just in case, Florida was hit again.

Precautions? Evacuations? With what and to where? Asked despairing Floridians when they heard the Governor declare such actions as 'mandatory'.

Governor Dessault convened a meeting of the state's Emergency Council to discuss their options. FEMA, the Dept of Homeland Security, Transport and Health, plus the Emergency Services, Heads of Hospitals and FPL were all summoned. It was, to a degree, an exercise in futility. Every department was overloaded, running out of money and resources. Another hurricane, no matter where it landed, would be catastrophic for the state. Coping with one Hurricane a season was difficult, two: almost impossible, three: terminal.

A weary looking Governor looked hopefully at the attendees and asked for suggestions, any suggestion, to cope with the impending cataclysm if Hurricane Thomas, by some 1000-1 chance hit the state? The group sitting in front of him were dejected, tired and bereft of ideas. Two '100 year' storms had smashed Florida in the space of two months. Another could be on the way. Nothing could prepare us for that eventuality they all claimed. And certainly nothing could be organized to help the millions who'd be left homeless with no prospect of help or rescue. With no electricity, and soon, though they didn't know it yet, no fuel and shrinking food supplies, they were in a hole they couldn't dig themselves out of.

So, Florida held its breath for ten days, then sighed with relief as Hurricane Thomas swept up the Gulf of Mexico heading for Louisiana and East Texas.

Unfortunately their luck didn't hold for long. Fifteen hundred miles to the North West, the events in Oklahoma had already hastened Florida's descent back into the 19th century.

To receive a free Kindle copy of *S.O.S: The Storm of all Storms,* when it's published go to: www.paulhrowney.com

About the Author

Paul H Rowney has spent most of his working life in magazine publishing. Born in England, he emigrated to America in 2004 and now lives near Nashville, Tennessee on a farm with his wife Sheri, seven dogs and a menagerie of other two and four legged animals.

His interest in a post-apocalyptic world started when he read 'Alas Babylon' by Pat Frank. 'French Creek' was his first book inspired by living in rural Kentucky and the idea this would be a good place to survive in a post-apocalyptic society.

Each year on his birthday friends join him for a 'Apaulcalyptic Party' where they experiment for a day living without the conveniences of the 21st century. It isn't easy.

Printed in Great Britain
by Amazon

28747158R00175